Hot Picks: A Convenient Marriage

MELANIE MILBURNE

D0713257

MILLS & BOON

First Published in Great Britain 2020
By Mills & Boon, an imprint of HarperCollins*Publishers*
1 London Bridge Street, London, SE1 9GF

HOT PICKS: A CONVENIENT MARRIAGE © 2020 Harlequin Books S.A.

Surrendering All But Her Heart © 2012 Melanie Milburne
Enemies at the Altar © 2012 Melanie Milburne
Deserving of His Diamonds? © 2012 Melanie Milburne

ISBN: 978-0-263-28107-1

MIX
Paper from
responsible sources
FSC™ C007454

This book is produced from independently certified FSC™ paper to ensure responsible forest management.

For more information visit: www.harpercollins.co.uk/green

Printed and bound in Spain
by CPI, Barcelona

SURRENDERING ALL
BUT HER HEART

CHAPTER ONE

'You'll have to see him.'

Natalie could still hear the desperation and plead-ing in her mother's tone even as she pressed the call button for the lift leading up to Angelo Bellandini's swish London office. The words had taken up resi-dence in her head. They had kept her awake for the last forty-eight hours. They had accompanied her like oversized baggage on the train all the way from her home in Edinburgh. They had clickety-clacked over the tracks until they had been like a mind-numbing mantra in her head.

'You'll have to see him. You'll have to see him. You'll have to see him.'

Not that she *hadn't* seen him in the last five years. Just about every newspaper and online blog had a photo or information about the playboy heir to the Bellandini fortune. Angelo Bellandini's fast-living lifestyle was the topic of many an online forum. His massive wealth—of which, to his credit, only half was inherited; the other half had been acquired through his own hard work—made him a force to be reckoned with.

And now she *had to reckon with him, on behalf of her wayward younger brother and his foolish actions.*

A prickle of apprehension fluttered like a faceless,

fast-footed creature down the length of her spine as she stepped into the glass and chrome capsule of the lift. Her hand shook slightly as she reached for the correct floor button.

Would Angelo even agree to see her, given the way she had walked out of his life five years ago? Would he hate her as much as he had once loved her? Would the passion and desire that had once burned in his dark brown gaze now be a blaze of hatred instead?

Her insides shifted uneasily as she stepped out of the lift and approached the reception area. Having grown up with comfortable wealth, she should not be feeling so intimidated by the plush and elegant surroundings. But when they had first met Angelo had never revealed to her the extent of his family fortune. To her he had been just a hard-working, handsome Italian guy, studying for a Master's degree in business. He had gone to considerable lengths to conceal his privileged background—but then, who was she to talk?

She had revealed even less about hers.

'I'm afraid Signor Bellandini is unavailable at present,' his receptionist said in a crisp, businesslike tone in response to Natalie's request. 'Would you like to make an appointment for some other time?'

Natalie looked at the model-gorgeous young woman, with her perfectly smooth blonde hair and clear china-blue eyes, and felt her already flagging self-esteem plummet like an anchor to the basement. Even though in the lift she had reapplied lip-gloss and run her fingers through her nondescript flyaway brown hair, it was hardly the same as being professionally groomed. She was aware her clothes looked as if they had been slept in, even though she hadn't slept a wink for the last twenty-four hours, and that her normally peaches and cream complexion was grey with worry. There were damson-coloured shadows under her eyes and her cheeks had a hollow look to them. But then that happened every year at this time, and had done so since she was seven years old.

She straightened her shoulders with iron-strong resolve. She was not going to leave without seeing Angelo, even if she had to wait all day. 'Tell Signor Bellandini I'm only in London for the next twenty-four hours.' She handed her personal business card over the counter, as well as the card of the hotel she had booked for the night. 'I can be contacted on that mobile number or at my hotel.'

The receptionist glanced at the cards and then raised her eyes to Natalie's. '*You're* Natalie Armitage?' she asked. '*The* Natalie Armitage of Natalie Armitage Interiors?'

'Er…yes.'

The receptionist's eyes sparkled with delight. 'I have some of your sheets and towels,' she said. 'I just adored your last spring collection. Because of me, all of my friends now have your stuff. It's so feminine and fresh. So original.'

Natalie smiled politely. 'Thank you.'

The receptionist leaned towards the intercom. 'Signor Bellandini?' she said. 'A Miss Natalie Armitage is here to see you. Would you like me to squeeze her in before your next client or make another appointment for later this afternoon?'

Natalie's heart stalled in that infinitesimal moment before she heard his voice. Would he sound surprised to find she was here in person? Annoyed? Angry?

'No,' he said evenly, his deep baritone and sexy accent like a silky caress on her skin. 'I will see her now.'

The receptionist led the way down an expansive corridor and smiled as she came to a door bearing a brass plaque with Angelo's name on it. 'You're very lucky,' she said in a conspiratorial undertone. 'He doesn't normally see clients without an appointment. Most people have to wait weeks to see him.' Her eyes sparkled again. 'Maybe he wants to slip between your sheets, so to speak?'

Natalie gave a weak smile and stepped through the door the receptionist had opened. Her eyes went straight to where Angelo was seated, behind a mahogany desk that seemed to have a football field of carpet between it and the door that had just clicked shut, like the door of a prison cell, behind her.

Her throat tightened. She tried to unlock it by swallowing, but it still felt as if a puffer fish was lodged halfway down.

He looked as staggeringly gorgeous as ever—maybe even more so. The landscape of his face had barely changed, apart from two deep grooves that bracketed his unsmiling mouth. His raven-black hair was shorter than it had been five years ago, but it still curled lushly against the collar of his light blue business shirt. His face was cleanly shaven, but the dark pinpricks of persistent masculine stubble were clearly visible along his lean cheeks and stubbornly set jaw. His thickly lashed eyes were the same deep, espresso coffee brown, so dark she could not make out his pupils or his mood.

He rose to his feet, but whether it was out of politeness or a desire to intimidate Natalie wasn't quite sure. At six foot four he was impressively, imposingly tall. Even in heels she had to crane her neck to maintain eye contact.

She sent the tip of her tongue out to moisten her

concrete-dry lips. She had to keep her cool. She had spent most of her life keeping her emotions under the strictest control. Now was not the time to show how worried she was about the situation with her brother. Angelo would feed off that and work it to his advantage. All she had to do was pay for the damage Lachlan had caused, then get out of here and never look back.

'Thank you for seeing me at short notice,' she said. 'I understand how busy you are. I won't take up too much of your time.'

Those incredibly dark, inscrutable eyes nailed hers relentlessly as he reached across to press the intercom. 'Fiona, postpone my engagements for the next hour,' he said. 'And hold all my calls. On no account am I to be interrupted.'

'Will do.'

Natalie blinked at him as he straightened. 'Look, there's really no need to interrupt your busy schedule—'

'There is every need,' he said, still holding her gaze with the force of his. 'What your brother did to one of my hotel rooms in Rome is a criminal offence.'

'Yes,' she said, swallowing again. 'I know. But he's been going through a difficult stage just now, and I—'

One of his jet-black brows lifted satirically. 'What "difficult stage" would that be?' he asked. 'Has Daddy taken away his Porsche or cut back his allowance?'

She pressed her lips together, summoning control over emotions that were threatening to spill over. How dared Angelo mock what her brother had to deal with? Lachlan was a ticking time bomb. It was up to her to stop him from self-destructing. She hadn't been able to save her baby brother all those years ago, but she would move heaven and earth to get it right this time with Lachlan.

'He's just a kid,' she began. 'He's only just left school and—'

'He's eighteen,' Angelo said through tight, angry lips. 'He's old enough to vote and in my opinion old enough to face up to the consequences of his actions. He and his drunken friends have caused over a hundred thousand pounds' worth of damage to one of my most prestigious hotels.'

Natalie's stomach nosedived. *Was he exaggerating?* The way her mother had described it had made her think it hadn't been much more than the cost of a carpet-clean and the replacement of a few furnishings—perhaps a repaint on one of the walls.

What had Lachlan been thinking? What on earth had made him go on such a crazy rampage?

'I'm prepared to reimburse you for the damage, but before I hand over any money I'd like to see the damage for myself,' she said, with a jut of her chin.

His dark eyes challenged hers. 'So you're prepared to foot the bill personally, are you?'

She eyeballed him back, even though her stomach was churning at the menacing look in his eyes. 'Within reason.'

His top lip curled. 'You have no clue about what you're letting yourself in for,' he said. 'Do you have any idea what your brother gets up to when he's out night-clubbing with his friends?'

Natalie was all too aware, and for the last few months it had been keeping her awake at night. She knew why Lachlan was behaving the way he was, but there was little she could do to stop him. Lachlan had been the replacement child after Liam had died—the lost son re-incarnated. Since birth he had been forced to live not his own life but Liam's. All the hopes and dreams their parents had envisaged for Liam had been transferred to Lachlan, and lately he had started to buckle under the pressure. She was terrified that one day soon he would go, or be pushed too far.

She already had one death on her hands. She could not bear to have another.

'How do you know Lachlan is responsible for the damage?' she asked. 'How do you know it wasn't one of his friends?'

Angelo looked at her with dagger-sharp eyes. 'The room was booked in his name,' he said. 'It was his credit card that was presented at check-in. He is legally responsible, even if he didn't so much as knock a cushion out of place.'

Natalie suspected her brother had done a whole lot more than rearrange a few sofa cushions. She had more than once witnessed him in the aftermath of one of his drinking binges. Lachlan wasn't a sleepy drunk or a happy, loquacious one. A few too many drinks unleashed a rage inside him that was as terrifying as it was sudden. And yet a few hours later he would have no memory of the things he had said and done.

So far he had managed to escape prosecution, but only because their rich and influential father had pulled in some favours with the authorities.

But that was here in Britain.

Right now Lachlan was at the mercy of the Italian authorities—which was why she had come to London to appeal to Angelo on his behalf. Of all the hotels in Rome, why had he stayed at one of Angelo Bellandini's?

Natalie opened her bag and took out her chequebook with a sigh of resignation. 'All right,' she said, hunting for a pen. 'I'll take your word for it and pay for the damage.'

Angelo barked out a sardonic laugh. 'You think after you scrawl your signature across that cheque I'll simply overlook this?' he asked.

She quickly disguised another swallow. 'You want more than one hundred thousand pounds?' she asked, in a voice that sounded too high—squeaky, almost.

He looked at her, his eyes meshing with hers in a lockdown that made the silence throb with palpable tension. She felt it moving up her spine, vertebrae by vertebrae. She felt it on her skin, in the ghosting of goose bumps fluttering along her flesh. She felt it— shockingly—between her thighs, as if he had reached down and stroked her there with one of his long, clever fingers.

He didn't say a word. He didn't need to. She could read the subtext of that dark, mocking gaze. He didn't give a toss about the money. It wasn't money he wanted. He had more than enough of his own.

Natalie knew exactly what he wanted. She had known it the minute she had stepped into his office and locked gazes with him.

He wanted her.

'Take it or leave it,' she said, and slammed the cheque on the desk between them.

He picked up the cheque and slowly and deliberately tore it into pieces, then let them fall like confetti on the desk, all the while holding her gaze with the implacable and glittering force of his. 'As soon as you walk out of here I'll notify the authorities in Rome to press charges,' he said. 'Your brother will go to prison. I'll make sure of it.'

Natalie's heart banged against the wall of her chest like a pendulum slammed by a prize-fighter's punch. How long would her brother last in a foreign prison?

He would be housed amongst murderers and thieves and rapists. It could be *years* before a magistrate heard his case. He was just a kid. Yes, he had done wrong, but it wasn't his fault—not really. He needed help, not imprisonment.

'Why are you doing this?' she asked.

His mouth lifted in a half-smile, his eyes taunting hers with merciless intent. 'You can't guess, *mia piccola*?'

She drew in a painfully tight breath. 'Isn't this taking revenge a little too far? What happened between us *is* between us. It has nothing to do with my brother. It has nothing to do with anyone but us.' *With me*, she added silently. *It's always been to do with me.*

His eyes glinted dangerously and his smile completely vanished until his lips were just a thin line of contempt. 'Why did you do it?' he asked. 'Why did you leave me for a man you picked up in a bar like a trashy little two-bit hooker?'

Natalie couldn't hold his gaze. It wasn't a lie she was particularly proud of. But back then it had been the only way she could see of getting him to let her go. He had fallen in love with her. He had mentioned marriage and babies. He had already bought an engagement ring. She had come across it while putting his socks away. It had glinted at her with its diamond eye, taunting her, reminding her of all she wanted but could never have.

She had panicked.

'I wasn't in love with you.' That was at least the truth…sort of. She had taught herself not to love. Not to feel. Not to be at the mercy of emotions that could not be controlled.

If you loved you lost.

If you cared you got hurt.

If you opened your heart someone would rip it out of your chest when you least expected it.

The physical side of things…well, that had been different. She had let herself lose control. Not that she'd really had a choice. Angelo had seen to that. Her body had been under the mastery of his from the first time he had kissed her. She might have locked down her emotions, but her physical response to him still echoed in her body like the haunting melody of a tune she couldn't forget no matter how hard she tried.

'So it was just sex?' he said.

Natalie forced herself to meet his gaze, and then wished she hadn't when she saw the black hatred glittering there. 'I was only twenty-one,' she said, looking away again. 'I didn't know what I wanted back then.'

'Do you know now?'

She caught the inside of her mouth with her teeth. 'I know what I don't want,' she said.

'Which is?'

She met his gaze again. 'Can we get to the point?' she asked. 'I've come here to pay for the damage my brother allegedly caused. If you won't accept my money, then what will you accept?'

It was a dangerous question to be asking. She knew it as soon as she voiced it. It hung in the ensuing silence, mocking her, taunting her for her supposed immunity.

She had *never* been immune.

It had all been an act—a clever ploy to keep him from guessing how much she'd wanted to be free to love him. But the clanging chains of her past had kept her anchored in silence. She couldn't love him or anyone.

Angelo's diamond-hard gaze tethered hers. 'Why don't you sit down and we can discuss it?' he said, gesturing to a chair near to where she was standing.

Natalie sank into the chair with relief. Her legs were so shaky the ligaments in her legs felt as if they had been severed like the strings of a puppet. Her heart was pounding and her skin was hot and clammy in spite of the air conditioning. She watched as he went back to the other side of his desk and sat down. For someone so tall he moved with an elegant, loose-limbed grace. His figure was rangy and lean, rather than excessively gym-pumped, although there was nothing wrong with the shape of his biceps. She could see the firm outline of them beneath his crisp ice-blue shirt. The colour was a perfect foil for his olive-toned skin. In the past she had only ever seen him in casual clothes, or wearing nothing at all.

In designer business clothes he looked every inch the successful hotel and property tycoon—untouchable, remote, in control. Her hands and mouth had traced every slope and plane and contour of his body. She could still remember how salty his skin tasted against her tongue. She still remembered the scent of him, the musk and citrus blend that had clung to her skin for hours after their making love. She remembered the thrusting possession of his body, how his masterful touch had unlocked her tightly controlled responses like a maestro with a difficult instrument that no one else could play.

She gave herself a mental slap and sat up straighter in the chair. Crossing her legs and arms, she fixed her gaze on Angelo's with a steely composure she was nowhere near feeling.

He leaned back in his own chair, with his fingers steepled against his chin, his dark gaze trained with unnervingly sharp focus on hers. 'I've heard anybody who is anybody is sleeping between your sheets,' he said.

She returned his look with chilly hauteur. 'I don't suppose *you* are doing so.'

His lips gave a tiny twitch of amusement, his dark eyes smouldering as they continued to hold hers. 'Not yet,' he said.

Natalie's insides flickered with the memory of long-ago desire. She'd fought valiantly to suppress it, but from the moment she had stepped into his office she had been aware of her body and its unruly response to him. He had always had that power over her. Just a look, an idle touch, a simple word and she would melt.

She couldn't afford to give in to past longings. She had to be strong in order to get through this. Lachlan's future depended on her. If this latest misdemeanour of his got out in the tabloids his life would be ruined. He was hoping to go to Harvard after this gap year. A criminal record would ruin everything for him.

Their father would crucify him.

He would crucify them both.

Natalie blamed herself. Why hadn't she realised how disenfranchised Lachlan was? Had she somehow given him some clue to her past history with Angelo? Had her lack of an active love-life made him suspect Angelo was the cause? How had he put two and two together? It wasn't as if she had ever been one to wear her heart on her sleeve. She had been busy building up her business. She had not missed dating. She'd had one or two encounters that had left her cold. She had more or less decided she wasn't cut out for an intimate relationship. The passion she had experienced with Angelo had come at a huge price, and it wasn't one she was keen to pay again.

She was better off alone.

'I understand how incredibly annoyed you are at

what my brother has supposedly done,' she said. 'But I must beg you not to proceed with criminal charges.'

His dark brow lifted again. 'Let me get this straight,' he said. 'You're *begging* me?'

Natalie momentarily compressed her lips in an attempt to control her spiralling emotions. How like him to taunt her. He would milk this situation for all it was worth and she would have to go along with it. He knew it. She knew it. He wanted her pride. It would be his ultimate trophy.

'I'm asking for leniency.'

'You're grovelling.'

She straightened her shoulders again. 'I'm asking you to drop all charges,' she said. 'I'll cover the damages— even double, if you insist. You won't be out of pocket.'

His gaze still measured hers unwaveringly. 'You want this to go away before it gets out in the press, don't you?' he said.

Natalie hoped her expression wasn't giving away any sign of her inner panic. She had always prided herself on disguising her feelings. Years of dealing with her father's erratic mood swings had made her a master at concealing her fear in case it was exploited. From childhood her ice-cold exterior had belied the inner turmoil of her emotions. It was her shield, her armour—her carapace of protection.

But Angelo had a keen, intelligent gaze. Even before she had left him she had felt he was starting to sum up her character in a way she found incredibly unsettling.

'Of course I want to keep this out of the press,' she said. 'But then, don't you? What will people think of your hotel security if a guest can do the sort of damage you say my brother did? Your hotels aim for the top end of the market. What does that say about the type of clientele your hotel attracts?'

A muscle flickered like a pulse at the side of his mouth. 'I have reason to believe your brother specifically targeted my hotel,' he said.

She felt her stomach lurch. 'What makes you think that?'

He opened a drawer to the left of him and took out a sheet of paper and handed it to her across the desk. She took it with a hand that wasn't quite steady. It was a faxed copy of a note addressed to Angelo, written in her brother's writing. It said: *This is for my sister.*

Natalie gulped and handed back the paper. 'I don't know what to say... I have never said anything to Lachlan about...about us. He was only thirteen when we were together. He was at boarding school when we shared that flat in Notting Hill. He never even met you.'

Nor had any of her family. She hadn't wanted Angelo to be exposed to her father's outrageous bigotry and her mother's sickening subservience.

'You must have said something to him,' Angelo said. 'Why else would he write that?'

Natalie chewed at her lip. She had said nothing to anyone other than that her short, intense and passionate affair with Angelo was over because she wanted to concentrate on her career. Not even her closest girlfriend, Isabel Astonberry, knew how much her break-up with Angelo had affected her. She had told everyone she was suffering from anxiety. Even her doctor had believed her. It had explained the rapid weight loss and agitation and sleepless nights. She had almost convinced *herself* it was true. She had even taken the pills the doctor had prescribed, but they hadn't done much more than throw a thick blanket over her senses, numbing her until she felt like a zombie.

Eventually she had climbed out of the abyss of misery and got on with her life. Hard work had been her remedy. It still was. Her interior design business had taken off soon after she had qualified. Her online sales were expanding exponentially, and she had plans to set up some outlets in Europe. She employed staff who managed the business end of things while she got on with what she loved best—the designing of her linen and soft furnishings range.

And she had done it all by herself. She hadn't used her father's wealth and status to recruit clients. Just like Angelo, she had been adamant that she would not rely on family wealth and privilege, but do it all on her own talent and hard work.

'Natalie?' Angelo's deep voice jolted her out of her reverie. 'Why do you think your brother addressed that note to me?'

She averted her gaze as she tucked a strand of hair behind her ear. 'I don't know.'

'He must have known it would cause immense trouble for you,' he said.

Natalie looked up at him again, her heart leaping to her throat. 'A hundred thousand pounds is a lot of money, but it's not a lot to pay for someone's freedom,' she said.

He gave an enigmatic half-smile. 'Ah, yes, but whose freedom are we talking about?'

A ripple of panic moved through her as she held his unreadable gaze. 'Can we quit it with the game-playing?' she said. 'Why don't you come straight out and say what you've planned in terms of retribution?'

His dark eyes hardened like black ice. 'I think you

know what I want,' he said. 'It's the same thing I wanted five years ago.'

She drew in a sharp little breath. 'You can't possibly want an affair with someone you hate. That's so... so cold-blooded.'

He gave a disaffected smile. 'Who said anything about an affair?'

She felt a fine layer of sweat break out above her top lip. She felt clammy and light-headed. Her legs trembled even though she had clamped them together to hide it. She unclenched her hands and put one to her throat, where her heart seemed to have lodged itself like a pigeon trapped in a narrow pipe.

'You're joking, of course,' she said, in a voice that was hoarse to the point of barely being audible.

Those dark, inscrutable eyes held hers captive, making every nerve in her body acutely aware of his sensual power over her. Erotic memories of their past relationship simmered in the silence. Every passionate encounter, from their first kiss to their blistering bloodletting last, hovered in the tense atmosphere. She felt the incendiary heat and fire of his touch just by looking at him. It was all she could do to stay still and rigidly composed in her chair.

'I want a wife,' he said, as if stating his desire for something as prosaic as a cup of tea or coffee.

Natalie hoisted her chin. 'Then I suggest you go about the usual way of acquiring one,' she said.

'I tried that and it didn't work,' he returned. 'I thought I'd try this way instead.'

She threw him a scathing look. 'Blackmail, you mean?'

He gave an indifferent shrug of one of his broad shoulders. 'Your brother will likely spend up to four years waiting for a hearing,' he said. 'The legal system in Italy is expensive and time consuming. I don't need to tell you he is unlikely to escape conviction. I have enough proof to put him away for a decade.'

Natalie shot to her feet, her control slipping like a stiletto on a slick of oil. 'You bastard!' she said. 'You're only doing this to get at me. Why don't you admit it? You only want revenge because I am the first woman who has ever left you. That's what this is about, isn't it? Your damned pride got bruised, so now you're after revenge.'

His jaw locked down like a clamp, his lips barely moving as he commanded, 'Sit down.'

She glared at him with undiluted hatred. 'Go to hell.'

He placed his hands on the desk and slowly got to his feet. Somehow it was far more threatening than if he had shoved his chair back with aggressive force. His expression was thunderous, but when he spoke it was with icy calm.

'We will marry as soon as I can get a licence. If you do not agree, then your brother will face the consequences of his actions. Do you have anything to say?'

She said it in unladylike coarseness. The crude words rang in the air, but rather than make her feel powerful they made her feel ashamed. He had made her lose control and she hated him for it.

Angelo's top lip slanted in a mocking smile. 'I am not averse to the odd moment of self-pleasuring, as you so charmingly suggest, but I would much rather share the experience with a partner. And, to be quite frank, no one does it better than you.'

She snatched up her bag and clutched it against her body so tightly she felt the gold pen inside jab her in the stomach. 'I hope you die and rot in hell,' she said.

'I hope you get some horrible, excruciatingly painful pestilent disease and suffer tortuous agony for the rest of your days.'

He continued to stare her down with irritatingly cool calm. 'I love you too, Tatty,' he said.

Natalie felt completely and utterly ambushed by the use of his pet name for her. It was like a body-blow to hear it after all these years. Her chest gave an aching spasm. Her anger dissolved like an aspirin in a glass of water. Her fighting spirit collapsed like a warrior stung by a poison dart. Tears sprang at the back of her eyes. She could feel them burning and knew if she didn't get out of there right now he would see them.

She spun around and groped blindly for the door, somehow getting it open and stumbling through it, leaving it open behind her like a mouth in the middle of an unfinished sentence.

She didn't bother with the lift.

She didn't even glance at the receptionist on her way to the fire escape.

She bolted down the stairs as if the devil and all his maniacal minions were on her heels.

CHAPTER TWO

NATALIE got back to her hotel and leant against the closed door of her suite with her chest still heaving like a pair of bellows. The ringing of her phone made her jump, and she almost dropped it when she tried to press the answer button with fingers that felt like cotton wool.

'H-hello?'

'Natalie, it's me…Lachlan.'

She pushed herself away from the door and scraped a hand through her sticky hair as she paced the floor in agitation. 'I've been trying to call you for the last twenty-four hours!' she said. 'Where are you? What's going on? Why did you do it? For God's sake, Lachlan, are you out of your mind?'

'I'm sorry,' he said. 'Look, I'm only allowed one call. I'll have to make it quick.'

Natalie scrunched her eyes closed, not wanting to picture the ghastly cell he would be locked in, with vicious-looking prison guards watching his every move. 'Tell me what to do,' she said, opening her eyes again to look at the view of the River Thames and the London Eye. 'Tell me what you need. I'll get there as soon as I can.'

'Just do what Angelo tells you to do,' Lachlan said. 'He's got it all under control. He can make this go away.'

She swung away from the window. *'Are you nuts?'* she said.

He released a sigh. 'He'll do the right thing by you, Nat,' he said. 'Just do whatever he says.'

She started pacing again—faster this time. 'He wants to marry me,' she said. 'Did he happen to mention that little detail to you?'

'You could do a whole lot worse.'

Her mouth dropped open. 'Lachlan, you're surely not serious? He *hates* me.'

'He's my only chance,' he said. 'I know I've stuffed up. I don't want to go to prison. Angelo's given me a choice. I have to take it.'

She gave a disgusted snort. 'He's given *me* a choice, not you,' she said. 'My freedom in exchange for yours.'

'It doesn't have to be for ever,' he said. 'You can divorce him after a few months. He can't force you to stay with him indefinitely.'

Natalie seriously wondered about that. Rich, powerful men were particularly adept at getting and keeping what they wanted. Look at their father, for instance. He had kept their mother chained to his side in spite of years of his infidelities and emotional cruelty. She could not bear to end up in the same situation as her mother. A trophy wife, a pretty adornment, a plaything that could be picked up and put down at will. With no power of her own other than a beauty that would one day fade, leaving her with nothing but diamonds, designer clothes and drink to compensate for her loneliness.

'Why did you do it?' she asked. 'Why his hotel?'

'Remember the last time we caught up?' Lachlan said.

Natalie remembered all too well. It had been a weekend in Paris a couple of months ago, when she had been attending a fabric show. Lachlan had been at a friend's eighteenth birthday party just outside of the city. He had been ignominiously tossed out of his friend's parents' château after disgracing himself after a heavy night of drinking.

'Yes,' she said in stern reproach. 'It took me weeks to get the smell of alcohol and vomit out of my coat.'

'Yeah, well, I saw that gossip magazine open on the passenger seat,' he said. 'There was an article about Angelo and his latest lover. That twenty-one-year-old heiress from Texas?'

She tried to ignore the dagger of jealousy that spiked her when she recalled the article, and the stunningly gorgeous young woman who had been draped on Angelo's arm at some highbrow function.

'So,' she said. 'What of it? It wasn't the first time he'd squired some brainless little big-boobed bimbo to an event.'

'No,' Lachlan said. 'But it was the first time I'd seen you visibly upset by it.'

'I wasn't upset,' she countered quickly. 'I was disgusted.'

'Same difference.'

Natalie blew out a breath and started pacing again. 'So you took it upon yourself to get back at him by trashing one of the most luxurious hotel rooms in the whole of Europe just because you thought I was a little peeved?'

'I know, I know, I know,' Lachlan said. 'It sounds so stupid now. I'm not sure why I did it. I guess I was just angry that he seemed to have it all together and you didn't.'

Natalie frowned. 'What do you mean?' she said. 'I'm

running a successful business all by myself. I'm paying for my own home. I'm happy with my life.'

'Are you, Nat?' he asked. 'Are you really?'

The silence was condemning.

'You work ridiculous hours,' Lachlan went on. 'You never take holidays.'

'I hate flying, that's why.'

'You could do a desensitising programme for that,' he said.

'I don't have time.'

'It's because of what happened to Liam, isn't it?' Lachlan said. 'You haven't been on a plane since he drowned in Spain all those years ago.'

Natalie felt the claws of guilt clutch her by the throat. She still remembered the tiny white coffin with her baby brother's body in it being loaded on the tarmac. She had seen it from her window seat. She had sat there staring at it, with an empty, aching, hollow feeling in her chest.

It had been her fault he had been found floating face-down in that pool.

'I have to go,' Lachlan said. 'I'm being transferred.'

Her attention snapped back to Lachlan's dire situation. 'Transferred where?' she asked.

'Just do what Angelo says, please?' he said. 'Nat, I need you to do what he wants. He's promised to keep this out of the press. I have to accept his help. My life is over if I don't. Please?'

Natalie pinched the bridge of her nose until her eyes smarted with bitter angry tears. The cage of her conscience came down with a snap.

She was trapped.

* * *

Angelo was finalising some details on a project in Malaysia when his receptionist announced he had a visitor. 'It's Natalie Armitage,' Fiona said.

He leaned back in his chair and smiled a victor's smile. He had waited a long time for this opportunity. He wanted her to beg, to plead and to grovel. It was payback time for the misery she had put him through by walking out on him so heartlessly.

'Tell her to wait,' he said. 'I have half an hour of paperwork to get through that can't be put off.'

There was a quick muffled exchange of words and Fiona came back on the intercom. 'Miss Armitage said she's not going to wait. She said if you don't see her now she is going to get back on the train to Edinburgh and you'll never see her again.'

Angelo slowly drummed his fingers on the desk. He was used to Natalie's obstinacy. She was a stubborn, headstrong little thing. Her independence had been one of the first things he had admired about her, and yet in the end it had been the thing that had frustrated him the most. She'd absolutely refused to bend to his will. She'd stood up to him as no one else had ever dared.

He was used to people doing as he said. From a very young age he had given orders and people had obeyed them. It was part of the territory. Coming from enormous wealth, you had power. You had privilege and people respected that.

But not his little Tatty.

He leaned forward and pressed the button. 'Tell her I'll see her in fifteen minutes.'

He had not even sat back in his chair when the door slammed open and Natalie came storming in. Her brown hair with its natural highlights was in disarray about her flushed-with-fury face. Her hands were clenched into combative fists by her sides, and her slate-blue eyes were flashing like the heart of a gas flame. He could see the outline of her beautiful breasts as they rose and fell beneath her top.

His groin tightened and jammed with lust.

'You…you *bastard*!' she said.

Angelo rocked back in his chair. *'Cara,'* he said. 'I'm absolutely delighted to see you, too. How long has it been? Four hours?'

She glowered at him. 'Where have you taken him?'

He elevated one brow. 'Where have I taken whom?'

Her eyes narrowed to needle-thin slits. 'My brother,' she said. 'I can't contact him. He's not answering his phone any more. How do I know you're doing the right thing by him?'

'Your brother is in good hands,' he said. 'That is as long as you do what is required.'

Her eyes blazed with venomous hatred. 'How can I trust you to uphold your side of the bargain?' she asked.

'You can trust me, Natalie.'

She made a scoffing sound. 'I'd rather take my chances with a death adder.'

Angelo smiled a thin-lipped smile. 'I'm afraid a death adder is not going to hold any sway with an Italian magistrate,' he said. 'I can get your brother out of harm's way with the scrawl of my signature.' He picked up a pen for effect. 'What's it going to be?'

He saw her eyes go to his pen. He saw the way her jaw locked as she clenched her teeth. Her saw the way her slim throat rose and fell. He saw the battle on her face as her will locked horns with his. He felt the energy of her anger like a high-voltage current in the air.

'You can't force me to sleep with you,' she bit out.

'You might be able to force me to wear your stupid ring, but you can't force me to do anything else.'

'You will be my wife in every sense of the word,' he said. 'In public and in private. Otherwise the deal is off.'

Her jaw worked some more. He could even hear her teeth grinding together. Her eyes were like twin blasts from a roaring furnace.

'I didn't think you could ever go so low as this,' she said. 'You can have anyone you want. You have women queuing up to be with you. Why on earth do you want an unwilling wife? Is this some sort of sick obsession? What can you possibly hope to achieve out of this?'

Angelo slowly swung his ergonomic chair from side to side as he surveyed her outraged features. 'I quite fancy the idea of taming you,' he said. 'You're like a beautiful wild brumby that bucks and kicks and bites because it doesn't want anyone to get too close.'

Her cheeks flushed a fiery red and her eyes kept on shooting sparks of ire at him. 'So you thought you'd slip a lasso around my neck and whip me into submission, did you?' she said, with a curl of her bee-stung top lip. 'Good luck with that.'

Angelo smiled a lazy smile. 'You know me, Tatty. I just love a challenge—and the bigger the better.'

Her brows shot together in a furious frown. 'Don't call me that.'

'Why not?' he said. 'I always used to call you that.'

She stalked to the other side of the room, her arms across her body in a keep-away-from-me pose. 'I don't want you to call me that now,' she said, her gaze determinedly averted from his.

'I will call you what I damn well want,' he said, feeling his anger and frustration rising. 'Look at me.'

She gave her head a toss and kept her eyes fixed on the painting on the wall. 'Go to hell.'

Angelo got to his feet and walked over to where she was standing. He put a hand on her shoulder, but she spun around and slapped at his hand as if it was a nasty insect.

'Don't you *dare* touch me,' she snarled at him, like a wildcat.

He felt the fizzing of his fingers where his hand had briefly come into contact with her slim shoulder. The sensation travelled all the way to his groin. He looked at her mouth—that gorgeous, full-lipped mouth that had kissed him with such passion and fire in the past. He had felt those soft lips around him, drawing the essence from him until he had been legless with ecstasy. She had lit fires of need over his whole body with her hot little tongue. Her fingers had danced over every inch of his flesh, caressing and stroking him, branding him with the memory of her touch.

Ever since she had left him he had waited for this moment—for a chance to prove to her how much she wanted him in spite of her protestations. His rage at being cut from her life had festered inside him. It had soured every other relationship since. He could not seem to find what he was looking for with anyone else. He had gone from relationship to relationship, some lasting only a date or two, none of them lasting more than a month. Lately he had even started to wonder if he had imagined how perfectly physically in tune he had been with her. But seeing her again, being in the same room as her, sensing her reaction to him and his to her, proved to him it wasn't his imagination.

She wouldn't be the one who walked out on him without notice this time around. She would stay with him until he decided he'd had enough. It might take a month or two, maybe even up to a year, but he would not give her the chance to rip his heart open again. He would not allow her that close again. He had been a passionate fool five years ago. From the moment he had met her he had fallen—and fallen hard. He had envisaged their future together, how they would build on the empire of his grandparents and parents, how they would be the next generation of Bellandinis.

But then she had ripped the rug from under his feet by betraying him.

She might hate him for what he was doing, but right now he didn't give a damn. He wanted her and he was going to have her. She would come to him willingly. He would make sure of that. There would be no forcing, no coercing. Behind that ice-maiden façade was a fiercely passionate young woman. He had unleashed that passion five years ago and he would do so again.

'In time you will be begging for my touch, *cara*,' he said. 'Just like you did in the past.'

Her expression shot more daggers at him. 'Can't you see how much I hate you?' she said.

'I can see passion, not hate,' he said. 'That is promising, *si*?'

She let out a breath and put more distance between them, her look guarded and defensive. 'How soon do you expect to get this ridiculous plan of yours off the ground?' she asked.

'We will marry at the end of next week,' he said. 'There's no point dilly-dallying.'

'*Next week?*' she asked, eyes widening. 'Why so soon?'

Angelo held her gaze. 'I know how your mind works, Natalie. I'm not leaving anything up to chance. The sooner we are married, the sooner your brother gets out of trouble.'

'Can I see him?'

'No.'

She frowned. 'Why not?'

'He's not allowed visitors,' Angelo said.

'But that's ridiculous!' she said. 'Of course he's allowed visitors. It's a basic human right.'

'Not where he is currently staying,' he said. 'You'll see him soon enough. In the meantime, I think it's time I met the rest of your family—don't you agree?'

Something shifted behind her gaze. 'Why do you want to meet my family?' she said. 'Anyway, apart from Lachlan there is only my parents.'

'Most married couples meet their respective families,' Angelo said. 'My parents will want to meet you. And my grandparents and uncles and aunts and cousins.'

She gave him a worried look. 'They're not all coming to the ceremony, are they?'

'But of course,' he said. 'We will fly to Rome on Tuesday. The wedding will be on Saturday, at my grandparents' villa, in the private chapel that was built especially for their wedding day sixty years ago.'

Her eyes looked like a startled fawn's. 'F-fly?'

'Si, cara,' he said dryly. 'On an aeroplane. You know—those big things that take off at the airport and take you where you want to go? I have a private one—a Lear jet that my family use to get around.'

Her mouth flattened obstinately. 'I'm not flying.'

Angelo frowned. 'What do you mean, you're not flying?'

She shifted her gaze, her arms tightening across her body. 'I'm *not* flying.'

It took Angelo a moment or two to figure it out. It shocked him that he hadn't picked it up before. It all made sense now that he thought about it.

'That's why you caught the train down from Edinburgh yesterday,' he said. 'That's why, when I suggested five years ago that we take that cut-price trip to Malta, you said you couldn't afford it and refused to let me pay for you. We had a huge fight over it. You wouldn't speak to me for days. It wasn't about your independence, was it? You're frightened of flying.'

She turned her back on him and stood looking out of his office window, the set of her spine as rigid as a plank. 'Go on,' she said. 'Call me a nut job. You wouldn't be the first.'

Angelo released a long breath. 'Natalie… Why didn't you tell me?'

She still stood looking out of the window with her back to him. '*Hi, my name's Natalie Armitage and I'm terrified of flying.* Yeah, that would have really got your notice that night in the bar.'

'What got my notice in that bar was your incredible eyes,' he said. 'And the fact that you stood up to that creep who was trying it on with you.'

He saw the slight softening of her spine and shoulders, as if the memory of that night had touched something deep inside her, unravelling one of the tight cords of resolve she had knotted in place. 'You didn't have to rescue me like some big macho caveman,' she said after a short pause. 'I could've taken care of it myself.'

'I was brought up to respect and protect women,' Angelo said. 'That guy was a drunken fool. I enjoyed hauling him out to the street. He was lucky I didn't rearrange his teeth for him. God knows I was tempted.'

She turned and looked at him, her expression still

intractable. 'I don't want to fly, Angelo,' she said. 'It's easy enough to drive. It'll only take a couple of days. I'll make my own way there if you can't spare the time.'

Angelo studied her dark blue gaze. He saw the usual obstinacy glittering there, but behind that was a flicker of fear—like a stagehand peeping out from behind the curtains to check on the audience. It made him wonder if he had truly known her five years ago. He had thought he had her all figured out, but this was a facet to her personality he had never even suspected. He had always prided himself on his perspicuity, on his ability to read people and situations. But he could see now that reading Natalie was like reading a complex multi-layered book.

'I'll be with you the whole time,' he said. 'I won't let anything happen to you.'

'That's hardly reassuring,' she said with a cynical look, 'considering this whole marriage thing you've set up is a plot for revenge.'

'My intention is not for you to suffer,' he said.

Her chin came up and her eyes flashed again. 'Oh, really?'

Angelo drew in a breath and released it forcefully as he went back behind his desk. He gripped the back of his chair as he faced her. 'Why must you search for nefarious motives in everything I do or say?'

She gave a little scoffing laugh. 'Pardon me for being a little suspicious, but you're surely not going to tell me you still care about me after all this time?'

Angelo's fingers dug deeper into the leather of his chair until his knuckles whitened. He didn't love her. He *refused* to love her. She had betrayed him. He was not going to forgive and forget that in a hurry. But he would *have* her. That was different. That had nothing to do with emotions.

He deliberately relaxed his grasp and sat down. 'We have unfinished business,' he said. 'I knew that the minute you walked in that door yesterday.'

'You're imagining things,' she said.

He put up one brow. 'Am I?'

She held his gaze for a beat, before she lowered it to focus on the glass paperweight on his desk. 'How long do you think this marriage will last?' she asked.

'It can last as long as we want it to,' Angelo said.

Her gaze met his again. 'Don't you mean as long as *you* want it to?' she asked.

He gave a little up and down movement of his right shoulder. 'You ended things the last time,' he said. 'Isn't it fair that I be the one to do so this time around?'

Her mouth tightened. 'I ended things because it was time to move on,' she said. 'We were fighting all the time. It wasn't a love match. It was a battlefield.'

'Oh, come *on*,' Angelo said. 'What are you talking about, Natalie? All couples fight. It's part and parcel of being in a relationship. There are always little power struggles. It's what makes life interesting.'

'That might have been the way you were brought up, but it certainly wasn't the way I was,' she said.

He studied her expression again, noting all the little nuances of her face: the way she chewed at the inside of her mouth but tried to hide it, the way her eyes flickered away from his but then kept tracking back, as if they were being pulled by a magnetic force, and the way her finely boned jaw tightened when she was feeling cornered.

'How *were* you brought up to resolve conflict?' he asked.

She reached for her bag and got to her feet. 'Look, I have a train to catch,' she said. 'I have a hundred and one things to see to.'

'Why didn't you drive down from Edinburgh?' he asked. 'You haven't suddenly developed a fear of driving too, have you?'

Her eyes hardened resentfully. 'No,' she said. 'I like travelling by train. I can read or sketch or listen to music. I find driving requires too much concentration—especially in a city as crowded as London. Besides, it's better for the environment. I want to reduce my carbon footprint.'

Angelo rose to his feet and joined her at the door, placing his hand on the doorknob to stop her escaping. 'I'll need you to sign some papers in the next day or two.'

Her chin came up. The hard glitter was back in her gaze. 'A prenuptial agreement?'

He glanced at her mouth. He ached to feel it move under the pressure of his. He could feel the surge of his blood filling him with urgent, ferocious need.

'Yes,' he said, meeting her gaze again. 'Do you have a problem with that?'

'No,' she said, eyeballing him right back. 'I'll have one of my own drawn up. I'm not letting you take away everything I've worked so hard for.'

He smiled and tapped her gently on the end of her nose. 'Touché,' he said.

She blinked at him, looking flustered and disorientated. 'I—I have to go,' she said, and made a grab for the doorknob.

Angelo captured her hand within his. Her small, delicate fingers were dwarfed by the thickness and length and strength of his. He watched her eyes widen as he slowly brought her hand up to his mouth. He stopped before making contact with his lips, just a hair's breadth from touching. He watched as her throat rose and fell. He felt the jerky little gust of her cinnamon-scented breath. He saw her glance at his mouth, saw too the quick nervous dart of her tongue as she swept it out over her lips.

'I'll be in touch,' he said, dropping her hand and opening the door for her. *'Ciao.'*

She brushed past him in the doorway and without a single word of farewell she left.

CHAPTER THREE

'CONGRATULATIONS,' said Linda, Natalie's assistant, the following morning when she arrived at work.

'Pardon?'

Linda held up a newspaper. 'Talk about keeping your cards close to your chest,' she said. 'I didn't even know you were dating anyone.'

'I'm…' Natalie took the paper and quickly scanned it. There was a short paragraph about Angelo and her and their upcoming nuptials. Angelo was quoted as saying he was thrilled they were back together and how much he was looking forward to being married next week.

'Is it true or is it a prank?' Linda asked.

Natalie put the paper down on the counter. 'It's true,' she said, chewing at her bottom lip.

'Pardon me if I'm overstepping the mark here, but you don't look too happy about it,' Linda said.

Natalie forced a smile to her face. 'Sorry, it's just been such a pain…er…keeping it quiet until now,' she said, improvising as she went. 'We didn't want anyone to speculate about us getting back together until we were sure it was what we both wanted.'

'Gosh, how romantic!' Linda said. 'A secret relationship.'

'Not so secret now,' Natalie said a little ruefully as

her stomach tied itself in knots. How was she going to cope with the constant press attention? They would swarm about her like bees. Angelo was used to being chased by the paparazzi. He was used to cameras flashing in his face and articles being written that were neither true nor false but somewhere in between.

She liked her privacy. She guarded it fiercely. Now she would be thrust into the public arena not for her designs and her talent but for whom she was sleeping with.

Her stomach gave another little shuffle. Not that she would be actually sleeping with Angelo. She was determined not to give in to that particular temptation. Her body might still have some sort of programmed response to him, but that didn't mean she had to give in to it.

She could be strong.

She *would* be strong.

And determined.

He wouldn't find her so easy to seduce this time around. She had been young and relatively inexperienced five years ago. She was older and wiser now. She hadn't fallen in love with him before and she wasn't about to fall in love with him now. He would be glad to call an end to their marriage before a month or two. She couldn't see him tolerating her intransigence for very long. He was used to getting his own way. He wanted a submissive, I'll-do-anything-to-please-you wife.

There wasn't a bone in Natalie's body that would bend to any man's will, and certainly not to Angelo Bellandini's.

'These came for you while you were at the lawyer's,' Linda said when Natalie came back to the studio a couple of hours later.

Natalie looked at the massive bunch of blood-red roses elegantly wrapped and ribboned, their intoxicating clove-like perfume filling the air.

'Aren't you going to read the card?' Linda asked.

'Er...yes,' Natalie said unpinning the envelope from the cellophane and tissue wrap. She took the card out and read: *See you tonight, Angelo.*

'From Angelo?' Linda asked.

'Yes,' Natalie said, frowning.

'What's wrong?'

'Nothing.'

'You're frowning.'

She quickly relaxed her features. 'I've got a few things to see to in my office at home. Do you mind holding the fort here for the rest of the day?'

'Not at all,' Linda said. 'I guess you'll have to leave me in charge when you go on your honeymoon, right?'

Natalie gave her a tight on-off smile as she grabbed her bag and put the strap over her shoulder. 'I don't think I'll be away very long,' she said.

'Aren't you going to take the roses with you?' Linda asked.

Natalie turned back and scooped them up off the counter. 'Good idea,' she said, and left.

Angelo looked at the three-storey house in a leafy street in the well-to-do Edinburgh suburb of Morningside. It had a gracious elegance about it that reminded him of Natalie immediately. Even the garden seemed to reflect parts of her personality. The neatly clipped hedges and the meticulous attention to detail in plants and their colour and placement bore witness to a young woman who liked order and control.

He smiled to himself as he thought how annoyed she

would be at the way things were now *out* of her control. He had the upper hand and he was going to keep it. He would enjoy watching her squirm. He had five years of bitterness to avenge. Five years of hating her, five years of wanting her, five years of being tortured by memories of her body in his arms.

Five years of trying to replace her.

He put his finger to the highly polished brass doorbell. A chime-like sound rang out, and within a few seconds he heard the click-clack of her heels as she came to answer its summons. He could tell she was angry. He braced himself for the blast.

'How dare you release something to the press without checking with me first?' she said as her opening gambit.

'Hello, *cara*,' he said. 'I'm fine, thank you. And you?'

She glowered at him as she all but slammed the door once he had stepped over its threshold. 'You had no right to say anything to anyone,' she said. 'I was followed home by paparazzi. I had cameras going off in my face as soon as I left my studio. I almost got my teeth knocked out by one of their microphones.'

'Sorry about that,' he said. 'I'm so used to it I hardly notice it any more. Do you want me to get you a bodyguard? I should've thought of it earlier.'

She rolled her eyes. 'Of course I don't want a bloody bodyguard!' she said. 'I just want this to go away. I want *all* of this to go away.'

'It's not going to go away, Natalie,' he said. 'I'm not going to go away.'

She continued to glare at him. 'Why are you here?'

'I'm here to take you out to dinner.'

'What if I'm not hungry?'

'Then you can sit and watch me eat,' he said. 'Won't that be fun?'

'You are totally sick—do you know that?' she said.

'Did you like the roses?'

She turned away from him and began stalking down the wide corridor. 'I hate hothouse flowers,' she said. 'They have no scent.'

'I didn't buy you hothouse flowers,' he said. 'I had those roses shipped in from a private gardener.'

She gave a dismissive grunt and pushed open a door leading to a large formal sitting room. Again the attention to detail was stunning. Beautifully co-ordinated colours and luxurious fabrics, plush sofas and crystal chandeliers. Timeless antiques cleverly teamed with modern pieces—old-world charm and modern chic that somehow worked together brilliantly.

'Do you want a drink?' she asked uncharitably.

'What are you having?'

She threw him a speaking glance. 'I was thinking along the lines of cyanide,' she said.

He laughed. 'Not quite to my taste, *mia piccola*,' he said. 'Can I have a soda and lime?'

She went to a bar fridge that was hidden behind an art deco cabinet. He heard the rattle of ice cubes and the fizz of the soda water and then the plop of a slice of lime. She fixed her own glass of white wine before she turned and passed his drink to him with a combative look on her face.

'I hope it chokes you,' she said.

He lifted the glass against hers in a salute and said, 'To a long and happy marriage.'

Her gaze wrestled with his. 'I'm not drinking to that.'

'What will you drink to?'

She clanged her glass against his. 'To freedom,' she said, and took a sip.

Angelo watched her as she moved across the room,

her body movements stiff and unfriendly. She took another couple of sips of her drink, grimacing distastefully as if she wasn't used to drinking alcohol. 'I drove past your studio on the way here,' he said. 'Very impressive.'

She gave him a quick off-hand glance over her shoulder. 'Thank you.'

'I have a project for you, if you're interested,' he said.

She turned and looked at him fully. 'What sort of project?'

'A big one,' he said. 'It's worth a lot of money. Good exposure for you, too. It will bring you contacts from all over Europe.'

She stood very still before him, barely moving a muscle apart from the little hammer beat of tension at the base of her throat. 'Go on,' she said, with that same look of wariness in her gaze.

'I have a holiday villa in Sorrento, on the Amalfi Coast,' he said. 'I bought another property nearby for a song a few months back. I'm turning it into a luxury hotel. I'm just about done with the structural repairs. Now it's time for the interior makeover. I thought it would be a good project for you to take on once we are married.'

'Why do you want me to do it?' she asked.

'You're good at what you do,' he said.

Her mouth thinned in cynicism. 'And you want a carrot to dangle in front of me in case I happen to find a last-minute escape route?'

'You won't find an escape route,' he said. 'If you're a good girl I might even consider using your linen exclusively in all of my hotels. But only if you behave yourself.'

The look she gave him glittered with hatred. 'You've

certainly got blackmail down to a science,' she said. 'I didn't realise you were this ruthless five years ago.'

'I wasn't,' he said, taking another leisurely sip of his drink.

She tightened her mouth. 'I'll have to think about it,' she said. 'I have a lot of work on just now.'

'How capable is your assistant?' Angelo asked.

'Very capable,' she said. 'I'm thinking of promoting her. I need someone to handle the international end of things.'

'It must be quite limiting, not being able to do the travelling yourself,' he said.

She lifted a shoulder in a dismissive manner. 'I manage.'

Angelo picked up a small photo frame from an intricately carved drum table next to where he was standing. 'Is this Lachlan as a toddler?' he asked.

Her deep blue gaze flickered with something as she glanced at the photo. 'No,' she said. 'It's not.'

Angelo put the frame back on the table and, pushing back his sleeve, glanced at his watch. 'We should get going,' he said. 'I've booked the restaurant for eight.'

'I told you I'm not having dinner with you,' she said.

'And I told you to behave yourself,' he tossed back. 'You will join me for dinner and you will look happy about it. I don't care how you act in private, but in public you will at all times act like a young woman who is deeply in love. If you put even one toe of one foot out of line your brother will pay the price.'

She glared at him, her whole body bristling with anger. 'I've never been in love before, so how am I going to pull that act off with any authenticity?' she asked.

Angelo gave her a steely look. 'Make it up as you

go along,' he said, and put his glass down with a dull thud next to the photo frame. 'I'll be waiting outside in the car.'

Natalie waited until he had left the room before she picked up his glass. She mopped up the circle of condensation left on the leather top of the table with the heel of her hand and then wiped her hand against her churning stomach.

Her eyes went to the photo of Liam. He was standing on the beach with a bucket and spade in his dimpled hands, his cherubic face smiling for the camera. It had been taken just hours before he died. She remembered how excited he had been about the shells he had found. She remembered the sandcastle they had built together. She remembered how they had come back to the pool with their parents to rinse off. She remembered how her mother had gone inside for a rest and her father had left her with Liam while he made an important phone call…

She gently straightened the photo frame with fingers that were not quite steady. And then, with a sigh that burned like a serrated knife inside her chest, she went to get ready for dinner.

The restaurant Angelo had booked was a popular one that attracted the rich and the famous. Natalie had been a couple of times before, but no one had taken much notice of her. This time everyone looked and pointed as she came into the restaurant under Angelo's escort. A couple of people even took photos with their phones.

She tried to ignore the feel of his hand at her back. It was barely touching her but it felt like a brand. She could feel the tensile strength of him in that feather-light touch. It was a heady reminder of the sensual power he had over her.

Still had over her.

The *maître d'* led them to a table and then bustled off to fetch drinks after he had handed them both menus.

She buried her head in the menu even though she had no appetite. The words were just a blur in front of her. She blinked and tried to focus. A week ago she wouldn't have dreamed it possible for her to be sitting with Angelo in a restaurant. Ever since their break-up she had kept her distance both physically and mentally. But now she was back in his world and she wasn't sure how she was going to get out of it. How long would their marriage last, given the irreconcilable differences between them? He had loved her once, but he certainly wasn't motivated by love now. Revenge was his goal.

It had taken five years for the planets to align in his favour, but Lachlan had provided the perfect set-up for him to make her pay for leaving him. A man as proud and powerful as he was would not be satisfied until he had settled the score. How long would he insist on her staying with him? He surely wouldn't tie himself indefinitely to a loveless marriage. He was an only child. He was thirty-three years old—almost thirty-four. He would want children in the not too distant future. He would hardly want *her* to be the mother of his heirs. He would want someone biddable and obedient. Someone who would grace his many homes with poise and grace. Someone who wouldn't argue with him or question his opinions. Someone who would love him without reservation.

'Are you still a strict vegetarian?' Angelo asked.

Natalie looked at him over the top of the menu. 'I

occasionally eat chicken and fish,' she confessed a little sheepishly.

His dark brows lifted. 'You were so passionate back then.'

She lowered her gaze to the menu again. 'Yes, well, I was young and full of ideals back then. I've realised since that life is not so black and white.'

'What else have you changed your mind about?' he asked.

She put the menu to one side. 'I haven't changed that much,' she said.

'Meaning you still don't want children?'

Natalie felt the all too familiar pain seize her. She thought of Isabel's little newborn daughter Imogen, of how it had felt to hold her in her arms just a couple of weeks ago—the soft sweet smell, the tiny little starfish hands that had gripped hers so firmly. It had brought guilt down on her like a guillotine.

'No,' she said. 'I haven't changed my mind about that.'

'So you're still the high-powered career girl?' he said.

She picked up her glass and raised it in a salute. 'That's me.'

His dark brown eyes kept holding hers. 'What about when you're older?' he asked. 'You're young now, but what about when your biological clock starts to ramp up its ticking?'

'Not every woman is cut out to be a mother,' she said. 'I'm not good with kids. I think I must have missed out on the maternal gene.'

'I don't believe that,' he said. 'I accept that there are some women who genuinely don't want to have children, but you're a born nurturer. Look at the way you're prepared to put your neck on the line for your brother.'

She gave a careless shrug. 'I hate the thought of ruining my figure,' she said. 'I don't want stretch marks or sagging boobs.'

He made a sound at the back of his throat. 'For God's sake, Natalie, surely you're not that shallow?'

She met his gaze levelly. 'No, but I'm convinced some of your recent lovers have been.'

He gave her a glinting smile. 'So you've been keeping track of me over the years, have you, *cara*?' he asked.

'Not at all,' she said, looking away again. 'It is of no interest to me whatsoever who you sleep with. I have no hold over you. We dated. We broke up. That's it as far as I'm concerned.'

'We didn't just date,' he said. 'We lived together for five and a half months.'

Natalie picked up her drink, just for something to do with her hands. 'I only moved in with you because my flatmate's boyfriend moved in with us and made me feel I was in the way,' she said. 'Anyway, five months is not a long time compared to some relationships.'

'It was a long time for me.'

'Only because you've been playing musical beds since you were a teenager,' she said.

'Now who's talking?' he asked, with a diamond-hard glitter in his gaze as it clashed with hers.

Natalie wasn't ashamed of her past, but she wasn't proud of it either. While not exactly a constant bed-hopper, like some of her peers, she had occasionally used sex as a way to bolster her self-esteem. But the physical sensations had meant nothing to her until she had met Angelo. Not that she had ever told him. While she had been totally open with him physically, emotionally she had always held him slightly distant. She wondered if that was why he had found her so attractive. He was used to women falling head over heels in love with him and telling him so right from the start.

But she had not.

'Careful, Angelo,' she said. 'Your double standards are showing.'

His jaw tensed as he held her look. 'How long did you date the guy you replaced me with?' he asked.

'Not long,' she said.

'How long?'

'Is this really necessary?' she asked.

'I want to know.'

'We went out for a couple of weeks,' she said.

'Who broke it off?'

Natalie found his intent look unsettling. 'I did,' she said.

'So who have you dated since?'

'No one you would know,' she said. 'I try to keep my private life out of the papers.'

'Well done, you,' he said. 'I try to, but it's amazing how people find out stuff.'

'How do you stand it?' she asked.

He gave a little shrug. 'I'm used to it,' he said. 'My family's wealth has always kept us in the spotlight. The only time it cooled off a bit was when I came to study in London. I enjoyed being anonymous—not that it lasted long.'

'You lied to me.'

'I didn't lie to you,' he said. 'I just didn't tell you I came from such a wealthy family. It was important for me to make it on my own. I didn't want my father's name opening any doors for me.'

'You've certainly made a name for yourself in your own right,' Natalie said. 'You have twice the wealth of your father, or so I've heard.'

'For someone who says they have no interest in what I do or who I see, you certainly know a lot about me,' he said with a sardonic smile.

She ignored his comment and picked up her glass again, took a sip. 'What have you told your family about me?' she asked.

'A version of the truth,' he said.

Natalie's eyes came back to his. 'The truth about you hating me and wanting revenge?' she asked with an arch look.

His dark brown eyes gleamed. 'I could hardly tell my parents I hate you, now, could I?'

'What *did* you tell them?'

His eyes kept on holding hers. 'I told them I had never stopped loving you,' he said.

She moistened her lips. 'And they…believed you?'

'They seemed to,' he said. 'Although the real test will be when they see us together. My mother, in particular, is a hard person to fool. You'll have to be on your toes with her.'

Natalie felt her insides quake at the thought of interacting with his parents and other members of his family. How would she do it? How would she play the role of a happy bride without revealing the truth of how things were between them? How long before someone guessed? How long before it was splashed all over the newspapers?

'Why do we have to get married?' she asked. 'Why couldn't we just have an…an affair?'

Those unfathomable brown eyes measured hers. 'Is that what you want?' he asked. 'An affair?'

She ran her tongue over her lips again. 'No more than I want to marry you. I was just making a point,' she said. 'It seems a bit over the top to go to all the trouble of getting married when ultimately we know it's going to end in divorce.'

'You seem very sure it will end in divorce,' he said.

Natalie's heart fluttered like fast moving wings against her breastbone. 'You can't want to be tied to me indefinitely?'

His eyes moved over her leisurely. 'Who knows? You might like being married to me,' he said. 'There will be numerous benefits to wearing my ring and bearing my name.'

She sat up like a puppet suddenly jerked backwards. 'I don't want your name,' she said. 'I'm perfectly happy with my own.'

A steely glint came into his eyes. 'You will take my name,' he said. 'And you will be proud of it.'

She glowered at him, her whole body trembling with anger. 'I will *not* change my name.'

Angelo's eyes warred with hers. 'You will do what I tell you to do,' he said, his voice low but no less forceful.

Natalie stood up so abruptly her chair knocked against the one behind it. Every eye turned to look at her but she was beyond caring. She tossed her napkin down on the table and scooped her purse up with the other.

'Find yourself another wife,' she said, and stormed out.

A camera went off in her face as soon as she stepped outside the restaurant.

'Miss Armitage?' A journalist pushed a microphone close. 'Can we have an exclusive on your current relationship with Angelo Bellandini?'

Natalie tried to avoid the reporter, but another member of the paparazzi cut her off as she tried to escape.

'We notice you're not wearing an engagement ring,' he said. 'Does that mean the wedding's off?'

'I...'

Angelo's arm came around her protectively and he gently led her away from the throng. 'Please give my fiancée some space,' he said.

'Mr Bellandini, do you have a comment to make on your engagement to Miss Armitage?' the first journalist asked.

Angelo's arm tightened around her waist a fraction. 'The wedding is going ahead as planned,' he said. 'I have an engagement ring already picked out for Natalie. I am giving it to her tonight when we get home. Now, please leave us to celebrate our engagement in privacy.'

Natalie was ushered to Angelo's car without further intrusion from the press. She sat back in her seat, her fingers white-knuckled around her purse.

'Don't *ever* do that again,' Angelo said as he fired the engine.

She threw him a cutting glance. 'I am not going to be ordered around by you.'

His hands gripped the steering wheel as tightly as she was clutching her purse. His knuckles looked as if they were going to burst through the skin.

'I will not tolerate you flouncing out on me like a spoilt child,' he said through gritted teeth. 'Do you have no sense of propriety? You do realise that little scene will be all over the papers tomorrow? What were you thinking?'

Natalie gave her head a toss. 'I'm not going to be bullied into changing my name.'

'Fine,' he said. 'It's obviously a sore point with you.

I'm prepared to compromise. I should've realised how important it was to you. It's your trademark.' He paused for a beat. 'I'm sorry.'

She slowly loosened her grip on her purse. 'Are the press always that intrusive?' she asked.

He let out a breath in a sigh. 'I hardly notice it any more,' he said. 'But, yes, they are. It won't last for ever. They'll lose interest once we're married.'

Natalie frowned as she looked at him. 'I hope people don't think I'm marrying you for your money.'

His lips lifted in the slightest of smiles. 'No, *cara*, they'll think it's my body you are after.'

She turned away to stare at the passing scenery, her lower body flickering with a pulse she had thought long ago quelled. 'I'm not going to sleep with you, Angelo,' she said.

'Are you saying that to convince me or yourself?' he asked.

Natalie couldn't have answered either way, so she changed the subject. 'Have you really got an engagement ring?' she asked.

'I have.'

'Do you not think I might have liked to choose it for myself?'

He threw her an exasperated look. 'In my family it's traditional for the man to choose the engagement ring,' he said.

She toyed with the catch on her purse for a moment or two. 'It's not the same one you bought five years ago, is it?' she asked.

'No,' he said.

She sneaked a glance at him but his expression was inscrutable. 'Did you give it to someone else?' she asked. 'As a present or something?'

He brought the car to a standstill outside her house before he answered. 'I donated it to a charity for their silent auction,' he said. 'There's some lucky girl out there now wearing a ring that cost more than most people's houses.'

Natalie chewed at the inside of her mouth. 'I never asked you to spend that amount of money on me.'

His swung his gaze to hers. 'No, you didn't, did you?' he said. 'But then it wasn't money you wanted from me, was it?'

She couldn't hold his look. 'I've seen what money can do to people,' she said. 'It changes them, and not always for the good.'

She felt his gaze studying her for endless seconds. 'What have you told your parents about us?' he asked.

She pressed her lips together. 'Not much.'

'How much?'

She looked at him again. 'It was my mother's idea for me to come and see you,' she said. 'I only did it for her sake.'

'And Lachlan's, presumably?'

Her eyes fell away from his. 'Yes...'

The silence stretched interminably.

'Are you going to ask me in?' he asked.

She gave him a pert look. 'Are you going to come in even if I don't?'

He brushed an idle finger down the curve of her cheek, his eyes focussed on her mouth, his lips curved upwards in a half-smile. 'If you don't want me then all you have to do is say so.'

I do want you.

The words were like drumbeats inside her head.

I want you. I want you. I want you.

She locked out that traitorous voice and pasted an

indifferent look on her face. 'Are you staying in town overnight?' she asked.

'No,' he said. 'I was hoping you'd offer me a bed for the night.'

Natalie felt her heart give a hard, sharp kick. 'I don't think that's such a good idea.'

'Why not?'

'Because... Because...'

'The press will think it odd if I don't stay with you,' he said, before she could think of an excuse. 'I'm not sure if you've noticed, but a car followed us back here. It's parked behind the red car.'

She checked in the side mirror. There was a man sitting behind the wheel with a camera's telephoto lens trained in their direction. Panic gripped her by the throat. Was this how it was going to be? Would she be hounded like a terrified fox with nowhere to hide?

Angelo opened his door and came around to where she was sitting, frozen in dread.

'He'll move on once we're inside,' he said. 'Just try to act naturally.'

Natalie got out of the car and allowed him to take her hand. She felt the strong grip of his fingers as they curled around hers. It was the same feeling she'd had when he had put his arm around her waist earlier.

She felt protected.

'Give me your keys,' he said.

She handed them over. 'It's the big brass one,' she said.

He unlocked the door and held it open for her to pass through. 'How long have you lived here?' he asked as he closed the door.

'Three and a half years.'

'Why Scotland? I thought you said you grew up in Gloucestershire?'

'My mother is a Scot,' she said. 'She grew up in the seaside village of Crail in Fife. I spent a lot of holidays there with my grandparents when I was young.'

'You didn't tell me that before.'

She gave a shrug as she placed her purse on the hall table. 'It didn't seem important.'

'What else didn't you tell me that didn't seem important?'

Natalie turned away from his probing look. 'Do you want a drink or something?'

He stalled her by placing a hand on her arm. 'Tatty?'

She looked down at his hand. How dark and masculine it looked against her paler skin. It dredged up memories she didn't want to resurface. She felt the rumble of them like tectonic plates rubbing against each other. An earthquake of sensation threatened to spill out like lava. She felt the heat of it bubbling like a furnace inside her.

'I asked you not to call me that,' she said.

His hand moved along her arm in a gentle caress. 'I don't always do what I'm told,' he said. 'I like bending the rules to suit me.'

Natalie tried to pull away but his fingers subtly tightened. She met his gaze—so dark and mesmerising—so in control. He knew he had her where he wanted her. She was at his mercy. Lachlan's freedom and future depended on her. Angelo knew she would not do anything to jeopardise it. Her little temper tantrum back at the restaurant had achieved nothing. He would always come after her and remind her of what was at stake.

'Why are you doing this?' she asked. 'You must know how it's going to end.'

His hooded gaze drifted to her mouth. 'I don't care how it ends,' he said. 'This is about the here and now.'

She looked at his mouth. Oh, how she wanted to feel those firm lips move against hers! She remembered the heat; she remembered the blistering passion that burned like a taper all over her flesh. She remembered the sexy thrust of his tongue as it came in search of hers.

Her breath caught in her throat as she felt the breeze of his breath skate over her lips. He lowered his mouth to just above hers. She swept her tongue over her lips, wanting him, aching for him to make the first move.

'Go on,' he said, in a low, husky, spine-melting tone. 'I know you want to.'

Natalie's stomach shifted like a speeding skater suddenly facing a sheet of broken ice. Could he read her so well even after all this time? She fought for composure, for self-control, for anything.

'You're mistaken,' she said coolly. 'I don't want any such thing.'

He brushed a finger over her tingling bottom lip. 'Liar.'

It took all of her resolve and then some to step back, but somehow she did it. She moved to the other side of the room, barricading herself behind one of the sofas set in the middle of the room. 'I think you should leave,' she said.

'Why?' he asked. 'Because you don't trust yourself around me?'

She sent him an arctic look. 'I'm not going to be a slave to your desires.'

'Is that what you think you'll be?' he asked. 'What about your own desires? You have them. You can deny them all you like but they're still there. I can feel it when I touch you.'

'What we had five years ago is gone,' Natalie said. 'You can't make it come back just to suit you.'

'It never went away,' he said. 'You wanted it to, but it didn't. You were scared of the next step, weren't you? You were scared of the commitment of marriage. You're still scared. What I'd like to know is why.'

'Get out.'

'I'm not going until I give you this.' He took a jeweller's box from inside his jacket pocket. But rather than come over to her he simply set it down on the coffee table. It reminded her of a gauntlet being laid down between two opponents.

'I'll have a car sent to collect you on Tuesday,' he said. 'Pack enough clothes for a week. We'll be expected to go on a honeymoon. If you e-mail me a list of the people you wish to invite to the ceremony I'll have my secretary deal with it.'

'What do you want me to wear?' she asked. 'Sackcloth and ashes?'

'You can wear what you like,' he said. 'It makes no difference to me. But do keep in mind that there will be photographers everywhere.'

'Do you really expect me to pack up my life here and follow you about the globe like some lovesick little fool?' she asked.

'We will divide our time between your place and mine,' he said. 'I'm based in London, but I plan to spend a bit of time in Sorrento until the development is near completion. I'm prepared to be flexible. I understand you have a business to run.'

She gave him a petulant look. 'What if I don't want you to share my house?'

'Get used to it, Natalie. I will share your house and a whole lot more before the ink is dry on our marriage certificate.' He went to the door. 'I'll see you on Tuesday.'

Natalie didn't touch the jeweller's box until he had left. She stood looking at it for a long time before she picked it up and opened it. Inside was an art deco design triple diamond ring. It was stunningly beautiful. She took it out of its velvet home and slipped it on her finger. She couldn't have chosen better herself. It was neither too loose nor too tight—a perfect ring for an imperfect relationship.

She wondered how long it would be before she would be giving it back.

CHAPTER FOUR

NATALIE was in a state of high anxiety by the time Tuesday came around.

She hadn't eaten for three days. She had barely slept. She had been dry retching at the thought of getting on a plane to Italy.

Angelo had called her each day, but she hadn't revealed anything of what she was going through. He had assured her Lachlan was out of harm's way. Her parents had called too, and expressed their satisfaction with the way things had turned out. Her father was greatly relieved that the family name hadn't been sullied by Lachlan's antics. Angelo had miraculously made the nasty little episode disappear, for which Adrian Armitage was immensely grateful. He'd made no mention of Natalie's role in fixing things. She had expected no less from him, given he had never shown an interest in her welfare, but she was particularly annoyed with her mother, who hadn't even asked her how she felt about marrying Angelo. But then Isla had married Natalie's father for money and prestige. Love hadn't come into it at all.

She felt annoyed too at having to lie to her friends—in particular Isabel. But strangely enough Isabel had accepted the news of her marriage with barely a blink of an eye. Her friend had said how she had always thought Natalie had unresolved feelings for Angelo since she hadn't dated all that seriously since. She thought Natalie's aversion to marriage and commitment had stemmed from her break up with Angelo. Natalie hadn't had the heart to put Isabel straight. As close as she was to her, she had never told Isabel about the circumstances surrounding Liam's death.

Natalie heard a car pull up outside her house. Her stomach did another somersault and a clammy sweat broke out over her brow. She walked to the door on legs that felt like wet cotton wool. It wasn't a uniformed driver standing there but Angelo himself.

'I...I just have to get my bag...' she said, brushing a loose strand of sticky hair back behind her ear.

Angelo narrowed his gaze. 'Are you all right?'

'I'm fine,' she said, averting her eyes.

He put a hand on her shoulder and turned her to look at him. 'You're deathly pale,' he said. 'Are you ill?'

Natalie swallowed the gnarly knot of panic in her throat. 'I have some pills to take.' She rummaged in her bag for the anxiety medication her doctor had prescribed. 'I won't be a minute.'

She went to the kitchen for a glass of water and Angelo followed her. He took the packet of pills from her and read the label. 'Do you really need to take these?' he asked.

'Give them to me,' she said, reaching for them. 'I should've taken them an hour ago.'

He frowned as he handed them to her. 'Do you take them regularly?'

She shook her head as she swallowed a couple of pills. 'No,' she said. 'Only in an emergency.'

He was still frowning as he led her out to the car. 'When did you develop your fear of flying?' he asked.

'Ages ago,' she said.

'What caused it?' he asked. 'Rough turbulence or a mid-air incident?'

She shrugged. 'Can't remember.'

His dark gaze searched hers. 'When was the last time you flew?'

'Can we get going?' she asked. 'I don't want to fall asleep in the car. You'll have to carry me on board.'

Angelo glanced at Natalie every now and again as he drove to the airport. She was not quite so pale now the medication had settled her nerves, but she still looked fragile. Her cheeks looked hollow, as if she had recently lost weight, and her eyes were shadowed.

Her concern over her brother was well founded. He had struck a deal with Lachlan, but already Lachlan was pushing against the boundaries Angelo had set in place. The staff at a very expensive private rehab clinic had called him three times in the last week to inform him about Lachlan's erratic and at times uncontrollable behaviour. He had organised a therapist to have extra sessions with him, but so far there had been no miraculous breakthrough. It seemed Lachlan Armitage was a very angry young man, hell-bent on self-destruction.

Speaking with Natalie's father had made Angelo realise how frustrating it must be to have a child who, no matter how much you loved and provided for him, refused to co-operate. Adrian Armitage had hinted at similar trouble with Natalie. Apparently her stubborn streak had caused many a scene in the Armitage household over the years. In spite of all of her father's efforts to get close to her she had wilfully defied him whenever she could. Angelo wondered if it was a cultural thing. He had been brought up strictly, but fairly. His parents had commanded respect, but they had more than earned it with their dedication and love for him. He hoped to do the same for his own children one day.

He turned off the engine once he had parked and gently touched Natalie on the shoulder. 'Hey, sleepy-head,' he said. 'Time to get going.'

She blinked and sat up straighter. 'Oh… Right…'

He put an arm around her waist as he led her on board his private jet a short time later. She was agitated and edgy, but he managed to get her to take a seat and put the belt on.

'Can I have a drink?' she asked.

'Sure,' he said. 'What would you like?'

'White wine,' she said.

'Are you sure it's a good idea to combine alcohol with those pills?' he asked.

She gave him a surly look. 'I'm not a child.'

'No, but you're under my protection,' he said. 'I don't want you getting ill, or losing consciousness or something.'

She started chewing her nails as the pilot pulled back. Angelo took her hand away from her mouth and covered it with his. 'You'll be fine, *cara*,' he said. 'You were in far more danger driving to the airport than you ever will be in the air.'

She shifted restively, her eyes darting about like a spooked thoroughbred's. 'I want to get off,' she said. 'Please—can you tell the pilot to stop? I want to get off.'

Angelo put his arm around her and brought her close against him. 'Shh, *mia piccola*,' he soothed. 'Concentrate on your breathing. In and out. In and out. That's right. Nice and slow.'

She squeezed her eyes shut and lowered her head to his chest. He stroked the silk of her hair, talking to her in the same calm voice. It took a lot longer than he expected but finally she relaxed against him. She slept for most of the journey and only woke up just as they were coming to land in Rome.

'There,' he said. 'You did it. That wasn't so bad, was it?'

She nodded vaguely and brushed the hair back off her face. 'Have I got time to use the bathroom?'

'Sure,' he said. 'Do you want me to come with you?'

Her cheeks pooled with colour. 'No, thank you.'

He gave her a mocking smile. 'Maybe next time, *si*?'

The press had obviously been given a tip-off somewhere between their arrival at the airport and Angelo's family villa in Rome. Natalie watched in dismay as photographers surged towards Angelo's chauffeur-driven car.

'Don't worry,' he said as he helped her out of the car. 'I'll handle their questions.'

Within a few moments Angelo had managed to satisfy the press's interest and sent them on their way.

An older man opened the front door of the villa and greeted Angelo. 'Your parents are in the salon, Signor Bellandini.'

'*Grazie*, Pasquale,' he said. 'Natalie, this is Pasquale. He has been working for my family for many years.'

'I'm very pleased to meet you,' Natalie said.

'Welcome,' Pasquale said. 'It is very nice to see Signor Bellandini happy at last.'

'Come,' Angelo said, guiding her with a hand resting in the curve of her back. 'My parents will be keen to meet you.'

If they were so keen, why hadn't they been at the

door to greet her instead of the elderly servant? Natalie thought bitterly to herself. But clearly there was a different protocol in the upper classes of Italian society. And Sandro and Francesca Bellandini were nothing if not from the very top shelf of the upper class.

Natalie could see where Angelo got his height and looks from as soon as she set eyes on his father. While an inch or two shorter than his son, Sandro had the same dark brown eyes and lean, rangy build. His hair was still thick and curly but it was liberally streaked with grey, giving him a distinguished air that was as compelling as it was intimidating.

Francesca, on the other hand, was petite, and her demeanour outwardly demure, but her keen hazel eyes missed nothing. Natalie felt them move over her in one quick assessing glance, noting her hair and make-up, the style and make of her clothes, the texture of her skin and the state of her figure.

'This is Natalie, my fiancée,' Angelo said. 'Natalie— my parents, Sandro and Francesca.'

'Welcome to the family.' Francesca was the first to speak. 'Angelo has told us so much about you. I am sorry we didn't meet you five years ago. We would've told him he was a fool for letting you go—*si*, Sandro?'

'*Si*,' Sandro said, taking her hand once his wife had relinquished it. 'You are very welcome indeed.'

Angelo's arm came back around her waist. 'I'll see that Natalie is settled in upstairs before we join you for a celebratory drink.'

'Maria has made up the Venetian room for you both,' Francesca said. 'I didn't see the point in separating you. You've been apart too long, no?'

Natalie glanced at Angelo, but he was smiling at his

mother. 'That was very thoughtful of you, *Mamma*,' he said.

Natalie had to wait until they were upstairs and alone before she could vent her spleen. 'I bet you did that deliberately,' she said.

'Did what?'

'Don't play the guileless innocent with me,' she flashed back. 'You knew your mother would put us in the same room, didn't you?'

'On the contrary. I thought she would go old-fashioned on me and put us at opposite ends of the villa,' he said. 'I told you she's incredibly insightful. She must have sensed how hot you are for me.'

Natalie glared at him. 'I'm not sharing that bed with you.'

'Fine,' he said unbuttoning his shirt. 'I'll let you have the floor.'

She frowned at him. 'What are you doing?'

He pulled his shirt out of the waistband of his trousers. 'I'm getting changed.'

Her eyes went the flat plane of his abdomen. He looked amazing—so masculine, so taut, so magnificently fit and tanned and virile. She swung away and went to look out of the windows overlooking the gardens.

'Why did you let your parents think it was you who ended our affair five years ago?' she asked.

'I didn't want you to get off to a bad start with them,' he said. 'I'm their only child. Parents can be funny about things like that.'

Natalie turned around. He was only wearing black underwear now. The fabric clung to him lovingly. Her insides clenched with greedy fistfuls of desire. She had kissed and tasted every inch of his body. She had taken him in her mouth, ruthlessly tasting him until he had collapsed with release. She had felt him move deep within her. She had felt his essence spill inside her. She had been as brazen as she could be with him and yet still he had always been a step ahead of her. He had pushed her to the limit time and time again. Her flesh shivered in memory of his touch. Her spine tingled and her belly fluttered. She drew in a breath as she saw his gaze run over her. Was he too thinking of the red-hot passion they had shared?

'I don't expect you to take the blame,' she said. 'I'm not ashamed of breaking off our relationship. I was too young to get married.'

'That won't cut it with my mother, I'm afraid,' he said. 'She was barely sixteen when she fell in love with my father. She has never looked at another man since.'

'Is your father faithful to her?'

He frowned. 'What makes you ask that?'

Natalie lifted a shoulder up and down. 'They've been together a long time. It's not uncommon for a man to stray.'

'My father takes his marriage vows seriously,' he said. 'He is exactly like my grandfather in that.'

'And what about you, Angelo?' she asked. 'Will you follow in their honourable footsteps, or will you have your little bits on the side if I don't come up trumps?'

He came over to where she was standing. Stopped just in front of her. So close she could feel her body swaying towards him like a compass searching for magnetic north. She fought against the desire to close the minuscule distance. She stood arrow-straight, stiff to the point of discomfort. Her heart was racing; the hammer blows were making her giddy, her breathing shallow and uneven.

Her resolve, God help her, was crumbling.

Angelo slipped a warm hand behind her head at the nape of her neck setting off a shower of sensation beneath the surface of her sensitive skin.

'Why do you fight with yourself so much?' he asked.

Natalie pressed her lips together. 'I'm fighting you, not myself.'

His fingers moved through her hair in a spine-tingling caress. 'We both want the same thing, *cara*,' he said. 'Connection, intimacy, satisfaction.'

She could feel her resolve slipping even further out of her control. Why did he have to look so damned gorgeous? Why did he have to have such melting brown eyes? Why did he have to have such amazing hands that made her flesh tingle with sensation? Why did he have to have such a tempting mouth?

For God's sake, why didn't he throw her backwards caveman-style on the bed and ravish her?

In the end it was impossible to tell who had closed the distance between their bodies. Suddenly she felt the hard ridge of his erection pressing against her belly. It was like putting a match to a decade of dried-out tinder. She felt the flames erupt beneath her flesh. They licked along every nerve pathway, from the top of her scalp to her toes.

Her mouth met his in a combative duel that had no hint of romance or tenderness about it. It was all about lust—primal, ravenous lust—that was suddenly let loose after being restrained for far too long. She felt the scorch of his lips as they ground against hers. And then his tongue thrust boldly through the seam of her lips, making her insides flip over in delight. Her tongue tangled with his, fighting for supremacy, but he wouldn't give in. She felt the scrape of her teeth against his; she even tasted blood but couldn't be sure whose it was. She fed off his mouth greedily, rapaciously, and little whimpers of pleasure sounded deep in her throat as he varied the speed and pressure.

He crushed her to him, one of his hands ruthlessly tugging her top undone so he could access her breast. She felt her achingly tight nipple rubbing against his palm. A wave of longing besieged her. She felt it flickering like a pulse between her thighs. She felt the honeyed moistness of her body preparing for his possession. She rubbed up against him intimately, the feminine heart of her on fire, aching, pulsing, contracting with a need so great it was overwhelming.

He kept kissing her relentlessly, his tongue diving for hers, conquering it with each and every sensual stroke. Her lips felt swollen but she didn't care. She kissed him back with just as much passion, nipping at him with her teeth in between stroking him with her tongue. He tasted just as she remembered him: minty and fresh and devastatingly, irresistibly male.

He tore his mouth from hers to suckle on her breast, his tongue swirling around her areola and over her nipple until her back arched in pleasure. She knew it would take very little to send her up into the stratosphere. She could feel the tremors at her core, the tension building and building, until she was close to begging him to satisfy that delicious, torturous ache.

He brought his mouth back to hers—a slower kiss this time. He took his time exploring her mouth, his tongue teasing hers rather than subduing it. She melted like honey in a hothouse. Her arms went around his neck. Her hands delved into the thick denseness of his hair. Her throbbing pelvis was flush against the hardness of his.

He raised his mouth from hers, his breathing heavy, his eyes dark and heavy-lidded and smouldering with desire. 'Tell me you want me,' he commanded.

Natalie was jolted out of his sensual spell with a resurgence of her pride. 'I don't want you,' she lied.

He gave a deep and very masculine-sounding mocking laugh. 'I could prove that for the lie that it is just by slipping my hand between your legs.'

She tried to back away but he held her fast. 'Get your hands off me,' she said through gritted teeth.

He slowly slid his hands down the length of her arms, his fingers encircling her wrists like handcuffs. 'You will come to me, *cara*, just like you did in the past,' he said. 'I know you too well.'

She held his gaze defiantly. 'You don't know me at all,' she said. 'You might know your way around my body, but you know nothing of my heart.'

'That's because you won't let anyone in, will you?' he said. 'You push everyone away when they get too close. Your father told me how difficult you are.'

Natalie's mouth dropped open in outrage. 'You discussed *me* with my father?'

His hands fell away from her wrists, his expression masked. 'We had a couple of conversations, yes,' he said.

'About what?'

'I asked for your hand in marriage.'

She gave a derisive laugh. 'That was rather draconian of you, wasn't it? And also hypocritical—because you wouldn't have let the little matter of my father's permission stand in the way of what you wanted, now, would you?'

'I thought it was the right thing to do,' he said. 'I

would've liked to meet him face to face but he was abroad on business.'

Natalie could just imagine the 'business' her father was working on. His latest project was five-foot-ten with bottle-blonde hair and breasts you could serve a dinner party off.

'I'm sure he didn't hesitate in handing me over to your care,' she said. 'I'm surprised he didn't offer to pay you for the privilege.'

His gaze remained steady on hers, dark and penetrating but giving nothing away. 'We also discussed Lachlan's situation.'

'I take it he didn't offer to postpone his *business* in order to be by Lachlan's side and sort things out?'

'I told him to stay away,' he said. 'Sometimes parents can get in the way when it comes to situations like this. Your father has done all he can for your brother. It's time to step back and let others take charge.'

'Which you just couldn't wait to do, because it gave you the perfect foothold to force me back into your life,' she said, shooting him a resentful glare.

Those piercing brown eyes refused to let hers go. 'You came to me, Natalie, not the other way around.'

A thought slipped into her mind like the thin curl of smoke beneath a door. 'My father was the one who contacted you, wasn't he?' she said, her eyes narrowed in suspicion. 'I only came to you because my mother begged me to. I would never have come to you otherwise. *He* put her up to it.'

'Your father expressed his concern for you when we spoke,' he said. 'It seems it's not only your brother with an attitude problem.'

Natalie stalked to the other side of the bedroom, her arms around her body so tightly she felt her ribs creak in protest. Her anger was boiling like a cauldron inside her. She wanted to explode. She wanted to hit out at him, at the world, at the cruel injustice of life. The thought of Angelo discussing her with her father was repugnant to her. She hated thinking of how that conversation would have played out.

Her father would have painted her as a wilful and defiant child with no self-discipline. He would have laid it on thickly, relaying anecdote after anecdote about how she had disobeyed him and made life difficult for him almost from the day she had been born. He would not have told of how he had wanted a son first, and how she had ruined his plans by being born a girl. He would not have told of his part in provoking her, goading her into black moods and tempers until he finally broke her spirit. He would not have told of how his philosophy of parenting was 'might is right', how tyranny took precedence over tolerance, ridicule and shame over support and guidance. He would not have told of how he had used harsh physical discipline when gentle corrective words would have achieved a much better outcome.

No, he would have portrayed himself as a long-suffering devoted father who was at his wits' end over his wayward offspring.

He would not have mentioned Liam.

Liam's death was a topic *no one* mentioned. It was as if he had never existed. None of his toys or clothes were at the family mansion. Her father had forced her mother to remove them as soon as Lachlan had been born. The photos of Liam's infancy and toddlerhood were in an album in a cupboard that was securely locked and never opened. Natalie's only photo of her baby brother was the one she had found in the days after his funeral, when everyone had been distraught and distracted. She had kept it hidden until she had bought her house in Edinburgh.

But for all her father's efforts to erase the tragedy of Liam's short life his ghost still haunted them all. Every time Natalie visited her parents—which was rare these days—she felt his presence. She saw his face in Lachlan's. She heard him in her sleep. Every year she had night terrors as the anniversary of his death came close.

With an enormous effort she garnered her self-control, and once she was sure she had her emotions securely locked and bolted down she slowly turned and faced Angelo. 'I'm sure you found that conversation very enlightening,' she said.

His expression was hard to read. 'Your father cares for you very deeply,' he said. 'Like all parents, he and your mother only want the best for you.'

Natalie kept her mouth straight, even though she longed to curl her lip. 'My father obviously thinks you're the best for me,' she said. 'And as for my mother—well, she wouldn't dream of contradicting him. So it's happy families all round, isn't it?'

He studied her for a heartbeat, his eyes holding hers in a searching, probing manner. 'I'm going to have a shower,' he said. 'My parents will have gone to a great deal of trouble over dinner. Please honour them by dressing and behaving appropriately.'

'Contrary to what my father probably told you, I *do* actually know how to behave in company,' she said to his back as he went towards the *en suite* bathroom.

He turned around and meshed his gaze with hers. 'I'm on your side, *cara*,' he said, with unexpected gentleness.

Her eyes stung with the sudden onset of tears. She

blinked and got them back where they belonged: con-
cealed, blocked, and stoically, strenuously denied. She
gave a toss of her head and walked back to the window overlooking the gardens. But she didn't let out her
breath until she heard the click of the bathroom door
indicating Angelo had gone.

Angelo was putting on some cufflinks when he heard
Natalie come out of the dressing room. He turned and
looked at her, his breath catching in his chest at the sight
of her dressed in a classic knee length black dress and
patent leather four-inch heels. Her hair was pulled back
in an elegant knot at the back of her head, giving her a
regal air. She was wearing diamond and pearl droplet
earrings and a matching necklace. Her make-up was
subtle, but it highlighted the dark blue of her eyes and
the creamy texture of her skin and model-like cheekbones. Her perfume drifted towards him—a bewitch-
ing blend of the wintry bloom of lily of the valley and
the hot summer fragrance of honeysuckle. A perfect
summation of her complex character: ice-maiden and
sultry siren.

How could someone so beautiful on the outside be
capable of the things her father had said about her? It
was worrying him—niggling at him like a toothache.
The more time he spent with her, the more he found new
aspects to her character that intrigued him.

Yes, she was wilful and defiant. Yes, she had a streak
of independence. Yes, she could be incredibly stubborn.

But she clearly loved her brother and was prepared
to go to extraordinary lengths to help him. How did
that fit in with Adrian Armitage's assessment of her as
totally selfish and self-serving?

'You look like you just stepped off a New York City catwalk,' he said.

She lifted a slim shoulder dismissively. 'This dress is three seasons old,' she said. 'I bought it on sale for a fraction of the cost.'

'I like your hair like that.'

'It needs cutting,' she said, touching a hand to one of her earrings. 'This is a good way to hide the split ends.'

'Why don't you like compliments?' he asked. 'You always deflect them. You used to do that five years ago. I thought it was because you were young back then, but you're still doing it.'

She stopped fiddling with her earring to look at him, her chin coming up. 'Compliment me all you like,' she said. 'I can handle it.'

'You're beautiful.'

'Thank you.'

'And extremely intelligent.'

She gave a little mock bow. 'Thank you.'

'And you have the most amazing body,' he said.

High on her cheekbones twin pools of delicate rose appeared, and her eyes moved out of reach of his. 'I haven't been to the gym in months.'

'You're meant to say thank you—not make excuses,' he pointed out.

She brought her gaze back. 'Thank you.'

'You're the most intriguing person I know.'

A mask fell over her face like a curtain dropping over a stage. 'You need to get out a little more, Angelo,' she said.

'You have secrets in your eyes.'

She stilled as if every cell in her body had been snap frozen. But then, just as quickly she relaxed her pose.

'We all have our secrets,' she said lightly. 'I wonder what some of yours are?'

'Who gave you that jewellery?' he asked.

She put a hand to her throat, where her necklace rested. 'I bought it for myself,' she said.

'Do you still have the locket I gave you from that street fair we went to?'

She dropped her hand from her neck and reached for her purse. 'Your parents will be wondering what's keeping us,' she said.

'My parents will think we've been catching up on lost time.'

Her cheeks fired again. 'I hope they don't expect me to speak Italian, because I'm hopeless at it.'

'They won't expect you to do anything you're not comfortable with,' he said. 'They're keen to welcome you as the daughter they never had.'

'I hope I live up to their lofty expectations,' she said, frowning a little. 'But then, I guess no one is ever going to be good enough for the parents of an only child.'

'I'm sure they will grow to love you if you show them who you really are,' he said.

'Yeah, like *that's* going to work,' she said, and picked up her wrap and wound it round her shoulders.

Angelo frowned. 'Why do you say that?'

'No one really gets to be who they truly are on the inside, do they?' she said. 'We all fall into line because of cultural conditioning and family expectation. None of us can say what we really want to say or do what we really want to do. We're hemmed in by parameters imposed on us by other people and the society we live in.'

'What would you do or say if those parameters weren't there?' he asked.

She gave one of her dismissive shrugs. 'What would be the point?' she asked. 'No one listens anyway.'

'I'm listening,' he said.

Her eyes fell away from his. 'We shouldn't keep your parents waiting.'

He brought her chin up with his finger and thumb. 'Don't shut me out, *cara*,' he said. 'For God's sake, talk to me. I'm tired of this don't-come-too-close-to-me game you keep playing.'

Her expression flickered with a host of emotions. He saw them pass through her eyes like a burgeoning tide. They rippled over her forehead and tightened her jaw, but she spoke none of them out loud.

'You won't let me in, will you?' he said.

'There's nothing *in* there.'

'I don't believe that,' he said. 'I know you try and pretend otherwise, but you have a soft heart and you won't let anyone get near it. Why? Why are you so determined to deny yourself human connection and intimacy?'

She stepped out of his hold and gave him a hardened look. 'Didn't my father tell you?' she said. 'I'm a lost cause. I'm beyond redemption. I have a streak of selfishness and self-preservation that overrides everything else. I care for no one but myself.'

'If that is so then why have you agreed to sacrifice yourself for your brother's sake?' he asked.

There was a hint of movement at her slim throat, as if she had tried to disguise a swallow. 'Lachlan isn't like me,' she said. 'He's sensitive and vulnerable. He doesn't know how to take care of himself yet, but he will. He just needs more time.'

'You're paying a very high price for his learning curve.'

She met his gaze levelly. 'I've paid higher.'

Angelo tried to break her gaze down with the laser force of his but she was indomitable. It was like trying to melt a wall of steel with a child's birthday cake candle. 'I won't give up on you, Natalie,' he said. 'I don't care how long it takes. I will not give up until I see what's written on your heart.'

'Good luck with that,' she said airily, and sashayed to the door. She stopped and addressed him over her shoulder. 'Are you coming or not?'

CHAPTER FIVE

NATALIE was handed a glass of champagne as soon as she entered the salon on Angelo's arm.

'This is such a happy occasion for us,' Francesca said. 'We were starting to wonder if Angelo would ever settle down, weren't we, Sandro?'

Angelo's father gave a benign smile as he raised his glass. 'Indeed,' he said. 'But we always knew he would only ever marry for love. It is a Bellandini tradition, after all.'

'Isn't it also twenty-first century tradition to do so?' Natalie asked.

'Well, yes, of course,' Francesca said. 'But that's not to say that certain families don't occasionally orchestrate meetings between their young ones to hurry things along. Parents often have a feel for these things.'

'I'm not sure parents should get involved in their children's lives to that extent,' Natalie said. 'Surely once someone is an adult they should be left to decide what and who is right for them?'

Sandro's dark brown eyes glinted as he addressed his son. 'I can see you have chosen a wife with spirit, Angelo,' he said. 'Life is so much more exciting with a woman who has a mind of her own.'

Francesca gave Sandro a playful tap on the arm.

'You've done nothing but complain for the last thirty-six years about *my* spirit.'

Sandro took her hand and kissed it gallantly. 'I adore your spirit, *tesoro mio*,' he said. 'I worship it.'

Natalie couldn't help comparing her parents' relationship to Angelo's parents'. Her parents spoke to each other on a need basis. She couldn't remember the last time they had touched. They certainly didn't look at each other with love shining from their eyes. They could barely be in the same room together.

'*Papa, Mamma,*' Angelo said. 'You're embarrassing Natalie.'

Francesca came over and looped an arm through one of Natalie's. 'Angelo tells me you are a very talented interior designer,' she said. 'I am ashamed that I hadn't seen your soft furnishings range until I searched for it online. I cannot believe what I have been missing. Do you not have an Italian outlet?'

'I've limited my outlets to the UK up until now,' Natalie said.

'But why?' Francesca said. 'Your designs are wonderful.'

'I'm not fond of travelling,' Natalie said. 'I know I should probably do more in terms of networking in Europe…'

'Never mind,' Francesca said, patting her arm reassuringly. 'Angelo will see to it. He is very good at business. You will soon be a household name and I will be immensely proud of you. I will tell everyone you are my lovely daughter-in-law and I will not speak to them ever again unless they buy all of your linen and use all of your treatments in their homes, *si*?'

Natalie thought of her father's dismissal of her latest range as 'too girly' and 'too Parisian'. She felt more affirmed after five minutes with Angelo's mother than she had in a lifetime with her father.

'I'll get my assistant to send you a catalogue,' she said. 'If you want a hand with anything I'd be happy to help.'

'Oh, would you?' Francesca's eyes danced with excitement. 'I've been dying to redecorate the guest rooms. I would *love* your help. It will be a bonding experience, *si*?'

'I'd like that,' Natalie said.

Francesca smiled. 'I have been so nervous about us meeting,' she said. 'But I am happy now. You are perfect for Angelo. You love him very much, no?'

'I... I...'

Francesca squeezed Natalie's forearm. 'I understand,' she said. 'You don't like wearing your heart on your sleeve, *si*? But I can see what you feel for him. I don't need you to say it out loud. You are not the sort of girl who would marry for anything but for love.'

Angelo came over and put an arm around Natalie's waist. 'So you approve, *Mamma*?' he said.

'But of course,' his mother said. 'She is an angel. We will get on famously.'

Dinner was a lively, convivial affair—again very different from meals taken at Natalie's family home. At the Armitage mansion no one spoke unless Adrian Armitage gave permission. It was a pattern from childhood that neither Natalie nor Lachlan had been courageous enough to challenge.

But in the Bellandini household, magnificent and imposing as it was, everyone was encouraged to contribute to the conversation. Natalie didn't say much. She listened and watched as Angelo interacted with his parents. They debated volubly about politics and religion and the state of the economy, but no one got angry or upset, or slammed their fist down on the table. It was like watching a very exciting tennis match. The ball of conversation was hit back and forth, but nothing but good sportsmanship was on show.

After the coffee cups were cleared Angelo placed a gentle hand on the nape of Natalie's neck. 'You will excuse us, *Mamma* and *Papa*?' he said. 'Natalie is exhausted.'

'But of course,' Francesca said.

Sandro got to his feet and joined his wife in kissing Natalie on both cheeks. 'Sleep well, Natalie,' he said. 'It is a very great privilege to welcome you to our family.'

Natalie struggled to keep her overwhelmed emotions back behind the screen she had erected. 'You're very kind...'

Angelo kept his hand at her back all the way upstairs. 'You didn't eat much at dinner,' he said. 'Are you still feeling unwell?'

'No,' she said. 'I'm not a big eater.'

'You're very thin,' he said. 'You seem to have lost even more weight since the day you came to my office.'

She kept her gaze averted as she trudged up the stairs. 'I always lose weight in the summer.'

He held the door of their suite open for her. 'My parents adore you.'

She gave him a vestige of a smile. 'They're lovely people. You're very lucky.'

Angelo closed the door and watched as she removed the clip holding her hair in place. Glossy brunette tresses flowed over her shoulders. He wanted to run his fingers through them, to bury his head in their fragrant mass.

'You can have the bed,' he said. 'I'll sleep in one of the other rooms.'

'Won't your parents think it rather odd if you sleep somewhere else?' she asked, frowning slightly.

'I'll think of some excuse.'

'I'm sure we can manage to share a bed for a night or two,' she said, looking away. 'It's not as if we're out-of-control, hormonally driven teenagers or anything.'

Angelo felt exactly like an out-of-control, hormonally driven teenager, but he thought it best not to say so. He wasn't sure he would be able to sleep a wink with her lying beside him, but he was going to give it a damn good try.

'You use the bathroom first,' he said. 'I have a couple of e-mails to send.'

She gave a vague nod and disappeared into the *en-suite* bathroom.

When he finally came back into the bedroom Natalie was soundly asleep. She barely took up any room in the king-sized bed. He stood looking at her for a long time, wondering where he had gone wrong with her. Had he expected too much too soon? She had only been twenty-one. It was young for the commitment of marriage, but he had been so certain she was the one for him he hadn't stopped to consider she might say no. It had been perhaps a little arrogant of him, but he had never factored in the possibility that she would leave him. All his life he had been given everything he wanted. It was part and parcel of being an only child born to extremely wealthy parents. He had never experienced disappointment or betrayal.

He had her now where he wanted her, but he wasn't happy and neither was she. She was a caged bird. She would not stay confined for long. She would do her duty to save her brother's hide but she would not stay with him indefinitely.

He slipped between the sheets a few minutes later and lay listening to the sound of her soft breathing. He ached to pull her into his arms but he was determined she would come to him of her own volition. He closed his eyes and willed himself to relax.

He was not far off sleep when he felt Natalie stiffen like a board beside him. The bed jolted with the movement of her body as she started to thrash about as if she were possessed by an inner demon. He had never seen her jerk or throw herself about in such a way. He was concerned she was going to hurt herself.

'No!' she cried. 'No! No! No! *Noooo*!'

Angelo reached for her, restraining her flailing arms and legs with the shelter of his body half covering hers. 'Shh, *cara*,' he said softly. 'It's just a bad dream. Shh.'

Her eyes opened wide and she gulped over a sob as she covered her face with her hands. 'Oh, God,' she said. 'I couldn't find him. I couldn't find him.'

He brushed the hair back off her forehead. 'Who couldn't you find, *mia piccola*?' he asked.

She shook her head from side to side, her face still shielded by her hands. 'It was my fault,' she said, the words sounding as if they were scraped out of her throat. 'It was *my* fault.'

He frowned and pulled her hands down from her face. 'What was your fault?'

She blinked and focussed on his face. 'I… I…' She swallowed. 'I—I'm sorry…'

She started to cry, her face crumpling like a sheet of paper snatched up by someone's hand. Big crystal tears popped from her eyes and flowed down her face. He had never seen her cry. He had seen her furiously angry and he had seen her happy, and just about everything in between, but he had never seen her in tears.

'Hey,' he said, blotting each tear as it fell with the pad of his finger. 'It's just a dream, Tatty. It's not real. It's just a horrible nightmare.'

She cried all the harder, great choking sobs that made his own chest feel sore.

'I'm sorry,' she kept saying like a mantra. 'I'm sorry. I'm sorry. I'm sorry.'

'Shh,' he said again. 'There's nothing to be sorry about.' He stroked her face and her hair. 'There...let it go, *cara*. That's my girl. Let it all go.'

Her sobs gradually subsided to hiccups and she finally nestled against his chest and fell into an exhausted sleep. Angelo kept on stroking her hair as the clock worked its way around to dawn.

He could not have slept a wink if he tried.

Natalie opened her eyes and found Angelo's dark, thoughtful gaze trained on her. She had some vague memory of what had passed during the night but it was like looking at something through a cloudy, opaque film.

'I hope I didn't keep you awake,' she said. 'I'm not a very good sleeper.'

'You're certainly very restless,' he said. 'I don't remember you being like that when we were together.'

She focussed her gaze on the white cotton sheet that was pulled up to her chest. 'I sleep much better in the winter.'

'I can see why you choose to live in Scotland.'

She felt a reluctant smile tug at her mouth. 'Maybe I should move to Antarctica or the North Pole.'

'Maybe you should talk to someone about your dreams.'

She got off the bed and snatched up a bathrobe to cover her nightwear. 'Maybe you should mind your own business,' she said, tying the waist strap with unnecessary force.

He got off the bed and came to stand where she was standing. 'Don't push me away, Natalie,' he said. 'Can't you see I'm trying to help you?'

She glared at him, her anger straining like an unbroken horse on a string bridle. 'Back off. I don't need your help. I was perfectly fine until you came along and stuffed everything up. You with your stupid plans for revenge. Who are *you* to sort out my life? You don't know a thing about my life. You just think you can manipulate things to suit you. Go ahead. See if I care.'

She flung herself away, huddling into herself like a porcupine faced with a predator. But her prickly spines felt as if they were pointing the wrong way. She felt every savage poke of them into her sensitive soul.

'Why are you being so antagonistic?' he asked. 'What's happened to make you like this?'

Natalie squeezed her eyes shut as she fought for control. 'I don't need you to psychoanalyse me, Angelo. I don't need you to fix me. I was fine until you barged back into my life.'

'You're not fine,' he said. 'You're far from fine. I want to help you.'

She kept her back turned on him. 'You don't need me to complicate your life. You can have anyone. You don't need me.'

'I do need you,' he said. 'And you need me.'

She felt as if he had reached inside her chest and grasped her heart in his hand and squashed it. She wasn't the right person for him. She could never be the right person for him. Why couldn't he see it? Did she have to spell it out for him?

'You deserve someone who can love you,' she said. 'I'm not capable of that.'

'I don't know what's happened in your life to make you think that, but it's not true,' he said. 'You do care, Natalie. You care about everything, but you keep your feelings locked away where no one can see them.'

She pinched the bridge of her nose until her eyes watered. 'I've stuffed up so many lives.' She sucked in a breath and released it raggedly. 'I've tried to be a good person but sometimes it's just not enough.'

'You *are* a good person,' he said. 'Why are you so damned hard on yourself?'

Natalie felt the anguish of her soul assail her all over again. She had carried this burdensome yoke since she was seven years old. Instead of getting lighter it had become heavier. It had dug down deep into the shoulders of her guilt. She had no hope of shrugging it off. It was like a big, ugly track mark on her soul.

It was with her for life. It was her penance, her punishment.

'When I was a little girl I thought the world was a magical place,' she said. 'I thought if I just wished for something hard enough it would happen.'

'That's the magic of childhood,' he said. 'Every child thinks that.'

'I truly believed if I wanted something badly enough it would come to me,' she said. 'Where did I get that from? Life isn't like that. It's never been like that. It's not like some Hollywood script where everything turns out right in the end. It's pain and sadness and grief at what could have been but wasn't. It's one long journey of relentless suffering.'

'Why do you find life so difficult?' he asked. 'You come from a good family. You have wealth and a roof over your head, food on the table. What is there to be so miserable about? So many people are much worse off.'

She rolled her eyes and headed for the bathroom. 'I don't expect you to understand.'

'Make me understand.'

She turned and looked at him. His dark eyes were so concerned and serious. How could she bear to see him look at her in horror and disgust if she told him the truth? She let out a long sigh and pushed against the door with her hand. 'I'm going to have a shower,' she said. 'I'll see you downstairs.'

Angelo was having coffee in the breakfast room when Natalie came in. She looked cool and composed. There was no sign of the distress he had witnessed during the dark hours of the night and first thing this morning. Her ice maiden persona was back in place.

He rose from the table as she came in and held out a chair for her. 'My mother has organised a shopping morning for you,' he said. 'She'll be with you shortly. She's just seeing to some last-minute things with the housekeeper.'

'But I don't need anything,' she said, frowning as she sat down.

'Aren't you forgetting something?' he asked. 'We're getting married on Saturday.'

Her eyes fell away from his as she placed a napkin over her lap. 'I wasn't planning on going to any trouble over a dress,' she said. 'I have a cream suit that will do.'

'It's not just your wedding, *cara*,' he said. 'It's mine

too. My family and yours are looking forward to celebrating with us. It won't be the same if you turn up in a dress you could wear any old time. I want you to look like a bride.'

A spark of defiance lit her slate-blue gaze as it clashed with his. 'I don't want to look like a meringue,' she said. 'And don't expect me to wear a veil, because I won't.'

Angelo clamped his teeth together to rein in his temper. Was she being deliberately obstructive just to needle him for forcing her hand? He regretted showing his tender side to her last night. She was obviously going to manipulate him to get her own way. Hadn't her father warned him? She was clever at getting what she wanted. She would go to extraordinary lengths to do so.

But then, so would he.

She had met her match in him and he would not let her forget it. 'You will wear what I say you will wear,' he said, nailing her with his gaze. 'Do you understand?'

Her eyes flashed like fire. 'Does it make you feel big and macho and tough to force me to do what you want?' she asked. 'Does it make you feel big and powerful and invincible?'

It made him feel terrible inside, but he wasn't going to tell her that. 'I want our wedding day to be a day to remember,' he said with forced calm. 'I will not have you spoiling it by childish displays of temper or passive aggressive actions that will upset other people who are near and dear to me. You are a mature adult. I expect you to act like one.'

She gave him a livid glare. 'Will that be all, master?' she asked.

He pushed back from the table and tossed his napkin

to one side. 'I'll see you at the chapel on Saturday,' he said. 'I have business to see to until then.'

Her expression lost some of its intractability. 'You mean you're leaving me here…alone?'

'My parents will be here.'

Her throat rose and fell over the tiniest of swallows. 'This is rather sudden, isn't it?' she said. 'You said nothing to me about having to go away on business. I thought you were going to be glued to my side in case I did a last-minute runner.'

Angelo leaned his hands on the table and looked her square in the eyes. 'Don't even think about it, Natalie,' he said through tight lips. 'You put one foot out of place and I'll come down like a ton of bricks on your brother. He will never go to Harvard. He will never go to any university. It will be years before he sees the light of day again. Do I make myself clear?'

She blinked at him, her eyes as wide as big blue saucers. 'Perfectly,' she said in a hollow voice.

He held her pinned there with his gaze for a couple of chugging heartbeats before he straightened and adjusted his tie. 'Try and stay out of trouble,' he said. 'I'll call you later. *Ciao*.'

CHAPTER SIX

THE private chapel at Angelo's grandparents' villa forty-five minutes outside of Rome was full to overflowing when Natalie arrived in the limousine with her father. The last few days had passed in a blur of activity as wedding preparations had been made. She had gone with the flow of things—not wanting to upset Angelo's parents, who had gone out of their way to make her feel welcome.

She had talked to Angelo on the phone each day, but he had seemed distant and uncommunicative and the calls hadn't lasted more than a minute or two at most. There had been no sign of the gentle and caring man she had glimpsed the other night. She wondered if he was having second thoughts about marrying her now he had an inkling of how seriously screwed up she really was.

Her parents had flown over the day before, and her father had immediately stepped into his public role of devoted father. Her mother was her usual decorative self, dressed in diamonds and designer clothes with a hint of brandy on her breath that no amount of mints could disguise.

Her father helped Natalie out of the car outside the chapel. 'You've done well for yourself,' he said. 'I thought you'd end up with some tradesman from the suburbs. Angelo Bellandini is quite a catch. It's a pity he's Italian, but his money more than makes up for that. I didn't know you had it in you to land such a big fish.'

She gave him an embittered look. 'I suppose I really should thank you, shouldn't I? After all, you're the one who reeled him in for me.'

Her father's eyes became cold and hard and his voice lowered to a harsh, dressing-down rasp. 'What else was I to do, you stupid little cow?' he asked. 'Your brother's future depended on getting on the right side of Bellandini. I'm just relieved he wanted to take you on again. Quite frankly, I don't know why he can be bothered. You're not exactly ideal wife material. You've got too much attitude. You've been like that since the day you were born.'

Natalie ground her teeth as she walked to the chapel along a gravelled pathway on her father's arm. She had learned long ago not to answer back. The words would be locked inside her burning throat just like every other word she had suppressed in the past.

They ate at her insides like bitter, poisonous acid.

Angelo blinked when he saw Natalie come into the chapel. His heart did a funny little jump in his chest as he saw her move down the aisle. She was wearing a gorgeous crystal-encrusted ivory wedding gown that skimmed her slim curves. It had a small train that floated behind her, making her appear almost ethereal, and she was wearing a short gossamer veil with a princess tiara that didn't quite disguise the chalk-white paleness of her face. She looked at him as she walked towards him, but he wasn't sure she was actually seeing him. She had a faraway look in her eyes—a haunted look that made him feel guilty for having engineered things the way he had.

He took both of her hands in his as she drew close. They were ice-cold. 'You look beautiful,' he said.

She moved her lips but there was no way he could call it a smile.

'Your mother chose the dress,' she said.

'I like the veil.'

'It keeps the flies off.'

He smiled and gave her hands a little squeeze as the priest moved forward to address the congregation. He felt her fingers tremble against his, and for the briefest moment she clung to him, as if looking for support. But then her fingers became still and lifeless in the cage of his hands.

'Dearly beloved,' the priest began.

'...and now you may kiss the bride.'

Natalie held her breath as Angelo slowly raised her veil. She blinked away an unexpected tear. She had been determined not to be moved by the simple service, but somehow the words had struck a chord deep inside her. The promises had reminded her of all she secretly longed for: lifelong love, being cherished, protected, honoured, worshipped...accepted.

Angelo's mouth came down and gently pressed against hers in a kiss that contained a hint of reverence—or maybe that was just wishful thinking on her part. Halfway through the service she had started wishing it was for real. That he really did love her. That he really did want to spend the rest of his life with her in spite of her 'attitude problem'.

The thought of her father's hateful words made her pull out of the kiss. If Angelo was annoyed at her breaking away he showed no sign of it on his face. He simply looped her arm through his and led her out of the chapel to greet their guests.

The reception was held in the lush, fragrant gardens at his elderly grandparents's spectacular villa, under a beautifully decorated marquee. The champagne flowed and scrumptious food was served, but very little made it past Natalie's lips. She watched as her father charmed everyone with his smooth urbanity. She watched in dread as her mother downed glass after glass of champagne and talked too long and too loudly.

'Your mother looks like she's having a good time,' Angelo remarked as he came back to her side after talking with his grandfather.

Natalie chewed at her lip as she saw her mother doing a tango with one of Angelo's uncles. 'Deep down she's really very shy, but she tries to compensate by drinking,' she said. 'I wish she wouldn't. She doesn't know when to stop.'

He took her by the elbow and led her to a wistaria-covered terrace away from the noise and music of the reception. Bees buzzed in the scented arras above them. 'You look exhausted,' he said. 'Has it all been too much for you?'

'I never thought smiling could be so tiring,' she said with a wry grimace.

'I should imagine it would be when you're not used to doing it.'

She looked away from his all-seeing gaze. He had a way of looking at her that made her feel as if he sensed her deep unhappiness. He'd used to tease her about taking life so seriously. She had tried—she had really tried—to enjoy life, but hardly a day passed without her thinking of all the days her baby brother had missed out on because of her.

'I like your grandparents,' she said, stepping on tip-toe to smell a purple bloom of wistaria. 'They're so devoted to each other even after all this time.'

'Are yours still alive?' he asked. 'You didn't put them on the list so I assumed they'd passed on.'

'They're still alive.'

'Why didn't you invite them?'

'We're not really a close family,' she said, thinking of all the stiff and awkward don't-mention-what-happened-in-Spain visits she had endured over the years.

Everything had changed after Liam had died.

She had lost not just her younger brother but also her entire family. One by one they had pulled back from her. There had been no more seaside holidays with Granny and Grandad. After a couple of years the beautiful handmade birthday presents had stopped, and then a year or two later the birthday cards had gone too.

A small silence passed.

'I'm sorry I couldn't arrange for Lachlan to be here,' he said. 'It's against regulations.'

She looked up at him, shielding her eyes against the bright sun with one of her hands. 'Where is he?'

'He's in a private clinic in Portugal,' he said. 'He'll be there for a month at the minimum.'

Natalie felt a surge of relief so overwhelming it almost took her breath away. She dropped her hand from her eyes and opened and closed her mouth, not able to speak for a full thirty seconds. She had been so terrified he would self-destruct before he got the help he so desperately needed. She had suggested a clinic a couple of times, but he had never listened to her. She had felt so impotent, so helpless watching him destroy his life so recklessly.

'I don't know how to thank you...I've been so terribly worried about him.'

'He has a long way to go,' he said. 'He wants help, but he sabotages it when it's given to him.'

'I know...' she said on a sigh. 'He has issues with self-esteem. Deep down he hates himself. It doesn't matter what he does, or what he achieves, he never feels good enough.'

'For your parents?'

She shifted her gaze. 'For my father, mostly...'

'The father-son relationship can be a tricky one,' he said. 'I had my own issues with my father. That's one of the reasons I came to London.'

Natalie walked with him towards a fountain that was surrounded by sun-warmed cobblestones. She could feel the heat coming up through her thinly soled high-heeled shoes. The fine misty spray of the fountain delicately pricked her face and arms like a refreshing atomiser.

'You've obviously sorted those issues out,' she said. 'Your father adores you, and you clearly adore and respect him.'

'He's a good man,' he said. 'I'm probably more like him that I'm prepared to admit.'

She looked at the water splashing over the marble dolphins in the fountain and wondered what Angelo would think if she told him what *her* father was really like. Would he believe her?

Probably not, she thought with a plummeting of her spirits. Her father had got in first and swung the jury. He had done it all her life—telling everyone how incredibly difficult she was, how headstrong and wilful, how cold and ungrateful. The one time she had dared to tell a family friend about her father's treatment of her it had backfired spectacularly. The knock-on effect on her mother had made Natalie suffer far more than any physical or verbal punishment her father could dish out.

It had silenced her ever since.

'I guess we should get back to the guests,' she said.

'It will soon be time to leave,' he said, and began walking back with her to the marquee. 'I'd like us to get to Sorrento before midnight.'

Natalie's stomach quivered at the thought of spending a few days alone with him at his villa. Would he expect her to sleep with him? How long would she be able to say no? She was aching for him, and had been since she had walked into his office that day. Her body tingled when she was with him. It was tingling now just from walking beside him. Every now and again her bare arm would brush against his jacket sleeve. Even through the barrier of the expensive fabric she could feel the electric energy of his body. It shot sharp arrows of awareness through her skin and straight to her core. She wanted him as she had always wanted him.

Feverishly, wantonly, urgently.

She was the moth and he was the flame that could destroy her, and yet she just couldn't help herself. But giving herself to him physically was one thing. Opening herself to him emotionally was another. If she showed him everything that was stored away inside her what would she do if he then abandoned her?

How would she ever be able to put herself back together again?

Natalie could barely recall the journey to Sorrento in the chauffeur-driven car. She had fallen asleep before they had travelled even a couple of kilometres. She had woken just after midnight as the car drew to a halt, to find her head cradled in Angelo's lap, his fingers idly stroking her hair.

'We're here,' he said.

She sat up and pushed back her loosened hair. 'I think I dribbled on your trousers,' she said, grimacing in embarrassment. 'Sorry.'

He gave her a lazy smile. 'No problem,' he said. 'I enjoyed watching you.'

The villa was perched high on a clifftop, overlooking the ocean. It had spectacular views over the port of Sorrento and the colourful villages hugging the coastline. With terraced gardens and a ground area twice the size of its neighbours, the villa offered a level of privacy that was priceless. Lights twinkled from boats on the wrinkled dark blue blanket of the sea below. The balmy summer air contained the sweet, sharp scent of lemon blossom from the surrounding lemon groves, and the light breeze carried with it the faint clanging sound of the rigging on a yacht far below.

Angelo left the driver to deal with their luggage as he led Natalie inside. 'My hotel development is much larger than this place,' he said. 'I'll take you there tomorrow or the next day.'

Natalie looked around at the vaulted ceilings and the panoramic arched windows, the antique parquet and the original terracotta floors. 'This is lovely,' she said. 'Have you had it long?'

'I bought it a couple of years ago,' he said. 'I like the privacy here. It's about the only place I can lock myself away from the press.'

'I suppose it's where you bring all your lovers to seduce them out of the spotlight?' she said before she could check herself.

He studied her as he pulled free his loosened tie. 'You sound jealous.'

'Why would I be jealous?' she asked. 'I don't have any hold over you. And you don't have any hold over me.'

He picked up her left hand and held it in front of her face. 'Aren't you forgetting something?' he asked. 'We're married now. We have a hold over each other.'

Natalie tried to get out of his grasp but his fingers tightened around hers. 'What possible hold do I have over you?' she asked. 'You forced me to marry you. I didn't have a choice. Five years ago I made the decision to walk out of your life and never see you again. I wanted to be left alone to get on with my life. But no; you had to fix things so I'd be at your mercy and under your control.'

'Stop it, Natalie,' he said. 'You're tired. I'm tired. This is not the time to discuss this.'

She tugged some more until she finally managed to break free. She stood before him, her chest heaving, her heart pounding and her self-control in tatters.

'Don't tell me to stop it!' she said. '*What* hold do I have over you? You hold all the cards. I know what you're up to, Angelo. I know how men like you think. You'll hoodwink me into falling in love with you and then you'll pull the rug from under my feet when I least expect it. But it won't work because I won't do it. I won't fall in love with you. I *won't*.'

He stood looking down at her with implacable calm. 'Do you feel better now you've got all of that off your chest?' he asked.

Goaded beyond all forbearance, she put her chin up and flashed him a challenging glare. 'Why don't you come and collect what you've bought and paid for right here and now?' she said. 'Come on, Angelo. I'm your little puppet now. Why don't you come and pull on my strings?'

A muscle flickered in his jaw as his dark-as-night gaze slowly moved over her body, from her head to her feet and back again. She felt it peel her ivory gown away. She felt it scorch through her bra and knickers. She felt it burn her flesh. She felt it light an inferno between her legs.

But then a mask slipped over his features. 'I'll see you in the morning,' he said. 'I hope you sleep well. *Buonanotte.*' He inclined his head in a brief nod and then turned and left.

Natalie listened to the echo of his footsteps on the terracotta floor fading into the distance until there was nothing left but the sound of her own erratic breathing...

The bedroom she'd chosen to sleep in was on the third floor of the villa. She woke after a fitful sleep to bright morning sunshine streaming in through the arched windows. She peeled back the covers and went and looked out at a view over terraced gardens. There was a sparkling blue swimming pool situated on one of the terraces, surrounded by lush green shrubbery. She could see Angelo's lean, tanned figure carving through the water, lap after lap, deftly turning at each end like an Olympic swimmer.

She moved away from the window before he caught her spying on him and headed to the shower.

When she came downstairs breakfast had been laid out on a wrought-iron table in a sunny courtyard that was draped on three sides in scarlet bougainvillaea. The fragrant smell of freshly brewed coffee lured her to the table, and she poured a cup and took it to the edge of the courtyard to look at the view over the port of Sorrento.

She turned around when she heard the sound of Angelo's tread on the flagstones as he came from inside the villa. He was dressed in taupe chinos and a white casual shirt that was rolled up past his wrists, revealing strong, masculine forearms. His hair was still damp; the grooves of his comb were still visible in the thick dark strands. He looked gorgeously fresh and vitally, potently alive.

'I thought you might've joined me for a swim,' he said.

'I'm not much of a swimmer,' she said, shifting her gaze. 'I prefer dry land sports.'

He pulled out a chair for her at the table. 'Do you want something hot for breakfast?' he asked. 'I can make you an omelette or something.'

Natalie looked at him in surprise. 'Don't you have a twenty-four-hour housekeeper at your beck and call here?'

'I have someone who comes in a couple of times a week,' he said. 'I prefer my time here to be without dozens of people fussing around me.'

'Oh, the trials and tribulations of having millions and squillions of dollars,' she said dryly as she sat down.

He looked at her with a half-smile playing about his mouth. 'You grew up with plenty of wealth yourself,' he said. 'Your father is a very successful investor. He was telling me about some of the ways he's survived the financial crisis. He's a very clever man.'

She reached for a strawberry from the colourful fruit plate on the table. 'He's very good at lots of things,' she said, taking a tiny nibble.

He watched her with those dark, intelligent eyes of his. 'You don't like him very much, do you?' he asked.

'What makes you say that?' she asked, taking another little bite of the strawberry.

'I was watching you at the reception yesterday,' he said. 'You tensed every time he came near you. You never smiled at him. Not even once.'

She gave a shrug and reached for another strawberry, focussing on picking off the stem rather than meeting his gaze. 'We have what you might call a strained relationship,' she said. 'But then he told you how difficult I was when you had that cosy little chat together, didn't he?'

'That really upset you, didn't it?'

'Of course it upset me,' she said, shooting him a hard little glare. 'He's good at swinging the jury. He oozes with charm. No one would ever question his opinion. He's the perfect husband, the perfect father. He doesn't show in public what he's like in private. You don't know him, Angelo. You don't know what he's capable of. He'll smile at your face while he has a knife in your back and you'll never guess it. You don't *know* him.'

The silence that fell made Natalie feel horribly exposed. She couldn't believe that she had said as much as she had said. It was as if a torrent had been let loose. The words had come tumbling out like a flood. A dirty, secret flood that she had kept hidden for as long as she could remember. Her words stained the air. The contamination of the truth even seemed to still the sweet sound of the tweeting birds in the shrubbery nearby.

'Are you frightened of him, *cara*?' Angelo asked with a frown.

'Not any more,' she said, giving her head a little toss

as she reached for a blueberry this time. 'I've taught myself not to let him have that power over me.'

'Has he hurt you in some way in the past?'

'What are you going to do, Angelo?' she asked with a woeful attempt at scorn. 'Punch him on the nose? Rearrange his teeth for him? Give him a black eye?'

His gaze became very dark and very hard. 'If anyone dares to lay so much as a finger on you I will do much more than that,' he said grimly.

A piece of her emotional armour peeled off like the sloughing of skin. It petrified her to think of how easily it had fallen away. Was this his plan of action? To conquer by stealth? To ambush her by making her feel safe and secure?

To protect her?

'You know, for such a modern and sophisticated man, deep down you're amazingly old-fashioned,' she said.

He reached for her hand. 'You have no need to be frightened of anyone any more, *cara*,' he said. 'You're under my protection now, and you will be while you're wearing that ring on your finger.'

Natalie looked at her hand in the shelter of his. The sparkling new wedding band and the exquisite engagement ring bound her to him symbolically, but the real bond she was starting to feel with him was so much deeper and more lasting than that.

And it secretly terrified her.

She pulled her hand out of his and took one of the rolls out of a basket. 'So, what's the plan?' she asked in a light and breezy tone. 'How are we going to spend this non-honeymoon of ours?'

His eyes continued to hold hers in a smouldering tether that made the base of her spine feel hot and tingly. 'How long do you think you'll be able to keep up this ridiculous pretence of not wanting me?' he asked.

She gave a false-sounding little laugh. 'You had your chance last night and you blew it.'

His eyes smouldered some more. 'I was very tempted to call your bluff last night.'

Hot, moist heat swirled between her legs as she thought of how dangerous and reckless her little taunt had actually been. Was that why she had issued it? Did some subconscious part of her want him to take charge and seduce her?

'Why didn't you?' she asked with a little lift of her brow.

'I don't like being manipulated,' he said. 'You wanted me to take the responsibility away from you. You don't like the fact that you still want me. You've taught yourself not to want or need anyone. It bugs the hell out of you that I stir you up the way I do, doesn't it?'

Natalie tried to push her emotions back where they belonged, but it was like trying to refold a map. She pushed back from the table with a screech of the wrought-iron chair-legs against the flagstones. 'I don't have to listen to this,' she said, slamming her napkin on the table.

'That's right,' he said mockingly. 'Run away. That's what you usually do, isn't it? You can't face the truth of what you feel, so you bolt like a scared rabbit.'

She glowered at him in fury, her fists clenched, her spine rigid. 'I am *not* a coward.'

He came to where she was standing, looking down at her with those penetrating eyes of his. She wanted to run, but had to force herself to stand still in order to discredit his summation of her character.

'How long do you think you can keep running?' he

asked. 'Hasn't anyone ever told you that your feelings go with you? You can't leave them behind. They follow you wherever you go.'

'I don't feel anything for you,' she said through barely moving lips.

He gave a deep chuckle of laughter. 'Sure you don't, Tatty.'

She clenched her teeth. 'Stop calling me that.'

'How are you going to stop me?' he asked with a goading smile.

She stepped right up to him and fisted a hand in the front of his shirt. 'Stop it, damn you,' she said, trying to push him backwards. But it was like a moth trying to move a mattress.

His dark gaze mocked her. 'Is that really the best you can do?'

She raised her other hand to slap him, but he caught it mid-air. 'Ah-ah-ah,' he chided. 'That's not allowed. We can play dirty, but not *that* dirty.'

Natalie felt the stirring of his erection against her, and her body responded with a massive tidal wave of lust. The erotic pulse of his blood thundering against her belly unleashed a deranged demon of desire inside her. She lunged at him, pulling his head down by grabbing a handful of his hair so she could smash her mouth against his. He allowed her a few hot seconds before he took charge of the kiss and pushed through her lips with the sexy thrust of his tongue, claiming her interior moistness, mimicking the intimate possession of hard, swollen male inside soft, yielding female.

She tried to take back control but he refused to relinquish it. He commandeered her mouth with masterful expertise, making her whole body sing with delight. One of his hands drove through her hair to angle her head for better access as he deepened the kiss. His other hand found her breast and cupped it roughly, possessively. Her flesh swelled and prickled in need, her nipples becoming hardened points that ached for the hot wet swirl and tug of his tongue. She moved against him, wanting more, wanting it all.

Wanting it *now*.

Her hands dug into his taut buttocks as she pulled him closer. He was monumentally aroused. She felt the rock-hard length of him and ached to feel him moving inside her. Her inner body secretly prepared itself. She felt the dewy moisture gathering between her thighs. She felt the tapping pulse of her blood as her feminine core swelled with longing. She didn't think she had ever wanted him so badly. She was feverish with it.

Her heart raced with excitement as he scooped her up and carried her indoors. But he didn't take her anywhere near a bedroom. He didn't even bother undressing her. He roughly lifted her sundress, bunching it up around her waist, and backed her towards the nearest wall, his mouth still clamped down on hers. He didn't waste time removing her knickers, either. He simply shoved them to one side as he claimed her slick, hot moistness with one of his fingers.

She gasped against his mouth and he made a very male sound at the back of his throat—a primal sound of deep satisfaction that made all the tight ligaments in her spine loosen. He tortured her with his touch. Those clever fingers got to work and had her shaking with need within moments. She clung to him desperately, her fingernails digging into his back and shoulders as he made her shatter into a million pieces. She sagged against him when the first storm was over. She knew there would be more. There always was with Angelo.

He was never satisfied until he had completely undone her physically.

She reached for the zip on his trousers and went in search of him. Her fingers wrapped around his pulsing steely length. He felt hot and hard and heavy with need. She blotted her thumb over the bead of moisture at his tip and a sharp dart of need speared her. He wanted her as badly as she wanted him. Hadn't it always been this way between them? Their coupling had always been a frenzied attack on the senses. Always fireworks and explosions. Always a mind-blowing madness that refused to be tamed.

He pulled her hand away and quickly applied a condom before pressing her back against the wall, thrusting into her so hard and so fast the breath was knocked right out of her. His mouth swallowed her startled gasp as he rocked against her with heart-stopping urgency.

The pressure built and built inside her again. The sensations ricocheted through her like a round of rubber bullets. It had been *so* long! *This* was what she had craved from him. The silky glide of his hard body, those powerful strokes and bold thrusts that made her shiver from head to foot. Her body was so in tune with his. Everything felt so right, so perfect. Her orgasm came speeding towards her, tightening all her sensitive nerve-endings and tugging at her insides, teasing as it lured her towards the edge of oblivion. She cried out as it carried her away on a rollercoaster that dipped and dropped vertiginously.

She was still convulsing when he came. She felt him tense, and then he groaned out loud as he shuddered and quaked with pleasure, his breathing heavy against her neck where he had pressed his face in that last crazy dash to the finish.

It was a moment or two before he stepped away from her. His expression was impossible to read as he did up his zip and tucked his shirt back into his trousers. Natalie felt a pang for the past—for a time when he would smile at her in a smouldering way, his arms holding her in the aftermath as if he never wanted to let her go.

She quickly suppressed that longing, however. She pushed her dress down and her chin up. 'Was that playing dirty enough for you?' she asked.

His dark, unreadable eyes held hers. 'For now.'

She felt a delicious little aftershock of pleasure ripple through her as his gaze went to her mouth. Was he thinking of how she'd used to pleasure him with it? He had done the same to her; so many times she had lost count. There had been few boundaries when it had come to sex. She had learned how to enjoy her body with him, how not to feel ashamed of its needs and urges. He had opened up a wild, sensual world to her that she had not visited since.

She moved away from the wall, wincing slightly as her tender muscles protested.

His expression immediately clouded with concern. 'Did I hurt you?'

'I'm fine.'

He put a hand around her wrist, his fingers overlapping her slender bones, his thumb stroking along the sensitive skin. 'I'm sorry,' he said. 'I shouldn't have taken things so fast. I should've taken my time with you, prepared you more.'

She gave him a nonchalant shrug and pulled out of his hold. 'Save the romantic gestures for someone you didn't have to pay for.'

A hard glitter came into his eyes. 'Is this really how

you want our relationship to run?' he asked. 'As a point-scoring exercise where we do nothing but attack each other?'

'If you're unhappy with how our relationship runs then you have only yourself to blame,' she said. 'You were the one who insisted on marriage. I told you I'm not cut out for it.'

'I wanted to give you the honour of making you my wife,' he said bitterly. 'But clearly you're much more comfortable with the role of a whore.' He took out his wallet and peeled off a handful of notes. Stepping up to her, he stuffed them down the cleavage of her dress. 'That should just about cover it.'

Natalie took the notes out and tore them into pieces, threw them at his feet. 'You'll need far more than *that* to get me to sleep with you again.'

'You're assuming, of course, that I would want to,' he said. And, giving her a scathing look, he turned and left.

CHAPTER SEVEN

NATALIE spent most of the day in her room. She heard Angelo moving about the villa but she refused to interact with him. She was determined to avoid him for as long as she could. Hunger was a minor inconvenience. Her stomach growled as the clock moved around but still she remained resolute.

It was close to eight in the evening when she heard the sound of footsteps outside her door, and then a light tap as Angelo spoke. 'Natalie?'

'Go away.'

'Open the door.'

She tightened her arms across her body, where she was sitting cross-legged on the bed. 'I said go away.'

'If you don't unlock this door I swear to God I'll break it down with my bare hands,' he said in a gritty tone.

Natalie weighed up her options and decided it was better not to call his bluff this time. She got off the bed, padded over to the door, turned the key and opened the door. 'Yes?' she said with a haughty air.

The lines that bracketed his mouth looked deeper and his eyes, though currently glittering with anger, looked tired. 'Can we talk?' he asked.

She stepped away from the door and moved to the

other side of the room, folding her arms across her middle. She didn't trust herself not to touch him. Her body had switched on like a high-wattage lightbulb as soon as he had stepped over the threshold. She could feel the slow burn of her desire for him moving through her. Her insides flickered with the memory of his possession. It was a funny sensation, like suddenly stepping on an uneven surface and feeling that rapid stomach-dropping free fall before restoring balance.

'Are you all right?' he asked.

She sent him a chilly look. 'Fine, thank you.'

He drew in a long breath and then released it. 'What happened this morning...I want to apologise. What I said to you was unforgivable.'

'You're right,' she said, shooting him another deadly glare. 'And, just for the record, I don't forgive you.'

He pushed a hand through his hair. Judging from the disordered state of it, it wasn't the first time that day he had done so. 'I also want to apologise for being so rough with you.' He swallowed tightly and frowned. 'I thought... I don't know what I thought. Maybe I didn't think. I just wanted you.' His eyes darkened as they held hers. 'I have never wanted anyone like I want you.'

Natalie's resolve began to melt with each pulsing second his eyes stayed meshed with hers. She felt the heat of longing pass between them like a secret code. It was there in his dark as night eyes. It was there in the sculptured contours of his mouth. It was there in the tall frame of his body, pulling her like a powerful magnet towards him. She felt the tug of need in her body; she felt it in her breasts, where they twitched and tingled behind her bra. And, God help her, she felt it rattle the steel cage around her heart.

'Apology accepted,' she said.

He came to her and gently cupped her right cheek in his hand, his eyes searching hers. 'Can we start again?' he asked.

She gave a little frown. 'Start from where?'

His mouth curved upwards. 'Hi, my name is Angelo Bellandini and I'm a hotel and property developer. I'm an only child of wealthy Italian parents. I help to run my father's arm of the business while working on my own.'

She gave a resigned sigh. 'Hi, my name is Natalie Armitage and I'm an interior designer, with an expanding sideline in bedlinen and soft furnishings.' She chewed at her lip for a moment and added, 'And I have a fear of flying...'

His thumb stroked her cheek. 'How old were you when you first got scared?'

'I was...seven...'

'What happened?'

She slipped out of his hold and averted her gaze. 'I'd rather not talk about it with a virtual stranger.'

'I'm not a stranger,' he said. 'I'm your husband.'

'Not by my choice,' she muttered.

'Don't do this, Natalie.'

'Don't do what?' she asked, glaring at him. 'Tell it how it is? You blackmailed me back into your life. Now you want me to open up to you as if we're suddenly inseparable soul mates. I'm not good at being open with people. I've never been good at it. I'm private and closed. It must be my Scottish heritage. We're not outwardly passionate like you Italians. You'll just have to accept that's who I am.'

The touch of his hands on her shoulders made every cell of her skin flicker and dance in response.

'You're much more passionate than you give yourself credit for,' he said. 'I've got the scratch marks on my back to prove it.'

Natalie felt that passion stirring within her. His body was calling out to hers in a silent language that was as old as time itself. It spoke to her flesh, making it tauten and tingle all over in anticipation. She wished she had the strength or indeed the willpower to step back from his magnetic heat, but her body was on autopilot. She pressed closer, that delicious ache of need starting deep in her core.

His mouth came down towards hers as hers came up, and they met in an explosion of sensation that made the flesh on her body shudder in delight. He flooded her senses with his taste—mint and male, heat and primal purpose. His tongue darted and dived around hers, subjecting it to a teasing tango that made her spine shiver and shake like a string of bottle caps rattling against each other. Heat pooled between her legs as he moved against her, the thickened length of him exciting her unbearably. She rubbed against him wantonly, desperate for the earth-shattering release that he alone could give her.

He pulled back slightly, his breathing heavy. 'Too fast.'

'Not fast enough,' she said and, pulling his head down, covered his mouth with her greedy one.

His hands worked on her clothes with deliberate attention to detail. She squirmed and writhed as he kissed every spot of flesh as he gradually exposed it. She tugged his shirt out of his trousers and with more haste than precision got him out of the rest of his clothes. She ran her hands over him reverentially. He was so strong and so lean, his muscles tightly corded, his skin satin smooth all but for the sprinkling of masculine hair that went from his chest in an arrow to his swollen groin. She stroked him with her hand, loving the feel of his reaction to her touch. She heard him snatch in a breath, his eyes glittering as she gave him a sultry look from beneath her lashes.

'If you're going to do what I think you're about to do then this show is going to be over before it gets started,' he warned.

She gave him a devil-may-care look and shimmied down in front of him. 'Then I'll just have to wait until the encore, won't I?'

'Dio mio,' he groaned in ecstasy as she took him into her mouth.

She used her tongue and the moistness of her saliva to take him to the brink. She would have pushed him over, but he stopped her by placing his hands on either side of her head.

'Enough,' he growled, and hauled her to her feet.

He carried her to the bed, laying her down and covering her, with his weight supported by his arms to avoid crushing her. His mouth took hers in a searing kiss as his hand caressed her breasts and that aching secret dark place between her thighs.

It was her turn to suck in a breath when he moved down her body to stroke her with his lips and tongue. She felt the fizzing of her nerves as he brought her closer and closer. Her release started far away, and then gathered speed and stampeded through her flesh. She lost herself in a whirlpool of sensation that made her feel weightless and boneless.

She opened her eyes to find him looking at her as he stroked a lazy finger down between her breasts. 'Do you want to finish me off with your hand?' he asked.

She gave him a little frown. 'Don't you want to come inside me?'

'I don't want to hurt you,' he said, gently circling one of her nipples. 'You might still be sore.'

She stroked her hand down his lean stubbly jaw. 'I want you inside me,' she said. 'I want *you*.'

His eyes held hers in a sensual lock that made her belly quiver. 'I'll take it easy,' he said. 'Tell me to stop if it hurts.'

'It's not as if I'm a virgin, Angelo,' she said, with a brittle little laugh to cover her unexpected emotional response to his tenderness. 'I can handle everything you dish out.'

His eyes smouldered as they held hers. 'Don't say you weren't warned,' he said, and covered her mouth with his.

Angelo lay on his side and watched Natalie sleep. From time to time he would pick up a silky strand of her hair and twirl it around one of his fingers.

She didn't stir.

Her stubborn refusal to open her heart to him was like a thorn in his flesh. It was as if she would do anything to stop him thinking she cared about him. He thought back to their break-up, to how she had announced without warning that she was leaving. Her bags had been packed when he'd come home from a three-day workshop in Wales. She had told him she had slept with someone she had met at the local pub. He had stood there in dumbstruck silence, wondering if she was joking.

Their relationship had been volatile at times, but he hadn't really thought she was serious about walking out on him. She had threatened to many times, but he had always thought it was just her letting off steam. He had planned to ask her to marry him that very night. He had wanted to wait until he got back from the workshop so she would have had time to think about how much she had missed him. But then she had shown him a photo on her phone, of her with a man, sitting at the bar, smiling over their drinks. The anger he had felt at seeing the evidence of her betrayal had been like a hot red dust storm in front of his eyes. She had stood there, looking at him with a what-are-you-going-to-do-about-it-look and he had snapped.

He wasn't proud of the words he had flailed her with. He was even more ashamed that he'd pushed her up against the wall like a cheap hooker and given her a bruising parting kiss that had left both of them bleeding.

He shuffled through his thoughts as he looked at her lying next to him like a sleeping angel.

She had *wanted* him to believe she had betrayed him. *But why?*

Hadn't he shown her how much he had loved her? He had said it enough times and shown it in a thousand different ways. She had never taken him seriously. Funny that, since she took life so seriously herself. She rarely smiled unless it was a self-effacing one. He couldn't remember ever hearing her laugh other than one of those totally fake cackles that grated on his nerves because he knew them for the tawdry imitation they were.

Why had she been so desperate to get him out of her life?

He was still frowning when she opened her eyes and stretched like a cat. 'What time is it?' she asked.

'You didn't do it, did you?' he asked.

A puzzled flicker passed through her gaze. 'Do what?'

'You didn't sleep with that guy from the bar.'

She made a business of sitting upright and covering herself with a portion of the sheet. 'I went home with him,' she said after a moment.

'But you didn't sleep with him,' he said. 'You wanted me to think you had. You wanted me to believe that because you knew me well enough to know I would never have let you go for anything less.'

A tiny muscle began tapping in her cheek and her eyes took on a defensive sheen. 'I wasn't ready for commitment. You were pressuring me to settle down. I didn't want to lose my freedom. I didn't want to lose my identity and become some nameless rich man's husband just like my mother.'

'You're nothing like your mother, *cara*,' he said. 'You're too strong and feisty for that.'

She got off the bed and wrapped herself in a silky wrap. 'I don't always feel strong,' she said. 'Sometimes I feel...' Her teeth sank into her bottom lip.

'What do you feel?'

She turned to the dressing table and picked up a brush, started pulling it through her hair. 'I feel hungry,' she said. She put the brush down and swung around to face him. 'What does a girl have to do around here to get a meal?'

Angelo knew it wasn't wise to push her. He had to be patient with her. She was feeling vulnerable and had retreated back to her default position. It was her way of protecting herself.

He only wished he had known that five years ago.

Natalie sat across from Angelo in a restaurant in Sorrento an hour later. He had given her the choice of eating in or out and she had chosen to go out. It wasn't that she particularly wanted to mingle with other people; it was more that she wanted to keep her head when around him. She couldn't do that so well when she was alone with him.

The passion they had shared had stirred up old longings that made her feel uneasy. She was fine with having sex with him—more than fine, truth be told. It was just she knew he would want more from her.

He had always wanted more than she was prepared to give.

How long before he would ask her to think about staying with him indefinitely? Then he would start talking about babies.

His mother had already dropped a few broad hints when she had helped her choose her wedding dress. Natalie's stomach knotted at the thought of being responsible for a tiny infant. She could just imagine how her parents would react if she were to tell them she was having a baby. Her mother would reach for the nearest bottle and drain it dry. Her father wouldn't say a word. He would simply raise his eyebrows and a truckload of guilt would land on her like a concrete slab.

Angelo reached across the table and touched her lightly on the back of her hand. 'Hello, over there,' he said with a soft smile.

Natalie gave him a rueful smile in return. 'Sorry... I'm hardly scintillating company, am I?'

'I don't expect you to be the life of the party all the time, *cara*,' he said. 'It's enough that you're here.'

She looked at his fingers entwined with hers. She had missed his touch so much in the years that had passed. She had missed the way his skin felt against hers, the way he felt under the caress of her hands. She had lain awake at night with her body crying out for his lovemaking. Her body had felt so empty. So lifeless without the sensual energy he shot through it like an electric charge.

'What are you thinking?' he asked, stroking the underside of her wrist with the broad pad of his thumb.

She met his chocolate-brown gaze and felt her insides flex and contract with lust. 'Do you want dessert?' she asked.

'Depends on what it is,' he said with a sexy glint.

She could barely sit still in her chair for the rocket blast of longing that swept through her. 'I'm not in the mood for anything sweet,' she said.

'What *are* you in the mood for?' Still that same sexy glitter was lighting his eyes from behind.

'Nothing that takes too much time to prepare.'

'I can be a fast order chef when the need arises,' he said. 'Tell me what you want and I'll deliver it as fast as humanly possible.'

Natalie shivered as he came behind her to pull out her chair for her. The fine hairs on the back of her neck stood up as his warm wine-scented breath coasted past her ear. She leaned back against him, just for a brief moment, to see if he was aroused.

He was.

She smiled to herself and walked out of the restaurant with him, her body already quaking in anticipation.

Angelo had barely opened the door of the villa when she slammed him up against the wall as if she was about to frisk him.

'Hey, was it something I said?' he asked.

Her dark blue gaze sizzled as it held his. 'You promised me dessert,' she said. 'It's time to serve me.'

The entire length of his backbone shuddered as she

ran her hand over his erection. 'Who's doing the cooking here?' he asked.

She gave him a wicked look and brazenly unzipped him. 'I want an appetiser,' she said.

It was all he could do to stand there upright as she sank to her knees in front of him. He braced himself by standing with his feet slightly apart. When she was in this mood there was no stopping her. He was just happy to be taken along for the ride.

And what a ride it was.

Fireworks went off in his head. He couldn't have held back if he had tried. She ruthlessly teased and caressed him until he was barely able to stand upright. His skin went up in a layer of goosebumps and his heart raced like a fat retiree at a fun run.

She stood up and gave him a wanton smile that had a hint of challenge to it. 'Top that,' she said.

'I can do that,' he said, and swept her up in his arms.

He took her to the master suite. He dropped her in the middle of the mattress and then pulled her by one ankle until she was right between his spread thighs. He leaned over her, breathing in her scent, his mouth coming down to claim her in a sensual feast that had her shuddering in seconds. She bucked and arched and screamed, and even batted at him with her fists, but he wouldn't let her go until he was satisfied that he had drawn every last shuddering gasp out of her.

She lay back and flung a hand over her eyes, her chest rising and falling. 'OK, you win,' she said breathlessly.

'It was pretty damn close,' he said, coming to lie next to her. He trailed a finger down the length of her satin-smooth arm. 'Maybe we should have a re-match some time soon, just to make sure?'

She rolled her head to look at him. 'Give me ten minutes.'

'Five.'

'You're insatiable.'

'Only with you.'

A tiny frown puckered her brow and she turned her head back to look at the ceiling. 'Have there been many?' she asked after a pause.

'Does it matter?'

She gave a careless shrug, but the tight set of her expression contradicted it. 'Not really.'

'I was never in love with anyone, if that's what you're asking.'

'I'm not.'

He sent his fingertip over the silky smooth cup of her shoulder. 'Is it so hard to admit you care for me?' he said.

She shoved his hand away and got off the bed. 'I *knew* you would do this,' she said in agitation.

'What did I do?'

She turned and speared him with her gaze. 'I don't love you,' she said. 'Is there something about those words you don't understand? I don't love you. I *like* you. I like you a lot. You're a nice person. I've never met a more decent person. But I'm not in love with you.'

Frustration made Angelo's voice grate. 'You don't *want* to love anyone, that's why. You do care, Tatty. You care so much it scares the hell out of you.'

She clenched her fists by her sides. 'I can't give you what you want,' she said.

'I want you.'

'You want more,' she said. 'You've said it from the beginning. You want a family. You want children. I can't give you them.'

'Are you infertile?'

She rolled her eyes heavenwards and turned away. 'I knew you wouldn't understand.'

He came over to her and took her by the upper arms. 'Then make me understand,' he said.

She pressed her lips together, as if she was trying to stop an outburst of unchecked speech from escaping.

He gave her arms a gentle squeeze. 'Talk to me, Tatty.'

Her eyes watered and she blinked a couple of times to push the tears back. 'What sort of mother would I be?' she asked.

'You'd be a wonderful mother.'

'I'd be a total nutcase,' she said, pulling away from him. 'I'd probably be one of those helicopter parents everyone talks about. I would never be able to relax. So much can happen to a child. There's so much danger out there: illness, accidents, sick predators on the streets and online. It's all too much to even think about.'

'Most parents manage to bring up their children without anything horrible happening to them,' he said. 'It's easy to look at what's reported in the press and think that the danger is widespread and unavoidable, but you're disregarding all the positive parenting experiences that are out there.'

'I just don't want to go there,' she said. 'You can't make me. No one can make me. You can't force me to get pregnant.'

'I sure hope you're on the pill, then, because I haven't always used protection.'

'Did you do that deliberately?' she asked with a hardened look.

'No, of course not,' he said. 'You were on the pill in

the past…I just assumed… OK, maybe I shouldn't have. I'm clear, if that's what's worrying you.'

'Yes, well, so am I,' she said. 'It's not like I've been out there much just lately.'

'Have you been "out there" at all?'

She tried to look casual about it, but he saw her nibble at the inside of her mouth. 'A couple of times,' she said.

'What happened?'

She gave him a withering look. 'I'm not going to discuss my sex life with you.'

'Did you have sex?'

She looked away. 'It wasn't great sex,' she said. 'More of a token effort, really. I don't even remember the guy's name.'

'What were you trying to prove?'

She looked at him sharply. 'What do you mean by that?'

'I've noticed you have a habit of using sex when you want to avoid intimacy.'

She pulled her chin back in derision. 'That's ridiculous,' she said. 'What sort of pop psychology is that? Isn't sex all about intimacy?'

'Physical, maybe, but not emotional,' he said. 'Emotional intimacy takes it to a whole different level.'

'That's way too deep for me,' she said, with an airy toss of her head. 'I like sex. I like the rush of it. I don't need anything else.'

'You don't want anything else because you're running away from who you really are,' he said.

'I'm sure you're a great big world expert on emotional intimacy,' she said with a scathing curl of her lip. 'You've had five different lovers in the last year.'

'So you *have* been counting.'

She stalked to the other side of the room. 'The Texan heiress was way too young for you,' she said. 'She looked like she was barely out of the schoolroom.'

'I didn't sleep with her.'

She gave a scoffing laugh. 'No, I can imagine you didn't. You would've kept her up way past her bedtime with your silver-tongued charm.'

Angelo ground his teeth in search of patience. 'I'm not going to wait for ever for you, Natalie,' he said. 'I have an empire that needs an heir. I've felt the pressure of that since I was twenty-one years old. If you can't commit to that, then I'll have to find someone else who will.'

She gave him a stony look. 'That's why you forced me into this farce of a marriage, isn't it?' she asked. 'It isn't just about revenge or nostalgic past feelings. It's a convenient way to get what you want. My brother played right into your hands.'

'This has nothing to do with your brother,' he said. 'This is between us. It's always been between us.'

Her slate-blue eyes were hard and cynical. 'Tell me something, Angelo,' she said. 'Would you have done it? Would you really have sent my brother to prison?'

He returned her look with ruthless determination. 'You're still the only person standing between your brother and years behind bars,' he said. 'Don't ever forget that, Natalie. His future is in your hands.'

She put up her chin, her eyes flashing their blue fire of defiance at him. 'I could call your bluff on that.'

He nailed her with his gaze. 'You do that, sweetheart,' he said. 'And see how far it gets you.'

CHAPTER EIGHT

NATALIE walked out in the moonlit gardens when sleep became impossible. She had tossed and fretted for the past couple of hours, but there was no way she could close her eyes without images of the past flickering through her brain like old film footage.

Tomorrow was the anniversary of her baby brother's death.

The hours leading up to it were always mental torture. Was that why she had practically thrown herself at Angelo, in an attempt to block it from her mind? She hadn't seen him since he had stalked out on her after delivering his spine-chilling threat.

She wanted to test him.

She wanted to see if he really was as ruthless as he claimed to be but it was too risky. Lachlan would have to pay the price.

She couldn't do it.

He had a future—the future that had been taken from Liam. Lachlan didn't just have his own life to live; he had that of his baby brother, too. No wonder he was buckling under the pressure. Who could ever live up to such a thing? Lachlan was his own person. He had his own goals and aspirations. But for years he had suppressed them in order to keep their parents happy. He had no interest in the family business. Natalie could see that, but their father could not or would not. Their mother couldn't see further than the label on the next bottle of liquor.

She gave a thorny sigh and turned to look at the shimmering surface of the pool that had appeared as if by magic in front of her. She generally avoided swimming pools.

Too many memories.

Even the smell of chlorine was enough to set the nerves in her stomach into a prickling panic. Before Liam's death she had loved the water. She had spent many a happy hour in the pool at Armitage Manor, practising what she had learned with Granny and Grandad at the beach at Crail. But after Liam had died the pool had been bulldozed and made into a tennis court.

She had never once picked up a tennis racket.

She looked at the moonlit water; a tiny breeze teased the surface. It was like a crinkled bolt of silver silk.

Had she come out here in a subconscious attempt to find some peace at last? Would she ever find peace? Forgiveness? Redemption?

A footfall behind her had her spinning around so quickly she almost fell into the water behind her.

'Couldn't you at least have said something before sneaking up on me like that?' she asked clutching at her thumping chest as Angelo stepped into the circle of light from one of the garden lamps.

'Can't sleep?' he asked.

She rubbed at her arms even though it was still warm. 'It's not all that late,' she said.

'It's three a.m.'

She frowned. 'Is it?'

'I've been watching you for the last hour.'

She narrowed her gaze. 'Don't you mean spying?'

'I was worried about you.'

She raised a brow mockingly. 'What?' she asked. 'You thought I might do something drastic rather than face the prospect of being tied to you for the rest of my life?'

'I was concerned you might go for a swim.'

Her eyebrow arched even higher. 'Do I have to ask your permission?'

'No, of course not,' he said, frowning. 'I was just worried you mightn't realise the danger of swimming alone late at night.'

A hysterical bubble of laughter almost choked her. 'Yeah, right—like I don't already know that,' she said with bitter irony.

His frown gave him a dark and forbidding look. 'You said you weren't a strong swimmer. I thought I should be with you if you fancied a dip to cool off.'

Natalie hid behind the smokescreen of her sarcasm. 'What were you going to do if I got into trouble?' she asked. 'Give me mouth to mouth?'

The atmosphere changed as if someone had flicked a switch.

His eyes smouldered as they tussled with hers. 'What a good idea,' he said, grasping her by the arms and bringing her roughly against him, covering her mouth with his.

His mouth tasted of brandy and hot male frustration. He was angry with her, but she could cope much better with his anger than his tenderness. He disarmed her with his concern and understanding.

She wanted him mad at her.

She wanted him wild with her.

She could handle that. She could pull against his

push. She could survive the onslaught of his sensual touch if she could compartmentalise it as a simple battle of wills, not as a strategic war against her very soul.

His lips ground against hers as his hands gripped her upper arms, his fingers biting into her flesh. She relished the discomfort. She was in the mood for pain. She kissed him back, with her teeth and her tongue taking turns. She felt him flinch as her teeth drew blood, and he punished her by driving his tongue all the harder against hers until she finally submitted.

She let him have his way for a few breathless seconds before she tried a counter-attack. She took his lower lip between her teeth and held on.

He spun her around, so her back was facing the pool, and with no more warning than the sound of his feet moving against the flagstones he tangled his legs with hers so she lost her footing. She opened her mouth on a startled gasp, fell backwards and disappeared under the water, taking him with her.

She came up coughing and spluttering; panic was like a madman inside her chest, fighting its way out any way it could. She felt the sickening hammer blows of her heart. She felt the acrid sting of chlorine in her eyes. She was choking against the water she had swallowed. It burned the back of her throat like acid.

'You...*you bastard*!' she screamed at him like a virago.

He pushed the wet hair out of his eyes and laughed. 'You asked for it.'

She came at him then. Hands in fists and teeth bared, she fell upon him, not caring if she drew blood or worse. She called him every foul name she could think of, the words pouring out of her like a vitriolic flood.

He simply held her aloft, and none of her blows and

kicks came to anything but impotent splashes against and below the water.

Suddenly it was all too much.

The fight went out of her. She felt the dismantling of her spirit like starch being rinsed out of a piece of fabric. She went as limp as a rag doll.

'Do you give up?' he asked, with a victorious glint in his dark eyes.

'I give up...'

His brows moved together and his smile faded. 'What's wrong?' he asked.

'Nothing,' she said tonelessly. 'Can I get out now? I—I'm getting cold.'

'Sure,' he said, releasing her, his gaze watchful.

Natalie waded to the edge of the pool. She didn't bother searching for the steps. She gripped the side and hauled herself out in an ungainly fashion. She stood well back from the side and wrung her hair out like a rope, and pushed it back over her shoulder. It wasn't cold, but she was shivering as if she had been immersed for hours in the Black Sea.

Angelo elevated himself out of the pool with a lot more athletic grace than she had. He came and stood in front of her, his hand capturing her juddering chin so he could hold her gaze. 'You didn't hurt yourself, did you?' he asked.

She flashed him a resentful look. 'It would be your fault if I had.'

'I would never have pushed you in if I didn't think it was safe,' he said. 'The water is deepest this end.'

She wrenched her chin out of his grasp and rubbed at it furiously. 'What if it had been the other end?' she asked. 'I could've been knocked out or even killed.'

'I would never deliberately hurt you, *cara*.'

'Not physically, maybe,' she said, throwing him a speaking glance.

A little smiled pulled up the corners of his mouth. 'So you're feeling a little threatened emotionally?' he asked.

She glowered at him. 'Not at all.'

His smile tilted further. 'It's the sex, *cara*,' he said. 'Did you know that the oxytocin released at orgasm is known as the bonding hormone? It makes people fall in love.'

She gave him a disparaging look. 'If that's true then why haven't you been in love with anyone since we were together? It's not as if you haven't been having loads and loads of sex.'

His eyes held hers in a toe-curling lock. 'Ah, but there is sex and there is *sex*.' His gaze flicked to her mouth, pausing there for a heartbeat before coming back to make love with her eyes.

Natalie felt her hips and spine soften. She felt the stirring of her pulse, the tap-tap-tap of her blood as it coursed through her veins. It sent a primal message to the innermost heart of her femininity, making it contract tightly with need.

'But you're not in love with me,' she said, testing him. 'You just want revenge.'

He stroked a light, teasing fingertip down the length of her bare arm, right to the back of her hand, before he captured her fingers in his and brought her close to his body. She felt the shock of touching him thigh to thigh like a stun gun. It sent a wave of craving through her that almost knocked her off her feet.

'I love what you do to me,' he said. 'I love how you make me feel.'

She could barely think with his erection pressing

so enticingly against her. Her body seeped with need. She felt the humid dew of it between her thighs. She looked up in time to see his mouth come down. She closed her eyes and gave herself up to his devastatingly sensual kiss.

His lips moved with hot urgency against hers, drawing from her a response that was just as fiery. Her tongue met his and duelled with it, danced with it, mated with it. Shivers of reaction washed over her body. She pressed herself closer, wanting that thrill of the flesh to block out the pain of the past.

But suddenly he put her from him. 'No,' he said. 'I'm not falling for that again.'

Natalie looked at him in confusion. 'You don't want to…?'

He gave her a wry look. 'Of course I want to,' he said. 'But I'm not going to until you tell me why you were out here, wandering about like a sleepwalker.'

Her gaze slipped out of the range of his. 'I wasn't doing any such thing.'

He pushed her chin up with a finger and thumb. 'Yes, you were,' he said, his gaze determined as it pinned hers. 'And I want to know why.'

Natalie felt her stomach churning and her shivering turned to shuddering. 'I told you. I often have trouble sleeping,' she said.

His eyes continued to delve into hers. 'What plays on your mind so much that you can't settle?'

She licked her dry lips. 'Nothing.'

His brow lifted sceptically. 'I want the truth, Natalie. You owe me that, don't you think?'

'I owe you nothing,' she said, with a flash of her gaze.

His eyes tussled with hers. 'If you won't tell me then

I'll have to find someone who will,' he said. 'And I have a feeling it won't take too much digging.'

Natalie swallowed in panic. If he went looking for answers it might stir up a press fest. She could just imagine the way the papers would run with it. She would have to relive every heartbreaking moment of that fateful trip. Her mother would be devastated to have her terrible loss splashed all over the headlines. Her father had managed to keep things quiet all those years ago, but it would be fair game now, in today's tell-all climate.

And then there was Lachlan to consider.

How would he feel to have the world know he was nothing but a replacement child? That he had only been conceived to fill the shoes of the lost Armitage son and heir?

She ran her tongue over her lips, fighting for time, for strength, for courage. 'I…I made a terrible mistake…a few years back…' She bit down on her lip, not sure if she could go on.

'Tell me about it, Natalie.'

Oh, dear God, *could* she tell him? How could she bear his shock and horror? Those tender looks he had been giving her lately would disappear. How she had missed those looks! He was the only person in the world who looked at her like that.

'Tatty?'

It was the way he said his pet name for her. It was her undoing. How could one simple word dismantle all her defences like a row of dominoes pushed by a fingertip? It was as if he had the key to her heart.

He had always had it.

He hadn't realised it the first time around, but now it was like the childhood game of hot and cold. He was getting warmer and warmer with every moment he spent with her.

Natalie slowly brought her gaze up to look at him head-on. *This is it*, she thought with a sinkhole of despair opening up inside her. *This is the last time you will ever see him look at you like that. Remember it. Treasure it.*

'I killed my brother.'

A confused frown pulled at his forehead. 'Your brother is fine, Natalie. He's safe and sound in rehab.'

'Not that brother,' she said. 'My baby brother, Liam. He drowned while we were holidaying in Spain...he was three years old.'

His frown was so deeply entrenched on his brow it looked as if it would become permanent. 'How could that have been your fault?' he asked.

'I was supposed to be watching him,' she said hollowly. 'My mother had gone inside to lie down. My father was there with us by the pool, but then he said he had to make a really important business call. He was only gone five minutes. I was supposed to be watching Liam. I'd done it before. I was always looking out for him. But that day... I don't know what happened. I think something or other distracted me for a moment. A bird, a flower, a butterfly—I don't know what. When my father came back...' She gave an agonised swallow as the memories came flooding back. 'It was too late...'

'Dear God! Why didn't you tell me this five years ago?' he asked. 'You never mentioned a thing about having lost a brother. Why on earth didn't you say something?'

'It's not something anyone in my family talks about. My father strictly forbade it. He thought it upset my mother too much. It was so long ago even the press have forgotten about it. Lachlan was the replacement child. As soon as he was born every photo, every bit of clothing or any toys that were Liam's were destroyed or given away. It was as if he had never existed.'

Angelo took her by the upper arms, his hold firm—almost painfully so. 'You were not to blame for Liam's death,' he said. 'You were a baby yourself. Your parents were wrong to lay that guilt on you.'

She looked into his dark brown eyes and saw comfort and understanding, not blame and condemnation. It made her eyes water uncontrollably. The tears came up from a well deep inside her. There was nothing she could do to hold them back. They bubbled up and spilled over in a gushing torrent. She hurtled forward into the wall of his chest, sobbing brokenly as his arms came around her and held her close.

'I tried to find him as soon as I noticed he wasn't beside me,' she said. 'It was barely a few seconds before I realised he was gone. I looked and looked around the gardens by the pool, but I didn't see him. He was at the bottom of the pool. I didn't see him. I didn't *see* him…'

'My poor little Tatty,' he soothed against her hair, rocking her gently with the shelter of his frame. 'You were not to blame, *cara*. You were not to blame.'

Natalie cried until she was totally spent. She told him other things as she hiccupped her way through another round of sobs. She told him of how she had seen Liam's tiny coffin being loaded on the plane. How the plane had hit some turbulence and how terrified she had been that his tiny body would be lost for ever. How she had sat in that wretched shuddering seat and wished she had been the one to drown. How her father had not said a word to her the whole way home. How her mother had sat in a blank state, drinking every drink the flight crew handed her.

She didn't know how much time passed before she eased back out of his hold and looked up at him through reddened and sore eyes. 'I must look a frightful mess,' she said.

He looked down at her with one of his warm and tender looks. 'I think you look beautiful.'

She felt a fresh wave of tears spouting like a fountain. 'You see?' she said as she brushed the back of her hand across her eyes. 'This is why I *never* cry. It's too damn hard to stop.'

He brushed the damp hair off her face, his gaze still meltingly soft. 'You can cry all you want or need to, *mia piccola*,' he said. 'There's nothing wrong with showing emotion. It's a safety valve, *si*? It's not good to suppress it for too long.'

She gave him a rueful look. 'You always were far better at letting it all hang out than me,' she said. 'It used to scare me a bit…how incredibly passionate you were.'

He stroked her hair back from her face. 'I seem to remember plenty of passion on your part too,' he said.

'Yes…well, you do seem to bring that out in me,' she said.

His hands slid down to hers, his fingers warm and protective as they wrapped around hers. 'I think it's high time you were tucked up in bed, don't you?'

Natalie shivered as his gaze communicated his desire for her. 'You want to…?'

He scooped her up in his arms. 'I want to,' he said, and carried her indoors.

Angelo lay awake once Natalie had finally dozed off. It had taken a while. In the quiet period after they had made love she had told him how today was the actual anniversary of her baby brother's death. It certainly explained her recent agitation and restlessness. He thought of her horrible nightmare the other night, how she had thrashed and turned and how worried he had been.

It all made sense now.

He still could not fathom why her parents had done such a heartless thing as to blame *her* for the tragic death of their little son. How could they have possibly expected a child of seven to be responsible enough to take care of a small child? It was unthinkably cruel to make her shoulder the blame. Why had they done it? What possible good did they think it would do to burden her with what was essentially their responsibility?

And where had the resort staff been?

Why hadn't Adrian Armitage aimed his guilt-trip on them instead of his little daughter?

His gut churned with the anguish of what she must have faced. Why had she not told him before now? It hurt him to think she had kept that dark secret from him. He had loved her so passionately. He would have given her the world and yet she had not let him into her heart.

Until now.

But she hadn't told him because she had trusted him. He had *forced* it out of her.

He picked up her left hand and rolled the pad of his thumb over the rings he had made her wear.

He had sought revenge, but it wasn't as sweet as he had thought. He hadn't had all the facts on the table. How differently would he have acted if he had known?

His insides clenched with guilt. He had railroaded her into marriage, not stopping to think of the reasons why she had balked at it in the first place. He had not taken the time to understand her, to find the truth about why she was so prickly and defensive. He had not made enough of an effort to get to know her beyond the physical. He had allowed his lust for her to colour everything else.

He had listened to those barefaced lies from her father. Listened and believed them. How could he ever make it up to her? How could he show her there was a way through this if only she trusted and leaned on him?

Or was it already too late to turn things around?

Angelo brought in a tray with coffee and rolls the next morning and set it down beside her. She opened her eyes and sat up, pushing her hair out of her face. 'I don't expect you to wait on me,' she said.

'It's no bother,' he said. 'I was up anyway.'

She took the cup of coffee he had poured for her. 'Thanks,' she said after a little pause.

'You're welcome.'

'I meant about last night,' she said, biting her lip.

Angelo sat on the edge of the bed near her thighs and took one of her hands in his. 'Would you have eventually told me, do you think?'

She lifted one shoulder up and down. 'Maybe—' She twisted her mouth. 'Probably not.'

'I've been thinking about your parents,' he said. 'I'd like to meet with them to talk through this.'

She pulled her hand out of his. 'No.'

'Natalie, this can't go on—'

'*No.*' Her slate blue eyes collided with his. 'I don't want you to try and fix things. You can't fix this.'

'Look, I understand this is a painful thing for all of you, but it's not fair that you've been carrying this guilt for so long,' he said. 'Your parents need to face up to their part in it.'

She put her coffee cup down with a splash of the liquid over the sides and slid out of the bed. She roughly wrapped herself in a robe and then turned and glared at him. 'If you approach my parents I will *never* forgive you,' she said. 'My mother has enough to deal with. It will destroy her if this is dragged up again. She's barely holding on as it is. And if this gets out in the press it will jeopardise Lachlan's recovery for sure.'

'I'm concerned about you—not your mother or brother,' he said.

'If you're truly concerned about me then you'll do what I ask.'

Angelo frowned. 'Why are you so determined to take the rap for something that was clearly not your fault?'

'It *was* my fault,' she said. 'I was supposed to be watching him.'

'You were a *child*, Natalie,' he said. 'A child of seven should not be left in charge of a toddler—especially around water. How would you have got him out even if you had seen him in time?'

Her features gave a spasm of pain. 'I would have jumped in and helped him.'

'And very likely drowned as well,' he said. 'You were too young to do anything.'

'I could've thrown him something to hold on to until help came,' she said, her eyes glittering with unshed tears.

'*Cara*,' he said, taking a step towards her.

'No,' she said, holding him off with her hands held up like twin stop signs. 'Don't come near me.'

He ignored her and put his hands on her shoulders. She began to push against his chest but somehow as he pulled her closer and she gripped his shirt instead. He brought his head down to hers, taking his time to give her time to escape if she wanted to.

'Don't fight me, *mia piccola*,' he said. 'I'm not your enemy.'

'I'm not fighting you,' she said, her gaze locked on his mouth. 'I'm fighting myself.'

He brushed her mouth with his thumb. 'That's what I thought.'

She gave him a rueful look. 'I can't seem to help myself.'

'You know something?' he said. 'Nor can I.' And then he covered her mouth with his.

CHAPTER NINE

A FEW days later Natalie was wandering around the renovation site of Angelo's hotel development, taking copious notes and snapping photographs as she went along. It was a spectacular development—a wonderful and decadent mix between a boutique hotel and a luxury health spa. Gold and polished marble adorned every surface. Tall arched windows looked out over the sea, or lemon groves and steep hills beyond framed the view. She couldn't believe he was giving her the work. It was a dream job. It would stretch her creatively, but it would springboard her to the heights of interior design.

'Are you nearly done?' Angelo asked as he joined her, after speaking to one of his foremen.

'Are you kidding?' she said. 'I've barely started. This place is amazing. I have so many ideas my head is buzzing.'

He put a gentle hand on the nape of her neck, making an instant shiver course down her spine. 'I don't want you to work too hard,' he said. 'We're supposed to be on honeymoon, remember?'

How could she forget? Her body was still humming with the aftershocks of his passionate possession first thing that morning.

Over the last few days Angelo had been incredibly

tender with her. She was finding it harder and harder to keep her emotions in check. He was unravelling her bit by bit, taking down her defences with every kiss and caress. The same blistering passion was there, but with it was a new element that took their lovemaking to a different level—one she had not experienced with him before. She wasn't ready to admit she loved him. Not even to herself. She knew she admired and respected him. She liked being with him and enjoyed being challenged by his quick intellect and razor-sharp wit.

But as for being in love…well, what was the point of even going there? She could not stay with him for ever. He had already told her what he wanted. He would not choose her over his desire for heirs.

'You have a one-track mind, Angelo,' she said in mock reproach.

He smiled a lazy smile and pressed a kiss to her bare shoulder. 'Are you going to deny you weren't just thinking about what we got up to this morning?' he asked.

Her belly shifted like a drawer pulled out too quickly as she thought of how he had made her scream with pleasure. 'Stop it,' she said in an undertone. 'The workmen will hear you.'

'So what if they do?' he said, nibbling on her earlobe. 'I am a man in love with his wife. Am I not allowed to tell the world?'

Natalie stiffened and pulled away. 'I think I'm just about done here,' she said. 'I can come back another time.'

'What's wrong?'

'Nothing.'

'You're shutting me out,' he said. 'I can see it in your face. It's like a drawbridge suddenly comes up.'

'You're imagining it,' she said, closing her notebook with a little snap.

'I won't let you do this, Tatty,' he said. 'I won't let you pull away. That's not how this relationship is going to work.'

She sent him a crystal-hard little glare. 'How *is* this relationship going to work, Angelo?' she asked. 'You want what I can't give you.'

'Only because you're determined to keep on punishing yourself,' he said. 'You want the same things I want. I know you do. Do you think I don't know you by now? I saw the way you looked at that mother and baby when we had coffee in that café yesterday.'

Natalie gave one of her *faux* laughs. 'I was looking at that mother in pity,' she said. 'Did you hear how loudly that brat was crying? It was disturbing everyone.'

'I saw your eyes,' he said. 'I saw the longing.'

She turned and began to stalk away. 'I don't have to listen to this.'

'There we go,' he said, with cutting sarcasm. 'And right on schedule too. Your stock standard phrase makes yet another appearance. I'm sick to death of hearing it.'

She turned back and looked at him. 'Then why don't you send me on my way so you don't have to listen to it any more?' she asked.

His eyes wrestled with hers, dark and glittering with frustration and anger. 'You'd like that, wouldn't you?' he said. 'You'd like to be let off the emotional hook. But I'm not going to do it. You will be with me until the day I say you can finally go.'

'I'm going back to the villa,' she said with a veiled look. 'That is if that's all right with you?'

He sucked in a harsh breath and brushed past her. 'Do what you like,' he said, and left.

* * *

When Natalie came downstairs at the villa a couple of hours later Angelo was on the phone. He signalled for her to wait for him to finish. He was speaking to someone in rapid-fire Italian, his full-bodied accent reminding her all over again of how much she had always loved his voice. It was so rich and deep, so sexy and masculine it made the skin on her arms and legs tingle.

'Sorry about that,' he said, pocketing his phone. 'I have a development in Malaysia that is proving a little troublesome. The staff member I sent over is unable to fix it. I have to go over and sort it out.'

She set her features stubbornly, mentally preparing for another battle of wills. 'I hope you're not expecting me to come with you,' she said. 'I have my own business interests to see to. I can't be on holiday for ever.'

His expression was hard to read. 'I have made arrangements for you to travel back to Edinburgh this evening,' he said. 'I will fly to Kuala Lumpur first thing tomorrow morning.'

The air dropped out of her self-righteous sails. She stood there feeling strangely abandoned, cast adrift and frightened. 'I see…'

'I'll fly to London with you,' he said. 'I'm afraid I haven't got time to do the Edinburgh leg, but one of my staff will go with you instead.'

'I don't need you to hold my hand,' she said with a hoist of her chin.

His dark brown eyes held hers in that knowing way of his. 'You'd better pack your things,' he said. 'We have to leave in an hour.'

The journey to London was surprisingly not as bad as Natalie had been expecting. Her anger at Angelo was enough of a distraction to keep her from dwelling on her fear. He hardly said a word on the flight. Once he had made sure she was comfortable he had buried his head in some paperwork and architectural plans and barely taken a break for coffee or a bite to eat.

Once they landed he introduced her to his staff member, and with a brief kiss to her mouth was gone.

Natalie watched him stride away as if he had just dumped a particularly annoying parcel at the post office and couldn't wait to get on with his day.

'This way, *Signora* Bellandini,' Riccardo said, leading the way to the gate for her flight to Edinburgh.

'It's Ms Armitage,' she insisted.

Riccardo looked puzzled. 'But you are married to *Signor* Bellandini now, *si*?'

'Yes, but that doesn't mean I no longer cease to exist,' she said and, hitching her bag over her shoulder, marched towards the gate.

Natalie was at her studio a couple of days later, leafing through the paper while she had a kick-start coffee before she opened the doors to her clients. Her eyes zeroed in on a photograph in the international gossip section. It was of Angelo, with his hand on the back of a young raven-haired woman as he led her into a plush hotel in Kuala Lumpur. The caption read: *'Honeymoon Over for Italian Tycoon?'*

A dagger of pain plunged through her, leaving her cold and sick and shaking. Nausea bubbled up in her throat—a ghastly tide of bile that refused to go back down. She stumbled to the bathroom at the rear of the office and hunched over the basin, retching until it was all gone. She clung to the basin with white-knuckled hands, clammy sweat breaking over her brow.

'Are you all right?' Linda's concerned voice sounded outside the door.

'I—I'm fine,' Natalie said hoarsely. 'Just a bit of an upset tummy.'

When she came out of the bathroom Linda was holding the newspaper. 'You know the press makes half of this stuff up to sell papers, don't you?' she said, with a worried look that belied her pragmatic claim.

'Of course,' Natalie said, wishing in this case it were true. How stupid had she been to think Angelo was starting to care about her? He had been playing her like a fool from day one. Reeling her in bit by bit, getting her to pour her darkest secrets out to him and then, when she was at her most vulnerable, swooping in and chopping her off at the knees with his cold-hearted perfidy.

Was this how her mother felt every time her father found a new mistress? How did she stand it? The emotional brutality of it was crucifying.

How could Angelo do this to her? Did he want revenge so much? Didn't the last week mean a thing to him? Had it all been nothing but a ruse to get her to let her guard down? How could he be so cold and calculating?

Easily.

He had never forgiven her for walking out on him. Her rejection of him had simmered for five years, burning and roiling deep inside him like lava building and bubbling up in a long-dormant volcano. He had waited patiently until the time was ripe to strike.

It hurt to think how easily she had been duped. How had she allowed him to do that to her? What had happened to her determination to keep her heart untouched?

Her heart felt as if it had been pummelled, bludgeoned. Destroyed.

'Do you know who the woman is?' Linda asked.

'No,' Natalie said tightly. 'And I don't care.'

'Maybe she's his assistant,' Linda offered.

Assisting him with what? Natalie thought as jealousy stung her with its deadly venom. Her mind filled with images of him in that wretched hotel with his beautiful 'assistant'. Their limbs entangled in a big bed, his body splayed over hers, giving the raven-haired beauty the pleasure it had so recently given *her*.

'Are you all right?' Linda asked again.

'Excuse me…' Natalie raced back to the bathroom.

When Natalie got home after work she wasn't feeling much better. Her head was pounding and her stomach felt as if it had been scraped raw with a grater.

She hadn't heard from Angelo—not that she expected him to contact her. No doubt he would be too busy with his gorgeous little dark-haired assistant. Her stomach pitched again and she put a hand on it to settle it, tears suddenly prickling at the backs of her eyes.

Her phone rang from inside her bag and she fished it out. Checking the caller ID, she pressed the answer button. 'How nice of you to call me, my darling husband,' she said with saccharine-sweet politeness. 'Are you sure you've got the time?'

'You saw the picture.'

Her hand tightened around the phone. 'The *whole world* saw the picture,' she said. 'Who is she? Is she your mistress?'

'Don't be ridiculous, Tatty.'

'Don't you *dare* call me that!' she shouted at him. 'You heartless bastard. How could you do this to me?'

'*Cara.*' His voice gentled. 'Calm down and let me explain.'

'Go on, then,' she challenged him. 'I bet you've already thought up a very credible excuse for why you had your hand on that woman's back as you led her into your hotel for a bit of rest and recreation. And I bet there was more recreation than rest.'

'You're jealous.'

'I am *not* jealous,' she said. 'I just don't like being made a fool of publically. You could have at least warned me this was how you were going to play things. I should've known you would have a double standard. One rule for me, a separate one for you. Men like you disgust me.'

'Her name is Paola Galanti and she's a liaison officer with my Malaysian construction team,' he said. 'She is having some difficulty dealing with a very male-dominated work environment.'

'Oh, so big tough Angelo had to come to her rescue?' Natalie put in scathingly. 'Another damsel in distress to rescue and seduce.'

'Will you stop it, for God's sake?' he said. 'Paola is engaged to a friend of mine. I have never been involved with her.'

'Why didn't you tell me your staff member was female when you told me you had to fly over there?' she asked.

'Because her gender has nothing to do with her position on my staff.'

'You still could have told me, rather than let me find out like that in the press,' she said, still bristling with resentment.

'Thus speaks the woman who didn't tell me a thing about her past until I dragged it out of her.'

Natalie flinched at his bitter tone. She bit her lip and

wondered if she was overreacting. Could she trust him? Could she trust anyone?

Could she trust herself?

'Fine,' she said. 'So now we're even.'

She heard him release a heavy sigh. 'Life is not a competition, Natalie.'

'When are you coming back?' she asked, after a tiny tense silence.

'I'm not sure,' he said, sighing again. 'I have a few meetings to get through. There's a hold-up with some materials for the hotel I'm building. It's all turning out to be one big headache.'

She suddenly thought of him all the way over there, in a steamy hot climate, dealing with language barriers and a host of other difficulties on the top of a decent dose of jet lag. How on earth did he do it? He ran not only his own company but a big proportion of his father's as well. So many people to deal with, so many expectations, so much responsibility.

'You sound tired,' she said.

'You sound like a loving wife.'

She stiffened. 'I can assure you I am nothing of the sort.'

'Missing me, *cara*?'

'Hardly.'

'Liar.'

'OK, I miss the sex,' she said, knowing it would needle him. Let him think that was all she cared about.

'I miss it too,' he said, in a low deep tone that sent a rolling firework of sensation down her spine. 'I can't wait to get home to show you how much.'

She felt the clutch of her inner muscles as if they were already twanging in anticipation. She tried to keep her voice steady, but it quavered just a fraction in spite of her efforts. 'I guess I'll have to be patient until then, won't I?'

'I bought you something today,' he said. 'It should arrive tomorrow.'

'You don't have to buy me presents,' she said, thinking of all the gold and diamonds her father had given her mother over the years—presumably to keep his guilt in check. 'I can buy my own jewellery.'

'It's not jewellery,' he said.

'What is it, then?'

'You'll have to wait and see.'

'Flowers? Chocolates?'

'No, not flowers or chocolates,' he said. 'What time will you be at home? I'm not sure the studio is the right place to have it delivered to.'

Natalie felt curiosity building in spite of her determination not to be out-manoeuvred by him. 'I'm working from home all day tomorrow,' she said. 'I have some design work to do on my next collection. I usually do that at home because I get interrupted too much at the studio.'

'Good,' he said. 'I'll make sure it arrives early.'

'Will you at least give me a clue?'

'I have to go,' he said. 'I'll call you tomorrow evening. *Ciao.*'

She didn't even get a chance to reply as he had already ended the call.

The doorbell rang at nine-fifteen. Natalie answered its summons to find a courier standing there, with a small pet carrier in one hand and a clipboard with paperwork in the other.

'Ms Armitage?' he said with a beaming smile. 'I have a special delivery for you. Could you sign here, please?' He handed her the clipboard with a pen on a string attached.

She took the pen and clipboard after a moment's hesitation. She scribbled her signature and then handed it back. 'What is it?' she asked, eyeing the carrier with a combination of delight and dread.

'It's a puppy,' the courier said, handing the carrier over. 'Enjoy.'

Natalie shut the door once he had left. The pet carrier was rocking as the little body inside wriggled and yelped in glee.

'I swear to God I'm going to kill you, Angelo Bellandini,' she said as she put it down on the floor.

She caught sight of a pair of eyes as shiny as dark brown marbles looking at her through the holes in the carrier and her heart instantly melted. Her fingers fumbled over the latch in her haste to get it open.

'Oh, you darling little thing!' she gushed as a furry black ball hurtled towards her, yapping excitedly, its tiny curly tail going nineteen to the dozen. She scooped the puppy up and it immediately went about licking her face with endearing enthusiasm. 'Stop!' she said, giggling as her cheek got a swipe of a raspy tongue. 'Stop, *stop*, you mad little thing. What on earth am I going to do with you?'

The puppy gave a little yap and looked at her quizzically with its head on one side, its button eyes shining with love and adoration.

Natalie felt a rush of nurturing instinct so strong it almost knocked her backwards. She cuddled the little puppy close against her chest and instantly, irrevocably, fell head over heels in love.

* * *

Angelo checked the time difference before he called. He'd had a pig of a day. His meetings hadn't gone the way he would have liked. He was finding it hard to focus on the task at hand. All he could think about was how much he missed Natalie.

Business had never seemed so tedious. He wasn't sure how it had happened, but in the last week or so making money had become secondary to making her happy. He wanted to see her smile. He wanted to hear her laugh. He wanted to see her enjoy life. God knew she hadn't enjoyed it before now. He wanted to change that for her, but she was so damned determined to punish herself. He still hadn't given up on the idea of confronting her parents. How could she ever be truly free from guilt unless they accepted their part in the tragic death of their son?

He pressed her number on his phone, but after a number of rings it went through to voicemail. He frowned as he put the phone down on his desk. Disappointment weighed him down like fatigue from a fever. His whole day had revolved around this moment and now she hadn't picked up.

He was halfway through a mind-numbing report on one of his father's speculative investments when his phone started jumping around his desk. He reached out and picked it up, smiling when he saw it was Natalie calling him back.

'How's the baby?' he asked.

'She peed on the rug in my sitting room,' she said, 'and on the one in my bedroom, and on the absolutely priceless one in the hall. She would've done worse on the one in the study, but I caught her just in time.'

'Oh, dear,' he said. 'I guess she'll get the hang of things eventually.'

'She's chewed a pair of designer shoes and my sunglasses,' she said. 'Oh, and did I mention the holes in the garden? She's been relocating my peonies.'

Angelo leaned back against his leather chair. 'Sounds like you've had a busy day.'

'She's mischievous and disobedient,' she said. 'Right at this very minute she is chewing the cables on my computer. Hey—stop that, Molly. *Bad* girl. Mummy is cross with you. No, don't look at me like that.' Natalie gave a little tinkling bell laugh—a sound he had never heard her make before. 'I *am* cross. I really am.'

He smiled as he heard an answering yap. 'You called her Molly?'

'Yes,' she said wryly. 'Somehow Fido or Rover doesn't quite suit her.'

'But of course,' he said. 'She comes from a pedigree as long as your arm. Both her father and mother were Best in Show.'

There was a little silence.

'Why a puppy?' she asked.

'I'm away a lot,' he said. 'I thought the company would be nice.'

'I have a career,' she said. 'I have a business to run. I haven't got the time to train a puppy. I've never had a dog before. I have no idea what to do. What if something happens to her?'

'Nothing will happen to her, Tatty,' he said. 'Not while you're taking care of her.'

'What about work?' she asked. 'I can't leave her alone all day.'

'So take her with you,' he said. 'It's your studio. You're the boss. You can do what you like.'

Another silence.

'When will you be back?' she asked.

'I'm not sure,' he said. 'Things aren't working out the way I want over here.'

'How is your assistant?'

'Tucked up in bed with her fiancé,' he said. 'I flew him out to be with her.'

'That was thoughtful of you.'

'Practical rather than thoughtful,' he said. 'She was missing him and he was missing her.'

A longer silence this time.

'Angelo?'

'Yes, *cara*?'

'Thank you for not buying me jewellery.'

'You're the only woman I know who would say that,' Angelo said. 'I thought diamonds were supposed to be a girl's best friend?'

'Not this girl.'

'You're going to have to let me buy you some eventually,' he said. 'I don't want people to think I'm too tight to spoil my beautiful wife with lavish gifts.'

'Being generous with money and gifts is not a sign of a happy relationship,' she said. 'My mother is dripping in diamonds and she's absolutely miserable.'

'Why doesn't she leave your father if she's so unhappy?'

'Because he's rich and successful and she can't bear the thought of going back to being a nobody,' she said. 'She's a trophy wife. She's not his soul mate and he isn't hers. By marrying him she gave up her name and her identity. She's an effigy of who she used to be.'

Angelo was starting to see where Natalie's stubborn streak of independence stemmed from. She was terrified of ending up like her mother—bound to a man who had all the power and all the influence. No wonder she had run at the first hint of marriage from him. No wonder she had fought him tooth and nail when he'd blackmailed her back into his life. He had unknowingly sabotaged his own happiness and hers by forcing her to marry him.

'It doesn't have to be that way between us, Tatty,' he said. 'Relationships are not inherited. We create them ourselves.'

'You created this one, not me,' she said. 'I'm just the meat in the sandwich, remember?'

'Even if Lachlan hadn't provided me with the opportunity to get you back in my life I truly believe I would have found some other way,' he said. 'I'd been thinking of it for months.'

'Why?'

'I think you know why.'

There was another little beat of silence.

'I have to go,' she said. 'Molly is running off with a pen. I don't want ink to get on the rug. Bye.'

Angelo put his phone down and let out a long sigh. His relationship with Natalie was a two steps forward three steps back affair that left both of them frustrated. Was it to late to turn things around? What did he have to do to prove to her he wanted this to work?

Would he have to let her go in order to have her return to him on her own terms?

CHAPTER TEN

A COUPLE of days later Natalie heard the deep throaty rumble of a sports car pulling up outside her house. She didn't have to check through the front window to see if it was Angelo. It wasn't the hairs standing up on the back of her neck that proved her instincts true but the little black ball of fluff that was jumping about, yapping in frenzied excitement at the front door.

She couldn't help smiling as she scooped Molly up in her arms and opened the door. 'Yes, I know,' she said. 'It's Daddy.'

Angelo reached for the puppy and was immediately subjected to a hearty welcome. He held the wriggling body aloft. 'I think she just peed on me,' he said, grimacing.

Natalie giggled. 'What do you expect?' she said. 'She's excited to see you.'

His dark eyes glinted as they met hers. 'And what about you, *cara*?' he asked. 'Are you excited to see me too?'

She felt her body tingle as his gaze read every nuance of her expression. She had no hope of hiding her longing from him. She didn't even bother trying. 'Do you want me to lick your face to prove it?' she asked.

'I can think of other places that would suit me much better,' he said.

An earthquake of need rumbled through her lower body. 'What about Molly?' she asked as he moved towards her.

'What *about* Molly?' he said as he released her hair from the knot she had tied on the back of her head.

'Don't you think she's a little young to be watching us…you know…doing it?'

'Good point,' he said, and scooped the puppy up in one hand. 'Where does she sleep?'

She chewed her lip. 'Um…'

He narrowed his eyes in mock reproach. 'You're not serious?'

'What was I supposed to do?' she asked. 'She cried for ages until I took her to bed with me. I felt sorry for her. She was missing her mum.'

He smiled indulgently and flicked her cheek with a gentle finger. 'Softie.'

'I told you I'd be a hopeless mum,' she said. 'I'd end up spoiling the kid rotten.'

'I think you'd make a terrific mother.'

She frowned and took the puppy from him. 'I'll put her in her carrier in the laundry…'

'Tatty?'

She stilled at the door. 'Don't do this, Angelo.'

'You can't keep avoiding the subject,' he said. 'It's an issue that's important to me.'

She turned around and glared at him. 'I know what you're doing,' she said. 'You thought by giving me a puppy to take care of it would magically fix things, didn't you? But I told you before. You can't fix this. You can't fix *me*. You can't fix the past.'

'How long are you going to keep punishing yourself?' he asked.

'I'm not punishing myself,' she said. 'I'm being realistic. I don't think I can handle being a parent. What if I turn out like my father? Having kids changes people. Some people can't handle it. They lose patience. They resent the loss of freedom and take it out on their kids.'

'You're nothing like your father,' he said. 'I find it hard to believe you are even related to him. He's nothing but an arrogant, selfish jerk. He doesn't deserve to have a daughter as beautiful and gentle and loving as you.'

Natalie felt a warm feeling inside her chest like bread dough expanding. She tried to push it down but it kept rising again.

She wanted to believe him.

She wanted it desperately. She wanted a future with him. She wanted to have his baby—more than one baby—*a family*. But the past still haunted her. Would there ever be a time when it wouldn't?

'I need more time...' she said, stroking the puppy's head as she cradled it against her. 'I'm not ready to make a decision like that just yet.'

He put his hands on her shoulders, his dark chocolate eyes meshing with hers. 'We'll talk about it some other time,' he said. 'In the meantime, I think Molly is just about asleep. It would be a shame not to make the most of the opportunity, *si*?'

She trembled with longing as he gently took the puppy from her and led her upstairs into a world of sensuality she was fast becoming addicted to.

How would she ever be able to survive without it?

Natalie was in the garden with Molly the following afternoon when Angelo came out to her.

'Look, Angelo,' she said excitedly. 'Molly has learned to shake hands. Watch. Shake, Molly. See? Isn't she clever?'

'Very.'

She swung her gaze to his but he was frowning. 'What's wrong?' she asked.

He paused for a moment as if searching for the right words. 'Your mother has been taken ill. She's in hospital. Your father just called.'

Natalie felt the hammer blow of her heart against her chest wall. 'Is she all right?'

'She has an acute case of pancreatitis,' he said. 'She's in intensive care.'

'I—I need to go to her.'

'I've already got my private jet on call at the airport,' he said. 'Don't waste time packing. I'll buy what you need when we get there.'

'But what about Molly?' she asked.

'We'll take her with us,' he said. 'I'll have one of my staff take care of her once we get there.'

The intensive care unit was full of desperately ill people, but none of them looked as bad as her mother–or so Natalie thought when she first laid eyes on her, hooked up to machines and wires.

'Oh, Mum,' she said, taking her mother's limp hand in hers. Tears blinded her vision and her chest ached as if someone seriously overweight was sitting on it.

'I've informed Lachlan,' Angelo said at her shoulder. 'I've sent a plane to collect him.'

She pressed her lips to her mother's cold limp hand. 'I'm sorry, Mum,' she said. 'I'm so sorry.'

Adrian Armitage came back in, after taking a call on his mobile out in the corridor. 'And so you should be,' he said with a contemptuous look. 'This is *your* fault. She wouldn't have taken up drinking if it hadn't been for you.'

Angelo stood between Natalie and her father. 'I think you'd better leave,' he said, in a voice that brooked no resistance.

Adrian gave him a disparaging look. 'She's got her claws into you well and good, hasn't she?' he said. 'I warned you about her. She's manipulative and sneaky. You're a damn fool for falling for it.'

'If you don't leave of your own free will then I will *make* you leave,' Angelo said, in the same cool and calm but unmistakably indomitable tone.

'She killed my son,' Adrian said. 'Did she tell you that? She was jealous of him, that's why. She knew I wanted a son more than a daughter. She killed him.'

'Natalie did not kill your son,' Angelo said. 'She was not responsible for Liam's death. She was just a child. She should never have been given the responsibility of watching over him. That was *your* job. I will not have you blame her for your own inadequacies as a parent.'

Natalie watched as her father's face became puce. 'You *dare* to question my ability as a parent?' he roared. 'That girl is a rebel. She's unmanageable. She won't give an inch. She's black to the heart.'

'That girl is *my wife*,' Angelo said with steely emphasis. 'Now, get out of here before I do something you will regret more than I ever will.'

'Mr Armitage?' One of the doctors had appeared. 'I think it's best if you leave. Come this way, please.'

Angelo's concerned gaze came to Natalie's. 'Are you all right, *cara*?' he asked, touching her cheek with a gentle finger.

'I've always known he hated me,' she said on a

ragged sigh. 'It's true what he said...I overheard him blasting my mother about it when I was about five or so. He wanted a son first. That's why I always felt I wasn't good enough. It didn't matter how hard I tried or how well behaved I was or how well I did at school, I could never be the son he wanted. And then when Liam died... well, that was the end of any hope of ever pleasing him.'

'Some people should never be parents,' he said with a furious look. 'I can't believe how pathetic your father is. He's a coward—a bully and a coward. I don't want you to ever be alone with him. Do you understand?'

Natalie felt another piece of her armour fall away. 'I understand.'

His fierce expression relaxed into tenderness as he cupped her cheek. 'I'm sorry I didn't know what your childhood was like, and even more sorry that you didn't feel you could tell me,' he said. 'The clues were all there but I just didn't see them.'

'I once told a family friend about my father's treatment of me,' she said in a quiet voice. 'It got back to my father. My mother...' She swallowed tightly over the memory. 'My mother drank really badly after that.' She looked back at her mother and gave another sigh. 'I don't want to lose her. I know she's not perfect, but I don't want to lose her.'

He put his hand over hers and squeezed it tightly. 'Then I'll move heaven and earth to make sure you don't.'

Natalie looked physically shattered by the time Angelo escorted her out of the hospital. Her mother showed some signs of improvement, but it was still too early to tell if the severe bout of pancreatitis would settle. The doctors had told them her mother would not live much longer unless she gave up drinking.

He put his arm around Natalie's waist as he led her out to the car he had organised. 'Lachlan should be here in the morning,' he said. 'In the meantime I think you should try and get as much rest as you can. You look exhausted.'

'I don't know how to thank you for everything you've done,' she said. 'You've been…amazing.'

He put an arm around her shoulders and drew her into his body. 'Isn't it about time someone stood up for you?' he said.

'Funny that it's you.'

'Why is that?' he asked.

She gave a little shrug. 'I just thought you'd be the last person to take my side.'

He pressed a kiss to the top of her head. 'Then you don't know me all that well, do you?'

Angelo took her to his house in Mayfair. It was an immaculately presented four-storey mansion, with beautiful gardens in front as well as behind. Wealth and status oozed from every corner of the building, both inside and out.

Natalie looked around even though she was almost dead on her feet. 'This is certainly a long way from that run down flat we shared in Notting Hill,' she said, once she had inspected every nook and cranny.

'I liked that flat.'

She gave him a wistful smile. 'Yes, I did too.'

'Come here.'

She came and stood in the circle of his arms. 'You'd better not tell my twenty-one-year old self about this,' she said. 'She would be furious with me for obeying your command as if I had no mind of my own.'

He smiled as he gathered her close. 'I won't tell her if you won't.'

She nestled up against him, loving the warmth and comfort and shelter of his body. She felt like a little beat-up dinghy that had finally found safe harbour during a tempestuous storm.

If only she could stay here for ever.

Over the next few days Natalie's mother improved enough to be moved to the private clinic Angelo had organised. Many years of heavy drinking had caused some serious liver damage. It would be a long road to recovery and, while her mother seemed ready to take the first tentative steps, Natalie wasn't keen to put any money on her succeeding. She had seen her mother's attempts to become sober too many times to be confident that this time would be any different.

Lachlan was another story. He seemed determined to get well, and had asked Angelo to send him back to Portugal once he was sure their mother was out of danger. He had started to talk to counsellors about his childhood; about the impossible burden it was to be the replacement child. Natalie could only hope this would be the turning point he needed to get his life back on track.

She hadn't seen her father since Angelo had spoken to him at the hospital. She suspected he was worried about running into Angelo again. It seemed pathetically cowardly to stop visiting his wife just to protect himself, but then, she wouldn't be able to bear to watch him pretending to be a loving, concerned husband when she had personally witnessed all his hateful behaviour over the years that told another story.

On the afternoon when Angelo took Lachlan to the

airport Natalie sat with her mother in the sun room
at the clinic. She had brought Molly along, hoping it
would lift her mother's spirits, but Isla barely gave the
puppy a glance.

'I wonder when your father's coming in?' she asked,
checking her watch for the tenth time. 'He hasn't been
to see me since I came here.'

Natalie felt frustrated that her mother couldn't or
wouldn't see that her father was only concerned about
himself. 'Mum, why do you put up with him?' she
asked.

'What are you talking about?' Isla said. 'What do
you mean?'

'He treats you like rubbish,' Natalie said. 'He's always treated you like rubbish.'

'I know you don't understand, but I'm happy enough
with my lot,' her mother said. 'He's a good provider. I
don't ever have to worry about working. I have the sort
of lifestyle other people only dream of having.'

'Mum, you could divorce him and still be well provided for,' Natalie said. 'You don't have to put up with
his bullying.'

'He wasn't always difficult,' Isla said. 'It was better
in the early days. It was a dream come true when he
asked me to marry him after I found out I was pregnant.
We were both so certain you were going to be a boy.
I even bought all blue clothes. I was happy to have a
daughter, but your father took it very hard. He got better after Liam was born. But then…'

Natalie's eyes watered and her throat went tight. It
was always the same. The same wretched anguish, the
same crushing guilt. Would there ever be a time when
she would be able to move on without it?

'I'm sorry…'

Isla checked her watch again. 'Do you think you could call the nurse for me?' she said. 'I want to go home. I'm sick of being here.'

'Mum, how can you think of leaving?' Natalie asked. 'You're supposed to stay on the program for at least a month.'

Her mother reached past Natalie to press the buzzer for the nurse. 'I belong at home with your father,' she said with an intractable look. 'I don't belong here.'

Angelo pulled up just as Natalie came out of the clinic. She had a deep frown on her forehead and her gait was jerky, as if she was terribly upset and trying her best to hide it. It amazed him how easily he could read her now. It was as if a curtain had come up in his brain. He could sense her mood from the way she carried herself. The very times she needed support she pushed him away. She got all prickly and defensive. He could see her doing it now.

He got out of the car and held open the door for her. 'What's wrong?' he asked, taking the wriggling puppy from her.

'Nothing.'

'Hey,' he said, capturing her chin and making her look at him. 'What's going on?'

Her eyes looked watery, as if she was about to cry. 'I really don't want to talk about it,' she said.

'Tatty, we *have* to talk about things,' he said. 'Especially things that upset us. It's what well-functioning couples do. I don't want any more secrets between us.'

'My mother is going to check herself out,' she said in a defeated tone. 'I can't stop her. I can't fix this. I can't fix her. I can't fix *any* of this.'

He brushed the hair back from her face. 'It's not your mess to fix.'

'I can't believe she thinks more of her position in society than her well-being,' she said. 'She doesn't love my father. She loves what he can give her. How can she live like that?'

'Some people want different things in life,' he said. 'You have to accept that. It doesn't mean you're going to be like that. You have the choice to do things differently.'

She was silent as he helped her in the car. She sat with Molly on her lap, her hands gently stroking her ears, her expression still puckered by a little frown.

'I'm sorry my family's dramas have taken up so much of your time,' she said after a long pause.

'It's not a problem,' Angelo said. 'What about your work? Is there anything I can do to help?'

'No, I've got everything under control,' she said. 'Linda is working on a few things for me. She's really excited about the Sorrento project. I e-mailed her the photos.'

'I know you'll do an amazing job,' he said. 'And my mother is excited about you helping her with the villa at home. It's her birthday next weekend. My father is bringing her to London to go to the theatre. They'd like to have a little celebration with us. You don't have to do anything. I'll get my housekeeper Rosa to prepare everything.'

She gave him a little smile that faded almost as soon as it appeared. 'I'll look forward to it.'

Angelo's parents arrived at his Mayfair house on Friday evening. Natalie had made up a collection of her linens for his mother as a present, but it was Molly that most interested Francesca.

They had barely come through the door when she scooped Molly out of Natalie's arms. 'Come to Nonna,' she said with a beaming smile. 'You will be good training for me, *si*? I can't wait to be a grandmother. I've already bought a new cot for Angelo's old nursery. It will be the first room you can help me redecorate, Natalie. I am so looking forward to it.'

Natalie felt her heart jerk in alarm. She glanced at Angelo, but he was smiling as if nothing was wrong. She felt the walls closing in on her. She felt claustrophobic. Panic rose inside her. She felt it spreading, making her head tight and her stomach churn.

'Got to keep the Bellandini line going,' Sandro said, with a teasing glint in his eye.

'Give us time,' Angelo said with an amused laugh. 'We've barely come off our honeymoon.'

'What if I don't want a baby?' Natalie said.

It was as if she had suddenly announced she had a bomb ticking inside her handbag. Sandro and Francesca stared at her with wide eyes and even wider mouths.

Francesca was the first to speak. 'But surely you can't be serious?'

Natalie tried to ignore Angelo's dark gaze. 'I'm not sure I want children.'

Francesca's face collapsed in dismay. 'But we've longed for grandchildren for years and years,' she said. 'I was only able to have one baby. I would have loved to have four or five. How can you not want to give Angelo a son?'

'Or a daughter,' Sandro said.

Angelo put his arm around Natalie's waist. 'This is a discussion Natalie and I should be having on our own.'

Francesca looked as if she was about to cry. 'You must make her change her mind, Angelo,' she said. 'Tell her how important it is to you. Our line of the family will die out with you. You can't let that happen.'

'Natalie is more important to me than carrying on the family line,' Angelo said. 'If she decides she can't face the prospect of having a child then I will have to accept that.'

Natalie saw the disappointment on his parents' faces. She saw a shadow of it in Angelo's expression too, even though he did his best to conceal it. Never had she felt more wretched about her past.

The evening went ahead as planned, but she felt on the outside the whole time. It was painful to watch Angelo's parents trying to enjoy themselves. They were clearly upset and uncomfortable.

She had spoilt his mother's birthday—just as she had spoilt everything else.

It was late by the time Angelo came up to their room. Natalie suspected he had been having a private discussion about her with his parents. The whole time she had been waiting for him she had worked herself into a state about how the conversation might have gone.

They would have been polite but concerned, wondering if he was serious about throwing his life away on a woman who could not give him what he most wanted.

He would have told them he loved her enough for it not to matter, but they would press him to have a rethink.

He had a responsibility.

It was his duty.

'Where have you been?' she asked, even before he had closed the door.

'I was seeing to some business,' he said, tugging at his tie.

'Did your parents tell you to divorce me?' she asked.

He frowned. 'Why would they do that?'

'Because I'm not going to be the breeding machine they so desperately want.'

'Tatty,' he said on a frustrated sigh, 'I think you need to take a step back from this and see it from my perspective.'

'Oh, I see it from your perspective, all right,' she said, throwing him a hard little glare. 'You think over time you'll eventually grind me down. You're working on me bit by bit. First it was Molly. Who knows what's next? A kitten, perhaps? But what if it doesn't work? What if I still don't want children?'

'What I said downstairs is true,' he said. 'You are far more important to me than adding to the family tree.'

Natalie *wanted* to believe him. She wanted to be confident that in two years, five years, even fifty years he would still be saying the same thing. She knew he loved her. He showed it in so many ways. She *felt* his love in his touch. She saw it in his gaze. She saw it now.

He tossed his tie to one side. 'How about you come over here and I'll show you just how important you are?' he said with a smouldering look.

She walked towards him on legs that trembled as desire rushed through her like a powerful drug. She had barely closed the distance between them when he grabbed her by the upper arms and crushed his mouth to hers. The kiss was hot, wet and urgent—just like the need that instantly flooded her. His tongue moved against hers, calling it into a sexy duel that made her senses shout and sing in rapture.

He kept his mouth clamped on hers as he walked

her backwards to the bed. He laid her down and began to rid himself of his clothes, all the while watching her with that slightly hooded I'm-about-to-make-love-to-you gaze of his.

'Aren't you going to take off your clothes?' he asked.

She gave him a sultry look. 'I don't know,' she said. 'Should I?'

'You'd better, if you still want them to be in one piece.'

A hot tingling sensation erupted between her thighs. 'This dress cost me a lot of money,' she said. 'I happen to love this dress.'

His eyes glittered as he came towards her. 'I love that dress too. But I think you look much better without it.'

Natalie shivered as he spun her around on the bed and released the zip at the back of her dress in one swift movement. Her bra and knickers were next, along with her shoes.

She tried to turn around but he laid a flat hand on her shoulder. 'Stay where you are,' he said.

She felt that delicious shiver again as his erection brushed against her bottom. It felt hard and very determined. She gave a little gasp as he entered her in a slick hard thrust that made every hair on her head tremble at the roots. He set a fast pace but she kept up with him. Each rocking movement of his hips, each stabbing thrust, sent another wave of pleasure through her. All her nerves were jumping in excitement. She felt the pressure building to a crescendo. Even the arches of her feet were tensed in preparation. Her orgasm was fast and furious. It rippled through her, making her shudder in ecstasy. He emptied himself with a powerful surge that sent another wave of pleasure through her.

But he wasn't finished with her yet.

He turned her and came down over her, his weight supported on one hand as he used the other to caress her intimately. She threw back her head and writhed in exquisite pleasure as he brought her to the brink before backing off again.

'Please,' she gasped as he ruthlessly continued the sweet torture.

'What do you want?' he asked.

'I want *you*.'

'How much?'

'Too much,' she gasped again.

'That makes two of us,' he said, and took her to paradise again.

Natalie stood beside Angelo as they farewelled his parents the following morning. Francesca and Santo each hugged her in turn, and on the surface they were as warm as ever, but she could tell they were struggling to accept the possibility that they would never hold a grandchild of their own in their arms.

Angelo took her hand as the driver pulled away from the kerb. 'I know what you're thinking.'

'They hate me.'

'They don't hate you.'

'I would hate me if I was them,' she said, pulling out of his hold and walking back inside.

'Tatty.'

She swung around to look at him once he had closed the front door. 'This is how it's going to be for the next however many years. Do you realise that, Angelo?' she asked. 'They're going to look at me with that crestfallen look, as if I've ruined both their lives.'

'You have not ruined anyone's life,' he said, blowing out a breath. 'They'll get used to it eventually.'

She felt a tight ache in her chest at how much he was giving up for her. She hadn't even told him she loved him. She wanted to, but it as if the words were trapped behind the wall of her guilt. She had bricked those three little words away and now she couldn't find them amongst the rubble of what used to be her heart.

'But will *you* get used to it?' she asked. 'What about in a couple of years? Five or ten? What about when all your friends have got kids? What if you hold someone else's baby in your arms and start to hate me?'

His expression tightened. 'I think we should shelve this topic until some other time.'

'Why is that?' she asked. 'Because I've touched on a nerve? Go on. Admit it. I've got you thinking about how it's going to be, haven't I?'

A muscle flickered at the corner of his mouth. 'You really are spoiling for a fight, aren't you?'

'I'm just trying to make sure you've looked at this from every angle.'

'You're the one who hasn't looked at this properly,' he bit back. 'Even now you're still punishing yourself for your brother's death, when it's obvious it's no one's fault but your parents'. They're totally inadequate, and always have been, and yet you continue to take the blame. You *have* to let it go, Tatty. You can't bring Liam back. You owe it to him to live a full life. I am sure if things were the other way around you would never have expected him to sacrifice his own happiness.'

She chewed at her lip. There was sense in what he was saying. She hadn't really thought about what Liam would have done if things were the other way around.

Angelo took her hand again and brought it up to his chest. 'Think about it, *cara*,' he said gently. 'What would Liam want you to do?'

Natalie thought of a newborn baby just like Isabel's. The sweet smell, the soft downy hair, the perfect little limbs and dimpled hands. She thought of a little baby that looked just like Angelo, with jet-black hair and chocolate-brown eyes. She thought of watching him or her grow up, each and every milestone celebrated with love and happiness. She thought of how the bond of a child would strengthen what Angelo already felt for her. Just having Molly had brought them closer. He was just as devoted to the little puppy as she was…

She suddenly frowned and glanced around her. 'Where's Molly?'

'She was here a minute ago,' Angelo said.

Natalie pushed past him. 'Molly?' She ran through the house, up and down the stairs, calling the puppy's name. There was no sign of her anywhere—just some of her toys: one of Angelo's old trainers and a squeaky plastic bone. She tried not to panic. She did all the self-talk she could think of on the hop.

Puppies were mischievous little things.

Perhaps Molly had found something new to chew and was keeping it to herself in a quiet corner.

Or maybe she was asleep somewhere and hadn't heard her name being called.

Puppies were either fully on or fully off.

Natalie came bolting back down the stairs just as Angelo was coming back through the front door. 'Have you found her?'

'She's not out on the street,' he said. 'I thought she might have slipped out when we were saying goodbye to my parents.'

'I can't find her.'

The words were a horrifying echo from the past. The gender had changed, but they brought up the very same gut wrenching panic. It roiled in her stomach like a butter churn going too fast. She felt her skin break out in a clammy sweat. Her heart hammered inside the scaffold of her ribs.

'I can't find her. I can't find her.'

'She's probably with Rosa in the kitchen,' Angelo said.

'I've already searched the kitchen,' she said. 'Rosa hasn't seen her.'

He reached for her arm to settle her. 'Tatty, for God's sake—stop worrying.'

Natalie wrenched her arm out of reach. Her heart felt as if it was going to burst through the wall of her chest. She could hardly breathe for the rising tide of despair and guilt.

It was her fault.

She couldn't even be trusted with a puppy. How on earth would she ever cope with a little baby?

'Tatty, calm down and—'

'Don't tell me to calm down!' she cried as she rushed out to the garden. Her lungs were almost bursting as she dashed along the flagstones to the lap pool in the garden.

The smell of chlorine sent her back in time.

She wasn't in the middle of London as a twenty-six-year-old. She was seven years old and she was in Spain and her little brother was missing. People were running about and shouting. Her father was shouting the loudest.

'Where is he? You were supposed to be watching him. *Where is he?*'

Her legs felt as if they were going to buckle beneath her. She couldn't speak for the thudding of her heart. Her skin was dripping in sweat. She could feel it tracking a pathway between her shoulderblades.

She ran along the edge of the pool, searching, searching, but there was no sign of a little body. There was nothing but a stray leaf floating on the surface.

She clutched at her head with both hands, trying to quell the sickening pounding of panic that had taken up residence inside. She was going to be sick. She felt the bubble of bile rise in her throat and only strength of will kept it down.

She had to find Liam. She had to find Liam. She had to find Liam.

'I've found her.'

Natalie's hands fell away from her head as Angelo appeared, carrying Molly in his arms. He was smiling as if her world hadn't completely shattered all over again.

'Here she is,' he said, holding her out to her.

She pushed the puppy away. 'No, take her away,' she said. 'I don't want her.'

Angelo frowned. '*Cara*, she's fine. She was in the wine cellar. Rosa must have accidentally locked her in when she put some new bottles down there a few minutes ago.'

Natalie tried to get her breathing back under control but she was still stuck in the past. All she could think of was her brother's limp little body being lifted from the pool. She could still hear the sound of water dripping from his shorts, from the T-shirt with the yellow lion on the front. She could hear it landing on the concrete.

She could still feel the accusing glare of the sun. It seemed to shine down on her like a scorching spotlight.

Your fault. Your fault. Your fault.

'Tatty?'

She looked at Angelo and suddenly it was all too

much. She had to get away. She could *not* do this. She could not be here.

'I have to leave,' she said. 'I can't do this any more.'

'Don't do this to me a second time, Tatty.'

'I have to do it,' she said tears welling in her eyes. 'I don't belong in your life. I can't give you what you want. I just can't.'

'We can work through this,' he said.

'*I* can't work through this!' She shouted the words at him as she teetered on the edge of hysteria. 'I can *never* work through this.'

'Yes, you can,' he said. 'We'll do it together.'

She shook her head at him. 'It's over, Angelo.'

His mouth pulled tight. 'You're running away.'

'I'm not running away,' she said. 'I'm taking control of my life. You forced me to come back to you. I didn't have a choice.'

His jaw locked. 'I can still send Lachlan to jail.'

She looked at him, with the puppy snuggled protectively against his chest. 'You're not going to do that,' she said. 'You were never going to do that. I *know* you, Angelo.'

'If you know me so well then you'll know if you walk out now I will never take you back,' he said through tight lips.

She felt the ache of losing him for ever settle like a weight inside her chest. It pulled on every organ painfully, torturously. 'I'm not coming back,' she said.

'Go, then,' he said, his expression closing like a fist.

It was the hardest thing she had ever done to turn and walk away from him. She put one foot in front of the other and willed herself to walk forward while everything in her protested.

Don't go. He loves you. He loves you no matter what.

This is the only chance you'll have at happiness. How can you walk away from it?

She allowed herself one last look as she walked out through the front door a few minutes later, bag packed, flight to Edinburgh booked. He was standing with Molly, who was struggling to break free from his arms and go to her. He had an unreadable expression on his face, but she could see the hint of moisture in his eyes.

She walked out of the door and closed it with a soft little click that broke her heart.

CHAPTER ELEVEN

'I HEAR Angelo's got a new lady-friend,' Linda said about a month later as she leafed through one of the gossip magazines during lunch.

Natalie felt a dagger of pain stab her, but she affected an uninterested expression as she put her untouched sushi in the little fridge. 'Good for him.'

'She looks pretty young,' Linda said. 'And she kind of looks like you. She looks devoted to the puppy. Here—have a look.'

Natalie pushed the magazine aside. 'I have work to do, and so do you.'

Linda pouted. 'Yeah, well, we'd have a lot more work to do if you hadn't quit on Angelo's Sorrento deal. Why would you let personal stuff get in the way of gazillions of pounds?'

Natalie gritted her teeth. 'I need to move on with my life.'

'Seems to me you can't really do that until you put the past behind you,' Linda said. She waited a beat before adding, 'Lachlan told me.'

Natalie frowned. 'You were speaking to Lachlan?'

'He calls me now and again to see how you're doing,' she said. 'He kind of told me about…everything. You know—about your little brother and all.'

'He had no right to talk to you about me.'

'He's worried about you,' Linda said. 'It sounds like he's got his stuff pretty much sorted. He thinks it's time you put your ghosts to rest, so to speak.'

'I've got my stuff sorted.'

'Yeah, so why are you so miserably unhappy?' Linda asked. 'You mope around with no energy. You don't eat. You look like you don't sleep.'

'I'm fine,' Natalie said, willing herself to believe it.

'Why don't you take a few days off?' Linda suggested. 'I've got things under control here. Kick back and have a think about things.'

'I have nothing to think about.'

Linda lifted one neat eyebrow. 'Are you sure about that?'

Natalie blew out a breath and finally came to a decision. She had been mulling it over for days. It would be Liam's birthday in a couple of days. She could at least put some flowers on his grave while she was there.

'I need to visit my parents,' she said. 'I won't be away long—just a day or two.'

'Take all the time you need,' Linda said, closing the magazine.

Her mother was the only one home when Natalie arrived.

'You could've called to warn me,' Isla said as Natalie entered the sitting room where her mother was holding a gin and tonic.

'I didn't think kids had to warn their parents when they were dropping by for a visit,' Natalie said.

'I hear Angelo's got himself a new lover.' Isla twirled her swizzle stick.

'I don't believe he's got a new lover,' Natalie said. 'He's not like Dad. He wouldn't betray me like that.'

'You left him.'

'I know…'

'Why on earth did you walk out on him?' Isla asked. 'He's as rich as Croesus and as handsome as the devil.'

'I can't give him what he wants,' Natalie said. 'I don't think I can have a child after what happened to Liam.'

There was an awkward little silence.

'It wasn't your fault,' Isla said on a little sigh. 'I've never blamed you—not really. I know it might've looked like it at times, but I was scared of what your father would do if I contradicted him. He can be quite nasty, as you well know. It wasn't your fault that Liam drowned. If anyone was to blame it was your father.'

Natalie stared at her mother. 'Why do you say that?'

'Because I had a headache when we came back from the beach and went inside to lie down,' she said. 'He said he'd watch you and Liam out by the pool.'

Natalie frowned. 'But he asked *me* to watch Liam. I remember him saying it. He said he had to make a really important call.'

Her mother gave her a worldly look. 'Do you really think it was *that* important?' she asked.

Natalie's stomach churned as realisation dawned. 'He was calling *his mistress*?'

Her mother nodded. 'One of the many he had on the side.'

'Why did you put up with it?' Natalie asked, choking back bitter tears. 'Why did you let him do that to you?'

'I told you why,' Isla said. 'I was scared of what he would do. I had nowhere else to go. There was nowhere else I wanted to go.'

'But you could've got help,' Natalie said. 'You

could've found a shelter or something. There are places for women to go when they're scared.'

'I don't expect *you* to understand,' Isla said. 'I know you want more from your life, with your fancy career and all, but I'm happy with my life. I have money and security. I would have lost all of that if I'd turned up to a shelter with a couple of kids in tow.'

Natalie stared at her mother as if she had never seen her before. Could her mother *really* be that shallow? Had she really sold her soul for diamonds?

'You don't even *like* him,' she said. 'How can you bear to live with him if you don't like him, much less love him?'

Isla raised one of her thin brows cynically. 'Are you telling me you're in *love* with your billionaire husband?' she asked. 'Come on, Natalie, what you really love is his money and what he can give you. It's what all women love. You're no different.'

'I love *everything* about Angelo,' Natalie said. 'I love his kindness. I love that he still loves me, even after I ran out on him. I love his smile. I love his eyes. I love his hands. I love every bit of him. I even love his family. They're not shallow and selfish like mine. They watch out for each other and take care of each other. They stay together because they want to be together, not just for the sake of appearances. I love him. Do you hear me? *I love him.*'

'You're a fool, Natalie,' her mother said. 'He'll break your heart. Men like him always do. They reel you in with their charm and then leave you high and dry.'

'I don't care if he breaks my heart,' Natalie said. 'It will be worth it just to have him for as long as he wants me.'

If he takes me back, she thought in anguish. *Did he really mean it when he said he never would?*

'And how long will that be?' Isla asked. 'You're beautiful now, but what about when your looks fade and you put on a few pounds and have a few more wrinkles than you'd like? What then, Natalie? Is he going to love you then?'

There was a sound at the door, and Natalie spun round to see her father saunter in.

'You have a hide to show your face here,' he said. 'Do you know what day it is?'

Natalie drew herself up to her full height. 'I do, actually,' she said. 'And I'm on my way to the cemetery now, to pay my respects to Liam. But when I leave I am *not* going to take the yoke of guilt with me. That's your burden, not mine. Liam would want me to move on with my life. He would have wanted me to be happy.'

'You killed him,' her father spat viciously, bits of spittle forming at the corners of his mouth. '*You* killed him.'

'I did *not* kill him,' Natalie said. 'I was too young to be left in charge of him. That was your duty of care— but you were too busy lining up another secret assignation with one of your mistresses.'

Her father's face reddened. 'Get out!' He thrust a finger towards the door. 'Get out before I throw you out.'

Natalie stared him down, feeling powerful for the first time in her life. 'You haven't got the guts to throw me out,' she said. 'You're a pathetic coward who has spent years hiding his guilt behind his innocent daughter. I'm not carrying it any more. I pity you and Mum. You've wasted your lives. You don't know the meaning of the word love.'

'I do love you, Natalie,' her mother said, sloshing her

drink as Natalie headed out through the door. 'I have always loved you. Even when you were born a girl instead of a boy I loved you.'

Natalie looked at her with a despairing look. 'Then where the hell have you been all my life?' she asked, and turned and left.

Angelo was trying to get Molly to use the garden as her toilet rather than the rug in his study. There had been a significant regression over the last month in the puppy's training. He hardly knew what to do with her. The young woman he had employed to train her had come with great recommendations, but had created a press fest that he would have given anything to avoid.

He could only imagine what Natalie was making of it.

He had got through each day that she had been gone with a wrenching ache in his chest. It was much worse than five years ago. He had thought he had loved her then, but now his love for her surpassed that by miles.

He had thrown himself into work, but he had no enthusiasm for building an empire he couldn't share with her.

He didn't care about the children thing.

He just wanted her.

He had wanted to go to her, to beg her to come back to him, but he knew she could only be his if she was free to make the choice to be with him—not because she had to be, but because she wanted to be.

'Signor Bellandini?' Rosa appeared at the back door. 'You have a visitor.'

He frowned irritably. 'Tell them to go away. I told you I don't want to be disturbed when I'm at home.'

'I think you might like to be disturbed in this case,' Rosa said.

Angelo looked past his housekeeper to see Natalie standing there. He blinked a couple of times, wondering if he was imagining her. But Molly clearly didn't have any doubt. She barrelled towards her with an excited yap, ears flapping, tail wagging frenetically. He watched as Natalie scooped her up and cuddled her against her chest.

'She's missed you,' he said before he could stop himself.

'I've missed her too,' she said, kissing the puppy's head.

'So,' he said. 'What can I do for you? Do you want me to sign the divorce papers? Is that why you're here? You could have sent them with your lawyer. You didn't have to come in person to rub it in.'

She set the puppy down at her feet and met his gaze. 'Did you really mean it when you said you would never take me back?' she asked.

Angelo tried to keep his expression impassive. 'Why do you ask?'

She ran her tongue over her lips and lowered her gaze. 'I was just kind of hoping you only said that to make me think twice about walking away.'

'You didn't walk away,' he said. 'You ran away.'

Her teeth snagged her bottom lip. 'Yes, I know... I'm not going to do that any more.'

Angelo was still not ready to let his guard down. 'Why are you here?'

She lifted her eyes back to his. 'I wanted to say...' She took a little breath and continued, 'I wanted to say I love you. I've wanted to say it for ages but I wasn't sure how. I couldn't seem to find the words. They were inside me, but I had to find a way to get them out.'

He swallowed the lump that had risen in his throat. 'Why now?' he asked. 'Why not a month ago?'

'I've talked to my parents since then,' she said. 'It turns out my father wasn't making an important business call that day. He was calling his mistress.'

Angelo frowned. 'And he let you carry the guilt all this time?'

'And my mother,' she said. 'I'm not sure I can forgive either of them. I'm still working through that.'

'I don't think you should ever see or speak to them again.'

'They're my parents,' she said. 'I have to give them the chance to redeem themselves.'

'I wouldn't be holding my breath,' he said. 'You're likely to get your heart broken.'

She looked up at him with a pained look. 'I know you've got someone else,' she said. 'I've seen the papers. I just wanted to tell you because…because…'

'She's a dog trainer,' Angelo said with a little roll of his eyes. 'And not a particularly good one. I don't think she knows a thing about puppies, to tell you the truth.'

Her eyes started to shine with moisture. 'Dogs are easy,' she said. 'It's kids that are difficult. But I reckon a dog is a great way to ease yourself into it.'

He held out his arms and she stepped into them. He hugged her so tightly he was frightened he was going to snap her ribs. 'We don't have to rush into anything you don't feel ready for,' he said. 'I'm just happy to have you back in my life.'

'I'm so sorry for what I've put you through,' she said. 'I love you so much. I couldn't bear to lose you all over again.'

He looked down at her tenderly. 'This last month has been torture,' he said. 'So many times I wanted to pick up the phone and call you. I even drove halfway to Edinburgh but then turned back. I thought if you came back it would have to be because it was the only place you wanted to be. I felt I had to let you go in order to get you back.'

She smiled up at him. 'This is the only place I want to be. Here with you.'

He stroked her face, loving the way her eyes were shining with happy tears instead of sad ones. 'Do you think it's too early in our marriage to have a second honeymoon?' he asked.

She stepped up on tiptoe and linked her arms around his neck. 'Is the first one over?' she asked with a twinkling look.

He smiled as he scooped her up in his arms. 'It's just getting started,' he said, and carried her indoors.

* * * * *

ENEMIES AT
THE ALTAR

To my niece Angie Fouche, who is a beautiful
and brave young woman. Love you. p.s. EEEE!!!!

CHAPTER ONE

ANDREAS got the call from his younger sister Miette in the early hours of the morning.

'Papà is dead.'

Three words that under normal circumstances should have evoked a maelstrom of emotion, but to Andreas they meant nothing other than he was now free from having to play happy families on the extremely rare occasions his path crossed with his father. 'When is the funeral?' he asked.

'Thursday,' Miette said. 'Will you come?'

Andreas glanced at the sleeping woman lying beside him in the king-sized hotel bed. He rubbed at his stubbled jaw and let out a frustrated sigh. It was just typical of his father to choose the most inconvenient time to die. This coming weekend in Washington DC was where he had planned to ask Portia Briscoe to marry him once his business here was complete. He even had the ring in his briefcase. Now he would have to wait for another opportunity to propose. There was no way he wanted his engagement and marriage to be forever associated with anything to do with his father, even his demise.

'Andreas?' Miette's voice pierced his reverie and his conscience. 'It would be good if you could be there, for me even if not for Papà. You know how much I hate funerals, especially after Mamma's.'

Andreas felt a claw of anger clench at his insides at the thought of their beautiful mother and how cruelly she had been betrayed. He was sure *that* had been what had finally killed her, not the cancer. The shame of finding out her husband was sleeping with the hired help while she was battling gruelling rounds of chemotherapy had broken her spirit *and* her heart.

And then, to add insult to injury, the brazenness of that witch Nell Baker and her trashy little sleep-around slut of a daughter Sienna had turned his mother's final farewell into a cheap and tawdry soap opera.

'I'll be there,' he said.

But that little hot-headed harlot Sienna Baker had better not.

The first person Sienna saw when she arrived at the funeral in Rome was Andreas Ferrante. At least her eyes registered it was him, but she had *felt* him seconds earlier in her body. As soon as she had stepped over the portal she had felt a shiver run up her spine and her heart had started a crazy little pitter-patter beat that was nothing like its normal, healthy, steady rhythm.

She hadn't seen him in years and yet she had *known* he was there.

He was sitting in one of the pews at the front of the cathedral. Even though he had his back towards her she could see he was as staggeringly gorgeous as ever. His aristocratic bearing was like an aura that surrounded him. He exuded wealth and power and status. His glossy raven-black head was several inches higher than any of the other black-suited men sitting nearby, his thick, slightly wavy hair neither long nor short, but cut and styled so it brushed against the collar of his shirt.

He turned his head and leaned down to say something to the young woman scated beside him. Just seeing the profile of his face made Sienna want to put a hand to her chest where her heart was flapping like a frantic fish suddenly flung out of its fish tank. For years she had dismissed his features from her mind. She had dared not think of him. He was a part of her past she was ashamed of—*deeply* ashamed. She had been so young and foolish, so immature and insecure. She hadn't thought through the consequences of twisting the truth. But then, who did at the age of seventeen?

And then, as if Andreas sensed her looking at him, he twisted his head and locked gazes with her. It was like a lightning strike when those hazel eyes hit hers. They narrowed and glared, pinning her to the spot like a bug on a corkboard.

Sienna pasted an indifferent smile on her face and, giving her silver-blonde head a toss, sashayed up the aisle and shimmied her way into a pew on the left hand side a few rows back from his.

She *felt* his anger.

She *felt* his rage.

She *felt* his fury.

It made her skin shiver. It made her vertebrae rattle like ice cubes in a glass. It made her blood race. It made her knees feel weak, as if someone had removed all of her strong stabilising ligaments and put overcooked noodles in their place.

But she showed none of that. Instead, she affected a cool poise that her teenage self, eight years ago, would have sorely envied.

The woman seated beside him was his latest mistress, or so Sienna had gathered from a recent press article. Portia Briscoe had lasted longer than any of his other lovers, which made Sienna wonder if the faint whisper she had heard of an impending engagement had any truth to it.

Not that she had ever thought of Andreas Ferrante as the falling in love type. To her he had always been the playboy prince of prosperity and privilege. When the time came he would choose a bride to suit his Old Money heritage. Just like his father and grandfather before him, love would not come into it at all.

Although, going on appearances alone, Portia Briscoe looked like the perfect candidate to be the next generation Ferrante bride. She was classically beautiful in a carefully constructed way. The sort of woman who never went anywhere without perfectly coiffed hair and expertly applied make-up. She was the type of woman who wouldn't dream of turning up at a funeral on a whim, in faded jeans with ragged hems and soiled trainers or, God forbid, a T-shirt that had suffered a food spill.

Portia Briscoe *only* wore exquisitely tailored designer couture. She even had toothpaste commercial teeth and porcelain skin that looked as if it had never suffered a blemish on it.

Unlike Sienna, who'd had to endure the torture of braces for two years and had only that morning had to reach for her concealer to cover a spot on her chin.

Andreas Ferrante would make sure his bride never put a designer-clad foot out of place. His bride wouldn't have a history of bad choices and reckless behaviour that had caused more pain and shame than she cared to think about.

No, his bride would be Perfect Portia, not shameful, scandalous Sienna.

Good luck to him.

As soon as the service was drawing to a close, Sienna slipped out of the church. She still wasn't exactly sure why she had felt compelled to pay her respects to a man in death she hadn't even liked in life. But she had seen the news in the press about his death from a heart attack and immediately thought of her mother.

Her mother Nell had *loved* Guido Ferrante.

Nell had worked for the Ferrante family for years, but not once had Guido acknowledged her as anything but his housekeeper. Sienna remembered all too well the scandal her mother had caused at Evaline Ferrante's funeral. The press had gone wild with it, like a pack of hyenas over a carcass. It had been one of the most humiliating experiences of her life. To see her mother vilified, to see her shamed in the most appalling way, was something Sienna still carried with her. She had sworn that day she would never be at the mercy of a powerful man. *She* would be the one in control. She would be the agent of her own destiny, not have her life dictated to by others who had been better born or had more money than her.

She would *never* fall in love.

'Excuse me, Miss Baker?' A well-dressed man in his late fifties approached. 'Sienna Louise Baker?'

Sienna set her shoulders squarely. 'Who wants to know?' she asked.

The man held out a hand. 'Allow me to introduce myself,' he said. 'I am Lorenzo Di Salle, Guido Ferrante's lawyer.'

Sienna took his hand briefly. 'Nice to meet you. Now, if you'll excuse me, I have to go.'

She had barely moved a step before the lawyer's words stopped her in her tracks. 'You are invited to be at the reading of Guido Ferrante's will.'

Sienna turned back around and stared at him with her mouth open. 'Pardon?'

'As a beneficiary to Signor Ferrante's estate you are—'

'A *beneficiary*?' she gasped. 'But why?'

The lawyer gave her a smile Sienna didn't much care for. 'Signor Ferrante has left some property to you,' he said.

'Property?' she said blankly. 'What property?'

'The Chateau de Chalvy in Provence,' he said.

Sienna's heart did a double shuffle. 'There must be some mistake,' she said. 'That was Evaline Ferrante's family home. Surely it should go to Andreas or Miette?'

'Signor Ferrante insisted it be left to you,' he said. 'There are, however, some conditions attached.'

Sienna narrowed her eyes. 'Conditions?'

Lorenzo Di Salle gave her a serpentine smile. 'The reading of the will is in the library at the Ferrante villa at three p.m. tomorrow. I look forward to seeing you there.'

Andreas prowled the length and breadth of the library feeling like a lion in a cat carrier. He hadn't been to his family home in years, not since the night Sienna had been found all but naked in his bedroom at the age of seventeen. The little she-devil had lied her way out of it, making him out to be some sort of lecher while she had maintained the act of innocent victim, a role she played all too well. Why else had his father included her in his will? She wasn't a blood relative. She was the housekeeper's daughter. She was nothing but a little gold-digging slut who had already married once for money. She had obviously inveigled her way into his ailing father's affections to get her greedy little hands on what she could, now that her elderly husband had died, leaving her practically penniless. His mother's estate in Provence was the one thing Andreas would do anything to keep out of Sienna's possession.

And he meant *anything*.

The door opened and Sienna Baker came breezing in as if she owned the place. At least today she had dressed a little more appropriately, but not by much. Her short denim skirt showed off the long slim length of her coltish sun-kissed legs and her white blouse was tied at her impossibly slender waist, showing a glimpse of the toned flesh of her abdomen. She didn't have a scrap of make-up on her face and her silver-blonde hair was loose around her shoulders, but even so she looked as if she had just stepped off a photo shoot.

The whole room seemed to suck in a breath and hold it. Andreas had seen it happen so many times. Her totally natural beauty was like a punch to the solar plexus. He had worked hard over the years to disguise his reaction, but even now he could feel the effect she had on him. He had felt it yesterday in the church. He had known the very minute she had arrived.

He had *sensed* it.

He glanced at his watch before throwing her a contemptuous glare. 'You're late.'

She gave him a pert look as she flipped her hair over one shoulder. 'It's two minutes past three, Rich Boy,' she said. 'Don't be so anal.'

The lawyer rustled his papers on the desk. 'Could we get started?' he asked. 'There's a lot to go through. Let's start with Miette…'

Andreas remained standing as the will was read out. He was glad his younger sister was well provided for, not that she needed it as she and her husband had a very successful investment business based in London, but it was a relief to know she hadn't been elbowed out by that brazen little blow-in. Miette had inherited the family villa in Rome and assets worth millions set in trust for her two young children. It was a satisfying result given that Miette—like Andreas—hadn't been all that close to their father over the last years of his life.

'And now we come to Andreas and Sienna,' Lorenzo Di Salle said. 'I think we should conduct this part of the reading in private. Just the two of you, if the others don't mind.'

Andreas felt his spine tighten. He didn't want his name bracketed with that little wildcat. It made him feel edgy. It had always made him feel that way. She was a tearaway who rocked his world in ways he didn't want.

Had *never* wanted.

He had stayed away from the family home because of her. For years he hadn't stepped over the threshold, not even to spend those few precious weeks with his mother before she died. Sienna's outrageous deceit had destroyed any chance of a working relationship with his father for the last eight years. Andreas blamed her for it all. She was a sly little vixen intent on her own gain.

He hated her with a vengeance.

The lawyer waited for the others to leave the library before he opened the folder in front of him. 'The Chateau de Chalvy in Provence is entailed to you both but on the proviso that you live together legally as man and wife for the minimum of six months.'

Andreas heard the lawyer's words but it took a moment for them to register. He felt a shockwave go through him. It was like being shoved backwards by a toppling bookcase. He couldn't get his throat unlocked to speak. He stood staring at the lawyer, wondering if he had imagined what he had just heard.

Sienna and him...married.

Legally tied.

Stuck together for six months.

It was a joke.

'This has got to be a joke,' Andreas said, raking a hand through his hair.

'It's no joke,' Lorenzo Di Salle said. 'Your father changed his will in the last month of his life. He was adamant about it. If you don't agree to marry each other within the time frame, the property will be handed over to a distant relative.'

Andreas knew exactly which distant relative the lawyer was referring to. He also knew how quickly his mother's ancestral home would be sold to feed the second cousin's gambling addiction. His father had laid the perfect trap. He had thought of everything, every get out clause and every escape route. He had made it impossible for Andreas to do anything but obey his orders.

'I'm not marrying him!' Sienna shot to her feet, her grey-blue eyes flaring in outrage.

Andreas flicked her a disparaging glance. 'Sit down and shut up, for God's sake.'

She pushed her chin up, her bottom lip going forward in a pout. 'I'm not marrying you.'

'I'm very glad to hear it,' Andreas said dryly and turned to the lawyer. 'There's got to be a way out of this. I'm about to become engaged. You have to make this go away.'

The lawyer lifted his hands in a gesture of defeat. 'The will is iron-clad,' he said. 'If either of you refuses to cooperate, the other automatically inherits everything.'

'What?' Andreas and Sienna spoke at once.

Andreas threw her a look before he addressed the lawyer. 'You mean if I don't agree to marry her she inherits Chateau de Chalvy, plus all the other assets?'

Lorenzo nodded. 'And if you do marry and one of you walks out before the six months is up, the one who stays inherits everything by default,' he said. 'Signor Ferrante set it up so neither of you have a choice but to marry each other and stay married for six months.'

'Why six months?' Sienna asked.

Andreas rolled his eyes as he muttered, 'Because any longer than that he knew I would probably end up on a murder charge.'

Sienna sent him a withering look. 'Only if you got in first.'

Andreas dismissed her comment by turning back to the lawyer. 'What happens at the end of six months if we do decide to stick it out?' he asked.

'You get the chateau and Sienna gets a pay-out,' the lawyer said.

'How big a pay-out?' Sienna asked.

Lorenzo named a sum that sent Andreas's brows sky-high. 'She gets that much for doing what exactly?' he asked. 'Flouncing around pretending to be the lady of the manor for six months? That's outrageous!'

Sienna curled her lip at him. 'I'd say it was pretty fair compensation for having to put up with you for six days, let alone six months.'

Andreas narrowed his eyes to paper-thin slits. 'You put him up to this, didn't you?' he said through clenched teeth. 'You got him to write this crazy will so you could get your greedy little hands on whatever you could.'

Her grey-blue eyes held his defiantly. 'I haven't seen or spoken to your father for five years,' she said. 'He didn't even have the decency to send me a card or flowers when my mother died, let alone attend her funeral.'

Andreas stared her down. 'Why did you come to his funeral if you hated him so much?'

Her chin stayed at a pugnacious height. 'Don't think I would've made a special trip because I damn well wouldn't,' she said. 'I was here for a dress fitting for my sister's wedding next month.'

'I heard about your long lost twin,' Andreas said. 'I read about it in the paper.' He curled his lip and added, 'God help us all if she's anything like you.'

She glared at him furiously. 'I came to your father's funeral out of respect for my mother,' she said. 'She would've come if she was still alive. Nothing on this earth would have stopped her.'

Andreas gave her a mocking look. 'No, not even common decency, it seems.'

She shot to her feet with a hand raised to slap him. He only managed to stop it from connecting with his jaw by grasping her wrist in mid-air. The shock of her soft silky skin against his fingers was like a power surge going through his body. He saw the sudden flare of her eyes as if she had felt it too.

A nanosecond passed.

Something entered the air between them, a primal, dangerous thing that had no name, no shape or form— *it was just there*.

Andreas dropped her wrist and stepped back from her, surreptitiously opening and closing his fingers to see if they were still able to function. 'You'll have to excuse Miss Baker—' he spoke to the lawyer again '—she has a reputation for histrionics.'

Sienna threw Andreas a filthy look. 'Bastard.'

The lawyer closed the folder and got to his feet. 'You have a week to come to a decision,' he said. 'I suggest you think about this carefully. There's a lot to lose on both sides if you don't cooperate.'

'I've already decided,' Sienna said, folding her arms across her chest. 'I'm not marrying him.'

Andreas laughed. 'Nice try, Sienna,' he said. 'There's no way you'd turn your back on that amount of money.'

She came and stood right in his body space, her chin up, her eyes flashing, her hands on her slim hips, her beautiful breasts heaving. He had never felt such raw sexual energy coming towards him in his life. His whole body jolted with it. It was like being zapped with a Taser gun. He felt it rush through every vein like a flood of roaring fire. His groin pulsated as she leaned in closer, close enough for him to smell the sweet honey scent of her breath as it danced over his face. 'You just watch me, Rich Boy,' she said and then she swivelled on her trainer-clad feet and left.

CHAPTER TWO

'IT SAYS here that Andreas Ferrante and his mistress have broken up,' Kate Henley, Sienna's flatmate, said a couple of days later. She looked up over the newspaper and frowned. 'Hey, I thought you said they were about to get engaged?'

Sienna turned her back to wash a perfectly clean cup in the sink. 'What Andreas Ferrante does or doesn't do is of no interest to me whatsoever.'

'Hang on a minute…' The paper rustled as Kate spread it out over the clutter of the breakfast table. 'Oh, my God! Is it true?'

Sienna turned to see her flatmate's eyes were as big as the saucer she had just put on the draining rack. 'Is what true?' she asked warily.

'It says you're the other woman,' Kate said, gaping at her like a fish. 'It says *you're* the reason they broke up.'

'Let me see that.' Sienna frowned as she snatched up the paper. She scanned the article, her heart galloping like a spooked thoroughbred.

Mega-rich French-Italian furniture designer Andreas Ferrante admits his secret involvement

*with former housekeeper's daughter Sienna Baker
destroyed his relationship with heiress Portia
Briscoe.*

'That's a downright lie!' Sienna slammed the paper
down, knocking over the milk carton in the process.
'Oh, shoot!' She grabbed a tea towel and mopped inef-
fectually at the mess while her mind ran on with fury.

'Why would he say something like that?' Kate asked
with a wrinkled brow.

Sienna ground her teeth as she rinsed the cloth at the
sink, splashing water everywhere in the process. 'He
wants me to marry him, that's why.'

'Erm…did I hear you correctly?' Kate asked. 'I *think*
you said he wants to marry you. Did you actually *say*
that?'

Sienna flung the milk-sodden tea towel in the sink.
'I did but I'm not marrying him,' she said with a scowl.

Kate clutched a hand to her chest theatrically. 'Be
still my heart,' she said. 'Andreas Ferrante—Florence-
based millionaire, no, make that *billionaire* playboy—
the most gorgeous-looking man on this planet—if not
the entire universe—wants you to marry him and you
said *no*?'

Sienna gave Kate an irritated look as she reached
past her to wipe the milk off the bottom of the peanut
butter jar. 'He's not that handsome.'

'Not handsome?' Kate gaped at her. 'What about his
bank account?'

'I'm not interested in his bank account,' Sienna said.
'I married once for money. I'm not doing it again.'

'But I thought you really loved Brian Littlemore,'
Kate said. 'You cried buckets at his funeral.'

Sienna thought of her late husband and how close she had become to him in the few months before he died. She had married him for protection and security, not love. It had been a knee-jerk reaction when her life had spun out of control soon after the death of her mother. After a horrifying incident in which she found herself in bed with a complete stranger after one too many drinks, Brian Littlemore had offered her security and respectability at a time in her life when she had neither. Like her, he had been forced to live a lie for most of his life, but during their marriage he had been honest with her in a way few people ever were. She had come to love him for it. As far as she was concerned, his secret had died with him. She would never betray his trust in her. 'Brian was a good man,' she said. 'He put his family before himself right to the day he died.'

'It's a pity he didn't leave you better provided for,' Kate said, reaching for the dishcloth. 'I guess you could always ask your rich twin sister to help you out with the rent if you don't manage to get a job in the next week or two.'

It still felt a little strange to Sienna to think of having a sister, let alone an identical twin. Gisele and she had been separated at birth when Sienna's mother had accepted a pay-out from the high profile Australian married man who had got her pregnant. Nell had taken Sienna and handed over Gisele to the childless couple, Hilary and Richard Carter, who had subsequently raised Gisele as their own. Nell had taken the secret to her grave. Sienna had found out quite by accident about Gisele's existence when she had been travelling in Australia a couple of months ago. She had only taken the trip on a whim when she'd seen a budget air fare online. She had always longed to go to Australia and, after Brian's death, it seemed a good opportunity to help her clear her head a bit before she made a decision about her future. A chance encounter in a department store had brought about her reunion with her twin.

Although Sienna loved Gisele dearly, she was still finding her feet with the relationship. Gisele had suffered a very bitter and painful breakup because of the sex tape scandal Sienna had been caught up in. Finding herself in that man's bed with no real memory of how she had got there had been such a shameful experience she had immediately left the country, thus having no idea of the fallout it had created for her sister. How that damning footage had got on the Internet and been wrongly linked to Gisele was something Sienna knew she would always feel dreadful about.

Gisele's fiancé Emilio had believed Gisele had betrayed him, and it had only been the discovery of the truth about Sienna's existence that had finally set things right. Their upcoming marriage in Rome was something she was looking forward to with bittersweet feelings. Her behaviour had almost wrecked Gisele and Emilio's lives. They had lost two precious years together and a baby. What could she ever do to make it up to them?

But Kate had made a very good point. She had to find a source of income and find it soon. Before he had become ill, Sienna had worked in the office of Brian's antiques business, but the family had stepped in after he had died and promptly sacked her. The trust fund Brian had left her had been just about gobbled up by the ongoing instability of the economy. Her dream of purchasing a home of her own had slipped out of her grasp, and there was no way—short of a miracle—for her to get it back.

Or was there?

Sienna thought of the money Guido Ferrante had bequeathed her. It was more than enough to buy a decent piece of real estate. The rest of it, invested sensibly, would set her up for life. She would be able to pursue her hobby of photography, perhaps even take it a step further and make a proper career out of it. How wonderful to be known for her talent instead of her mistakes and social blunders. How wonderful to be on the other side of the lens for a change, to be the one taking the pictures instead of being the subject.

She chewed at her lip as she thought of the conditions put on the will. Six months married to her worst enemy. It was a high price to pay, but then the reward at the end surely compensated for it?

It wasn't as if it had to be a *real* marriage.

An involuntary shiver rippled over her skin at the thought of lying in Andreas's strongly muscled arms, with his long hair-roughened legs entangled with hers, with his...

Sienna dried her hands on a fresh tea towel before she picked up her bag and keys. 'I'm going away,' she said. 'I'm not sure when I'll be back. I'll send you the money for the rent.'

Kate swung around with the empty milk carton in one hand and a wet dishcloth in the other. 'Away where?'

'To Florence.'

Kate's eyes bulged. 'You're going to say yes?'

Sienna gave her a grim look. 'This could turn out to be the longest six months of my life.'

'Six months?' Kate frowned in confusion. 'Isn't marriage meant to be until death us do part?'

'Not this one,' Sienna said.

'Aren't you going to pack?' Kate asked, eyes still out on stalks. 'You can't just turn up dressed in torn jeans and a T-shirt. You'll need clothes, lots and lots of clothes and shoes and make-up and stuff.'

Sienna flung her handbag strap over her shoulder. 'If Andreas Ferrante wants me to dress like one of his mistresses he can damn well pay for it. Ciao.'

'Signor Ferrante is in a design team meeting and cannot be disturbed,' the receptionist informed Sienna.

'Tell him his fiancée is here,' Sienna said with a guileless smile.

The receptionist's eyes widened as they took in Sienna's travel-worn appearance. 'I'm not sure…' she began uncertainly.

'Tell him if he doesn't see me right now the wedding won't go ahead,' Sienna said with a don't-mess-with-me look.

The receptionist reached for the intercom and spoke in Italian to Andreas. 'There's a young woman here who claims to be your fiancée. Do you want me to call Security?'

Andreas's deep mellifluous voice sounded over the system. 'Tell her to wait in Reception.'

Sienna leaned over the desk and swung the speaker her way. 'Get your butt out here, Andreas. We have things to discuss.'

'The boardroom,' he said. 'Ten minutes.'

'Out here *now*,' Sienna said through gritted teeth.

'*Cara*,' he drawled, 'such impatience fires my blood. Have you missed me terribly?'

Sienna pasted a false smile on her face for the sake of the receptionist. 'Darling, you can't imagine how *awful* it's been without your arms around me. I'm going crazy for you. It's been absolute torture to be without your kisses, your touch and your body doing all those wonderful things to—'

'Let's keep some things private, shall we?' he interjected coolly.

Sienna smiled at the now goggle-eyed receptionist. 'You wouldn't know it to look at him, but he has the most amazingly huge—'

'Sienna,' Andreas clipped out, 'get in here right *now*.'

Sienna slipped off the desk and gave the receptionist a fingertip wave. 'Isn't he adorable?'

The boardroom was empty by the time Sienna arrived. Andreas had a face like thunder and the air was crackling with palpable tension.

'What the hell do you think you're doing?' he asked even before she had closed the door.

Sienna threw him a contemptuous glare. 'Apparently we're engaged,' she said, clicking the door shut with considerable force. 'I read about it in the press.'

His mouth went to a flat line. 'I'm not the one who leaked that to the media.' He raked a hand through his hair. 'You know what they say about a woman scorned.'

Sienna raised her brows. 'Perfect Portia did that? Wow, I bet she didn't read that in the Good Girl's Guide to Avoiding Social Slip-Ups.'

His brows snapped together. 'I was about to ask her to marry me,' he said. 'She has a right to be upset.'

'My heart bleeds,' Sienna said on an exaggerated sigh.

He threw her a flinty look. 'Bitch.'

She smiled at him sweetly. 'Bastard.'

The air crackled some more.

Andreas paced the floor, his hand tracking another ragged pathway through the thick pelt of his hair. 'We have to find a way to manage this,' he said. 'Six months and we'll be free of this. I've looked at it from every angle. There's no way out of it. We just have to do what's expected. We can both win.'

Sienna pulled out one of the ergonomic chairs and sat down, swinging it from side to side as she watched him work the floor. 'What's in it for me?' she asked.

He stopped pacing to look at her, his frown deepening. 'What do you mean what's in it for you? You get a truckload of money at the end of it.'

She held his hazel gaze. 'I want more.'

His mouth tightened even further. 'How much more?'

'How about double?'

His jaw worked for a moment. 'A quarter.'

'A third,' she said, holding his look.

He slammed his hands on the table right in front of her, his face so close to hers she could smell the good quality coffee on his breath. 'Damn you to hell and back, you're not getting any more,' he said. 'The deal stands as it stands. I'm not negotiating on it.'

Sienna rolled her chair back and rose to her feet in one fluid movement. 'I guess that's it then,' she said. 'If you want me to marry you then you'll have to pay for the privilege.'

She was at the door when he finally spoke. 'All right,' he said on a heavily expelled breath. 'I'll give you a third on top of what my father bequeathed to you.'

Sienna turned to face him. 'You want that chateau real bad, don't you?'

His expression was rigid with tension. 'It belonged to my mother,' he said. 'I will do anything it takes to keep it out of the hands of my greedy, profligate second cousin.'

'Even marry me?'

He gave a humourless chuckle. 'I can't believe I'm saying this, but yes, I can actually think of worse things than marrying you.'

'Your imagination is streets ahead of mine because I *can't* think of anything worse than being married to you,' she said as she resumed her seat.

The air tightened like a steel cable.

Sienna felt his gaze run over her. It felt like a hot caress on her skin. His eyes seemed to sear the flesh off her bones. She felt naked under his scrutiny.

But then he *had* seen her naked, or almost.

She cringed at the memory. She had wanted him to be her first lover. She had dreamt about it for months. She had fantasised about him rescuing her from the life of drudgery she and her mother had been forced to live. All those years of never knowing what house they would be living in next. Not knowing what school or suburb she would be residing in. Her childhood had been a patchwork of packing up and leaving, of trying to fit in a new place, of trying to make friends with people who already had enough friends. She had always felt the odd one out. She didn't belong upstairs or downstairs.

But everything had changed when her mother had got the position as housekeeper at the Ferrante villa in Rome. It was the most stunning property, with fabulous gardens and a massive swimming pool and tennis court. It had felt like paradise after years of living in a variety of cramped and mouldy inner city flats.

It had been the first time in her life Sienna had seen her mother truly happy and settled. She hadn't wanted it to end. In her immature mind she'd had it all planned. Andreas, the son and heir of the Ferrante fortune, would fall in love with her and marry her. He was the handsome playboy prince, she was the pretty but penniless pauper, but their love and desire for each other would overcome that. She had been determined that he would notice her for once instead of treating her like an annoying puppy that hadn't been properly housetrained. To him, she had always been the cleaning lady's brat. He had even called her *enfant terrible.*

But this night it would be different. He hadn't been home in months. This time he would see the change in her. He would see her for the sexually mature young woman she had believed herself to be.

She had seen his hazel eyes follow her all evening when she had helped bring in the family's meal. She had sensed his male appraisal as she brought in the coffee and liqueurs to the *salone.* His nostrils had flared when she had leant down to place his cup beside him, as if he was breathing in her fragrance. Her hair had brushed against his arm and she had felt the electric current of awareness shoot through her body. He had looked at her then with those green and brown-flecked eyes of his and she had known he wanted her.

She had *felt* it.

She had waited for him in his bedroom, draping herself alluringly across his bed, dressed only in her knickers and bra, nervous but excited at the same time. Her body had tingled all over in anticipation.

The door had opened and Andreas had stood there for a moment, his eyes drinking in the sight of her. But then he seemed to give himself a mental shake and his expression immediately locked down, becoming stony, marble-like. 'What the hell do you think you're playing at?' he growled. 'Get dressed and get out.'

Sienna had been crushed. She had been so certain he wanted her. She had seen it. She had felt it. She had sensed it in the air. The heavily charged atmosphere had practically exploded with erotic tension. The same tension she could see in his body even though he had done his best to hide it. 'I want you to make love to me,' she said. 'I know you want me. I've known it for ages.'

His mouth had been so tight it looked as if it had been drawn there with a thin felt tip pen. 'You're mistaken, Sienna,' he said. 'I have no interest in you whatsoever.'

Sienna had got off the bed and approached him. It had been brazen of her and impulsive but she had wanted to prove to him that what she felt was not just a figment of her youthful imagination. 'I want you, Andreas,' she said in a sultry tone as she reached for him.

Andreas had grasped her by the upper arms just as the door opened...

Sienna blinked herself out of the past. She didn't want to remember that dreadful scene between Andreas and his father. She didn't want to remember the unforgivable lies she had told. She had been desperate, terrified that her mother would lose the job she loved so much. The words had come tumbling out, a river of nonsense that she had regretted ever since. Andreas had never come home again, not even when his mother lay dying.

When Sienna looked up Andreas was standing behind the boardroom table, his steely gaze focused on her. 'There are some practicalities we need to sort out,' he said.

She resisted the urge to moisten her bark-dry lips. 'Practicalities?'

'The will states we have to live together as man and wife,' he said. 'That means you will have to sleep wherever I sleep.'

Sienna shot to her feet so fast the chair toppled over behind her. 'I'm not sleeping with you!'

He rolled his eyes as if dealing with an imbecile. 'Not in the same bed, Sienna, but under the same roof,' he said. 'We have to put on a show for the public.'

She blinked at him. 'You mean we have to act as if we really wanted to be married to each other?'

He continued to look at her with that unwavering hazel gaze. 'As much as it pains me to say this, yes, we will have to act as if we're in love.'

'Are you out of your mind?' she gasped. 'I can't do that! Everyone knows how much I hate you.'

'Likewise,' he said dryly, 'but it's only for six months and it's only when we're in public. We can wrestle each other to the ground when we're alone.'

Sienna felt her cheeks flame with colour as the images his words conjured up flooded her brain. 'I haven't the faintest clue how to wrestle.'

'Perhaps I could teach you,' he said with a slanting smile that contained a hint of mockery and something else she didn't even want to think about identifying. 'The only thing you have to remember is the winner is the one who finishes on top.'

Sienna turned away so he couldn't see how hot and bothered she felt. Her body felt as if it were on fire. Her

skin was prickling all over as she thought of his strong
lean body pinning hers beneath his. 'How soon do we
have to…you know…make things official?'

'As soon as possible,' he said. 'I've applied for a
special licence. It should come through any day now.'

'And what sort of wedding do you have in mind?'
she asked, turning to look at him again.

'You're surely not hankering for a white wedding?'
he said with a mocking arch of one of his eyebrows.

She gave him a flippant look in return. 'It's supposed
to be the bride's day.'

'You've already been a bride.' He held her gaze for
a microsecond before adding in disgust, 'To a man old
enough to be your grandfather.'

Sienna raised her chin at him. 'At least I loved him.'

His lip curled. 'You loved his money, you trashy little gold-digger,' he said. 'Did he make you earn every
penny by opening your legs on command?'

She gave him her wild-child smile, the one the
press had documented time and time again—the one
that painted her as a sleep-around-slut on the make.
'Wouldn't you like to know?' she asked.

He flung himself away from the table, thrusting his
hands deep in his trouser pockets as if he didn't trust
himself not to shake her till her teeth rattled.

Sienna found it exhilarating to know she had yanked
his chain. He was always so cool and in control, but
there was a side to him only she brought out. It was his
primitive side, the raw male side that wanted to domi-
nate and subdue her. The thought of him making her
submit to him made her skin lift in a shiver.

She would fight him tooth and nail.

* * *

Andreas took some steadying breaths. She was doing it deliberately, of course. Trying her best to get under his skin, to prove nothing had changed in spite of the passage of time. How could one woman have such an effect on him?

He was *not* a slave to lust.

He had abhorred that in his father, how he had betrayed his wife of more than thirty years to bed a common tart.

Andreas prided himself on his self-control. He had the normal urges of any full-blooded male, but he always chose his partners with discretion. The women he slept with had class and poise. They were not headstrong harpies. They did not stir in him such unbridled passion.

He *never* lost his head.

But something about Sienna inflamed him and he had no control over it. He wanted to drive himself in her as hard and deeply as he could. He wanted to rut her like a wild animal did a random mate. He wanted to tame her, to have her submit to him in every way possible. His body ached and burned for her feverishly.

She was the forbidden fruit he had always prided himself he *could* resist.

That was no doubt why his father had set things up the way he had. He had known the temptation Sienna had always been for him. His father could not have thought of a worse punishment than tying her to him, dangling her under his nose, day in and day out. What had he been thinking? Had his father really hated him that much?

Andreas turned back to face Sienna. She was sitting down again, her jeans-clad legs propped up on the desk, her arms folded across her chest, which pushed her beautiful breasts upwards, looking every bit the impudent schoolgirl called into the headmaster's office. She had a lamentable disrespect for authority. She was wilful and defiant. She didn't know the meaning of the word respect. She could be surly and then sunny in the blink of an eye. She could be a sultry siren one second and an innocent waif the next.

He didn't have a clue how he was going to manage this farcical arrangement, but manage it he would, even if it meant sleeping with her to get her out of his system once and for all.

Every drop of his blood sizzled at the thought.

'Where are you staying?' he asked.

'I haven't found a place yet,' she said. 'I only just flew in.'

'Where are your things?'

'I didn't bring anything with me,' she said. 'I thought I'd leave the wardrobe arrangements up to you. I figured the stuff I normally wear won't suit.'

He stared at her incredulously. 'You came here with nothing but the clothes you're wearing?'

She gave him a feisty look. 'If I'm going to act the part, I need to dress for it. But you can pay for it, not me.'

'I have no problem with footing the bill,' Andreas said. 'It just seems a little unconventional, if not impetuous, for a young woman of your age to fly about the globe with nothing but jeans and a T-shirt and a handbag. Most of the women I know carry enough make-up and toiletries to sink a ship.'

'I'm very low maintenance,' she said.

'I very much doubt it,' he muttered.

She lowered her slim legs to the floor with a movement that was both coltish and graceful. 'I'll need a place to stay until we make things official,' she said. 'A five-star hotel will do nicely.'

'You can stay at my villa.' He scribbled the address on a sheet of paper and pushed it across the desk to her. 'I want you right under my nose where I can keep an eye on you.'

'You think I'll spill my guts to the press like your ex-fiancée did?' she asked with an insolent smile as she popped the folded paper inside her bra.

'Technically, she wasn't my fiancée,' he said, tearing his gaze away from the tempting sight of her pert breasts. 'I hadn't got that far. I had bought a ring, however. You can borrow it if you like.'

She gave him a slitted-eye glare. 'Don't even think about it, Rich Boy,' she said. 'I want my own ring, not someone else's.'

Andreas came over to where she was standing. He could feel the force field of her as soon as he crossed that invisible line. Her summery fragrance assaulted his nostrils, a combination of flowers and feminine warmth that was as heady as any mind-altering drug. This close, he could see the tiny dusting of freckles over the bridge of her retroussé nose and the tiniest of chickenpox scars above her left eyebrow.

Almost of its own volition, his gaze flicked down to her mouth.

Lust gave him a knockout punch in the gut when he saw the way the tip of her tongue darted out to leave a glistening layer of moisture on those plump, ripe lips.

He fought his leaping pulse back under control, dragging his gaze back to her glittering one. 'This is all a game to you, isn't it?' he said.

Her top lip curled at him and her grey-blue eyes glittered. 'You were going to kiss me, weren't you?'

Andreas ground his teeth until he thought he'd have to eat jelly for the rest of his life. 'I want to throttle you, not kiss you,' he said.

'You put one finger on me and see what happens,' she said, matching him stare for stare.

Andreas already knew what would happen. He could feel it in his body. It was thundering through his veins like a torpedo. He couldn't think of a time when he had felt such forceful, uncontrollable desire. It was like being a hormone-driven teenager all over again. Dynamite couldn't do more damage than Sienna in temptress mode. 'Get out of my sight,' he ground out savagely.

She put up her chin. 'Say please.'

He strode over to the door, holding it open pointedly. 'Out.'

She tossed the silver-blonde curtain of her hair back behind her shoulders. 'If I'm going to stay at your place I'll need a key,' she said.

'The housekeeper will let you in,' Andreas said. 'I'll call her now and tell her to expect you.'

'What will you tell her and the rest of your staff about us?' she asked.

'I don't make a habit of exchanging confidences with the household staff at any of my residences,' he said. 'They will assume it's a normal marriage, just like everyone else.'

A little frown appeared over her grey-blue eyes. 'Even though we won't be sharing a room?'

Andreas felt that punch to his gut again. He could think of nothing more tempting than rolling around his bed with her legs wrapped around his waist, his body buried to the hilt in hers. His blood thickened and pulsed as he thought of how it would feel to finally satiate this need he had harboured so long. He would have his fill of her once and for all. In six months he would walk away. He would finally be immune. Free. In control.

'It's very common for people with villas the size of mine to occupy different suites,' he said. 'It doesn't make sense to cram into one room when there are thirty others to choose from.'

Her eyes went wide. 'That big, huh?'

'It's bigger than my father's.'

A little smile played about the corners of her mouth. 'I just bet it is,' she said.

Andreas took out his wallet and handed her a credit card. 'Here,' he said, handing it to her. 'Go shopping. Get your hair and nails done. Have coffee. Have a meal. I won't be back till late. Don't wait up.'

She took the card from him without touching his fingers and popped it in her bag. She moved past him in the doorway, not touching but close enough for every hair on his body to stand to attention and for every blood vessel to expand and throb. He was about to let out the breath he was holding when she suddenly stopped and turned back to look at him. 'Do you have any idea why your father did this?' she asked.

'No idea at all.'

She chewed at her lower lip for a moment, a shadow passing like a cloud over her face. 'He must have really hated me…'

'What makes you think that?' he asked, frowning at

her. 'This is about me, not you. My father hated me as much as I hated him.'

A little beat of silence passed.

'I'd better get going,' she said with an overly bright smile. 'So many things to buy, so little time. Ciao.'

Andreas closed the door once she had left and leant back against it heavily, a frown tugging at his forehead. Half an hour with Sienna was like being in the middle of a hurricane with nothing but a paper parasol for protection.

How was he going to get through six months?

CHAPTER THREE

SIENNA took a taxi to Andreas's Tuscan estate once she had finished shopping. The Renaissance-style villa was a few kilometres outside Florence, set amongst acres of olive groves and vineyards in the Chianti region of Tuscany, made famous for its wine. The fading afternoon sunshine cast a spectacular light over the fresh growth on the vines. Flowers in an array of bright colours tumbled from baskets hanging near the entrance to the villa. It was breathtakingly beautiful and a jolting reminder of the wealth Andreas had been born into and had never questioned. Sure, he had forged his own way with his furniture designs, but he had never had to worry about bills not being paid or where the next meal was coming from. It was hard not to feel a teensy bit jealous. Why did he even want his mother's wretched chateau in Provence when he had all of this?

The thought of owning a property like the chateau made Sienna wonder if she should set about making him default on the will by making it impossible to live with her. It was a tempting thought: a chateau of her own, her own patch of paradise. It wasn't as if Andreas would be left homeless or anything. He had homes everywhere. The one in Florence was his base, but she knew for a fact he had a villa in Barbados as well as one somewhere in Spain.

The door of the villa opened and a motherly-looking woman who introduced herself as Elena smiled as she ushered Sienna in. 'Signor Ferrante told me you would be arriving this evening,' she said. 'I have made up the Rose Suite for you.' She winked knowingly. 'It is right next to his.'

Sienna forced a smile. 'That was very thoughtful of you.'

'It is no trouble,' Elena said. 'I was young and madly in love once. I met my husband and within a month we were married. I knew Signor Ferrante would change his mind about that one.'

Sienna frowned slightly. 'Erm…"That one"?'

Elena made a noise that sounded something like a snort. 'Princess Portia. She was never happy. I had to fetch and carry. She did not like red meat. She did not like cheese. She only ate this. She only ate that. I nearly went crazy.'

'Maybe she was thinking of her figure,' Sienna offered generously.

The housekeeper gave another snort of disapproval. 'She is not the right one for Signor Ferrante,' she said. 'He needs a woman who is as passionate as he is.'

Sienna couldn't help wondering exactly what Andreas had told his housekeeper about their relationship or whether Elena had assumed their whirlwind courtship had come about because they had suddenly fallen deeply in love. Or, even more worryingly, could the housekeeper see something in Sienna that she desperately wanted to keep hidden? It wasn't as if she still had a crush on Andreas or anything. She didn't love him. She hated him. But that didn't mean his physical presence didn't disturb her. It did, and way too much. 'You seem to know him very well,' she said.

Elena smiled. 'He's a good man. He's very generous and hard-working, too. He helps in the vineyard whenever he can, and the orchards. You knew him before? I read about it in the paper. Your *mamma* used to work for his family, *sì*?'

'*Sì*,' Sienna said. 'My mother took up the position as head housekeeper when I was fourteen. Andreas wasn't living at home then, of course, but we ran into each other from time to time.'

'Friends to lovers, *sì*?' Elena said, smiling broadly.

'Erm…something like that.'

'I can see the fire in your eyes,' Elena said. 'He will be happy with you. I can tell these things. You will make good babies with him, *sì*?'

Sienna felt her face grow hot. 'We haven't talked about kids. It's been a bit of a whirlwind affair, actually.'

'The best ones are,' Elena said with matronly authority. 'Come, I'll show you your new home. You'll want to settle in before Signor Ferrante gets back.'

Sienna followed the cheery housekeeper on a tour of the villa. It was even bigger than she had expected. Room after room, suite after suite, all beautifully and tastefully decorated. It occurred to her that in a villa this size she could pass six months without even running into Andreas, or anyone else for that matter.

'I'll leave you to shower and change,' Elena said. 'I will set up the dinner before I leave.'

'You don't live here?' Sienna asked.

'I live in the farmhouse next to the olive grove,' Elena said. 'My husband, Franco, works for Signor

Ferrante too. If you want anything we are only a phone call away. I will be back in the morning around ten. Signor Ferrante likes a bit of privacy. He has lived with servants all his life. I understand he wants his space.'

Sienna hadn't factored in actually being alone with Andreas. Alone with servants was a whole lot different than *alone*. It put a completely different spin on things. Could she trust him to keep his distance? The chemistry between them was volatile, to say the least. She knew it wouldn't take much to set things off. If that tense little moment in his boardroom was anything to go by, things could get pretty intense in a flash and what would she be able to do about it? It wasn't as if she had any immunity, not really. She put on a good front but how long was that going to last? He had only to look at her a certain way and her insides coiled with lust.

It was ironic because sex was something she had never really taken to with any great enthusiasm. Although she had partied, and partied hard after Andreas's rejection, it had been months and months before she had even thought about dating, and even when she had finally gone out with a couple of young men her age, the intimate encounters had left her cold. She had felt nothing for either of her partners and they clearly had felt nothing for her. And then, after the shameful night that had found her in a stranger's bed, she had locked herself away in a sex-less and safe marriage of convenience. Before that night, whenever the press had portrayed her as a sleep-around-slut, she had laughed it off, pleased that she was getting some attention, even if it wasn't positive. *She* had known the truth about herself and that had been all that mattered. But now the label had a ring of truth to it she dearly wished she could remove.

After she had unpacked and showered and changed, Sienna came downstairs. The villa seemed rather empty without the warm and friendly chatter of the housekeeper. She picked at some food and poured herself a glass of wine, feeling restless and irritable.

Maybe she should have thought about this a little more before she went any further. It wasn't the first time her impulsive nature had got her into trouble. Was it too late to back out?

The money stopped her thoughts of escape in their tracks. What was she thinking? It was like any other unpleasant job that had to be done. A six-month contract that would be over before she knew it. She would receive a handsome pay-out for her trouble.

There was that T word again. Trouble.

She had a habit of attracting it, no matter what she did. Was she forever destined to be at the mercy of circumstances she couldn't control? Was it her fault her mother had kept her and given away her sister?

Jealousy was something Sienna didn't want to feel around her twin, but she couldn't help feeling a little cheated by how things had panned out. Gisele had grown up well provided for. She'd had a private education and gone on fabulous exotic holidays. She had lived in the same gorgeous house all of her childhood. She hadn't had to pack up her things every few months or so when someone got tired of her mother's laziness or cheek. She'd had a father to watch out for her, to provide for her and protect her from those who preyed upon the vulnerable.

Sienna, on the other hand, had grown up a whole lot

faster than her peers. She'd learnt early on that there were few people you could trust. Everyone was out for his or her own gain.

And now she was no different.

She would get what she could out of this and move on. She would milk Andreas for every penny she could before she walked out of his life.

For good.

Sienna was on to her second glass of wine when she heard Andreas's car. The deep throaty roar of the engine made her stomach clench unexpectedly. His fast car, fast-living lifestyle was something that had always attracted her even as it annoyed her. He had probably never had to push start a car in his life. He had never had to make his own bed or butter his own toast. He hadn't been born with just a silver spoon in his mouth, but an entire dinner service. He ate from fine bone china and drank from crystal glasses. He had everything that money could buy and then some.

How she hated him for it.

Andreas came in to find Sienna lying on her stomach on his leather sofa with a half drunk glass of wine in her hand and the remote control to his big screen television in the other. Her hair was pulled back in a high ponytail and she was wearing close-fitting black yoga pants and a loose hot-pink top that had slipped off one of her sun-kissed shoulders. Her feet were bare as she swung her lower legs back and forth in a slow motion kicking action. She looked young and nubile and so damned sexy he felt a tight ache deep in his groin.

'Hard day at the office?' she asked without even looking his way as she flicked through the channels.

He tugged at his tie to loosen it. 'You could say that.'
He shrugged off his jacket and tossed it over the end
of the other sofa. 'Making ourselves at home, are we?'

She took a sip of her wine before she answered.
'Having a blast,' she said. 'You make great wine, by
the way. I like your housekeeper too. We're already
best friends.'

'You're not supposed to make friends with the servants,' he said, frowning.

She muted the television and swung her legs down
to sit up. 'Why's that?' she asked. 'Because they might
forget their place and get too close to you?'

Andreas let out a carefully controlled breath. 'They're
employees, not friends,' he said. 'They do the work and
they get paid. There's nothing else that's required of
them.'

She got off the sofa and padded over to where he was
standing with her loose-limbed sensual gait. She looked
up at him with those big sparkling-with-mischief grey-
blue eyes of hers and he felt his groin tighten another
excruciating notch. It was all he could do to stand there
without hauling her against him to show her how much
he lusted after her. But he had decided he would have
her when *he* said so, not because she thought she could
manipulate him at will.

'Have you eaten?' she asked.

'What is this?' he asked with a mocking look.
'Wifely duties 101?'

She lifted that deliciously bare shoulder of hers in a
little shrug, her mouth going to a resentful pout. 'Just
trying to be helpful,' she said. 'I thought you looked
tired.'

'Maybe that's because I haven't slept a wink since I

heard about my father's will,' Andreas said, rubbing a hand over his face, which was in need of a shave.

He walked over to the bar and poured himself a glass of the wine Sienna had opened. He took a couple of sips before swinging his gaze back to her. 'I've got the licence. I pulled a few strings. We can get married next Friday.'

Her eyes widened a fraction but her voice when she spoke was all sass. 'You move fast when you want something, don't you, Rich Boy?'

'No point in dragging things out,' he said. 'The sooner we marry, the sooner we can get a divorce.'

'Sounds like a plan.'

Andreas narrowed his gaze in sharp focus. 'What's that supposed to mean?'

Her slim brows lifted archly. 'Exactly what I said,' she said. 'You seem to have it all figured out,'

'I do,' he said. 'We marry and then at the end of six months we end it. Simple.'

'What did you tell Elena about us?' she asked.

'Nothing, other than we're getting married as soon as possible.'

'You must have said more than that,' she said, toying with the end of her ponytail.

'Why do you think that?' he asked.

She lifted her golden shoulder up and down again. 'She seems to think we're madly in love,' she said.

'Most people are when they marry,' Andreas said, taking another mouthful of wine.

A beat of silence ticked past.

'Were you in love with Portia Briscoe?' Sienna asked.

Andreas's brows shot together. 'What sort of question is that?' he asked.

She tilted her head on one side, her finger tapping against her lips. 'No, I don't think you loved her,' she said. 'I think you liked her well enough. She ticked all the boxes for you. She comes from money, she knows what cutlery to use and she dresses well and never has a hair out of place. She never says the wrong thing or rubs people up the wrong way. But grab-you-in-the-guts love? Nope. I don't think so.'

'You're a fine one to harp on about true love,' he said. 'You weren't in love with Brian Littlemore. You barely knew him when you waltzed him down the aisle before his wife was even cold in her grave.'

'Actually, I did know him,' she said with an imperious air. 'I'd met him well before his wife died.'

Andreas gave her a disgusted look. 'And no doubt you opened your legs for him then too. Did he pay you? Or did you give him one for free to get him so hot and hungry the poor old fool couldn't help himself?'

Sienna's eyes flashed at him with undiluted venom. 'You have a mind like a sewer,' she said. 'You sit up there in your diamond-encrusted, gold-inlaid ivory tower of yours, passing judgement on people you don't even know from a bar of soap. Brian was a decent man with a big heart. You haven't even got a heart. All you've got inside your chest is a lump of cold, hard stone.'

Andreas took a measured sip of his wine. 'Your loyalty to your late husband is touching, *ma chérie*,' he said. 'But I wonder if you would be so loyal if you knew he had another lover the whole time he was with you.'

Her eyes flickered before moving away from his. He watched as she moved back to where she had left her glass of wine. She picked it up and cradled it in her hands without drinking any of it. 'We had an open marriage,' she said, still not looking at him. 'It gave us both the freedom to do what we wanted as long as we were both discreet about it.'

Andreas wondered if he should have been quite so blunt with her. There had been nothing in the press about her late husband's affair. He had heard it second-hand and not from a particularly reliable source. But if she was hurt or upset by the news she was doing a good job of concealing it. Admittedly, she was standing stiffly, almost guardedly, but neither her expression nor her tone showed any sign of emotional carnage.

'You knew about his mistress?' he asked.

She turned to look at him, a little puzzled frown pulling at her brow. 'His…mistress?'

'The woman he was seeing,' he said. 'His lover.'

She gave a little laugh that seemed totally out of place. It sounded almost…relieved. 'Oh, *her*…' she said. 'Yes, I knew about her right from the start.'

'And you married Littlemore anyway?' he asked, frowning deeply.

She met his gaze with a directness he found jarring. 'I did it for the money,' she said. 'The same reason I'm marrying you. It's only for the money.'

Andreas felt his jaw clamp down in anger. She was so brazen about her gold-digging motives. Had she no shame? No self-respect? What sort of laughing stock would she try and make of him during their six-month marriage? She had no sense of propriety. She was as selfish and self-serving as she had been as a teenager. She would do anything to get as much out of this situation as she could. He could practically see the dollar signs flashing in her eyes. 'While we're on the subject of money,' he said, 'I want to make a few things clear, right from the start. Throughout the duration of our marriage, I will not tolerate any behaviour on your part that leads to speculation in the press that this is not a normal relationship. If you don't behave yourself there will be consequences. Do I make myself clear?'

She gave him one of her insolent schoolgirl looks. 'Perfectly.'

He drew in a breath for patience and slowly released it. 'Secondly, I will not be made a fool of by your practice of leaping in and out of bed with a host of unsavoury men,' he said. 'That means no boudoir photos and no seedy little sex tapes uploaded to the Internet or social networking sites. Got it?'

Her cheeks turned a cherry-red, he presumed from anger at being reminded of the sex tape incident that had occurred a little over two years ago, for which her twin sister had inadvertently taken the rap. He'd missed the scandal as he had been abroad at the time, but, after reading about her twin's recent reconciliation with her fiancé, the thing that had struck him most was that Sienna hadn't come forward at the time. To be fair, she hadn't known she even had a twin then, but it was just typical of Sienna's inability or unwillingness to take responsibility for her actions. She didn't give a toss what anyone else suffered because of her reprehensible behaviour. She just barrelled her way through life with no thought or care for what anyone else was feeling.

'There won't be any slip-ups,' she said stiffly.

'There had better not be,' he warned.

She turned away from him and drained her glass,

putting it down with a little rattle against the coffee table. 'Will that be all?' she asked.

Andreas pressed his lips together. Her subdued tone was a new one. He hadn't heard her use it before. How did she do it? How did she switch things so deftly to make him feel as if *he* had overstepped the mark? 'If it is any consolation to you, I will also refrain from any behaviour that could compromise our arrangement,' he said, ploughing a hand through his hair. 'It's only for six months. A bout of celibacy is supposed to re-energise the soul and sharpen the intellect, or so I've heard.'

She gave him a little smile, that old familiar spark back in her gaze. 'Do you think you'll last the distance?' she asked.

Andreas wasn't prepared to put any money on it. Not with her looking so damned hot and gorgeous without even trying. 'I'll take it one day at a time,' he said, deliberately running his gaze over her from head to toe and back again.

She held his look but he noticed one of her shoulders rolling as if she suddenly found her clothes prickly against her skin. 'Good luck with that,' she said in an airy tone.

He refilled his wine glass and took a couple of mouthfuls before he turned to look at her again. 'By the way, I'd appreciate you making an effort to buy something suitable to wear to the wedding. I'm not sure yoga pants or tattered jeans are going to set a new trend in bridal gear, no matter how good you look in them.'

Sienna raised her brows at him. 'My, oh, my, a compliment from the impossible-to-impress Signor Ferrante,' she said. 'Wonders will never cease.'

Andreas frowned at her in irritation. 'What are you talking about? I've complimented you plenty of times.'

'Remind me of one,' she said, folding her arms across her chest as she tilted one hip forwards in a pose of youthful scepticism. 'My memory seems to have completely failed me.'

He rubbed at the back of his neck. 'What about the time you were going to that school dance when you were sixteen or thereabouts,' he said. 'You were wearing a crinkly candy-pink and white dress. I said you looked pretty.'

She gave him a resentful look. 'You said I looked like a cupcake.'

Andreas felt a smile tug at his mouth. 'Did I really say that?'

'You did.'

'Well, then, what I probably meant to say was you looked good enough to eat,' he said.

The air seemed to thicken in the ensuing silence.

'You probably should take a little more care with your diet,' Sienna said. 'Too much sugar is bad for you.'

'Yes, but once in a while it's good to have a little of what you fancy, don't you think?' Andreas said.

'Only if you can keep control,' she said, holding his look with a haughty air he found incredibly arousing. 'For some people, one taste is never going to be enough. They can't just have one square of chocolate. They have to have the whole bar.'

His gaze swept over her slim figure again. 'You're obviously not speaking from personal experience,' he said. 'I could just about span your waist with my hands.'

'Lucky genes, I guess.'

Andreas saw a flicker of something move through

her gaze. 'What are you going to tell your sister about this arrangement between us?' he asked.

She rolled her lips together for a moment. 'I feel uncomfortable about lying to her, but I don't want her to worry about me either,' she said. 'I think it's best if I stick to the script for now.'

'We should probably tidy up a few details then,' Andreas said. 'Like how we came to fall in love so quickly.'

Sienna gave him one of her worldly looks. 'Do you really think people are going to believe you fell in love with me? We have nothing in common. I'm a cleaning lady's kid from the wrong side of the tracks. You've had more silver spoons in your mouth than most people have had hot dinners. Men with your sort of heritage don't marry trailer trash. It's just in fairy tales where that sort of thing happens. Not in real life.'

Andreas frowned. 'That's rather a harsh way to speak of your background,' he said. 'I have never once referred to you as trailer trash.'

'You don't have to,' she said. 'I see it in your eyes every time you look at me.'

He felt a little stab of guilt. He had called her plenty of other things in the past and none of them were any less disparaging. 'Look, Sienna,' he said. 'I realise we have some ill feeling because of our history. But I'm prepared to put that aside for the moment in order to get through this period.'

She chewed at her lower lip in a childlike manner he found at odds with what he knew of her. 'Are you saying you forgive me?' she asked.

'I wouldn't go as far as saying that,' he said. 'What you did was unforgivable.'

'Yes,' she said, biting down on her lip again. 'I know…'

Andreas ratcheted up his resolve. She was toying with him, trying to appeal to his better side to get herself off the hook. He wasn't buying it for a moment. Behind that forgive-me-I-was-too-young-to-know-what-I-was-doing façade was a conniving little social-climbing trollop who was on a mission to land herself a fortune. She might have fooled his father into writing her into the will, but it wasn't going to work on him.

He scooped up his jacket from the sofa. 'I'm going to be tied up for the next few days,' he said. 'I hope you can stay out of mischief until Friday.'

'It'll be a piece of cake,' she said.

He gave her a droll look before he left. 'Just stick to one slice, OK?'

CHAPTER FOUR

WHEN Sienna came down after a shower the next morning there was no sign of Andreas. Elena hadn't yet arrived so it gave her some time to wander about and get her bearings. She made a cup of tea and took it out onto a wisteria-covered terrace. She felt the heat of the sun-warmed flagstones through the bare soles of her feet as she walked towards one of the wrought iron chairs. She sat and looked out at the expansive view. There were a hundred shades of green and a thousand fragrant smells and sounds to dazzle her senses.

She put her cup down and went back inside to get her camera from her handbag. It was compact but high-tech enough to allow her to capture images that took her fancy. She went back down to the terrace and beyond, snapping away in bliss, losing track of time as she explored the gardens.

She was aiming for a shot of a bird on a shrub when she caught sight of a dog skulking in the distance. She lowered the camera and, shading her eyes with one of her hands, peered to see if anyone was with it. It seemed to be alone and, by the look of its sunken-in sides, half starving.

Sienna looped her camera strap around her wrist and

walked towards the dog. 'Here, boy,' she called when she got a little closer. 'Come here and say hello.'

The dog looked at her warily, the back of its neck going up in stiff bristles.

Sienna was undaunted. She crouched down and crooned to the dog softly, holding out her hand for it to smell. The dog crept closer, its body low to the ground, the hackles going down and its tail giving the tiniest of wags. 'Good boy,' she said. 'That's right; I won't hurt you. Good dog.'

Just as she was about to see if the dog's worn collar had an identifying tag on it, there was a sound behind her and the dog tore off, disappearing into the nearby woods with its tail tucked between its legs.

'You little fool,' Andreas said. 'You'll get yourself bitten. That dog is a stray. Franco was supposed to shoot it days ago.'

Sienna rose from her crouching position but, even so, he seemed to tower over her. 'But it's wearing a collar!' she said. 'It must belong to someone. Maybe it's just lost and can't find its way home.'

'It's a flea-bitten mongrel,' he said. 'Any fool can see that.'

Sienna scowled at him. 'I suppose you only allow pure-bred dogs with pedigree papers the thickness of three phone books on your precious property.' She brushed past him to go back to the villa. 'What a stuck-up jerk.'

He caught her arm on the way past, swinging her round to face him. 'You shouldn't be wandering around down here without shoes,' he said. 'Are you completely without sense?'

Sienna tugged at his hold but it tightened like a vice.

She felt the sexy rasp of his callused fingers on her wrist and her stomach gave a little fluttery flip-flop. She met his hard hazel eyes and something shifted in the atmosphere. Her gaze slipped to his mouth. He hadn't yet shaved and the sexy pepper of his stubble sent another shockwave of awareness through her. He smelt of man and heat and hard work, a potent smell that stirred her feminine senses into a mad frenzy. Could he tell how much he got under her skin? Could he sense it? Was that why he kept looking at her with those smouldering eyes? 'What would you care?' she said. 'I'd be better off to you dead, wouldn't I?'

His brooding frown cut deeper into his tanned forehead. 'That's a crazy thing to say,' he said. 'Why would I want you dead?'

'Because you'd automatically inherit the chateau,' she said. 'You wouldn't have to go through a marriage you didn't want to a woman you hate more than anyone else in the world.'

'You hate me just as much as I hate you, so we're pretty square on that,' he said. 'Or are you hiding a secret affection for me, hmm?'

She gave him a withering look. 'You have got to be joking.'

He tugged her closer, flush against his rock-hard body. The heat of his arousal was like a brand against her belly. 'You like to tease and tantalise, don't you, *cara*?' he said. 'You like the power. It's like a drug to you, to have men falling over themselves to possess you. I see it in your eyes. They dance with sensual intent. You can't wait to have me fall at your feet. But I won't do it. I won't let you play your seductress games with me. I will have you on my terms, not yours.'

Sienna pushed against his chest with the flat of her hands but, while it put some distance between their upper bodies, it made their lower connection all the more intense. She felt the thundering roar of his blood against her, the rigid length of him taking her breath clean away.

The air sizzled with sexual electricity.

She felt the force of it like waves of searing heat rippling over her skin. She felt her heart rate pick up and her inner core clenched and released, clenched and released, in a primitive rhythm of need.

She wondered if he was going to kiss her. His eyes had dropped to her mouth in an infinitesimal moment of sensual suspense that made her heart beat all the faster. She sent her tongue out over her lips, wondering what he would taste like. Would he be rough or smooth? Forceful or gentle?

'Damn you,' Andreas ground out as he put her from him roughly. 'Damn you to hell.'

Sienna let out a ragged breath as she watched him stride back the way he had come. She put a hand to her chest where her heart was beating like a maniacal metronome. She felt light-headed and shaky on her feet, her body still tingling from the hard male contact of his. That primitive pulse of longing was still thrumming deep inside her and she couldn't seem to turn it off.

She looked down at her wrist where her camera was swinging from its strap. The imprint of his fingers was almost visible on her skin. She touched the tender area with the fingertips of her other hand, her stomach slipping like a skater who had mistimed a manoeuvre.

She was in trouble with a capital T.

* * *

Sienna didn't see Andreas until the evening before the wedding. Elena told her he had been called away to some important business in Milan but Sienna wondered if he was keeping his distance for as long as possible before they were thrust together as man and wife.

The days flashed past as she fielded phone calls from Gisele and her flatmate Kate in London. Somehow she managed to convince her twin she was madly and blissfully in love with Andreas and couldn't wait to get married. As Gisele's wedding was in a few weeks' time and the guest list had blown out considerably, Gisele was nothing but supportive of Sienna's plan for a simple witnesses-only ceremony so she and Andreas could be left alone by the press.

Kate didn't buy into the 'we suddenly fell in love' story but, as a hopeless romantic herself, she was convinced Andreas would finally come to his senses and want Sienna to stay with him for ever.

Sienna didn't like to disabuse her friend of the impossibility of such an outcome. His refusal to forgive her was not the only stumbling block to their relationship. She had long ago given up her foolish dream of him falling in love with her. And, as for her falling in love with him, well, that was *not* going to happen.

Sienna went shopping a couple of times under the escort of a very willing Franco, who faithfully carried her bags and waited patiently in the car while she had her hair and beauty treatments done.

There was also a visit to a lawyer's office where Andreas had set up the signing of a prenuptial agreement. Sienna understood it was part and parcel of many modern marriages, and she totally understood Andreas's motivations given the wealth he had at his disposal, but even so it rankled that he didn't trust her to walk away without a legal tussle when the time was up on their marriage.

The rest of the time Sienna spent working on befriending the dog, whom she called Scraps. He had built up enough confidence to take titbits of food from her hand, but he wouldn't allow her to touch him as yet. She was prepared to be patient, however. And she had made Franco promise he wouldn't shoot him, no matter what orders Andreas gave to the contrary.

Sienna had not long fed the dog and settled him in one of the buildings close to the villa when she heard the roar of Andreas's car come up the driveway that curved through the property, fields of vines on one side, olive groves on the other. A church bell calling the faithful to Mass sounded in the distance, a peaceful sound that was totally at odds with the tension she could feel building in her body as soon as Andreas came into view.

She watched as he unfolded his long, lean length from the low-slung vehicle. He had loosened his tie and his shirtsleeves were rolled up past his strongly muscled wrists. His suit jacket was hooked through one of his fingers and was slung over his shoulder, his briefcase in his other hand.

His eyes ran over her shorts and T-shirt, resting a heart-stopping moment on the upthrust of her breasts, before meshing with her gaze. 'Isn't it supposed to be bad luck to see the bride before the wedding?' he asked.

'That's the morning of the wedding,' she said. 'I don't think the night before counts.'

He gave a slight movement of his lips that could only be very loosely described as a smile, and a half one at that. 'Glad to hear it,' he said. His footsteps crunched over the gravel as he came to where she was standing. 'Elena tells me you have a new conquest.'

'That would be Scraps,' Sienna said, rocking on her feet. 'I've just tucked him in for the night.'

One brow curved in an arch over his eye. 'Scraps?' he said.

'It's what he likes to eat,' she said. 'Plus it's sort of a tribute to his mixed heritage.'

His mouth quirked upwards in that almost smile again. 'Original.'

'I thought so.'

He indicated for her to go ahead of him into the villa. 'How has your week been?' he asked.

'I've shopped myself silly,' Sienna said. 'Thanks for the use of the car, by the way. Franco quite fancies himself as a chauffeur. I think you should get him fitted for a uniform.'

Andreas closed the door and placed his car keys on a marble table in the foyer. 'I've ordered a car for you,' he said. 'It should be here some time next week.'

'I hope it's an Italian sports car,' Sienna said, just to needle him. 'I'll be the envy of all my friends. It's the ultimate status symbol.'

He gave her a derisive look. 'It will get you from A to B without mishap, that is if you drive with any sense of responsibility. But, judging by what you do in your personal life, I'm not holding my breath.'

'I'll have you know I'm a very safe driver,' Sienna said, following him into the *salone*. 'I've never had an accident or even copped a speeding fine. Parking tickets, well, now, that's another thing.'

'So you have a history of outstaying your welcome,

do you?' he asked as he poured himself a drink. 'I'll have to make a note of that.'

Sienna threw him a haughty look. 'If you think I'll stay even a minute over the six months, then you are seriously deluded,' she said.

He looked at her with his unwavering hazel gaze. It seemed more brown than green in the subdued lighting of the *salone*. But then she had noticed lately that his eyes seemed to change with his mood. 'Just as long as we're both clear on the terms of this arrangement,' he said. 'I don't want any complications. And you, *cara,* are nothing if not a magnet for complications.'

Only Andreas could make a term of endearment sound like an insult, Sienna thought. But she had to concede that he was right about the complications. Other people had such simple, uncomplicated lives. She seemed to go from one stuff-up to another. It was as if she had been cursed since birth. But then, maybe she had. Born out of wedlock to a man who had used her mother and then tossed her aside when he was done with her, taking one of her babies for a sum of money to pay for her silence.

It didn't get more complicated or cursed than that.

Sienna suddenly realised Andreas was still watching her with that slightly narrowed focused gaze of his. 'Are you going to offer me a drink or should I just help myself?' she asked.

'Pardon my oversight,' he said. 'What would you like?'

'White wine,' she said. 'The one from your vineyard. It's my favourite.'

He handed her a chilled glass of wine but, just as she reached for it, his brows moved together as he saw the fading marks on her arm. 'What happened to your wrist?' he asked.

Sienna put her hand back down by her side. 'Nothing.'

He put the wine aside and reached for her hand, gently turning over her wrist to look at the full set of his fingerprints there. She saw his face flinch with shock. 'Did I do this to you?' he asked.

'It's nothing,' she said. 'I bruise easily, that's all.'

Her stomach folded over as the pad of his thumb gently moved across the purple stain of his touch. 'Forgive me,' he said in a voice so deep it felt as if it had come from beneath the floor at their feet.

She swallowed as his eyes meshed with hers. 'Really, Andreas, it's nothing…'

'Does it hurt?' he asked, still gently cradling her wrist in the warmth of his hand.

Sienna wasn't used to this tender, more considerate side of him. It made something inside her melt like molasses under the blaze of a hot summer sun. A dangerous melting that she should not allow, but somehow she couldn't prevent it. It flowed through her like a slow-moving tide, all the way through the circuitry of her veins, loosening her spine and all of her ligaments until she felt as if she would end up in a pool of longing at his feet. Her swiftly indrawn breath hitched against something in her throat. 'No…'

He brought her wrist up to his mouth, his lips barely touching the sensitive skin, but it set off a shower of sensations that travelled all the way up her arm and shoulder, making every hair on her head lift away from her scalp.

His eyes were the darkest she had ever seen them. 'It won't happen again,' he said. 'I can assure you of that.

You have no reason to fear for your safety while living under my protection.'

'Thanks for the reassurance,' Sienna said, pulling her hand out of his with a sassy little smile to hide her vulnerability, 'but I've never been scared of you.'

'No, you haven't, have you?' he said, still studying her intently.

Sienna picked up the wine he had poured for her earlier. 'So, I take it we're not going on a honeymoon?' she said before taking a sip.

'On the contrary,' he said, 'I thought we should go to Provence. It's a perfect opportunity to pretend we are taking some time together. I want to see how the Chateau de Chalvy estate is being run. My father appointed a husband and wife team to manage it quite a few years back. I'd like to reacquaint myself with them.'

'Why don't you go on your own?' Sienna said. 'It's not as if you really need me to tag along. I'll only get in the way or say something I shouldn't or dress inappropriately.'

'Sienna, we are getting married tomorrow,' he said with an expressive roll of his eyes. 'People will think it highly unusual if within hours of the ceremony we go our separate ways. That's not how newly married couples behave.'

'But what about Scraps?' she asked. 'I can't just leave him. I've only just got him to trust me. He probably won't take food off Franco or Elena. He might starve or run away again.' She narrowed her gaze at him pointedly and added, 'Or get shot.'

Andreas let out a breath. 'Is that mangy-looking mongrel really that important to you?'

'Yes,' Sienna said. 'I've never had a pet before. I was

never allowed to have one because we always lived in a flat or other people's houses. I've always wanted my own dog. Dogs don't judge you. They love you no matter how little or much money you have and they don't give a toss about whether or not you come from a posh suburb or a trailer park. I've always wanted to be...' She suddenly checked herself. God, how embarrassing. What was she thinking, blurting out all those heartfelt longings as if she was a soppy fool?

Andreas was looking at her quizzically. It was the sort of look that suggested he was seeing much more than she wanted him to see.

Sienna lifted a shoulder in an indifferent shrug as she took another sip of her wine. 'Now that I think of it, maybe Elena could toss him a bone or two,' she said. 'I won't be able to take him with me when I leave in six months, anyway. Best not to get too attached.'

'Why won't you be able to take him with you?' Andreas asked, frowning slightly.

'I want to travel,' Sienna said. 'I don't want to be tied down. I'll have enough money by then to go where I want when I want. It's what I've always dreamed of doing. Having no responsibilities other than to please myself. That's what I'd call the perfect life.'

'It sounds rather pointless and shallow to me,' he said. 'Don't you want more for your life than a never ending holiday?'

'Nope,' Sienna said. 'Give me nine to five partying any day, as long as someone else is paying for it.'

A muscle worked like a hammer at the side of his mouth, while his eyes had gone all hard and glittery. 'You really are a piece of work, aren't you?'

'That's me,' Sienna said, draining her wine glass

before holding it out to him. 'Can you pour me another one?'

Andreas threw her a disgusted look. 'Get it yourself,' he said and strode out of the *salone*, snapping the door shut behind him.

The following morning Elena arrived earlier than usual to help Sienna prepare for the ceremony. She bustled about like a mother hen, gushing about how beautiful Sienna looked as she dressed in a slim-fitting cream dress, the purchase of which had hit Andreas's credit card a little more heavily than Sienna cared to think about.

'Signor Ferrante is going to be…how you say?' Elena said. 'Knocked out by you, *si*?'

Sienna gave the housekeeper what she hoped passed for a convincing smile. 'I'll be glad when this bit is over,' she said, smoothing a hand over her abdomen. 'My stomach feels like a hive of bees.'

'Wedding jitters,' Elena said reassuringly. 'It happens to every bride.'

Sienna didn't feel like a bride. She felt like a fraud. She thought of her twin sister preparing for her big day with Emilio and she felt a twinge of something that felt very much like pain. When she was a little girl she had dreamed of a white wedding with all the trimmings: a church filled with fragrant flowers, with bridesmaids and flower girls and a cute little ring-bearer. She had envisaged a horse-drawn carriage and footmen just like Cinderella. She had imagined a handsome husband who would look down at her as he lifted back her veil with such love and adoration that her heart would swell like a balloon.

But then her dreams and reality had always had a problem socialising.

'Come,' Elena said. 'Franco has brought the car around. It's time to leave.'

Andreas was waiting at the foot of the stairs when Sienna came down. He hadn't been sure what to expect. He had wondered if she would appear in her signature torn denim or a ridiculously short skirt or even bare feet. He hadn't been expecting a vision in designer cream satin that was so stylish and yet so elegantly simple it quite literally took his breath away.

Her silver-blonde hair was up in a classic French roll that showed off her swan-like neck to perfection. Her make-up was understated but somehow it worked brilliantly to showcase the luminosity of her flawless skin. Her grey-blue eyes had a hint of eye shadow and her lashes were long and lustrous with mascara. Her model-like cheekbones were defined by a subtle sweep of bronzer and her lips adorned with a glisten of pink-tinted lipgloss.

The only thing she lacked was jewellery.

An elbow of remorse nudged him in the ribs. He should have thought to buy her something but he had assumed she would spend up big all by herself since he had given her carte blanche on the credit card he had issued her with.

'You look magnificent,' he said. 'I don't think I've ever seen you look quite so beautiful.'

'Amazing what a bit of money splashed around can do,' she said in a flippant tone. 'You don't want to know what this dress cost. And don't get me started on the shoes.'

He took her hand as she stepped from the last stair, a smile tugging at the corners of his mouth. 'At least you're wearing them,' he said. 'I was wondering if you might go without.'

'Watch this space,' she said with a wry twist of her mouth. 'These are what I call car-to-the-bar shoes. They're not meant for walking unless you want to end up with seriously deformed toes.'

Andreas was aware of Elena and Franco hovering in the background, looking suspiciously like the proud parents of the bride. In the space of a week Sienna had charmed them, along with the feral dog. She certainly had a way about her that was unlike any other woman he had associated with before. But then she was very good at fooling people into believing she was all sweetness and light, when underneath that friendly façade was a cold and calculating little madam who—like her mangy dog—could lash out and bite when you were least expecting it.

Andreas turned to Franco. 'Give us a few minutes, there's something I have to give Sienna before we leave.'

'Sì, signor.'

'Come,' Andreas said to Sienna, leading her by the hand towards his study. 'I have something for you.'

'God, my feet are already killing me,' Sienna said, click-clacking beside him.

'This won't take long,' Andreas said, closing the door once they were inside the study.

'Have you bought me a present?' she asked with bright interest in her eyes.

Another sharp elbow of guilt nudged him. 'No,' he said. He opened the safe and took out the box that contained a pearl and diamond necklace and matching droplet earrings. 'These are just on loan.'

'They're beautiful,' Sienna said, peering at them for a moment before straightening. 'But if you bought them for your ex, then forget about it. I'd rather go without.'

Andreas lifted the necklace off its bed of maroon velvet. 'These belonged to my mother,' he said. 'She wore them on her wedding day.'

She looked at the jewels without touching them. 'I'm not sure your mother would appreciate me wearing her jewellery.' She raised her eyes to his. 'It seems a bit… tacky, given the circumstances, don't you think?'

Andreas rolled his thumb over one of the pearls as he looked at her. 'Every Ferrante bride has worn them,' he said. 'They are a family heirloom.'

'Oh…well, then,' she said, turning her back to him. 'That's different. I wouldn't want to break with tradition or anything.'

Andreas fastened the necklace around her neck, his fingers fumbling over the catch as his skin came into contact with the silk of hers. 'You smell nice,' he said. 'Is that a new perfume?'

'If you wanted me to stick to a budget then you should have said so,' she said, turning around to scowl at him.

Andreas handed her the earrings. 'I think you've shown remarkable restraint,' he said. 'But then it's early days yet.'

She clipped on the earrings, still giving him the evil eye as she did so. 'There,' she said once she was done. 'How do I look?'

'Breathtaking,' he said.

'Good,' she said. 'It's not every day a girl like me

gets to marry a billionaire. I want to make the most of every single minute of it.'

Andreas held open the door, his jaw set in a tight line. *Not if I can help it*, he said beneath his breath as she sashayed past him.

Sienna had thought her marriage ceremony to Brian Littlemore had been a bit on the sterile and impersonal side but it had nothing on the clinical detachment of the service Andreas had organised. The vows were nothing like the ones she had composed in her girlish dreams. They were stilted and formal and she'd even been forced to say the O word. Obey.

She was fuming by the time it was almost over. Her lips felt as if they'd been stitched in place. Her teeth were half a centimetre down from grinding and her back was rigid with tension.

'You may kiss the bride.'

The words jolted her out of her simmering fury. 'I don't think—'

Andreas drew her closer, one of his hands in the small of her back, the other holding the hand that had not long ago received the slim gold band that now bound her to him as his wife. 'Relax, *ma chèrie*,' he said in an undertone. 'This one is for the cameras.'

'What cam—?'

A flash went off but it wasn't from any lurking cameras. It was a flare inside Sienna's brain that almost took the top of her head off. As soon as Andreas's lips touched down on hers she felt a tectonic shift of her equilibrium. The world seemed to tilt on its axis.

His lips were firm and yet soft.

Warm and yet dry.

He tasted of…she wasn't quite sure. It was something she had never tasted before and yet it was incredibly addictive.

She wanted more.

She *craved* more.

Her hands went to the front of his chest. She could feel his heart thudding beneath her palm. It mimicked the erratic rhythm of hers. He felt warm and male and vital. He felt strong and capable and arrantly potent.

His tongue stroked along the seam of her lips, a bold and commanding stroke that didn't ask permission for entry, but rather *demanded* it.

She opened to him on a soft little whimper, her stomach dropping in delight as his tongue deftly found hers. She felt the stirring of his arousal, the hot, hard length of him swelling against her as his mouth wreaked sensual havoc on hers. She moved closer, an instinctive, almost involuntary shift against him that evoked a husky-sounding groan from his throat as he deepened the kiss even further.

'Ahem…' The celebrant cleared his throat. 'I have another ceremony in five minutes.'

Sienna stepped out of Andreas's hold, her heart still galloping like a racehorse on steroids. Her mouth was tingling, every nerve alive with feeling, her lips swollen and sensitive from the pressure of his. She ran the tip of her tongue over them and tasted his hot male potency. Her stomach gave another tripping movement as she looked up at his darkly hooded gaze…

A flash went off but this time it was the surge of the paparazzi.

'Looks like it's show time,' Andreas said grimly and,

taking her hand in his, led her towards the pack of journalists and photographers.

Sienna's emotions were in such turmoil she didn't want to examine them too closely. She had responded with such wantonness to Andreas. She had forgotten everything but the feel of his mouth on hers. The whole world had ceased to exist in that heart-stopping moment when he had kissed her with such fiery passion and intent. She had felt the primal rhythm of his blood through the surface of his lips. She hadn't wanted the kiss to end. Her insides were still trembling from the sensual onslaught of being in his arms.

It was at least an hour before they could escape. Her face felt stiff from all the fake smiling. Her head was aching and her feet were throbbing by the time they got back to where Franco was waiting for them in the car.

'That went remarkably well,' Andreas said once the partition between the driver and the passenger section was closed.

'You think?' Sienna bent down to prise off her shoes. 'Ouch! I've got blisters.'

'Elena will probably have an intimate dinner set up for us back at the villa,' he said. 'She's a hopeless romantic so just go along with it.'

'She reminds me of my flatmate Kate back in London,' Sienna said, closing her eyes and flinging her head back against the headrest in bone-aching fatigue. 'She thinks you're going to fall in love with me before the end of this and beg me to stay with you for ever.'

'I hope you put her straight on that.'

'I did,' she said flatly. 'She forgot to factor in the fact that I wouldn't stay on even if you paid me.'

Andreas gave a mocking laugh. 'If the price was right you'd stay.'

Sienna turned her head on the headrest to glare at him. 'Even you don't have enough money to buy me, Rich Boy,' she said. 'And, just for the record, I am *not* going to obey you.'

He gave her a supercilious smile. 'You just promised to do so in front of a legally appointed celebrant.'

'I don't care,' she said, throwing her head back and closing her eyes again. 'I am *not* going to bend to your will.'

'So what was that kiss all about?' he asked.

Sienna jerked upright in her seat to glower at him. 'That was your doing, not mine,' she said. 'I was all geared up for the hands-off clinical deal we'd agreed on and then you sideswipe me with a wedding kiss. That was low. That was *really* low.'

His look was smouldering, and it centred on her mouth just long enough to set her lips tingling all over again. 'It was a good kiss,' he said. 'I can see why you have the reputation you have. I was starting to think how it would feel to have those lips of yours on my—'

'Will you stop it, for God's sake?' Sienna hissed at him. 'My lips are going nowhere near your...your whatever. We're meant to be keeping this strictly to the terms.'

He was still looking at her mouth with that hooded dark gaze. 'We could always adjust the goalposts a little to suit our needs,' he said. 'After all, six months is a long time to be celibate.'

'It's not a long time for me.'

The words seemed to hang suspended in the air for a moment.

'How long is a long time for you?' Andreas asked.

Sienna felt the weight of his gaze but resolutely kept her head facing forward. 'How long is a piece of string?' she asked.

She heard him give a snort of derision. 'You have no idea, do you?' he said. 'Do you even know the names of some of the men you've slept with?'

'Not all of them,' Sienna answered with ironic truthfulness. 'Some men don't require a personal introduction before they sleep with you.'

Andreas let out a breath of disgust. 'You are such a shameless gold-digging whore,' he said. 'Don't you have any self-respect?'

'Plenty,' Sienna said, lifting her chin. 'I could've settled for the deal your father set up, but I know you'll pay more to have what you want. And you want it. You want it so badly you'll do anything to stop me from taking it from you.'

His hands went to white-knuckled fists on the armrests each side of him. 'You'd better believe it,' he said. 'Don't say you weren't warned.'

CHAPTER FIVE

As soon as the car pulled up in front of his villa, Andreas wanted to head to the furthest reaches of the property to put as much distance as he could between him and Sienna. He wanted to regroup before she made him lose control completely. But for the sake of Franco and Elena's presence he was forced to play the role of devoted husband, which included carrying his new bride over the threshold of the villa. He could already feel his blood simmering at the thought of holding her against his body.

Sienna gave a little gasp as he scooped her up in his arms. 'What are you doing?' she asked.

'It's considered bad luck not to carry one's bride over the threshold,' he said and strode to the door being held open by his housekeeper, who was smiling broadly.

Andreas felt his skin grow hot and tight where Sienna's arms had looped around his neck. Her right breast was pressed against his thumping heart and the fragrance of her alluring perfume teased his nostrils. She was lighter than he had expected and she fitted against him like a glove. He tried not to look at her mouth. Tried not to remember how it had felt to taste her moist hot sweetness. The taste of her lingered on his tongue; it was a potent potion as addictive as a drug. One taste was not going to be enough. It was never going to be enough. But then he had always known that. He had fought it for so long. This raw need to have her as his had been a part of his life for so long he had no idea how to subdue it. It was an ache that resided deep within him. It would not go away, no matter how much he distracted or disciplined himself.

He wanted her.

He lowered her to the floor by sliding her down the length of his body, his blood roaring in response to her curves as they brushed against him.

He wanted her and he would have her.

He heard the soft intake of her breath and saw the flare of her pupils as her eyes meshed with his. The barrier of their clothes was no barrier at all. They might as well have been standing there naked.

Sienna glowered up at him. 'Was that really necessary?'

'But of course,' Andreas said. 'Elena and Franco were watching.'

'Yeah, well, no one's watching now,' she said. 'Let's just step back into our true characters and tear strips off each other again.'

He gave a soft deep chuckle and pressed her even closer with his hand on the shapely curve of her bottom. 'Why the hurry, *ma petite*?' he said. 'I'm getting to like the feel of you against me. You like it too, *sì*?'

Her eyes were pools of stormy grey and blue. 'This is not part of the plan,' she said, but she didn't do anything to push him away. If anything her body shifted closer, a subtle movement that sent another hot lightning rod of lust straight to his groin.

'Is it not?' he asked with a mocking smile. 'You've planned this from the start. You want me to think twice about ending this marriage when the time is up.' He captured one of her hands and pressed his lips to each and every fingertip, watching as her eyes darkened with desire. 'And what better way than to entice me into your bed as soon as you can?'

Her gaze flicked to his mouth, her tongue sweeping over her lips. 'That's not what I'm planning at all,' she said in a breathless voice. 'I don't want to be married to you any longer than I have to be.'

Andreas's fingers tightened on hers. Her hand was dainty and small in the grasp of his. He could have broken her fingers with just the slightest pressure. He was so close to her he could feel her body warmth radiating through him. She smelt of summer, of jasmine and honeysuckle and red-hot temptation. The skin of her hand was soft against the roughness of his. He felt her fingers move experimentally against the cup of his palm, whether to test his hold or tease him, he wasn't quite sure. It shouldn't have had anywhere near the sensual impact it had. It felt as if she had dipped her hand down the front of his trousers and touched him flesh on flesh.

He brought his mouth down to hers for the second time that day, and for the second time in his life a seismic shift knocked him sideways.

She tasted of sweet, hot, forbidden longings. He couldn't get enough of her delicious moistness. He fed off her with a greed he hadn't known existed. He savaged her mouth like a hungry beast on a rampage.

It was rapacious. It was primitive. It was raw male lust let off the leash. He hadn't realised how out of control a kiss could get until he thrust through the seam of her lips in search of her tongue.

Hers was hot and moist and brazen. It danced with his in a tango that was as sexy as anything he had ever experienced. It shot fireworks off in his head. Desire filled him so tightly he thought he would explode. His teeth scraped against hers. She bit him and he bit her back. It only made him want her more.

He thrust a hand at the back of her head, his fingers burying deep into her scalp as he explored her mouth with a thoroughness that left both of them breathless. His hand found her breast. It filled his palm with sensual heat, the tight bud of her nipple pressing against him. She felt so damn good, so feminine and soft. His need pulsed and pounded against her belly.

He wanted her naked.

He wanted to see her silky skin, every gorgeous inch of it. He wanted to taste her feminine heat, to move his lips and tongue against her to make her scream with ecstasy. He wanted to drive himself deep within her honeyed warmth, to feel the tight grip of her body contracting around him as she came.

He started to lift up the skirt of her dress but she suddenly stepped back, turning away from him with her arms going across her body as if she were suffering a chill. 'I'm sorry, Andreas,' she said. 'I don't want to continue with this.'

'Is this part of your technique?' Andreas asked. 'To tempt and to tease?'

Her cheeks flushed with delicate colour. 'It was unfair of me to give you the wrong impression,' she said. 'I didn't mean to mislead you.'

'The impression you gave me is that you want me just as much as I want you,' he said.

'Yes, well, I'm sorry about that but I had no idea that was going to happen every time you kiss me,' she said with a return to her haughty air. 'Maybe you should keep your mouth to yourself for the rest of the time we have together.'

'Ah, but that would not be half as much fun, would it, *ma belle*?' he asked. 'I quite like kissing you. I am developing rather a hunger for it, actually.'

She challenged him with those incredible grey-blue eyes and that stubborn little uptilted chin. 'Then you'll have to satisfy your appetite elsewhere. I'm not going to be a rich man's mistress.'

'You're not my mistress,' he said. 'You're my wife.'

'Same difference, as far as I can see,' she threw back.

Andreas fought down his frustration and anger. She had been toying with him all along and he had been fool enough to fall for it. She knew how much he wanted her. It wasn't as if he could hide it. She had sensed it. Damn it, she had *felt* it.

And she wanted him. He'd have to be blind not to see it. He felt it in her kiss, in her touch and in the way she had pressed herself closer as if she had wanted to climb into his skin.

He would not rest until he had her where he wanted her.

Where he had always wanted her.

Sienna was the one woman who could make him lose all sense of control. He had sensed it all those years ago and had fought it determinedly.

But now was different.

Now there was nothing to stop them exploring the

heat and passion that was flaring between them every time they were in the same room.

He could hardly wait.

Sienna closed her bedroom door and leant back against it, her heart thumping like a jackhammer. Her breathing was still out of control and her insides quivered with a longing so intense she could barely stand up. They had been married only a matter of a couple of hours and already things were spinning dangerously out of control. She didn't want to feel this level of attraction, not to Andreas Ferrante, not to a man who hated her as much as he desired her. But what was she to do? Her mind said *no* but her body kept saying a resounding *yes*. It completely disregarded her common sense. Instead, it was set on a pathway to sensual hedonism that she could not control. She didn't want to end up like her mother, madly in love with a man who only saw her as a convenient outlet for his lust. Unrequited love for Andreas's father had destroyed her mother. After Guido Ferrante had rejected her so publicly, Nell had sunk into an alcohol and prescriptions drugs binge that had eventually killed her.

Sienna wasn't prepared to go down the same path of destruction. She was determined to keep her heart well guarded. Andreas was by far the most attractive man she had ever met and his kisses were a temptation she couldn't seem to resist, but that didn't mean she had to fall in love with him. She had thought herself in love with him as a teenager, but that had just been a youthful crush, an infatuation that had got totally out of hand. She was no longer that foolish star-struck teenager caught up in the fantasy of thinking a well-born rich and powerful man was the answer to all of her problems.

Things would be different this time.

She would do what other young women her age did and what men had been doing for centuries. She would separate her emotions from her physical needs. Sex would be just sex. Love would not come into it at all.

Sienna joined Andreas in the *salone* for the intimate celebration Elena had taken such delight in setting up for them. The housekeeper was clearly in her element, a beaming smile was spread across her face as she brought in an ice bucket and a bottle of vintage champagne.

'I have left everything ready for you in the dining room,' she said. 'You will prefer to be alone, *si*? It will be much more romantic.'

'*Grazie*, Elena,' Andreas said. 'I'm sure it will be delightful.'

'Thank you for going to so much trouble,' Sienna chimed in. 'I saw the dining room on my way past. It looks fabulous with all the candles and the food smells absolutely delicious.'

'Enjoy,' Elena said and bustled out, closing the door softly as she left.

Sienna went over to where Andreas was standing and handed him his mother's pearl necklace and earrings. 'I thought I'd better hand these back before I get too attached to them,' she said. 'I'm sure your next bride will appreciate the chance to carry on the tradition.'

He took them from her with an unreadable expression on his face. 'Thank you,' he said.

'So,' she said with forced brightness. 'Champagne, huh?'

'Yes,' he said. 'Would you like some?'

'Why not?'

Sienna watched as he unpeeled the foil cover and unwound the wire before he popped the cork. A soft flutter like wings passed over the floor of her belly as she thought of those hands on her breasts and other parts of her anatomy. He had beautiful hands. Not soft and unused to hard work, but strong and capable.

She took the bubbling glass of champagne from him and was about to take a sip when his voice stalled her.

'Shouldn't we make a toast?'

'Sure,' she said, holding her glass up. 'What shall we drink to?'

He clinked his glass against hers, his eyes holding hers in a steely little lockdown that made her spine tingle. 'To making love, not war.'

She looked at him archly. '*Love*, Andreas?' she said. 'Don't you mean sex?'

His eyes glinted smoulderingly as he gave her a half-smile. 'You want it as much as I do,' he said. 'There's no point pretending otherwise.'

Sienna gave a little indifferent shrug. 'I admit the thought of seeing what you're like in bed holds a certain fascination,' she said. 'But I don't want you getting any ideas that *if* we conduct an intimate relationship it will mean anything to me other than the satiation of physical lust.'

He held her gaze for a pulsing moment. 'If?'

She gave him a defiant look. 'If.'

He took a leisurely sip of his champagne. 'I think we both know this thing between us is not going to go away,' he said. 'The thing is, it can only last as long as six months. By that time we will both have achieved what we want and will be free to move on with our lives.'

Sienna toyed with the champagne flute with her fingers, determined to rattle his chain as much as she could. It was an impish urge in her she couldn't quite control. 'What if you want me to stay a little longer?' she asked. 'What if you get so used to having me around you don't want to let me go?'

His hazel eyes drilled into hers with burning intensity. 'I will let you go, Sienna,' he said. 'Make no mistake about that. You are not the woman I want to be my wife or the future mother of my children.'

Sienna wasn't expecting his cutting response to hurt, but it had and deeply. Having children of her own was a subject she had put to the back of her mind. It was one of those things she didn't want to think about. Her childhood had been so unsettled and chaotic, and her mother's example of mothering so poor, she had always felt worried she might not be a good mother herself. But to hear Andreas say she was a totally unsuitable candidate as the mother of his children made her feel crushed in that closely guarded centre of her being. No woman wanted to hear that sort of insult. It felt as if she had been stabbed in the heart. The pain was so acute and so raw it momentarily took her breath away. She was annoyed at herself for feeling so upset. It wasn't like her to be so emotionally ambushed by a throwaway comment.

She quickly disguised her feelings by pasting an insolent smile on her face. 'Just as well, because I'm not planning on ruining my figure any time soon for a brood of obnoxious brats,' she said. 'Even a billionaire's ones.'

Andreas's eyes hardened. 'Is your twin sister as selfish and shallow as you?' he asked.

Sienna took a sip of her champagne. 'You can find out for yourself when you meet her in a few weeks,' she said. 'I'm going to be her bridesmaid. You'll be expected to attend the wedding with me in Rome. Won't that be fun?'

'I can hardly wait,' he said dryly.

Sienna sat down and flung one leg over the other, idly swinging her ankle up and down. 'So, this proposed honeymoon,' she said. 'When do we leave?'

'Tomorrow morning,' he said. 'I can only be away a couple of days, three at the most. I have a lot of work on at the moment.'

'Is it absolutely necessary I come with you?' she asked.

'We've already had this discussion, Sienna,' he said a little impatiently. 'I'm sure your dog will survive the separation from you. I have already spoken to Franco about making sure it is taken care of.'

She gave him a narrow-eyed look. 'You're not going to get rid of him while my back is turned, are you?'

'While I don't share your enthusiasm for the mutt, I can see you've taken him on as some type of project,' he said. 'I just hope you won't be disappointed when he fails to live up to your expectations. He's half wild and quite possibly dangerous. You shouldn't let your guard down around him in case he reverts to form.'

'You sound as if you care about my welfare, Andreas,' Sienna said giving him a teasing smile. 'How touching.'

Andreas put his barely touched drink down. 'We should go and eat,' he said. 'I don't want the food to be spoiled.'

While the wedding ceremony had not been in line with Sienna's dreams, the wedding breakfast Andreas's housekeeper had prepared certainly was. Dish after delectable dish of local produce had been laid out in the dining room. There were hot dishes and cold ones, main ones and gorgeous desserts. Elena had even made a wedding cake. It was only a small one but it had been decorated with marzipan and white royal icing with fresh flowers as decoration. It even had a bride and groom on the top, and a silver knife with a satin ribbon tied around the handle lay ready.

It was a jarring reminder that none of this was for real.

'Gosh, will you check this out,' Sienna said. 'Elena's made us a wedding cake. Isn't that sweet?' She leaned down to peer at the plastic figures standing together. 'And the groom even looks like you, see? He looks all stiff and formal.'

Andreas gave her an irritated look. 'She shouldn't have gone to so much trouble.'

'No point complaining,' Sienna said as she picked up a plate. 'You're the one who insisted on telling everyone this is the real deal.'

'And what would you have done in my place?' he asked in an embittered tone. 'Told everyone you know—including the world's media—that you've been manipulated by your father into marrying a sleep-around gold-digging slut? I would be laughed out of town, if not the country.'

The words echoed in the silence.

Sienna put the plate she was holding down on the sideboard with calculated precision in case she was tempted to throw it at his face. Then, turning to face him, she gave him the coldest look she could muster. 'Enjoy your dinner,' she said. 'I hope it damn well chokes you.'

She moved past him to leave but he blocked her with his body. 'Sienna,' he said.

Sienna refused to even look at him. 'Get out of my way,' she said through tight lips. 'I don't want to talk to you.'

He put a hand on the top of her nearest shoulder but she jerked back out of his grasp. 'Don't you dare touch me,' she said, glaring at him furiously. 'I can't bear it when you touch me.'

His green and brown-flecked eyes challenged hers. 'We both know that's not true.'

'It *is* true,' she said. 'I hate you. I hate the way you think you can just crook your little finger and get what you want just because you're rich and powerful. You can't have me.'

'I *can* have you,' Andreas said with steely conviction. 'I can have you any time I want. That's what you're frightened of, isn't it, Sienna? You don't like it that you want me. You like it when you're in the driver's seat, but you can't be with me. You can't call the shots with me, *ma chérie*, because I'm not playing by your rules.'

Sienna tried to get past him again but he made a roadblock with his arm. Her belly tingled when she came into contact with those strongly corded muscles and she immediately sprang back as if he had burned her. 'Move out of my way or I'll hit you,' she warned.

His mouth curled upwards mockingly. 'Go on, I dare you,' he said. 'Show me what a little guttersnipe you really are.'

The hair trigger on her temper suddenly snapped. Sienna flung herself at him. She felt the tornado of her anger and frustration propel her forwards with such force she surprised even herself. Her fist landed a punch to his abdomen but it bounced off as if she had struck a slab of stone.

She slapped at his face but his hand came up and deflected it with a deftness that was as swift as it was effective.

She tried to kick him in the shins but somehow his thighs were so close to hers all she could do was make little shuffling movements with her feet that did nothing other than remind her how seriously outmatched she was.

There was only one avenue left and it wasn't one she normally used. She couldn't even understand why she was using it now. It bubbled up from nowhere, catching her off guard. Emotions she normally hid under layers of sass and cheek suddenly rose to the surface. She burst into tears but, thank God, it worked like a charm.

Andreas dropped his hold as if she were on fire. 'What the hell?' he said.

Sienna knew she wasn't the prettiest crier on the planet. Not only did her nose go bright red but it streamed as well, and her eyes got pink and swollen, and if she really got going she couldn't speak past the hiccups.

'Sienna,' he said, taking her by the upper arms. 'Stop it. Stop crying. Stop it right now.'

'I...I can't,' she blubbered.

He let out a whooshing breath. 'I'm sorry,' he said. 'I pushed you too far. I can't seem to help myself.' He pulled her into the cradle of his arms, one of his hands pressing against the back of her head. 'Come on, *ma petite*. Don't cry, please. I didn't meant to upset you like this.'

Sienna should have pushed back from him at that point but something about the warm, strong protective circle of his arms struck a chord inside her that insisted she stay right where she was. It felt good to have his heart beating right against her cheek. It felt amazing to have his hand pressed against her head in such a gentle and tender manner. It felt wonderful to have his other arm around her in a band of iron that made her feel safe in a way she had never felt before. His body felt so warm and solid. So dependable, so fortress-like she wanted to stay there for ever.

The breeze of his warm breath ruffled her hair when he spoke. 'This is not like you, *ma belle*. Has today been too much for you? I should have realised. You've had a lot to do to prepare. Leaving your flat and your friends in London, moving in with me and handling the press's interest in us. It's a lot to cope with in a very short time.'

Sienna gave a big noisy sniff and he dug in his pocket for a handkerchief. 'Here,' he said. 'Dry your eyes, *cara*.'

She buried her nose in the clean linen and pulled herself together with an effort. 'Sorry,' she said. 'I don't know what came over me. I don't do this normally.'

He brushed her hair out of her eyes with a gentle hand. 'I've been a brute to you,' he said. 'It's not helping anything, is it? We're stuck together and we have to make the most of it. It won't make the time go any faster by trading insults.'

Sienna rolled his handkerchief into a soggy ball in her hand. 'I'm sorry about hitting you.'

He gave a wry smile. 'I didn't feel a thing.'

She pressed her lips together, feeling a little more exposed and vulnerable than she cared for. 'Would you mind if I gave dinner a miss?' she asked. 'I think I'll have an early night. I have a bit of a headache.'

'Can I get you anything for it?' he asked. 'Some painkillers?'

She shook her head. 'No, I'll be fine. I always get a headache when I cry. It'll pass.'

She moved across to the door, stopping to turn to face him before she left. 'I'm really sorry, Andreas,' she said.

'You don't have to apologise,' he said. 'I was the one who was out of line.'

She chewed at her bottom lip for a moment. 'I'm not only talking about just now...'

His whole body stilled, as if every muscle and cell inside him had come to a sudden halt. His expression was like a mask, not even his eyes gave anything away.

It seemed a very long time before he spoke. 'Go to bed, Sienna,' he said. 'I will see you in the morning.'

Sienna slipped out of the room, closing the door softly behind her and, with a heart that felt like a dumb-bell inside her chest, quietly made her way upstairs.

CHAPTER SIX

DURING the journey to Provence Sienna could sense Andreas was making an effort to be polite and solicitous towards her. Whether it was for the benefit of any lurking press, or whether it was because he had taken on board her attempt to apologise for her behaviour all those years ago was still open to question.

Andreas had explained on the way in the car from Marseille that the chateau had been in his mother, Evaline's, family for generations, but since his uncle Jules had died some years ago without leaving an heir, the place had been left to Andreas's father in Evaline's will.

Although he didn't say anything specific, Sienna could tell Andreas was intensely frustrated that his mother hadn't changed her will before she'd died. Sienna knew for a fact that Evaline had found out about Guido's affair with Sienna's mother Nell several weeks before her death, but she had been desperately ill with aggressive rounds of chemotherapy. Sienna suspected Evaline hadn't had the energy or wherewithal to correct things before it was too late. She also suspected Evaline had been hopeful that her husband's affair was just a one-off thing that would soon pass.

As Andreas drove up the long entrance to the chateau, Sienna drew in a breath of wonder. She had seen pictures of the Chateau de Chalvy in the past, but it was completely different witnessing the exquisite beauty of the centuries-old chateau face to face.

Lavender fields lay in front of the chateau, while rolling green hills and pastures and the mountains beyond were its backdrop. A distant field of bright red poppies danced in the warm summer breeze. The air was fresh and fragrant and the birdsong from the shrubbery in the chateau's gardens was such a delight to hear after the bustle and busyness of the airport.

The tempting thought of actually owning this piece of paradise came back, but stronger this time. It dangled like an irresistible lure in front of her. If Andreas left her before the six months was up, all of this would be hers. Every hectare of fertile land, every ancient stone of the chateau and its surrounding buildings, every bloom of every fragrant flower and every blade of grass would be legally hers.

It made her heart thump excitedly. Was it mercenary of her to want a place like this? No one would be able to kick her out. No one would be hammering on the door for unpaid rent. She would feel secure for the first time in her life. She would have a roof over her head that no one could take away. It would be hers and hers alone.

But it could only be hers if Andreas called an early end to their marriage.

As Andreas was helping her from the car, the estate manager Jean-Claude Perrault and his wife Simone greeted them. The French couple were obviously keen to show Andreas that they were worthy caretakers of his mother's beloved estate, although their formality with Sienna was annoying. According to the Perraults, Sienna might be Andreas's wife, but she was a foreigner, and a British one at that.

After refreshments were served, Jean-Claude suggested he take Andreas on a quick tour of the property while Simone helped Sienna to settle in.

Sienna followed the Frenchwoman upstairs to where a suite had been specially prepared for their stay. Heirloom linen had been taken out of storage and washed and ironed, and the big walnut bed dusted and polished. Sienna didn't like to tell Simone that she and Andreas weren't actually sharing a room, so she just smiled and complimented Simone on the lovely décor and the fresh flowers sitting on the antique dressing table and on a chest of drawers.

'This has always been the bridal suite,' Simone said. 'For centuries, Chalvy brides have started their married life here. It has the best view of the lavender fields. It is a pity you can't stay longer. It is a very short honeymoon, but then Monsieur Ferrante is a very busy man, no?'

'Very busy,' Sienna agreed.

'I'll leave you to rest,' Simone said, some of her earlier formality softening slightly. 'Dinner will be served at eight-thirty. I have organised a chef from the village to prepare a celebratory meal for you both.'

'That was very kind of you,' Sienna said.

'Not at all,' Simone said. 'This is the first time in many years that Monsieur Ferrante has been to the Chateau de Chalvy estate. It is a time to celebrate both that and your marriage. Jean-Claude and I are happy he is finally settled. For a time we wondered if he would be like his uncle and never marry.'

'You mean Andreas's uncle Jules?'

Simone nodded as she smoothed the perfectly neat bedcover. 'He was very much a playboy,' she said. 'Definitely not a one-woman man, if you know what I mean. His sister Evaline, on the other hand, only ever had eyes for Andreas's father. She fell in love with him as a teenager. It was a happy marriage until…' She gave a discomfited smile, two spots of colour pooling high on her cheekbones. 'I should not be gossiping like one of the village girls. Forgive me. I forgot your connection to the family. I did not mean to offend you.'

'It's all right,' Sienna said. 'I understand my mother's involvement with Andreas's father caused a lot of pain for a lot of people.'

'I suppose no one really knows what goes on in a marriage other than the two people involved,' Simone said with a little sigh. 'Evaline loved Guido to the day she died, but I suspect he might not have loved her at all. Some men are like that, especially rich men. They can have anyone they want and they know it.'

Sienna couldn't have agreed more. Didn't her marriage to Andreas prove it?

'I have a problem,' Sienna said as soon as she found Andreas in the garden of the chateau. She had spied him from the window of their suite and had immediately come down to speak to him. He was standing on some flagstones next to a fishpond where some frogs were croaking volubly. Water lilies floated on the surface of the pond and every now and again a flash of bright orange came to the top as a goldfish came in search of food.

'Let me guess,' Andreas said with a flicker of his signature mocking smile. 'You forgot your hair straighteners?'

She gave him a speaking glance. 'I am *not* sharing a room with you,' she said, 'especially the bridal suite. Do you have any idea of the trouble Simone has gone to? It's like she was expecting royalty to arrive. There are flowers on just about every surface and the linen your great-great-great-grandparents slept in has been brought out of storage and is on the bed, for God's sake!'

He took her arm and looped it through one of his and led her away from the fishpond to a long avenue of yew trees that led to a magnificent fountain. 'There are workers about, *ma chérie*,' he said. 'Keep your voice down.'

Sienna felt her breast brush against his arm and suppressed a shiver of forbidden delight. 'You have to do something, Andreas,' she insisted.

'There's no need to get all het up about it,' he said. 'It's only for a couple of nights. Besides, we can't break with the Chalvy tradition. Every new bride spends her first night there with her husband. It's been that way for hundreds of years.'

She stopped in her tracks and glared up at him. 'You knew about this all along, didn't you?' she said. 'You knew it and didn't warn me.'

'To be quite honest, I'd forgotten about the tradition until you mentioned the linen,' he said. 'My grandmother was the last Chalvy bride, as my mother married my father in Italy and only came back for occasional visits well into their marriage. And my uncle never married, so you are the first new bride to stay here since.'

'Aren't you forgetting a minor detail here?' Sienna asked. 'I'm not a Chalvy bride. I'm a Ferrante bride.'

Something moved at the back of his eyes as they held hers, something dark and pulsing. 'According to the tradition, a bride is a bride no matter who she belongs to,' he said.

Sienna narrowed her eyes at him. 'I don't belong to you, Andreas,' she said. 'And you'd better not forget it.'

His lips curved upwards as he captured both of her hands in his and brought her closer. 'Stop scowling and start smiling like a blushing bride, *cara*,' he said. 'There's a gardener clipping a hedge about twenty metres away.'

Sienna felt the brush of Andreas's hard male body against her stomach and a flare of heat rushed through her. Her gaze went to his mouth, that beautiful, sinfully sculpted mouth that had already done so much damage to her equilibrium. It was impossible to ignore the way her body reacted to his. His proximity, his touch, even his hazel gaze sent an electric jolt of awareness through her. Her breasts rose to sensitive peaks against his chest as he brought her a little bit closer, and then her stomach plunged when he lowered his mouth to hers.

His lips were firm but gentle as they played with hers: a soft press, a lift-off, another soft press and then a slightly firmer, more insistent one. Then his tongue stroked over her bottom lip, making it tingle and fizz with sensation. She opened to him on a soft gasp and her stomach plummeted even further when his tongue masterfully took control of hers. He cajoled it into an erotic duel, leaving her in no doubt who was going to win the sensual war in the end. He'd had her at his mercy from the first moment his lips touched hers. She was boneless within seconds, leaning into him, desperate to feel more of his magical touch...to feel the urgency of his need against hers...to feel the potency of his raw male desire. It made her feel dizzy with longing. The need crept through her like a stealthy opponent on a covert mission. She didn't want to feel so out of control but her body was hungry for every erotic feeling he was tempting her with.

He drove a splayed hand through her hair, tilting her head so he could kiss her deeper and longer, the rough stubble of his jaw scraping along her softer skin. She lost herself in the frenzied fever of his kiss. It was urgent, it was boldly insistent and, with that captivating edge of taboo about it, it made her forget about the past or the future. She was totally in the moment and the moment was all about him and how he made her feel.

His hand went from her head to slide down to the dip in her spine, pulling her against the jut of his erection. It was shockingly, shamelessly intimate. It made every sensible thought fly out of her head. She was suddenly and totally reduced to raw physical need.

His mouth lifted off hers as his gaze drilled smoulderingly into hers. 'Still want separate bedrooms?' he asked.

Sienna drew in a sharp little breath that was connected to something deep in the pit of her belly. 'I'm starting to see there could be some benefits to airing that musty old linen,' she conceded wryly.

He gave a spine-tingling chuckle as he cupped her face in his hands. 'I like how you make me laugh, *ma petite*,' he said. 'You don't kowtow to me like a lot of women do. I like that you are spirited and feisty. You always stand your ground with me.'

Sienna wished she could find some ground to stand on, but right now she was on the rockiest platform she had ever occupied. She was teetering on the edge of throwing caution to the wind and diving head first into a passionate affair with Andreas, no matter what the cost to her ultimately. She looked into his gaze and felt another layer of her resolve peel away like a slough of old useless skin.

She wanted him.

She had *always* wanted him.

She could have him for six months.

The thought was more than a temptation. It was a statement of intent. The rationalisations began in her head. It was a finite time. She would be able to walk away when it was over. She knew the rules from the outset and so did he. It was a convenient arrangement, a no-strings affair that had benefits for them both. She wouldn't fall in love with him and he wouldn't fall in love with her. It would be an exciting erotic interlude to pass the time while they were shackled together in marriage. God knew she could do with the experience of a red-hot affair. Her body was craving an outlet for the sensuality denied her for so long.

Andreas stroked the broad pad of his thumb over Sienna's bottom lip, his hazel eyes meshing with hers in simmering heat. 'You know how much I want you,' he said. 'You've known it from the start. I think my father must have known it too, otherwise why would he have orchestrated this?'

Sienna salved her tingling lips with a quick darting sweep of her tongue. 'I meant what I said last night,' she said. 'I'm sorry I acted the way I did when I was seventeen. I panicked when your father came in. I didn't want my mother to lose her job. It was the first time I'd seen her really happy. I didn't want to be the one who wrecked everything for her. I didn't think things would get so out of hand. I didn't think you would leave and never come back.'

'There were lots of reasons I didn't come back,' he said, dropping his hands from her face to walk with her back towards the chateau. 'My father and I always had a difficult relationship. We locked horns on many things. He didn't want me to pursue my furniture design work. But I wanted to work for my wealth, not simply inherit it from him and his father and grandfather before him. I wanted to make my own way, not stand on anyone's shoulders. My father took that as a slight. He liked to have control, but I refused to play by his rules.'

Sienna walked alongside him, wondering if he would ever forgive her for her shameless behaviour. She had made his already strained relationship with his father so much worse. No wonder he hated her so much. She had ruined any chance of him making peace before his father had died. How could she expect him to overlook that as just a bit of immaturity on her part? 'I didn't re-alise the reason my mother was so happy was because she was having an affair with your father,' she said after a little silence. 'I think I would've acted differently if I'd known about that at the time.'

He stopped walking and turned to look down at her, an embittered frown slicing between his dark brows. 'Your mother wanted a quick leg up in life,' he said. 'She ruthlessly set her sights on my father. He was to be her next meal ticket. To this day I don't understand why he was so foolish to get involved with a shame-less slut like her.'

'My mother loved him,' Sienna said, glaring at him for painting such a tawdry picture of her mother. 'He was the only man she had ever loved. She told me a few days before she died. Her life before that had been a litany of meaningless affairs. But once she met your father she fell deeply in love. She was devastated when he refused to acknowledge her publicly. I think she thought after your mother passed away that he would marry her.'

Andreas's expression was cynical. 'Are you sure it was him she loved or the lifestyle he could give her?' he asked.

Sienna gave him another flinty glare. 'I don't expect you to understand what love feels like,' she said. 'You're exactly like your father in that sense. You take what you want from people and give nothing back. Emotion doesn't come into it. Your life is a series of cold, hard business deals conducted one after the other.'

'Ah, but is that not just like you?' Andreas asked with a sardonic slant to his mouth. 'You married Brian Littlemore for money. You have married me for exactly the same reason. Is that not rather cold and business-like? You want money in exchange for your body, but you will not give your heart.'

'Do you *want* my heart, Andreas?' she asked with a deliberately taunting look.

His gaze ran over her like the scorching stroke of a naked flame. 'I think you know what I want,' he said. 'It's what we both want. And tonight there is nothing to stop us from having it.'

She lifted her chin at him. 'I haven't said I'll sleep with you.'

He bent his head and pressed a brief but searing kiss to her mouth. 'Not yet, but you will,' he said, flashing one of his satirical smiles. 'You won't be able to help yourself.'

'Let's see about that, shall we?' she said.

He touched her cheek with a soft brushstroke of one of his fingers, his eyes burning hers with the glinting fire of his. 'I can hardly wait,' he said and, with another mocking smile, he left.

CHAPTER SEVEN

SIENNA felt in an edgy mood by the time she joined Andreas for pre-dinner drinks downstairs. She had successfully managed to avoid him since their meeting in the garden but she had been aware of him all the same. She had heard him come upstairs to shower and change for dinner. She had imagined him standing under the showerhead as she had done only minutes before, his body lean and tanned, all rippling muscles and toned naked male flesh. Her stomach had triple somersaulted at the thought of standing there with him, of feeling his hard body dividing the softness of hers to claim her as his. Her body seemed to be intent on having what her mind tried so valiantly to resist. Her traitorous body was clamouring for more of his touch, for more of his kisses, for flesh on flesh contact—for everything.

And Andreas—damn him—knew it.

Sienna entered the large *salon* overlooking the chateau's formal garden with her nerves jangling in irritation. 'Where are Jean-Claude and Simone?' she asked. 'Aren't they joining us?'

Andreas gave her a crooked smile that made his eyes glint. 'It's our honeymoon, *ma chérie*,' he said. 'Four's a crowd, don't you think?'

She averted her gaze and reached for the champagne he had poured for her. 'I can see why you wanted to secure this place,' she said to change the subject. 'It's very beautiful.'

'My mother loved it here,' he said. 'She wanted her grandchildren to grow up like Miette and I did, with both French and Italian cultural experiences.'

Sienna looked at the bubbles in her glass, trying not to think of Andreas's future children running about the chateau and its gardens. It was unsettling to think of him with some other faceless woman on his arm, a woman he had selected as prime wife material. Or maybe he would take Portia Briscoe back once his brief marriage to Sienna was over. But that thought was even more upsetting. The more she knew of Andreas, the less suited Portia seemed to be for him. Couldn't *he* see that?

'Was Miette upset that the chateau was left to you and not to her?' Sienna asked after a little silence.

'My sister was more upset it was co-inherited by you,' he said. 'She is worried you will do everything in your power to make me default.'

Sienna could see why his sister would feel the way she did about her. Their relationship during the time she had lived with the family had been fraught with tension. Many a petty or bitchy argument had broken out between them, which, to be fair, Sienna knew she was largely responsible for. She had been insanely jealous of Miette as the only daughter of the Ferrante dynasty. To Sienna, Miette was everything she was not. Miette had two parents who adored her, an older brother who was loving and protective towards her, and she had grown up with the sort of wealth that meant she never had to worry about anything other than what designer brand to choose over another. Like Andreas, Miette had been to the best schools and university. Miette had even spent a year at a Swiss finishing school before she'd moved to London, where she had met her now equally well-heeled husband. Miette's life was the dream life Sienna had always wanted for herself. 'What did you say to her?' she asked before taking a sip of her drink.

'I told her not to worry,' he said. 'I am well aware of the tricks you might feel compelled to play.'

Sienna shrugged off his comment. 'Well, you can assure her I only want the money,' she said. 'The chateau is nice and all that, but what would I do with a place this size? I'd have to sell it. I could never afford to maintain it. The heating bills in winter must be crucifying.'

Andreas took a sip of his drink, still watching her with his hazel eyes. 'Just so you know, Sienna,' he said. 'I will not be tricked out of inheriting this property. You can do the time the nice way or the hard way but, either way, I am not leaving until I inherit what rightly belongs to my family.'

'Fine,' Sienna said, throwing him a testy look. 'But the same goes for you. I'm not going to be forced out by your brooding, boorish behaviour or your bad moods.'

Andreas gave an ironic chuckle. 'You're a fine one to talk of bad moods,' he said. 'You've been spoiling for a fight from the moment you stepped in the room. I can see it in your eyes. They've been flashing like sheet lightning for the last five minutes.'

Sienna glared at him. 'Maybe that has something to do with your own chicanery in making sure I have no choice but to sleep in your bed,' she said.

'What is the problem with sharing a bed that is large

enough to house a family of five?' Andreas asked. 'I bet I won't even notice you're there.'

She set her mouth. 'Just another nameless woman lying beside you, eh? Nice one, Andreas. You have such class.'

'Are you jealous?' he asked.

'Of course not!' Sienna gave her head a toss. 'It's just that I don't like the thought of you suddenly forgetting who's lying beside you. You might take liberties that I'm not comfortable with.'

'Take liberties?' He gave a little snort of amusement. 'You sound like someone out of a Regency period drama. What, are you worried I might see one of your naked ankles or wrists, are you? I've seen a lot more of you than that, Sienna, and you know it. So, too, did most of the cyber world when your little bedroom peccadillo was aired, so don't play the outraged virgin card with me. It just won't wash.'

Sienna turned away so he couldn't see the way her cheeks coloured up. She concentrated on drinking her champagne, desperately trying to appear cool and collected when inside she was anything but. She hated him for reminding her of that wretched event. How like him to needle her with her past, the past she wanted to forget about, the past she wished had never happened. She pretended it didn't hurt but it did. Every time she saw a photo or snippet about herself in the press she cringed in shame. How could her life have come to that?

'Dinner will be waiting for us,' Andreas said after a moment. 'I hope you're hungry?'

Sienna gave him one of her arch looks. 'It sure beats making small talk, doesn't it?' she said and sashayed past him to the dining room.

* * *

Dinner was a tense affair. Sienna knew she wasn't help-ing things by being prickly but she resented the way Andreas always saw the worst in her. He assumed she would try to wangle him out of his inheritance, but if it weren't for the money she needed to kick-start her life she would have already defaulted so he could have the chateau. She wanted to be free of him just as much as he wanted to be free of her.

Well, maybe that wasn't quite true, she thought as she toyed with her glass. The physical fascination she felt for him was something that drew her to him irrespec-tive of the ill feeling between them. She could feel the tension of it brewing in the air. It was an atmospheric change that occurred every time they were on their own.

Knowing he wanted her made her need for him all the harder to ignore. She could feel the traitorous pulse of it in her blood, the way her insides clenched every time his gaze encountered hers. Those tense little eye-locks unfurled something deep inside her until she had to look away or betray herself completely.

'More wine?' Andreas offered.

Sienna covered her glass with her hand. 'I think I've had enough, thank you.'

There was a ghost of a smile in his eyes. 'Always wise to know when to stop, *si*?' he said.

She gave him a direct look. 'Do you know when to stop, Andreas?' she asked. 'Or do you keep going just because you can?'

He sat back and surveyed her for a moment before he answered. 'I don't believe in losing control in any area of my life.'

She raised a questioning brow at him. 'Not even dur-ing sex?'

He continued to hold her gaze with an intensity she found both thrilling and unsettling. 'It depends on what you mean by losing control,' he said. 'If you mean do I lose myself in the moment of orgasm, then yes, that is exactly what happens.'

Sienna knew her face was hot. She could feel it. So too was her body. Just the thought of him losing control—*having an orgasm*—with her was enough to send her senses spinning all over the place.

'You're blushing, *ma belle*,' he said with a slanting smile.

'I'm not blushing,' she retorted. 'It's hot in here.'

He rose from the table and opened one of the windows, letting in the fragrant night air. 'Better?' he asked, turning back to face her.

Sienna felt the caress of his gaze. It touched her from head to foot, lingering on the upthrust of her breasts just long enough for the fiery combustion of her need to engulf her.

She felt the tingle of her flesh as he came towards her, his eyes still doing that erotic little tussle with hers, as if he was already making love with her in his mind, running through the images of their naked limbs entangled, their bodies joined in the most intimate way possible.

Her body shivered involuntarily. She could almost feel his hard male presence inside her. It started as a tiny flicker and then it became a pulse that was like a distant drumbeat inside her, growing in intensity as each sensually charged second passed.

Sienna swallowed as he came towards her with slow but purposeful strides. Her heart gave a stumble as he stood right beside her chair, the tip of his index finger lifting her chin to face him. 'What are we going to do about this tricky little situation between us, hmm?' he asked.

She rose to her feet as if he had drawn her up by tugging on invisible puppet strings. Her body was within a hair's breadth of his, her insides coiling tightly with lust. 'I don't know,' she said a little too huskily. 'Ignore it?'

His mouth tilted in that sexy smile again as his thumb brushed over her bottom lip. 'Sounds like a good idea in theory,' he said. 'How do you propose we do that in practice?'

Sienna swept her tongue over her lip where his thumb had just been and tasted the salt of him. A shockwave of longing rippled through her. She felt the rush of her blood and the hot tingle of feminine want darted like an expertly aimed arrow deep inside her. 'I don't know,' she said, trying to keep her tone light and unaffected. 'Do you have any suggestions?'

His hazel eyes pulsed as they held hers. 'Just the one,' he said in a deep gravel-rough voice.

Her gaze drifted to his mouth and her heart gave another little tripping movement. 'I sure hope it's a good one,' she said so softly it was barely audible.

'It is,' he said and, taking her by the upper arms and pulling her against him, chest pressed to chest, he bent his head and covered her mouth with his.

His lips were neither soft nor hard but somewhere right in between. They moved with mesmerising magic on the surface of hers before he took things to another blistering level with the bold and commanding thrust of his tongue.

It was like a flame let loose amongst bone-dry tinder. The kiss was suddenly hot and hard and urgent, just as hot and hard and as feverishly urgent as his body pressed against hers.

His hands went from their grip on her upper arms to slide down to her waist, one hand slipping behind her to press in the small of her back to hold her against the heated trajectory of his body. She moved against him, an instinctive and utterly primal movement that signalled her rapidly escalating need for him.

His mouth explored hers with spine-tingling expertise. His tongue played with hers, teasing and flirting at first, but then with increasing demand as his desire to mate took hold. She felt it in his body, the way he hardened and throbbed against her. Her body responded automatically. It softened and melted against him, her desperate need to get closer taking over whatever objections her scrambled mind tried to put up.

One of his hands skimmed over her breast in a teasing motion that set every nerve beneath her skin on fire. She whimpered against his mouth, pushing closer, desperate to have him hold her, to caress her, to touch her, to brand her with his lips and tongue.

He continued to kiss her deeply as his hand came back, firmer this time, cupping her, caressing her through the thin barrier of her dress and lacy bra. It was like torture not to have him as close as she wanted him. But then, as if he read her mind, or her body, or indeed both, he slid the shoulder of her dress aside. His warm dry hand on the skin of her neck and shoulder made her flesh sing with delight. He pushed the strap of her bra aside and then lowered his mouth to her skin. She shuddered in response when his tongue grazed the soft skin stretched tightly over her collarbone.

She snatched in a breath when he pushed the lace cup

of her bra away. Her belly clenched with a hard fist of desire as his warm breath skated over her naked breast before his mouth closed over her achingly tight nipple. Thousands of fiery explosions went off beneath her skin at that toe-curling caress. His teeth and tongue teased her into a frenzy of want she had never imagined possible. The sensation of having his mouth suck on her made the hair on her head tingle at the roots.

Sienna slid her hands up his chest to work on his buttons; one by one she released them, kissing each section of his hot salty skin as she exposed it.

He made a deep sound at the back of his throat as she went lower, his hands fisting in her hair as she got to his waistband. The jut of his erection tented his trousers and she boldly touched him, caressing the length of him, delighting in the feel of him as he shuddered in response.

He made another deep guttural sound and pulled her down with him to the floor, his mouth slamming back down on hers as he pinned her with his weight. It was a bruising kiss but she was with him all the way, nipping at his lower lip, her teeth tugging and pulling at him in a desperate urge for satiation. His tongue thrust and stroked, cajoled and teased and finally tamed hers. In between hot searing kisses he got her dress off and her bra and knickers in a wild tangle of fabric and limbs that made Sienna's heart race with excitement. She only got his shirt off and his belt. There was barely time for the application of a condom before her head snapped back on the carpeted floor as he drove into her with a thick, hard thrust that made her cry out in sharp and sudden discomfort.

He froze above her. 'What's wrong?'

'Nothing,' Sienna said, quickly averting her eyes from his. 'It's been a long time, that's all.'

He captured her chin and made her look at him. 'How long?' he asked.

Sienna caught her bottom lip with her teeth. 'A while...'

His frown deepened, making a criss-cross of lines over his forehead and between his eyes. 'How long is a while?' he asked.

She gave a little shrug, secretly holding her breath. 'I can't really remember.'

His eyes were narrowed in focus. 'You mean it is a while since you slept with your husband?' he said.

Sienna found it hard to lie to him when she was facing him eye to eye. 'I never slept with Brian,' she said.

His face blanched, his eyes shrinking back in their sockets as if she had struck him across the face. 'What?' he asked.

'It was a marriage of convenience,' she said. 'Brian wanted a wife in name only. I wanted the respectability of marrying well. It was a mutually satisfying agreement.'

Andreas pulled away from her and got to his feet in an agitated manner. He zipped up his trousers and then snatched up his discarded shirt and handed it to her. 'Here,' he said in a gruff tone. 'Put this on while I get your things.'

Sienna slipped her arms through the long sleeves and wrapped herself in his warmth and smell. His shirt didn't offer the same dignity as her clothes would have done but at least it covered her nakedness.

She watched as he gathered up her clothes from the floor, his hands folding them with meticulous care when only minutes ago he had been all but ripping them from her body. His brow was furrowed with a preoccupied frown as if he was having trouble processing what she had told him.

He came back over and handed the tidy pile to her, his eyes meshing with hers. 'I hurt you,' he said, his voice grave. 'I'm sorry.'

'You didn't hurt me…not really,' Sienna said.

'Why didn't you tell me?' he asked, still frowning.

'Tell you what?' she said. 'That I haven't had sex in ages? You wouldn't have believed me. The press make it pretty clear I'm up for it with anyone any time. Why would you take my word over theirs?'

'Why do you let them write that stuff without defending yourself?' he asked.

She gave an indifferent shrug. 'I don't care what people think. I know what's true. That's all that matters.'

'Why didn't you have a normal marriage with Brian Littlemore?' he asked. 'He paraded you about enough times. You were always at some gala event hanging off his arm like a trophy. Was it really all an act?'

Sienna wished she'd kept her mouth shut. What was *with* her tonight? Such honesty and openness was totally out of character. Before she knew it she'd be spilling the beans on Brian's 'mistress', the male lover he had adored even before he had married his wife Ruth and fathered three children with her. It wasn't her secret to tell. She had promised Brian on his deathbed she would honour his decision to protect his children from the knowledge of his true sexual orientation. But she realised she would have to be a little more careful around Andreas. He wasn't the sort to be fobbed off and lied to. His sharp intelligent gaze saw too much as it was.

'I'd rather not talk about it,' she said, hugging her pile of clothes close to her body. 'Brian was good to me. I don't regret being married to him. He looked after me.'

Andreas screwed up his face. 'He had a mistress, for God's sake,' he said. 'How could you have so little self-respect to allow that to continue right under your nose?'

Sienna squeezed her clothes even tighter against her body. 'I told you I don't want to talk about it.'

He studied her for a long moment, his gaze narrowing slightly. 'You married him soon after the sex tape scandal, didn't you?' he asked. 'It was only a few weeks or so, wasn't it?'

She kept her expression closed. 'What of it?'

'What happened that night?' he asked. 'What happened that made you suddenly run off and marry a man nearly forty years older than yourself?'

Sienna couldn't hold his penetrating gaze. She stared at the middle of his chest instead. Her chest felt tight and heavy with all the regret she carried inside. She had made such a mess of her life and her sister's. Maybe it was time to air some of her guilt. To confess how awful she felt about what had happened. Why she felt compelled to confess it to Andreas was something she would have to think about later.

'I was out drinking with friends,' she said. 'The girls I hung around with were regular binge drinkers but I never let myself get totally wasted. But that night…I must have had more than I realised or not drunk enough water or something. I don't remember much other than waking up in some guy's hotel room. I didn't know who he was. He was naked. I was naked. I was so ashamed of myself. For the first time I started to feel like the slut the press had always painted me. Before, I used to laugh it off when they wrote something about me being a bed-hopper because I'd only had sex twice.' She gave a little humourless laugh. 'By today's standards, I'm practically still a virgin. But after that night I felt like I deserved it for not taking responsibility for my actions.'

'Did you ever consider you might have been the victim of a drink spike?' Andreas asked, frowning.

Sienna tried to shrug it off. 'I did wonder about that but, even so, it was still my fault for being so careless,' she said. 'I should've chosen my friends a little more carefully. I think they enjoyed seeing me pulled down a peg or two. I was always the one who kept her head. That night certainly put an end to that.'

'Sienna,' he said heavily, 'you were a victim of a crime. Why didn't you report it to the police?'

'Who would have believed me?' she asked. 'Like mother, like daughter, everyone would've said. Anyway, I didn't know if a crime *had* been committed. The tape showed me kissing that guy and him kissing me and his arms and hands all over me, but there was no way of knowing if anything else had happened.'

Andreas let out a stiff curse, his hand dragging over his face again. 'I can't get my head around this,' he said. 'Why didn't you say something when the press named your sister as the woman in that tape?'

Sienna shifted her gaze from his. 'I didn't know about any of that,' she said. 'As soon as I woke up in that hotel room I caught the next flight out of the country. I wanted to get as far away from it as I could. That's when Brian stepped in. I rang him in a bit of a state from the airport. We'd met at a function a few years before and really hit it off in a friends-only way. He was like a father to me, the father I'd never had. He offered me a safe haven. I didn't think twice when he suggested we marry as soon as possible. I wanted the respectability. I wanted to feel safe.'

Andreas lifted her chin up so her gaze met his. 'Why have you let everyone believe such scurrilous lies about you?' he asked.

Sienna could feel her carefully constructed composure cracking. She was used to acting all tough and resilient but it was hard to keep that façade in place when Andreas seemed so tender and concerned. 'Can we drop this topic?' she said. 'It's in the past. I'd like to leave it there.'

'Sienna, you can't just brush something like this aside,' he said. 'You've let everyone—including me— believe you're a gold-digging slut when you're no such thing.'

She raised her chin away from the pressure of his fingertip. 'I might not be a slut but I still want the money,' she said. 'That makes me a gold-digger, doesn't it?'

He stared her down. 'That's what you want everyone to believe,' he said. 'Why do you do that? What do you hope to achieve by making everyone hate you?'

'People hate a lot more easily than they love,' she said. 'It's just the way things are. I do it too. I'm good at it. Look at just now, for example. I was prepared to sleep with you, even though I hate your guts.'

He continued to look at her for a lengthy moment, those hazel eyes searching hers until her heart jumped and thumped behind the wall of her chest. He touched her cheek with his fingertip; it was hardly more than a brushstroke but it made every pore of her skin reach up on tiptoe to feel more of his touch. 'If you didn't hate me before, then you surely do so now,' he said with a touch of ruefulness. 'I was rough with you.'

Sienna swallowed a tight tangled knot inside her throat. 'It wasn't that bad,' she said, affecting what she hoped was a casual tone. 'Anyway, I probably should've said something.'

He gave a self-deprecating grunt. 'Do you think I would've believed you?'

She acknowledged that with a wry on-off smile. 'Probably not.'

'Do you know the man's name?' Andreas asked.

Sienna felt a ripple of panic roll through her. 'Leave it, Andreas, please. I don't want Gisele to be reminded of it all again. She's about to get married. I know what the press would do if you went looking for justice on my behalf. There's enough CCTV footage of me coming in and out of nightclubs to make me look like the biggest lush out. You know how lawyers can twist things to build a case for the defence. I just want to forget about it.'

'You can't keep running away from unpleasant stuff, Sienna,' he said.

She hoisted her chin. 'I'm not running away,' she said. 'I'm moving forward, for my sake as well as Gisele's.'

He held her gaze for a moment before he tucked a strand of her hair behind her ear, as one would do to a small child. Sienna didn't feel like a child, however. His touch against the sensitive skin of her ear made her shiver with womanly want and need. She felt him inside her still, a tender ache where her flesh had been stretched by his hot, hard presence.

What would it feel like to have him totally possess

her? To have him move inside her in the throes of passion? To have him lose control in the soft, moist cocoon of her body? To feel her own body respond to his in a rhythm as old as time?

The silence throbbed with the erotic tension Sienna could feel in her body. She saw it in the dark heat of his eyes. It smouldered there in the black ink spill pools of his pupils. She felt the slow burn of his gaze move over her face like a lighted taper, scorching her like a blowtorch when it came to rest for a tantalising moment on her mouth.

Her heart gave a swift hard kick against her ribcage. Her tongue came out to moisten the arid landscape of her lips. Her stomach lifted and fell a thousand feet as he brushed that same gentle fingertip he had used on her cheek over the surface of her lips, a faint movement that sent every nerve into a frenzy of want.

His hand suddenly dropped from her face and just as swiftly a shutter came down on his features. 'I think it's best for the time being if we keep our distance from each other,' he said. 'I'll sleep in one of the spare rooms.'

Sienna hid behind the screen of her sarcasm. 'Frightened you might get too attached now I'm not the bed-hopping harlot you once thought I was?' she asked.

He held her look with cool but implacable determination. 'I want this chateau, Sienna,' he said. 'I am prepared to do whatever is required to obtain it. Neither of us needs the complication of a relationship that to all intents and purposes has been thrust upon us for reasons as yet unclear. If it hadn't been for my father's will, I would never have considered you as a temporary partner, let alone a life one. I suspect you would not have considered me either.'

'You're spot on there,' she said. 'You're the last person I would consider spending the rest of my life with. Can you imagine the fights we'd have? You're so anal you get antsy when the tea towels aren't aligned.'

'And you're so chaotic you're like a whirlwind,' he said, but he softened it with a wry smile. 'I still find it hard to believe you came from the womb of a woman who made a living out of being tidy.'

'Yeah, well, she might have been good at tidying up other people's messes, but she wasn't so crash hot at sorting out her own,' Sienna said with a little slump of her shoulders. 'I spent most of my childhood wondering where we'd be living the next week. Mum would say or do something she shouldn't and the next thing I'd be packing all my things. I lost count of how many schools I attended over the years. The time with your family was the longest we'd stayed anywhere. I didn't want it to end.'

Andreas took one of her hands in his, toying with her fingers, one by one. 'I had no idea things were so difficult for you,' he said. 'I always thought you were a bit of a brat, but now I can see why you flounced around with such an attitude all the time. You felt terribly insecure.'

'I shouldn't complain,' Sienna said, trying to ignore the sensations firing up her arms from the warm stroke of his fingers against hers. 'Plenty of people have it so much worse.'

He brought her hand up to his mouth and gently kissed her bent knuckles. 'I should let you get to bed,' he said, giving her hand one last gentle squeeze before releasing it. 'Is there anything I can get or do for you? Perhaps run a hot bath for you?'

Sienna could see the concern in his eyes. It made

her feel delicate and feminine, a startling and somewhat unsettling change from having to act tough and streetwise around him. 'No, I think I can manage to turn on the taps for myself,' she said with a crooked smile. 'Thanks all the same.'

He continued to study her for a long pulsing moment. Sienna suspected those green and brown-flecked eyes could see right through her shabbily erected façade. That brief moment of physical intimacy had changed the dynamic between them and she wasn't sure how it could be changed back. The air was thick with the sensual energy their brief but passionate encounter had unleashed. It swirled like a current, a wild vortex that could so easily carry her way out of her depth if she wasn't careful.

'What happened here tonight…' He frowned as if searching for the right words. 'I don't know how to make it up to you. I've misjudged you, misunderstood you and insulted you. I hope you will find it in your heart to forgive me.'

'Wow, I really like this nice guy thing you've got going,' Sienna said. 'Maybe I won't hate you quite so much if you keep that up for the next six months.'

His eyes pulsed with something dark and intense as they held hers. 'You don't hate me, *ma petite*,' he said. 'In fact, I have a feeling you have never hated me.'

She challenged him with another lift of her chin. 'You surely don't think I'm still harbouring that silly little teenage crush on you, do you?' she said. 'That was a long time ago, Andreas. I might not have as much experience as other women my age, but I can assure you I haven't been saving myself for you.'

'Why haven't you got involved with anyone?' he

asked. 'It can't have been for lack of opportunity. Men fall over themselves to be with you. I've seen it with my own eyes. You can stop a speeding train with your looks.'

'I saw my mother move from one shallow hook-up after the other,' Sienna said. 'I saw what it did to her self-esteem. I was always picking up the emotional pieces. I felt like the parent a lot of the time. I guess it turned me off the thought of allowing someone that close who could turn around and hurt you. Besides, I want to be appreciated for more than my looks. I have dreams and aspirations. I'm not a narcissistic airhead. Unfortunately, a lot of men can't see past the physical stuff, or maybe they don't want to.'

He moved his fingertips across the sensitive skin on the slope of her lower jaw in a soft-as-air caress that set her nerves into a frenzied dance. 'You're a complex little thing, aren't you, *cara*?' he said.

'No more complex than the next person,' she said, shooting him a look from beneath her lashes. 'And not half as complex as you.'

A wry smile tipped up the corners of his mouth. 'Perhaps we are more alike than we are different, *si*?'

'I don't think we have much in common at all,' Sienna said, barely able to breathe with his fingers tracing back and forth along the line of her jaw.

He trailed a fingertip over her bottom lip before dropping his hand back down by his side. 'Perhaps you're right,' he said as he moved over to open the door for her. 'Call me if you need anything during the night. I'll only be a few doors down the hall.'

She gave a vague nod and moved past him in the

doorway, trying not to notice his warm body so close she could have touched it. 'Goodnight.'

The only answer she got was the soft, but no less definite, closing of the door.

CHAPTER EIGHT

ANDREAS paced the floor for hours after Sienna had left. Her perfume lingered in the air. He could even smell it on his skin. He could still taste the sweetness of her in his mouth in spite of the three stiff drinks he had consumed since.

The shock of finding out she had never had a sexual relationship with her late husband had left him more than a little dumbfounded. Just about everything he had believed about her was wrong. He had thought she had prostituted herself by marrying for money. To find the marriage had been nothing more than a paper arrangement had completely stunned him.

And that wasn't even half of it. He couldn't get his head around the fact that she had so little experience. She'd only had two sexual partners and she was twenty-five years old. For all these years she had played the role of a hardened tart. The press had constantly portrayed her as an easily picked up party girl and she had done nothing to discourage that view. The circumstances of the sex tape scandal had obviously affected her deeply, as indeed they would most young women. Andreas suspected she had hidden behind the label of gold-digger because that was Sienna's way of hiding her hurt, by toughing it out and pretending it didn't matter one jot, when of course it did.

Guilt gnawed at his conscience. He had pulled her to the floor like a common whore. Desire and lust had got the better of him. It had got the better of both of them. She had been just as willing, but it didn't make him feel any less responsible.

He had physically hurt her.

He groaned out loud and paced some more. He had acted *exactly* like his father. He had been intent on slaking his lust with no thought to the consequences. He dragged a hand through his hair. Was this what his father had wanted to teach him? To show him how hard it was to resist the lure of lust?

Had his desire for Sienna been so obvious? He had done his best to hide it. He had disciplined himself to ignore her on his visits or, at the very least, treat her as if she was just a kid. He had watched her bloom into young womanhood. From visit to visit she had morphed from a pimply fourteen-year-old to a sultry siren of ripe sensuality at seventeen. His rejection of her had been the honourable thing to do, and yet he wondered if that and not her mother's antics had caused her to hit the party scene in a defiant attempt to save face.

By the time she was eighteen or so she had a reputation as a wild party girl. A 'nightclub nymphet', some journalist in London had labelled her. Night after night she had teetered out of clubs and hotels with her gaggle of giggling girlfriends.

And then at the age of twenty-two she had suddenly married a man old enough to be her grandfather. Everyone had called her a greedy little gold-digger. He had done it himself. He had thrown the newspaper aside in disgust when he had read about it on one of his visits to England. He had sworn and cursed and called her every filthy name under the sun.

His chest tightened and cramped with its weight of guilt.

Sienna was nothing like the person he'd thought she was. For years she had hidden behind a façade to protect herself from being hurt. Behind that tough smart-mouth exterior was a vulnerable young woman, a young woman who had never felt safe and secure. He had made the mistake of assuming she was just like her mother, on the take for whatever she could get.

But Sienna was nothing like Nell Baker. She wasn't a social climbing harlot with no sense of propriety. Sienna had more pride than he had given her credit for.

Every insult he had flung at her came back to haunt him. She had thrown back her own insults with a feistiness of spirit he had always secretly admired. Defiance had glittered from her sparkling grey-blue eyes in every one of their exchanges. He had found it invigorating to spar with her. She always gave as good as she got. It was verbal foreplay. A little game they had played for as long as he could remember.

He closed his eyes as he thought of how she had felt wrapped so tightly around him. The silky warmth of her had engulfed him. His body still ached and pulsed with the burden of desire. It was a pounding ache that reverberated through his flesh.

He wanted her.

That desire was nothing new to him, but somehow now it was stronger than ever. He had tasted the sweet pleasure of her; it was like a drug he could no longer resist.

He drew in a breath and slowly released it as he

looked out at the moonlit fields of the estate. Six months and all of this would be his. Sienna would get her pay-out and he would inherit what was rightly his.

He knew she wanted the money. She was currently out of work and the funds her late husband had left her were just about gone. He was confident it was enough to keep her by his side for the allotted time. An affair between them would be an added bonus.

He closed the curtains with a flick of his hand.

He had a feeling that keeping her with him was not going to be the problem. Letting her go at the end of the six months might very well prove to be the biggest hurdle he had yet to face.

Sienna woke the next morning to a knock on the bed-room door. She pushed the hair out of her eyes and sat upright. 'Come in.'

Andreas came in with a tray with fresh croissants and a pot of fragrant steaming coffee. 'I thought you might like breakfast in bed,' he said.

'Is this another Chalvy bridal tradition?' she asked.

His lips moved in the semblance of a smile as he set the tray down over her knees. 'One of many,' he said.

'Well, as much as I'd like to keep the ghosts of this place happy, I'm afraid there's no way I can drink cof-fee at this time of the morning,' she said. 'I'm a tea girl. Call me British if you must but, in spite of living all those years in Italy, I can't quite get used to starting the day without my cup of tea.'

He gave a little eye roll as he whipped the coffee pot off the tray. 'I should've guessed,' he said. 'Give me five minutes and I'll be back with your tea.'

Sienna tilted her head at him. 'You wouldn't last five

minutes as a servant, Andreas,' she said. 'You have to accept all commands and requests with grace and poise.'

'Perhaps you could give me some lessons,' he said.

'You already know I'm absolute rubbish at following orders,' she said. 'As soon as someone tells me to do something I always want to do the opposite. I think it's a personality flaw or something.'

'I'll have to make sure I say the opposite of what I want you to do then,' he said. 'It's called reverse psychology, *si*?'

'Something like that,' she said.

Sienna picked at one of the croissants once he had gone, licking the buttery crumbs off her fingers. She had slept fitfully last night. Her body had thrummed with need for hours, and then, when she had finally drifted off to sleep, she had dreamed of Andreas. She had dreamed of his mouth and hands pleasuring her, touching her, caressing her, of him making her body sing with delight.

She squeezed her legs together and felt that tiny intimate ache where he had been. It made her belly feel all fluttery, like a thousand moth wings moving inside her. She put a hand over her stomach, trying to stop the sensation, but if anything it intensified.

The door opened after a few minutes and Andreas came in bearing a pot of tea. 'Your tea, Madame,' he said with a bow.

'Way too obsequious,' Sienna said, smiling at him. 'Your employer would automatically assume you're pilfering the silver or something.'

An answering smile flickered in his eyes. 'Perhaps I do have an ulterior motive,' he said as he poured her a cup of tea.

Sienna took the cup off the tray, burying her nose in

the steam rising from its surface rather than meet his gaze. 'So I take it this breakfast in bed routine is a guilt trip, not a tradition?' she said.

'How do you expect me not to feel guilty?' he asked. 'I spent most of last night pacing the floor over what happened.'

Sienna kept staring at the steamy mist rising from her tea. 'You're making too big an issue out of it,' she said. 'Let's just forget it ever happened.'

He brushed a strand of hair away from her face. 'Look at me, Sienna,' he said.

She drew in a breath and looked into his eyes. Her belly did that moth wing thing again and her heart skipped a beat. His face was cleanly shaven. His breath smelt of mint. His eyes looked tired, however. There were thumbprint-sized shadows beneath them. Had he too spent most of last night wondering what it would have felt like to make love properly? Had his body throbbed and ached for hours as hers had done? Had he dreamt of her as she had dreamt of him? It was so hard to tell what he was thinking or feeling. He had never been one for showing much in the way of expression. She had only seen him smile a handful of times.

His fingers brushed against her cheek as his eyes held hers. 'I overstepped the mark. I take full responsibility for it. I broke the rules we set down. It was a mistake I promise won't be repeated, not unless it's what you want. If you want a six-month affair, then, of course, I would consider it.'

Of course, Sienna thought cynically. She would be a convenient plaything to pass the time, just like her mother had been for his father. He would walk away when the time was up and leave her without a flicker of regret. Within months, if not weeks, he would go on to marry some other beautiful woman with a blue blood pedigree and fill his precious villas with his gorgeous little black-haired heirs.

How would she cope with it?

The same way she coped with everything else. She would put on a brave face. She would show him she could play him at his own game. She could be just as ruthless and mercenary as him. When the time was up she would walk away without a single regret, or at least none that he could see. 'I don't think an affair between us would work out,' she said. 'I think it's best if we stick to our original agreement.'

If he was surprised or disappointed by her response he showed no sign of it on his face. 'Very well,' he said, rising from where he had perched on the edge of the bed. 'I have some business to go over with Jean-Claude. I probably won't see you until this evening.'

'I'm sure I'll find something to amuse myself with,' Sienna said. 'Maybe I'll find a wolf or a wild boar in the woods to tame.'

His lips twitched as he looked down at her. 'I noticed your camera the other day,' he said after a moment. 'I thought you liked being in front of the lens, not behind it.'

'Yes, well, that just goes to show how little you know me, doesn't it?' she said.

His eyes held hers in a beat or two of silence.

'Does anyone know the real you, *ma petite*?' he asked.

Sienna gave a little shrug. 'I have friends, if that's what you're asking.'

'A person can have hundreds of friends but it doesn't mean anyone knows who they really are when they are alone.'

She gave him an arch look. 'Who are you when you're alone, Andreas?' she asked. 'Or aren't you ever alone? I bet there's always some willing woman to keep you company or some bowing and scraping servant to cater to your every whim.'

'It is one of the burdens of being born into wealth,' he said. 'One is rarely left alone. There are people always keen to be with you, but it is never clear if they want to be with you because they genuinely like your company or because they want something from you.'

'Given a choice, I'd rather live life from your side of the tracks than mine,' Sienna said. 'Besides, who needs genuine friends when you have loads and loads of money?'

He looked at her unwaveringly for a long moment. 'Do you really believe that, Sienna?' he asked. 'Do you really think being rich will make you truly happy?'

'I'll let you know once the money drops into my account in six months' time,' she said, picking up the rest of her croissant. 'Mind you, I reckon a chateau thrown in for free would bring a smile to my face.'

His mouth flattened to a thin line. 'You are *not* getting the chateau,' he said.

'Lighten up, Andreas,' she said. 'I'm only joking. I don't want your precious chateau. It's probably haunted by all your stuffy old relatives anyway.'

'Try and stay out of trouble today,' he said, with his brooding frown still in place. 'And remember, if you speak to anyone, we're supposed to be on our honeymoon.'

She arched a brow at him. 'You're the one rushing off to work the first chance you get.'

He came back to stand next to the bed, his eyes raking over her smoulderingly. 'Changed your mind already, have you, *cara*?' he said.

Sienna felt those gossamer wings brush over her belly again as she brought her eyes up to meet his glittering ones. 'Not yet,' she said. 'You can't give me what I want.'

He cupped her cheek with his hand as his eyes held hers captive. 'What do you want, Sienna? A promise of forever?'

She forced herself not to blink. 'Of course not,' she said. 'Neither of us is the forever type.'

His thumb moved over the surface of her bottom lip. 'We could be good together for a while, *ma cherie*,' he said. 'It seems a shame not to take advantage of the situation we find ourselves in. You and me, alone and legally married. Why not explore the possibilities, *si*?'

Sienna couldn't think when he looked at her like that. Those hazel eyes promised sensual heaven. That mouth had already tempted her beyond endurance. She wanted him even though she knew it would probably end badly. How long could she say no, especially after that deliciously hot taste of sensuality last night?

She drew in a breath as he brought his mouth inexorably closer. The feather-light brush of his lips against hers made her senses skyrocket. The gentle pressure called every nerve into play, making her lips tingle and fizz like champagne underneath her skin. He lifted his mouth away but for a microsecond her lips clung to his. It seemed her body was determined to betray her, no matter what she said to the contrary. Need pulsed inside her. Rampant hungry need that only he could satisfy. She had always known it. He was her physical nemesis. No one came close to making her feel what he did. His touch, his kisses and his caresses all made her blood race through her veins and her heart gallop in excitement. She wanted to feel his complete possession. She wanted him to satisfy this aching longing that just wouldn't go away.

He gave her cheek a light brush with his fingertip, his eyes dark and intense as they held hers. 'Have you really only had two partners?' he asked.

'Yes,' Sienna said. 'I know the press have always made me out to be a sensual hedonist but, to tell you the truth, I felt awkward and uncomfortable having sex. I just wanted to get it over with. I didn't feel anything much at all.'

'That's probably because you weren't in tune with the other person physically,' he said. 'The first few times you have sex you shouldn't rush it. You need time to get to know your body's needs and rhythm. I rushed things last night because I thought you were more experienced. It will be different the next time. I'll make sure of it.'

Sienna felt her insides tremble with anticipation. Could she risk everything to indulge in a red-hot fling with him? It would be a sensuous feast she could sustain herself with for the rest of her life. But could she keep her feelings well clear of it?

It was a gamble she felt more and more tempted to take.

'You sound pretty certain there's going to be a next time,' she said. 'Isn't that a little arrogant of you?'

'There's a difference between arrogance and confidence,' he said. 'I'm confident we're going to be dynamite together, but I'm not so arrogant to assume it's going to last.'

It wasn't quite the answer Sienna was looking for.

It seemed to suggest he had only a passing interest in her. She was more of a novelty to him than a person of any lasting value. 'Does any woman hold your interest longer than a month or two?' she asked.

'Some more than others.'

'What about Portia Briscoe?' she asked. 'You were going to marry her. What were you going to do once you got bored? Have a little affair on the side, just like your father did?'

A flicker of heat passed through his gaze. 'My father made promises to my mother he later broke,' he said. 'I made no such promises to Portia. She knew what I wanted in a wife and she was prepared to provide it.'

'She's not the right person for you, Andreas,' Sienna said. 'Your housekeeper Elena thinks so and, quite frankly, so do I.'

His top lip curled. 'I suppose you think you're a much better candidate, do you?'

'No, but obviously your father thought so,' Sienna said. 'I can't see why else he would have done this. He must've wanted you to stop and think about what you were doing. Perhaps he didn't want you to lock yourself into a loveless marriage for the rest of your life.'

Andreas's eyes clashed with hers. 'So he locked me into a hate-filled one with you?'

'Only for six months,' she reminded him.

He looked at her for a long moment. 'You know, it was a whole lot easier hating you when I thought you were a money-hungry trollop,' he said. 'Now I know more about you, it seems rather unfair to maintain such negative feelings.'

'What are you saying, Andreas?' Sienna asked with

a deliberately goading smile. 'That you're falling a tiny bit in love with me?'

'I'm no more in love with you than you are with me,' he said, his expression locking down like a shutter over a window. 'What we feel for each other is lust. There's no other fancy way of putting it. And, in my opinion, the sooner it burns itself out the better.' And, without another word, he left, clipping the door shut behind him.

Later that day Sienna was coming back from photographing the lavender fields when she saw Andreas in the distance. He was walking through the vineyard, inspecting the vines as he went along the rows.

She raised her camera and zoomed in to frame him in a series of shots. She captured him deep in thought. She captured him squinting against the late afternoon sun. She captured him picking a leaf from a vine and running it through his fingers, his brow furrowed in a frown. And then, as if he suddenly became aware of being watched, he turned and looked directly at her.

Sienna lowered the camera as he walked towards her. She watched as his long legs ate up the distance, the muscles of his thighs bunching with every step. Her belly gave an excited little quiver. He looked so arrantly male, dressed in dark blue denim jeans and a close-fitting white T-shirt. Every honed and toned muscle stretched against the fabric, reminding her of the potent power of his body. She had felt that hard male body move inside hers.

She wanted to feel it again.

He came and stood right in front of her, his towering height almost blocking the sun from her view. 'Are you going to let me see what you've been up to?' he asked.

Sienna positioned herself beside him and pressed the buttons on her camera to recall the shots. 'You make a good study when you're not aware of the camera,' she said. 'But that's like most people. It's hard to get a natural shot of someone when they know they're being watched.'

His eyes met hers. 'These are good,' he said. 'How long have you been doing this?'

Sienna shrugged dismissively as she turned off the camera. 'A while.'

He took the camera from her and turned it back on, scrolling through the archive of pictures she had loaded. 'You've got a good eye,' he said, looking at her again. 'Is this a hobby or is it what you want to do? To pursue a career in photography?'

Sienna took the camera from him, her fingers briefly coming in contact with his. 'I lost my office job when Brian died,' she said. 'His family didn't want me working in the business. It made me think about being my own boss instead of being at the mercy of other people all the time. Of course it will take me a while to build up the business, but I'd like to have a go at it. I could never afford decent equipment before. I'd need a much better camera for official portraits and wedding photography and I'd need to rent a studio. I couldn't afford to do that before. But after this six months is over... well, I'll be laughing all the way to the bank, won't I?'

His expression was deeply thoughtful. 'So why did you encourage me to think you only wanted the money for a layabout holiday and endless partying?' he asked.

She shifted her gaze from his as she put the camera back inside its vinyl case. 'I might not make it as a photographer,' she said. 'There's pretty stiff competition out there. I'm under no illusions that I'm any more talented than anyone else.'

'Where would you like to base yourself?' he asked.

'London,' Sienna said. 'But I could travel to other places on assignment. It'd be fun travelling around to take pictures all over the world. I could even do a book, you know, like one of those super-glam coffee table ones.' She flashed him a little smile. 'You could tell everyone you knew me before I was famous.'

'I'm sure you'll do very well,' he said, a small frown forming between his eyes. 'You seem to have rather a knack for falling on your feet.'

She tucked a strand of hair behind her ear that the light breeze had been playing with. 'What will you do with this place once you inherit it?' she asked. 'Are you going to base yourself here or Florence, or travel between the two?'

His eyes held hers in a brooding little lockdown. 'It is not yet certain that I will inherit it,' he said. 'It would be foolish of me to make plans at this stage. I'll take a wait and see approach.'

Sienna frowned at him. 'You don't trust me, do you?'

'This is a valuable property,' he said. 'It surely can't have escaped your notice that it's worth five or six times what you will get in the pay-out. Why should I trust you?'

'No, indeed,' she said, throwing him a blistering look. 'Why should you?'

He let out a breath of irritation. 'Sienna, I realise I've made some errors of judgement with you in the past, but I would be a fool to take it for granted that you'll abide by the terms of the will. We haven't been married a week. How do you know what you'll feel in six weeks from now, let alone six months?'

'I know exactly what I'll feel,' she said, glaring at him. 'I'll still hate you.'

'Best you keep on doing that,' he said, turning to walk back towards the vineyard. 'It will make the end much easier for both of us.'

'Why are we leaving so soon?' Sienna asked as Andreas loaded their bags in the car later that evening. He had given her very little notice. He had sent a message via Simone, telling her to pack as they were leaving to catch the next available flight. 'I thought you said we were staying for two or three days.'

'I've seen what I came here to see,' he said as he snapped the boot shut and came around to open her door for her. 'The Perraults are managing things just fine. I have other things I need to see to in Florence. I have a business to run.'

'Aren't you worried what the press will think of you cutting short your honeymoon?' she asked once they were on their way.

He sent her a brief unreadable glance. 'I thought you were desperate to get back to your feral dog?'

'So you're doing this for me?' Sienna asked with a sceptical look. 'Somehow, I don't think so.'

'I'm doing it for both of us,' he said and put his foot down on the accelerator.

Sienna didn't see much of Andreas after they got back from France. Each day he left early in the morning and returned well after she had gone to bed. It annoyed her that he had just left her to her own devices, not even having the decency to communicate with her, other than via the housekeeper or a short text. It made her feel like an uninvited guest who was being tolerated, rather than welcomed.

But then, that was exactly what she was. Andreas had planned his life with meticulous precision. She had never been a part of it. She was the last woman he would ever have considered marrying. But his father's will had changed everything. So, too, had that brief moment of intimacy. Yet ever since that night Andreas had kept his distance.

Her heart gave a funny little spasm. He could easily find someone else. He might have already recruited someone to satisfy his needs. There were hundreds of women who would do anything to be his mistress. Would she have to pretend not to notice for the rest of the time they were stuck together in this arrangement? Was he doing it to make her default on the will? After all, she was the one with the most to lose. All he had to do was wait it out and he could claim what was rightly his. Her lack of experience was probably the biggest turn-off for someone with his level of expertise. He probably couldn't wait to get rid of her now she was of no further use to him.

Sienna was sure Elena was well aware that Andreas didn't share a bed with his new wife, but the housekeeper was either too discreet or polite to mention it in any of her interactions with her.

Elena had mentioned something about a furniture design collection Andreas was working on, commissioned by a wealthy American businessman, and how it was taking up a lot of his time. 'He barely sleeps when he is working on a special project,' she said. 'He spends hours and hours at his office. Once it is finished he will be able to relax a little, *si*? Maybe he will take you away somewhere special for a proper honeymoon. It is lonely here all day on your own.'

'I'm not lonely,' Sienna insisted. 'I have Scraps to keep me company.'

Elena gave her an indulgent smile. 'It will be easier when you have a *bambino* or two to keep you busy, *sì*?'

Sienna pushed the thought of a dark-haired hazel-eyed chubby baby out of her mind. She thought instead of a home of her own in London, a luxury home with a studio and a garden and money in the bank—lots and lots of money.

That was her goal, not marriage and babies.

When Sienna came downstairs for dinner towards the end of the week Andreas was in the *salone* sipping an aperitif. His gaze skimmed over her coffee-coloured dress before meshing with hers. 'I was expecting you to send word via Elena that you wouldn't be joining me for dinner,' he said.

Sienna held her head at an imperious angle. 'I considered it, but then I thought that would be letting you off the hook,' she said. 'I'd much rather annoy you with my presence since you seemed to be actively avoiding it for the past week.'

A half-smile kicked up one side of his mouth. 'Feeling neglected, are we?'

She took the glass of wine he had poured for her, giving him a hardened look. 'Not at all,' she said. 'I just can't help wondering what your housekeeper thinks of our relationship, with you spending every minute you can at work while I'm stuck here twiddling my thumbs.'

'She is employed to keep order in the villa, not to speculate on my private life,' he said. 'She knows she would be fired immediately if she spoke out of turn. Anyway, if you're bored, why not take the car out I bought you?'

'I'm not bored,' Sienna said. 'I've got plenty to do; it's just I don't like having to pretend things are normal between us when they're not.'

'There's one way to change that,' he said with a glinting look in his eyes. 'We can make them normal. You can move into my bed tonight.'

Sienna felt her stomach do a flip turn. 'How can you be so clinical about this?' she asked. 'We don't even like each other.'

'Liking one another has nothing to do with it,' he said. 'Physical compatibility is what matters. I've had lovers I didn't like much at all, but they were perfectly fine as sexual partners.'

'Have you ever been in love?' Sienna asked.

'No,' he said. 'It's not that I don't believe it exists. I've seen it and admire it in others. I just haven't felt that level of attachment.' He took a sip of his drink. 'What about you?'

'I think my twin got all the love genes instead of me,' she said. 'I don't think I've ever seen two people more in love than Gisele and Emilio. Their wedding is in three weeks. You haven't forgotten, have you? I called your secretary to put it in your diary. I'm going to go a couple of days before to help with things. I'll meet you at the hotel.'

'No, I haven't forgotten,' he said. 'I'm looking forward to meeting them both, particularly your sister.'

'We're nothing alike,' Sienna said. 'Well, apart from looks, I mean.'

'You must have more in common than looks,' he said.

'Not much,' she said. 'Don't get me wrong. I adore her. She's so sweet and caring I can't help but love her. But because we haven't shared the same parents, or the same experiences, we want different things for our lives. I wonder if it would have been different if we had grown up together. I guess we'll never know now.'

He studied her for a moment as if he was memorising her features in fine detail. 'I wonder if I'll be able to tell you apart.'

'I'll give you a tip-off,' Sienna said. 'My sister will be the one wearing white and she'll have a big smile on her face. Oh, and a wedding band on her finger to match the fabulous diamond engagement ring Emilio gave her.'

'That reminds me.' Andreas put his drink to one side. 'I have something for you,' he said. He took an antique ring box out of his pocket and handed it to her. 'You might recognise it. It belonged to my mother and my grandmother before her.'

Sienna opened the tiny box to find the diamond and sapphire dress ring she had often admired on Evaline Ferrante's hand, nestled in the groove of black velvet. 'I do recognise it,' she said, looking up at him with a little frown. 'But shouldn't you be keeping such an heirloom for your future bride?'

'If you don't like it then I'll get you something else,' he said.

Sienna wasn't sure what to make of his expression or his curt tone. 'Of course I like it,' she said, putting it on her finger. 'I've always thought it was a gorgeous ring. But I'll give it back to you when we get divorced. That would only be fair.'

'Fine,' he said, refilling his glass. 'But I've noticed you don't seem to have a lot of jewellery.' He took a sip of his drink. 'What happened to all the diamonds you had dripping from you when you were with Littlemore?'

'I gave them back to his family,' she said. 'I didn't feel comfortable keeping them.'

He gave her another one of his thoughtful looks. 'I got the impression from what was reported in the press that his family never accepted you,' he said. 'At times they were quite vitriolic in their comments.'

'Yes, well, they loved their mother dearly and didn't want anyone to take her place,' Sienna said. 'I totally understood where they were coming from.'

'Do you think they would have accepted his mistress any better?'

She shifted her gaze from his. 'No.'

'And yet, by all accounts, he had been involved with her a long time,' he said. 'It seems strange he didn't offer to marry her instead of you.'

She shrugged off his comment and took a sip of her wine.

He continued to study her. 'You're very loyal to Littlemore, aren't you?' he said.

Sienna forced herself to meet his gaze. 'Why wouldn't I be? He was good to me.'

'There's more to it, isn't there?' he asked. 'It's been niggling at me for days. Why didn't he marry his mistress? Why marry a woman younger than one of his daughters instead of the mistress he had kept for all those years?'

'Maybe his mistress was already married,' she said.

Andreas lifted her chin with his index finger, locking his gaze with hers. 'That's not the reason, though, is it?' he said.

Sienna remained silent. The intense scrutiny of

his hazel gaze made her heart beat faster and faster. It was harder and harder to hide anything from him. He seemed to see through the layers of her skin to the very heart of her.

'Brian Littlemore wasn't involved with a woman, was he?' Andreas said. 'His long-term lover was a man.'

Sienna swallowed tightly. 'That's not true.'

'Don't lie to me, *cara*,' he said. 'I hate being lied to. Don't you think you've told enough lies by now? Surely you can be honest with me over this. It will go no further than this room.'

She chewed at her lip. 'How did you find out?' she asked. 'No one is supposed to know. Brian didn't want his children to find out. He was worried it would hurt them. He didn't think they'd understand. If this gets out in the public arena it will hurt so many people.'

'It's not common knowledge, as far as I know,' he said. 'I came to the conclusion myself so it's likely others will do so as well. But if it goes public, I can't see how you should be blamed.'

'Brian wanted to protect his family,' Sienna said. 'He came from a very conservative background. His parents would've disowned him if they'd known. He did all the things that were expected of him. He got married and raised a family. Even after his wife died he still had to maintain the lie. Do you know how hard that was on him? He was trapped. You mustn't let anyone know about it. You mustn't, Andreas. So many people will get hurt.'

He stroked her chin with his thumb, back and forth like a slow-moving metronome. 'You care more about his family's feelings even though they've trashed you any time they could in the press?'

Sienna looked into his warm hazel eyes and felt something reposition itself in her chest. A soft little gear change of emotion that was totally unexpected and deeply unsettling. She didn't want to lose her grip on her feelings. She wanted to keep her emotions under lockdown. Falling in love with Andreas would be the biggest mistake of her life so far. She couldn't afford to let her feelings get involved. She had to be strong enough to walk away when the time was up. 'I care about what Brian wanted,' she said. 'He trusted me. I didn't want to betray that trust.'

Andreas's eyes held hers in an intimate lock that made her insides flutter. His thumb was still doing that mesmerising little caress that made her feel as if her nerves were pirouetting beneath the surface of her skin. 'So you were prepared to let me carry on thinking you were a gold-digger?' he said as his hand fell away from her face. 'Does my opinion of you mean absolutely nothing to you at all?'

Sienna swept the surface of her lips with a quick dart of her tongue. 'I figured after this six months is up it won't be relevant what you think of me,' she said. 'We don't mix in the same circles. We probably won't see each other again.'

Something passed through his gaze as it held hers. 'That will be a shame, don't you think?' he said.

'Why?'

'Because I have a feeling I'm going to miss doing this,' he said, and lowered his mouth to hers.

CHAPTER NINE

Sienna felt the warm, gentle pressure of his lips as they met hers. It was a slow kiss, no sense of urgency or out of control passion, just his lips moving at a leisurely pace as they explored the softness of hers.

She returned the kiss in much the same way, slow and soft, touching down, lifting off, touching down again, varying the pressure ever so slightly, but not the speed.

It was a getting-to-know-you kiss. It felt like a romantic first kiss between two people who were attracted to each other, but were mindful of overstepping the boundaries too early. A kiss where the two parties were taking tentative steps to see how well they worked together intimately.

No other parts of their bodies were touching. He didn't gather her to him. He didn't put his arms on her shoulders or her waist. She didn't put her hands on his chest or around his neck. Only their lips bridged the gap between them, but, even so, Sienna felt a roar of heat go through her. Her insides melted like the wax of a candle under a powerful heat source.

After endless dreamy minutes, Andreas slowly lifted his mouth away. His expression was faintly bemused as he looked down at her. 'You have such a soft, kiss-able mouth,' he said. 'It's surprisingly soft given how razor-sharp your tongue can be.'

Sienna couldn't hold back a rueful smile. 'Yes, well, you do seem to bring the shrew out in me at times.'

He made a little sound of amusement, a deep and to-tally male sound that made her belly quiver like unset aspic. His hand came up to cup her cheek, his thumb lazily stroking her skin as his eyes made love with hers. 'You haven't always brought out the best in me either,' he said. 'But maybe, once this period of time is up, we can walk away from this as friends. Do you think that's possible, *ma petite*?'

Sienna felt her breath come out in a little flutter but she hoped he hadn't noticed. 'I'm not sure I could ever get used to thinking of you as a friend,' she said play-fully. 'I guess I'll have to find someone else to sharpen my claws on, won't I?'

He stroked her cheek one last time before dropping his hand back down by his side. 'I bet it won't be half as much fun with someone else,' he said, his expres-sion now inscrutable.

Sienna had a feeling he wasn't just talking about their verbal sparring. The crazy thing was, she couldn't imagine kissing another man now. She couldn't imagine another man holding her and caressing her and mak-ing love to her.

She only wanted Andreas.

She gave herself a swift mental slap. He wanted the chateau, not her. She was a means to an end. In six months it would all be over. He would walk away from her, just as his father had done to her mother.

This wasn't forever.

'No, perhaps not,' she said. 'But I won't know that until I try, will I?'

His eyes flickered as if something behind them had momentarily become unstuck. 'We should have dinner,' he said, putting his glass down as if it had suddenly turned into a poisoned chalice. 'I still have some work to see to afterwards.'

'Do you ever take time to relax?' Sienna asked. 'You can't possibly go at this pace for weeks on end. It's not healthy.'

'I have a lot of people depending on me for their incomes and their futures,' Andreas said, scraping a hand through his hair. 'My father's death couldn't have come at a worse time.'

'I'm quite sure he didn't plan to die just then to personally inconvenience you,' Sienna said in a dry tone.

'Don't bet on it,' he said with an embittered scowl.

'You didn't really hate him, did you, Andreas?' she asked.

He held her look for a moment before he let out a long breath. 'I used to look up to him when I was a young child,' he said. 'I wanted to be just like him when I grew up: successful and wealthy. But as I got older I started to see that, like most people, he had a dark side. He was driven by his emotions. He was selfish and at times outrageously ruthless in getting what he wanted. He exploited the love my mother felt for him. I don't think he ever truly loved her. I think he only married her because he knew she would never challenge him. She would just accept whatever he did without question. She could've left him over his affair with your mother but she didn't. She stayed until the bitter end.'

'Sounds like your father didn't want you to make

the same mistake in your choice of a bride, don't you think?' Sienna asked.

His gaze narrowed. 'What do you mean?'

'Perfect Portia,' she said. 'The wife who would never do or say the wrong thing. The wife who would meekly turn a blind eye when her handsome, charming, virile husband took up with someone else every now and again. That was the sort of marriage you had planned, was it not?'

His frown closed the space between his brows. 'You don't know what the hell you're talking about.'

'Don't I?' she asked with an arch of one brow.

He threw her an irritated look as he wrenched open the door. 'I've changed my mind about dinner,' he said. 'I'm going back to the office. I'll see you when I see you.'

Andreas came home the following evening to find Sienna wasn't home. The villa felt completely different without her in it. The air didn't have that intoxicating trace of her perfume lingering in it, and the scatter cushions on the sofas were all neatly propped in place. There were no half empty cups or glasses littered about, and the television wasn't blaring with some inane reality show or the sound system shuddering with noise that he wouldn't even go as far as calling music.

It was quiet and peaceful, ordered and neat, but sterile.

A bit like his life.

He quickly dismissed the thought and snatched up his phone and rapidly dialled her number. 'Where are you?' he asked as soon as she answered.

'I'm on my way back now,' she said. 'I'm about ten minutes away.'

'Back from where?'

'I've been...erm...at the doctor's,' she said.

His heart gave a sudden lurch. 'The doctor?' he said. 'Why? What's wrong? Are you sick?'

'Not really...'

He heard the hesitancy in her tone. 'What's going on?' he asked.

'I had a bit of an accident,' she said. 'I had to have a couple of stitches in my hand. Nothing serious, however.'

'An accident?' His heart jerked again. 'What happened? Are you all right?'

'I'm fine but you have to promise you won't get rid of Scraps.'

Andreas frowned as he clutched the phone until his knuckles whitened. 'Did that mongrel attack you?'

'It was my fault,' she said. 'I tried to get too close to him. I tried to put some ointment on his sore leg but he wouldn't let me. He snapped at me in pain, not spite.'

'I told you to keep away from that dog,' Andreas said. 'Are you all right to drive? Why didn't you get Franco to take you? Pull over and I'll come and get you. Where are you?'

'Stop fussing, Andreas,' she said. 'You're really starting to scare me. You sound just like a doting husband.'

Andreas drew in a sharp breath and strode over to the windows to scan the driveway of the estate to see if he could see her in the distance. 'That's an expensive and very powerful car you're driving,' he said. 'It needs two hands on the wheel, not one.'

'I won't hurt your precious car,' she said and hung up on him.

* * *

Sienna pulled up in front of the villa but didn't even get time to turn the engine off before Andreas had the driver's door open.

'You silly little fool,' he railed at her as he helped her out. 'Why didn't you call me as soon as it happened?'

'I didn't want you to overreact,' she said. 'It's just a scratch.'

He gently picked up her thickly bandaged hand. 'How many stitches?' he asked.

Sienna considered fibbing but decided against it. 'Five,' she mumbled.

'Five?' His eyes flared in alarm. 'That's not a scratch. You could have lost a finger or even your hand.'

'Well, I didn't so everything's all right, isn't it?' she said.

'That dog has to go,' he said trenchantly. 'I will see that Franco destroys it first thing in the morning. And if he won't do it, then I'll do it myself.'

Sienna glared at him as she cradled her hand against her stomach. 'You do that and I swear to God I'll never speak to you again.'

His hazel eyes collided with hers. 'Why are you so determined to rescue a dog that clearly doesn't want to be rescued?' he asked.

She raised her chin at him. 'He does want to be rescued,' she said. 'He just doesn't know who to trust. He'll get there in the end. I just have to be patient.'

Andreas let out a curt swear word as he cupped her by the elbow to lead her into the villa. 'You're going to give me a heart attack one day, *ma petite*,' he said. 'I didn't realise one small woman could cause such chaos.'

Sienna threw him a pert look. 'Just as well I won't be around any longer than a few months, isn't it?' she said. 'Once this is over you can settle back into your boringly ordered life and forget all about me.'

He shouldered open the heavy front door of the villa as she stalked past. 'I can hardly wait,' he muttered darkly.

CHAPTER TEN

SIENNA woke during the night and had trouble going back to sleep as the local anaesthetic had worn off. The painkillers the doctor had given her were still in her handbag in the car. With all the fuss Andreas had made, she had forgotten to bring it with her into the villa. She tossed off the covers and padded downstairs, turning on the minimum of lights as she went.

She walked past Andreas's study and saw the thin line of light shining from beneath the door. She heard the tapping of his computer keyboard and the squeak of leather as he shifted in his chair. There was a pause in the tapping as she heard him mutter a very rude word, and then the tapping resumed.

She tiptoed past in her bare feet, but one of the floor-boards protested volubly and suddenly Andreas's study door was flung open and he stood there towering over her. 'What are you doing?' he said.

'I'm going out to the car.'

His brows slammed together over his eyes. 'Whatever for?'

'I forgot to bring in my bag,' she said. 'The painkillers the doctor gave me are inside it.'

'Why didn't you ask me to get it for you?'

'I didn't think of it till now.'

'Go back upstairs,' he said, rubbing a hand over his weary-looking features. 'I'll bring it up to you.'

Sienna went back to her room and sat propped up against the pillows. Within a few minutes Andreas came in, carrying her bag as well as a glass of water. She took the pills and he set the glass on the bedside table.

'Does it hurt much?' he asked.

'A little,' Sienna said. 'Just a dull throb.'

A little silence passed.

Sienna felt the drumbeat of her heart as his gaze meshed with hers. One of his hands was resting on the bed within a hair's breadth of hers. She felt the magnetic pull of his body, the sensual tug on her flesh, as if all of the organs and cells inside her body wanted to shift to be perfectly aligned with his.

His thumb moved just a fraction and stroked against the little finger of her undamaged hand. It was such a tiny touch and yet it made a tumultuous storm of feeling erupt inside her. Her skin tingled all the way up her arm. Her heart picked up speed and her insides flexed and coiled with unbridled need.

His hooded gaze slipped to her mouth. It felt as if he had physically kissed her. Her lips burned and fizzed and she had to sweep her tongue out over them to dampen down the sensation.

He raised a hand to her face, his touch so gentle it felt as if he were wearing kid gloves. He traced the pad of his finger over the cushion of her bottom lip. It was such an achingly intimate caress—the moisture of her lips and the dryness of his fingertip meeting in an erotic moment that stirred something deeply primal in the core of her being.

'I want you,' Sienna said on a whisper of sound.

Andreas's eyes locked on hers, dark, intense and serious. 'Is that the painkillers talking or you?' he asked.

'It's me,' she said, touching her hand to the stubbly skin of his jaw. 'I want you to make love to me.'

He covered her hand with his and, lifting it from his face, pressed a kiss to the middle of her palm, his tongue moving against the sensitive flesh in an erotic stroke that sent her senses into a tailspin. 'I want you too,' he said. 'It's driving me crazy. *You've* been driving me crazy, do you know that?'

Sienna shivered as he leaned in to kiss the skin of her neck just below her ear. 'We're both a little crazy, don't you think?' she said. 'Hating each other and yet wanting each other.'

His mouth brushed over hers, a light-as-air, teasing kiss that made her want to scream out loud for more. 'Total craziness, that's what it is,' he said, sliding one of his hands underneath the curtain of her hair as he gently drew her closer.

Sienna closed her eyes as his mouth came back down on hers. His lips moved with gentle urgency against hers. The undercurrent of lust that flowed between them made her blood race like high-octane fuel through her veins. Every thudding heartbeat made her longing for him rise to a feverish level. She could feel it building inside her body. A tug and release sensation that resided deep in her womb, making her hot and moist and restless for the full possession of his body.

His tongue commanded entry to her mouth and with a soft sigh of pleasure she opened to him. He played with her tongue, dancing with it, cavorting and teasing it into submission.

Electric shocks arced down her spine when his hand moved to cover her breast. The barrier of her thin night-wear was no barrier at all. If anything, the movement of the fine fabric against her nipple intensified the sensa-tion. But then he pushed the fabric aside and took her nipple and areola in his mouth. It was an explosion of feeling that made her flesh sizzle and shiver with de-light. His tongue teased her nipple by rolling over it and circling it, making all the tiny super-sensitive nerves dance in excitement. He uncovered her other breast and subjected it to a similar heart-stopping sensual assault, making her breathing and heart rate go into a frenzied mismatched rhythm.

His mouth came back to her as he gently eased her back on the bed, his weight supported by one of his el-bows. 'Let's get rid of this, shall we?' he said, peeling away her nightwear.

Sienna shucked herself out of it, feeling strangely at ease with him without the covering of her clothes. His gaze devoured her hungrily. It made her flesh sing with delight as his eyes took in every curve and con-tour of her body.

'You're incredibly beautiful,' he said, sliding a hand down over the jut of her hipbone. 'So slender and your skin is like silk.'

'I want to touch your skin,' Sienna said, starting to work on the buttons of his shirt, but she didn't get very far with only one hand.

'Hold that thought,' he said. He lifted himself off the bed and stood there, looking down at her as he undid each button of his shirt, shrugging it off his shoulders before unfastening the waistband of his trousers.

Sienna's eyes followed his every movement with

breathless anticipation. Seeing him totally naked for
the first time made her breath stall like a misfiring engine. He was all strongly corded muscles and lean and
tanned planes. Masculine hair was lightly sprinkled
over his chest in a T shape, arrowing down to his groin,
where his erection jutted boldly.

He fished a condom out of his wallet and joined her
on the bed again. 'Are you sure about this?' he asked.
'It's not too late to stop. I don't want to hurt your hand.'

'It *is* too late, and I've forgotten all about my hand,'
Sienna said. 'I want this. I want you.'

His mouth came down and sealed hers with a long
passionate kiss that set her flesh alight. He took his time
caressing every inch of her body, making her aware of
herself in a way she had never been before. She hadn't
realised the pleasure spots she possessed. She hadn't
known how delicious it felt to have his mouth on the
undersides of her breasts, or the way it felt to have his
hands stroke the silky skin of her inner thighs. She
hadn't known how it would feel to have him gently
separate her feminine folds with his fingers and then
with the stroke and flicker of his tongue. Her body responded with a sensual energy that took her completely
by surprise. It was like a giant wave of sensation that
she could not stop even if she tried. It snatched her up
in its powerful surge of momentum, tossed her about
and flung her out the other side, spent, limbless, breathless and dazed.

Sienna blinked her eyes open and looked at Andreas.
'Wow...' she said.

His hazel eyes glittered. 'It gets better.'

'You can top that?' she said with an incredulous look.

He gave her a smile that made her insides quiver all

over again. 'I'll take it slowly,' he said. 'You're tiny and I don't want to hurt you. Just relax, try not to clamp up. You're meant to stretch to accommodate me.'

Sienna sighed with pleasure as he positioned himself so as not to crush her with his weight. She loved the feel of his hair-roughened thighs and the way his hands were so gentle, almost worshipful, as they caressed her. Tasting the feminine essence of her body on his mouth was a new experience, but a totally erotic one. He kissed her lingeringly while his fingers played with her, making sure she was moist and relaxed before he eased into her slowly, pausing as her body got used to his thickness, before going deeper. She felt her inner walls wrap around him; the sensation of him moving inside her made her spine instantly melt. She moved against him experimentally and her belly somersaulted as she heard him give a deep groan of pleasure. 'Am I wowing you?' she asked, sliding her uninjured hand up and down his strongly muscled back.

He swept a strand of her hair away from her face with a tender movement of his hand. 'Most definitely,' he said and, with a spasm of pleasure passing over his face, he took her with him to paradise.

Andreas lay on his side, watching as Sienna slept. She was curled up on her side facing him, her little bandaged hand resting in the space between them. Her hair was a tousled cloud over the pillow. The scent of her was on his skin, the taste of her both sweet and salty on his tongue.

He had made love many times with many women. It was a physical union that he enjoyed. But somehow, making love with Sienna was something else, some-

thing infinitely more pleasurable, more deeply satisfying—a mind-blowing experience that touched him
where no one else had been able to reach before.

But then she constantly surprised him. That was part
of her alluring charm. He never knew what to expect
from her. She was totally, and yet somehow delightfully, unpredictable.

She suddenly opened her eyes and gave him one of
her breath-snatching smiles. 'I had this amazing dream,'
she said. 'This amazingly gorgeous-looking and disgustingly rich guy made love to me. I hate his guts in
real life, but in my dream we made magic together.
Wasn't that a weird dream?'

Andreas smiled crookedly as he stroked a lazy finger
down her cheek. 'Are you sure you hate him so much
in real life?' he asked.

She pretended to think about it. 'Mmm, maybe not
as much as I did before, but I'm not in love with him
or anything.'

'So what's the plan?' he asked. 'A short affair to get
him out of your system?'

She tiptoed her fingers up his sternum, making his
heart leap like a mad thing behind the cage of his ribs.
'That's the plan,' she said, meshing her gaze with his.
'Five months, give or take a day or two, ought to do it,
don't you think?'

Andreas studied her soft plump mouth for a moment.
'What if the amazingly gorgeous-looking, disgustingly
rich guy wanted you to stay a little longer?' he asked.

Her grey-blue eyes stilled for a moment. Then she
blinked and asked, 'Why would he want that?'

He slowly coiled a strand of her silver-blonde hair

around his index finger. 'Maybe he likes having you around to mess up his ordered life,' he said.

She gave a little gurgle of laughter. 'I can't quite see it, somehow,' she said, doing that sexy little tiptoe thing again. 'We'd drive each other nuts.'

Andreas felt an arrow of lust stake him in the groin when her fingers suddenly changed direction, step by exquisite step, as they made their way down to dance tantalisingly over his erection. He snatched in a breath when she boldly circled him with her hand, her soft skin like a silky glove.

She gave him a sultry little smile and bent her head to him, her hair tickling his abdomen and thighs, as she stroked her tongue over his engorged flesh. He groaned out loud as she licked him like a shy, tentative kitten. But then she suddenly turned into a wild rampaging tigress and consumed him whole. Shudders of delight rocked through him as she fed off him hungrily.

He tried to pull away but she pressed him back down with a determined hand. 'Stay,' she said.

'You don't have to do this,' he said, fighting for control.

'You did it to me.'

'That was different,' he said, breathing raggedly.

'"All's fair in love and war",' she said in a sing-song voice.

'So which is this?' he asked. 'Love or war?'

She gathered her hair in one hand before curling it over one shoulder, her eyes glinting with mischief and daring. 'This is war,' she said, and then lowered her mouth and claimed victory.

CHAPTER ELEVEN

In the weeks leading up to her twin's wedding Sienna settled into Andreas's life as if she had always been in it. They didn't discuss the future by tacit agreement, although their affair was as blisteringly hot as ever. She had wondered if Andreas's ardour would cool over time but it hadn't any more than hers had. She had been constantly surprised by her body's capacity for pleasure. His mix of tenderness and daring as a lover repeatedly took her breath away. He would only have to look at her a certain way and she would shudder in anticipated pleasure. She had become more adventurous as her confidence grew. She delighted in catching him off guard, seducing him when he least expected it.

He had been generous to her in showering her with gifts. He had bought her a sophisticated camera and a computer of her own to store her files of pictures. He had encouraged her to have copies professionally printed and had even hung some framed ones in his office in Florence.

Sienna wondered if they would still be hanging there when their marriage came to its inevitable end.

The other project Andreas had helped her with was Scraps. With careful handling and patience, the dog was now totally at ease around them. Andreas drew the line at having the dog inside the villa, but Sienna was content that Scraps was at least healthy and happy and comfortable with the staff as well as her and Andreas.

For once in her life the press left her alone. They seemed to have accepted that she and Andreas were a happily married couple and, apart from an occasional snap of them having dinner or attending a function together, there was no hint of scandal or anything untoward.

Sienna knew it wouldn't last but she tried not to think about it. She was becoming very good at not thinking about things that troubled her. Denial had become her closest companion. As soon as a worrying or wayward thought entered her head she would immediately dismiss it, like her feelings for Andreas, for instance. She absolutely refused to think beyond the fact that she no longer hated him. What she actually felt for him was locked behind a door inside her head marked private and off-limits.

She just didn't want to go there.

As to what Andreas felt about her, she knew was equally dangerous to examine too closely. He had a goal in mind and within a few rapidly passing months he would achieve it. He would be able to claim his inheritance and move on with his life. She didn't like to presume she would continue to be a part of it.

He never spoke of his feelings. He was attentive and affectionate, and even teasing and playful at times, but occasionally she would catch him looking at her with a frown pulling at his brow. It was as if he wasn't quite sure what to do with her. She suspected she delighted and frustrated him in equal measure.

One such time was a couple of days before Sienna was due to leave for Rome to help her sister prepare for her wedding. Andreas came into the bedroom they shared just as Sienna was sorting out what to take with her. She had been determined to take a leaf from his book and become better organised. She had planned to be packed well and truly in advance—there would no longer be any last minute mad grabs or flying off without packing appropriately. The bed was strewn with clothes and the floor with shoes, but that was all under control, or it would have been if he hadn't come home earlier than she had expected. 'Hi,' she said with a bright smile. 'You're home early.'

His brooding frown looked as if it had been stitched to his brow. 'Do you have to take everything out of the wardrobe every time you get dressed?' he asked.

Sienna lifted her chin, more than a little stung by his surly mood. 'I'm packing.'

A muscle jerked at the side of his mouth. 'What?'

'I'm leaving for Rome, remember?' she said, turning to fling a pair of jeans on to the not-taking-this pile on the floor. 'I'm going to my sister's wedding. I told you about it, not that you probably listened. Of course, it's entirely up to you whether you come or not. No one is pressuring you. I can imagine going to a real wedding where the couple actually love each other will be quite an eye-opener for you.'

'What the hell is that supposed to mean?' he asked.

'Figure it out for yourself,' she said as she pushed past him to fetch a suitcase.

He shackled one of her wrists with his hand, turning her round to face him. 'What's got into you?' he asked.

'What's got into *me*?' Sienna asked. 'You're the one

who came home like a bear with a thorn in his paw.'
She shoved at his chest with her free hand. 'Take your
hands off me.'

A burning gleam entered his hazel gaze as it collided with hers. 'You wanted my hands on you twice
last night and this morning,' he said. 'I've been getting
shivers all day just thinking about what you did to me
in the shower.'

She threw him a caustic glare that belied her quivering insides. 'Well, I don't want them on me now.'

He tugged her closer, his pelvis hard against hers, his
desire warring with her will. 'Prove it,' he said.

'I don't have to prove anything,' she said, giving
him another shove, but it was like trying to shift a sky-
scraper.

He put a hand at the base of her spine, holding her
to the hardened probe of his erection. 'One kiss and I'll
let you go,' he said.

'All right,' Sienna said, determined to show him she
could resist him. She would rise to the challenge the
same way she dealt with all of her traitorous thoughts.
She would block it from her mind. 'Give me your best,
Rich Boy.'

His mouth came down but, instead of completely
covering hers, his lips teased the side of her mouth,
making every nerve twitch and writhe in rapture. She
fought against the desire to turn her head that tiny fraction so her mouth was right under his. She scrunched
her eyes closed and tried to ignore the way her body
was responding to his as if on automatic. Her spine
loosened as he shifted his attention to the other side of
her mouth. His stubble caught on her skin, sending a
lightning bolt of desire to her core.

'You're cheating,' she said, a little shocked at how breathless she sounded.

'How am I cheating?' he asked, moving up to suck on her earlobe.

Sienna shivered. 'You said one kiss, but you haven't even kissed me.'

'I'm working my way up to it,' he said, coming back to that incredibly sensitive corner of her mouth where her top lip joined her bottom one.

She let out a wobbly breath as his tongue came out to stroke along the partially open seam of her mouth. He still hadn't pressed his lips to hers and yet she was thrumming like a tuning fork struck against a hard object.

Finally she could stand it no longer. She grabbed at his head with her hands, digging her fingers into his scalp as she pressed her mouth to his. He took immediate control by going in search of her tongue, the sensual and commanding thrust of his destroying any hope of her resisting him. She slammed her body up against his, rubbing herself against his arousal, delighting in the crackling sexual energy that fired between them at the intimate contact.

He growled against her mouth as he walked her backwards to the clothes-strewn bed. 'Get your clothes off.'

'Off the bed or off me?' she asked, tearing at his shirt, popping buttons with scant disregard for the designer label it bore.

'Let's start with you,' he said, pulling off her T-shirt as if it were nothing more than tissue paper.

Sienna landed on the mattress with a gasp as he came down on top of her. Somehow her jeans and knickers had met the same fate as her T-shirt. She was naked and sizzling with need as he parted her, thrusting into her with a groan of primal pleasure that made the skin on her arms come up in a fine sandpaper of goose bumps.

He set a rhythm that was breathtakingly fast, his strongly muscled body pumping into hers with raw urgency until she was screaming out loud her release. She wrapped her legs around his waist, desperate to hold on to the exquisite sensations for as long as she could. She sobbed as the final waves coursed through her. She had never felt such exhilarating pleasure. It racked her body with its aftershocks just as his release burst out of him. She felt every shuddering pulse of his body as he spilled. She felt the way the muscles of his back and shoulders finally relaxed under the soothing stroke of her hands.

In that quiet moment of the aftermath, she felt the carapace of her closely guarded heart fall away as if chipped at by a sharpened chisel.

It terrified her.

She could not allow this to happen.

She had to squash it before it took hold.

'Get off me,' she said, pushing against him.

Andreas frowned as he moved to let her get up. 'What's wrong, *ma petite*?'

Sienna shoved her hair back from her face. 'Why do you always switch languages?' she asked irritably. 'It totally confuses me.'

'You understand both Italian and French,' he said. 'It doesn't confuse you at all.'

'I *am* confused,' she said, snatching up a wrap to cover her nakedness.

He rose from the bed and came over to where she was standing with her back towards him. He put his hands on her shoulders, his breath skating past her ear as he drew her back towards him. 'What's confusing you, *cara*?' he asked.

Sienna turned to face him. 'I'm sorry,' she said, letting her shoulders go down in a slump. 'I think I'm letting my sister's wedding get to me. It's so...so starkly different from ours.'

His eyes searched hers. 'And that's a problem for you?'

She shifted her gaze from his. 'No,' she said, fiddling with a dress on the bed that was now in desperate need of an iron. 'Why should it be? It's not the same thing at all. We're not in love or planning a future together. We both want what we can get out of this arrangement. This little affair we've got going is all well and good for now, but I don't want to be tied to you in the long term any more than you want to be tied to me.'

A long silence ticked past, measured by the rustling of her increasingly haphazard sorting.

'Do you want some help packing?' Andreas asked. 'It looks like you need it.'

Sienna turned and faced him again. 'I can do it by myself,' she said. 'I think it's time I learned how to sort out the mess of my own making.'

'This is not your mess,' he said, frowning as he raked his hair with his fingers. 'This is my father's.'

'Is it?' she asked, giving him a world-weary look. 'Is it really?'

He held her gaze for a long moment. 'I suspect my father wanted to teach me a lesson,' he said. 'He wanted me to understand how hard it is to choose between what I think I want and what I really need.'

'So have you figured it out yet?' she asked.

He continued to hold her gaze. 'I already know what I want,' he said. 'I'm not sure, however, that it's what I need.'

'And what is it that you want, Andreas?' she asked. 'More money? More fame and notoriety?'

He took her by the upper arms and pulled her close, making her heart beat triple time as she felt his body stirring against her belly. 'I think you already know the answer to that,' he said and pressed his mouth down firmly on hers.

CHAPTER TWELVE

'You look absolutely amazing,' Sienna said as she made one last adjustment to Gisele's veil. 'Emilio is going to be speechless when he sees you.'

Gisele smiled as she squeezed Sienna's hands in hers. 'I think Andreas is going to have a similar reaction when he sees you,' she said. 'You look stunning.'

'Thanks...' Sienna slipped her hands out of Gisele's and moved to the dressing table so she could do a last minute touch-up of her make-up before Hilary, Gisele's mother, came back from the suite next door where the hairdresser was styling her hair. With all the bustle of getting ready, it was the first time Sienna had been alone with her sister.

'Is everything all right?' Gisele asked.

Sienna met her twin's grey-blue gaze in the mirror. It still startled her sometimes to see an identical replica of herself standing there. They were so physically alike it was uncanny, and yet they were so different. 'I'm fine,' she said, forcing a bright smile to her lips.

Gisele came over and put a gentle hand on Sienna's bare shoulder. 'You and Andreas are happy together, aren't you?' she asked. 'It was such a whirlwind courtship, I just wondered if—'

'Of course we're happy,' Sienna said, dipping the lipstick brush in a pot of lip-gloss. 'We're just peachy.'

'You don't have any regrets about having such a small wedding?' Gisele asked.

Sienna's hand trembled slightly as she painted her lips with the lipgloss. 'No, why should I?'

Gisele caught her gaze in the mirror. 'I saw you looking at me when Mum was helping me into my dress,' she said. 'You had such a sad look on your face. I realised then how difficult it must have been for you, getting married without your mother to help you. Is that why you kept things so simple?'

Sienna put the lip brush down with a little clatter on the dressing table. 'I'm not like you, Gisele,' she lied. 'A big wedding has never interested me. For one thing, I'd be rubbish at organising it. I'd probably forget to invite someone terribly important or not order the right colour flowers. Anyway, can you see me wearing white? I wouldn't make it to the church without spilling something on it or tripping over the train or something.'

Gisele smiled and tucked a wayward strand of Sienna's hair back into the elegant style the hairdresser had arranged earlier. 'You're good for Andreas,' she said, putting her hands on Sienna's shoulders and meeting her gaze in the mirror once more. 'I could tell from last night's dinner that he has a tendency to be a little formal and distant. It probably comes from his wealthy background. He doesn't feel comfortable letting people get too close until he works out whether he can trust them or not. I see the way he looks at you. It was as if he can't quite believe his luck to have found someone who loves him for who he is, not for what he can provide.'

Sienna reached for the bronzer brush, even though

she really didn't need it given that her cheeks were doing a perfectly fine job of blushing all by themselves. 'He is lucky to have me,' she said. 'We're lucky to have each other.' *Even if it's only for another few months*, she thought.

'He'll make a wonderful father,' Gisele said. 'Have you talked about when you'll start a family?'

Sienna averted her gaze. 'I'm not…He's not…We're not…ready…'

Gisele smiled. 'It's just I have some news for you,' she said. 'I wondered if that was why you and Andreas married in such a rush. I got all excited. I thought it'd be so cool if we were pregnant together.'

Sienna swung around on the stool so quickly her head spun. 'You're pregnant?' she said.

'Yes,' Gisele said, beaming radiantly. 'Emilio is beside himself with pride. We haven't told anyone, other than Mum. I wanted you to be one of the first to know. We're having twins.'

'Twins!' Sienna grabbed Gisele's hands, desperately trying to ignore the sudden pang of envy that seized her. It was wrong of her to feel jealous. It was hideous of her. It was selfish. She wasn't the one who had longed for a family since she was a young girl. Sienna had no idea of what to do with a baby. She hadn't even held one in her arms.

What right did she have to wonder what it would be like to carry a pregnancy to full term? To feel those tiny limbs growing and moving inside her? To hold that precious little bundle soon after it was born? To smell that sweet innocent smell and stroke that soft fluffy head?

A wave of longing rushed through her. It set off an ache that felt like a weight pressing down on her heart.

There would be no sweet-smelling babies for her. Andreas had already made it clear how unsuitable he thought her as a mother for his children. He had left nothing to chance. Every time they had made love he had used protection.

The ache tightened in her chest like a spanner working on a nut and bolt.

Just as Sienna couldn't imagine having someone else kiss her or make love to her, she couldn't imagine having someone else's baby. She didn't *want* anyone else's baby.

'Do you know if they're identical?' she asked, thinking of those little limbs wrapped around each other like she and Gisele had been.

'Yes,' Gisele said. 'The ultrasound showed they're sharing the same placenta.'

'And what about the sex?' Sienna asked. 'Do you know if they're boys or girls?'

'Boys,' Gisele said, placing a hand on her only very slightly rounded tummy. 'After losing Lily, I never thought I'd be able to face a pregnancy again, but this time I just know it's going to be different. It *feels* different.'

The door of the suite opened and Hilary came in, looking every inch the stylishly coiffed and very proud mother of the bride. 'Ready, darling?' she said to Gisele. 'Emilio is eagerly awaiting his beautiful bride.'

Sienna handed Gisele the bridal bouquet, forcing an I'm-so-happy-for-you-smile to her lips, while inside her heart felt as if it were being backed over by an earthmover.

She had already forfeited love.

Would she have to forfeit motherhood as well?

* * *

Andreas felt his heart do a couple of leapfrogs in his chest as Sienna walked up the aisle ahead of her twin sister. She was wearing a floor-length latte-coloured satin gown with a cream bow tied over her left hip. Her hair was up in an elegant style that gave her a distinctly regal air. She was breathtakingly beautiful, but then, so too was her twin sister.

He tore his eyes away from Sienna to look at Gisele as she floated up the aisle in an ivory satin gown and a stunning veil and diamond tiara. Before the bridal party dinner last night he had only seen photographs of her in the press. The likeness, even in print, was amazing but meeting her in the flesh had been totally surreal. It was like looking at a mirror image of Sienna.

It occurred to him then, with an unexpected twinge of guilt, that this was what Sienna would have looked like as a proper bride if he had married her under normal circumstances.

Had *she* wanted something like this?

He felt another ferocious fist of guilt grab at his gut.

Didn't most young women dream of having their day as a fairy tale princess?

As the service got underway he watched to see if any of the heartfelt vows that were being exchanged were affecting Sienna. She stood looking at her sister and the handsome groom with a smile on her lips, but Andreas wasn't sure if that glittery moisture in her eyes was from happiness or something else. She looked rather pale, he thought, and once or twice he saw her lick her lips, from nervousness or dryness, he couldn't quite tell.

Andreas was surprised to find the service so moving. He had attended weddings before and, while he had mostly enjoyed them, he had not felt a lump of emotion suddenly stick like a nut halfway down his throat when the groom promised to love and protect his bride.

Emilio Andreoni was clearly a man deeply in love. His voice cracked unashamedly as he slipped the wedding band on Gisele's finger. Gisele looked up at him with absolute devotion, tears of joy shining in her eyes.

Andreas felt ashamed of how his marriage to Sienna had been such a sterile, businesslike affair. She hadn't looked at him with her eyes full of love. Hers had glittered with hatred. Their clinical, emotionless union made a mockery of one so sacred and deeply poignant as this. How had his life become such a tawdry sideshow alley game of smoke and mirrors?

He caught Sienna's eye across the church. She smiled at him but it was a weak movement of her lips that didn't involve her eyes. She looked away again, focusing her gaze on the bride and groom as they exchanged their first kiss as a married couple.

Andreas wondered if she was thinking of *their* first kiss. Their mouths had never touched until they had exchanged those meaningless vows. He was reminded of the electric shock of that kiss every time he had kissed her since. It was a power surge in his flesh. He could feel it now just thinking about it. His body ached for her. His blood thrummed with it. He had expected the pulse of lust to wane a little by now, but if anything it had increased. Would the five months left of their marriage contract be enough to satisfy him?

Because she was part of the bridal party, Sienna was separated from Andreas for most of the reception. It made his hunger for her all the more intense. He couldn't wait until the formalities were over so he could stake his claim. His whole body prickled with annoyance when she danced with the best man as part of the bridal waltz routine. Andreas clenched and unclenched his fists under the table as he watched the best man's arms go around her and bring her up close.

Jealousy was a new experience for him. He could not remember ever feeling it before. He bristled with it. It made his teeth grind together. It made his jaw ache. It made his blood boil.

His gaze narrowed. Was Sienna *flirting* with that guy? She was smiling up at him with that dazzling smile of hers. Her left hand was on the guy's shoulder and her right encased in the grasp of his. Her body was moving in time to the music, a slow romantic waltz that had her pelvis brushing against the best man's every now and again as her feet tangled with his.

Andreas strode across the dance floor and laid a firm hand on the best man's shoulder. 'I'd like to dance with my wife,' he said.

The best man dropped his hold on Sienna and stepped back. 'Sure,' he said with an easy smile. 'She's a fabulous dancer. I have two left feet but she made me dance like a pro.'

Andreas ground his teeth behind his stiff smile. 'She is indeed an expert at executing tricky manoeuvres.'

Sienna's grey-blue gaze collided with his once the best man had gone. 'What the hell are you playing at?' she asked in a hushed voice. 'You interrupted the bridal party waltz, for God's sake.'

Andreas turned her so she wasn't facing the wedding guests. 'I had to step in before you made a complete fool of yourself,' he said. 'You were practically crawling into that guy's skin.'

She glowered up at him. 'I was not!'

He tugged her against him. 'The only man you should be getting up close and personal with is me,' he said. 'We're married, remember?'

'Only for another five months,' she said, challenging him with her haughty gaze. 'After that, I'm free to be with anyone I want and you won't be able to do a thing to stop me.'

He whipped her around as the music changed tempo, his groin alive with want as her slender thighs bumped against his. 'I wouldn't dream of trying,' he said, 'but for now you are my wife and I expect you to act accordingly.'

Her eyes flashed at him like blue lightning. 'I'm not really your wife,' she said. 'This is just an act, a stupid little game of charades. I'm surprised no one has already guessed we're not the real deal. I'm sure Gisele already suspects something.'

'What makes you think that?' Andreas said, holding her close to him as another couple glided past.

'She kept grilling me on why we got married so quickly and why I hadn't gone for a big wedding,' she said, frowning and chewing at her lip as if the conversation had somehow distressed her.

Andreas deftly led her off the dance floor to a secluded area behind a column. He kept his arms around her, his body thrumming with need with her standing thigh to thigh with him. 'Are you disappointed we didn't have a proper wedding?' he asked.

She pulled her chin back against her neck in a gesture of scorn. 'Are you joking? Of course I'm not disappointed. What we have is a sham. It was bad enough lying in front of a celebrant, let alone a priest and a huge congregation. Anyway, it's different for Gisele. She loves Emilio and he loves her. They have their whole lives to look forward to.'

Andreas held her gaze for a beat or two. A shadow had passed through her eyes and her beautiful white teeth began to nibble at her bottom lip again. He pushed against the soft pillow of her lip with the pad of his fingertip. 'What's wrong?' he asked.

She jerked her head away from his touch. 'Nothing.'

'I know you better than that, *ma petite*. You always do that to your lip when you're brooding or mulling over something.'

She drew in a breath and then let it out on a long exhalation. 'I'm being stupid and sentimental,' she said, slipping out of his hold. 'Weddings do that to me, or at least ones like this.'

'Yes, well, it was certainly a very moving service,' Andreas conceded. 'Anyone can see Emilio and Gisele belong together. I've never seen a more radiant bride.'

'Gisele's pregnant,' she said. 'She's having twins.'

'That's wonderful news,' he said. 'You must be very happy for her.'

'I am…It's just…' She bit her lip again and dropped her eyes from his.

'Just what?' he asked, cupping the side of her face to bring her gaze back in line with his.

Her eyes shimmered for a moment but then she blinked and her gaze cleared. 'Just as well you're using protection,' she said lightly as she slipped out of his hold. 'Can you imagine the snotty nosed little brats we would make? If we had twins, I bet they'd fight like demons from the moment of conception. I'd probably get stretch marks from all the punches and kicks going on inside.'

Andreas felt a primal tug deep and low in his groin. He pictured Sienna ripe with his seed, her body swelling as each week and month passed. He thought of two little baby girls with silver-blonde hair, or two little boys with jet-black hair, or one of each. He imagined seeing them born, holding them in his arms, loving and protecting and providing for them for as long as he drew breath.

He put a brake on his thoughts like a speeding driver trying to avoid a crash.

In a matter of months he would have everything sewn up the way he wanted it. He would have the chateau and Sienna would have her money. He didn't need or want the complication of being tied forever with her. Their passion would burn out. Their marriage had come about for all the wrong reasons.

He would *not* be a slave to lust.

It would burn out.

It *had* to burn out.

'We should get back to the reception,' he said. 'Everyone will be wondering what's happened to us.'

CHAPTER THIRTEEN

It was late by the time they got back to their room at the hotel. Sienna kicked off her shoes and tossed her wrap on to the bed. She felt tired and overwrought. Her emotions had been building to a crescendo all evening. Andreas's brooding silence hadn't helped. He had barely spoken a word to her during the remainder of the reception. He had danced with her but it had felt as if he were just going through the motions, just like their relationship.

Their marriage was a lie.

It was a farce compared to her sister's. It made her feel like a fraud. It made her feel cheap and tainted. How could she have signed up for something so far from what she longed and yearned for?

She couldn't carry on like this, telling lie after lie after lie. How long before Andreas saw through it? How long before everyone saw through it? She would become an object of pity, just like her mother. She would be known as the woman not good enough, not beautiful enough or smart enough to hold her man.

'I'm going out,' Andreas said.

Sienna frowned. 'What? Now? It's almost one in the morning.'

'I feel like some air.'

She shrugged as if she didn't care either way. 'Don't expect me to wait up for you,' she said, pulling the pins from her hair and tossing them on to the dressing table willy-nilly.

A stiff silence passed.

'I have to fly to Washington DC for a few days,' he said. 'I've organised for Franco to collect you in the morning.'

'You don't want me to come with you?' she asked, meeting his gaze in the mirror.

His expression was unreadable. 'I'll be busy with meetings,' he said. 'The businessman I'm doing a collection for wants me to meet a colleague of his.'

Sienna loathed the feeling of being dismissed like a mistress who no longer held the same fascination and appeal. Was this how her mother had felt? Discarded? Betrayed? Unlovable? Worthless?

Her heart contracted as she looked at Andreas's stony expression. She was not important to him. How could she have let things get to this? She had betrayed every one of her values. He had used her to get what he wanted. He felt secure now she had succumbed to his seduction. After all, he had nothing to lose. If she left him now, he would still get what he wanted, what he had always wanted. He wanted a wretched old pile of bricks and mortar, not her. She had been a silly little fool to imagine otherwise.

She kept her expression cool and collected. 'Aren't you worried about what people will think of us being in separate countries when we've only been married a month?' she asked.

'I have a business to run,' he said. 'I don't want to be distracted when I'm working on such a big contract.'

'Fine,' Sienna said, throwing him a casual look to cover the wrenching pain she was feeling inside. 'I guess I'll see you when I see you.'

He didn't answer but the door closing on his exit was answer enough.

'What do you mean she's not here?' Andreas said when he got back to his villa in Tuscany a week later.

Elena lifted her hands in a don't-blame-me manner. 'She told me to tell you it's over,' she said. 'She doesn't want to be married to you any more.'

Andreas sucked in a furious breath. 'When did she leave?'

'The day after her sister's wedding,' Elena said. 'I tried to talk her out of it but she was very stubborn about it. She'd made up her mind.'

'Why didn't you call me and tell me this days ago?' he asked.

'She made me promise.'

'You are employed by me, not her,' Andreas railed at her. 'You should have informed me the minute she left.'

Elena gave him an accusing look. 'Maybe you should have called her every day like a loving husband would have done,' she said. 'Maybe then she wouldn't have run away.'

Andreas clawed a hand through his hair. 'Where the hell is she?' he asked.

'She didn't say where she was going,' Elena said. 'I don't think she wants you to know. She left this for you.' She handed him his mother's ring.

Andreas closed his fingers over the ring until it bit

into his palm. He had thought he'd had the upper hand by distancing himself for a few days but Sienna had turned the tables on him. Didn't she want the money? If she left him she would automatically default. She wouldn't get a penny. A month ago that would have pleased him no end. Now, all he could think about was getting her to come back.

He reached for his phone and rapid-dialled her but it went straight to voicemail. He shoved his phone back in his pocket and glared at Elena. 'She must have left some clue as to where she was going,' he said. 'Did she take her passport?'

'I think so,' Elena said, sighing heavily. 'Scraps is pining for her. He won't eat. I'm worried about him.'

Andreas gave a scornful grunt as he raked his fingers through his hair. 'Shows how much she cares about him.'

'She loves him,' Elena said.

'If she loved him she'd be here with him, not running off to God knows where,' he said.

'Maybe she doesn't know if he loves her back,' Elena said with a direct look.

Andreas glowered at her. 'Don't you have work to do? Some cushions to straighten or some clothes to fold and iron.'

'Sì, signor,' she said, 'but without Signora Ferrante here there is not much for me to do. She makes this place come alive, no?'

Andreas went out to the barn but Scraps barely lifted his head off his paws. His woebegone eyes followed Andreas's movements as he crouched down in front of him. 'What's this I hear about you not eating?'

The dog let out a mournful little whine.

'She won't answer her phone,' Andreas said, absently scratching behind the dog's tattered ears. 'I've left hundreds of messages. She's doing it deliberately, you know. She wants me to beg her to come back. But I'm not going to do it. If she wants to default, then that's her business. It's not as if I'm going to lose out if she pulls the plug on our relationship. I still get the chateau. That's all I ever wanted in the first place.'

Scraps gave a low growl, his tawny eyes staring unblinkingly at Andreas.

Andreas pulled his hand away and exhaled heavily. 'OK, I know what you're thinking. You're thinking I'm an idiot for lying to myself for so long.' He sent his fingers through his hair and let out another sigh. 'And you'd be right. I don't care about the chateau. I don't want to live there, not unless she's with me. I don't want to live here without her either. The place is so formal and...*tidy*.' He coughed out a humourless laugh. 'I hate the way she leaves her mess everywhere. Do you know she *always* leaves the lid off the toothpaste? It drives me crazy. But I'd give anything to have her with me driving me crazy right now. I don't know where she is or who's she's with.' His gut clenched in anguish and dread. 'I don't know if I can get her back. What am I supposed to do? Crawl on my belly and beg her to come back to me?'

Scraps gave his threadbare tail a wag against the dusty floor, his eyes still staring wisely at Andreas.

'You're right,' Andreas said, sighing heavily again. 'I'm crazy about her. I'm never going to get her out of my system, am I? We're not talking about lust here. It's never been about lust, has it? What was I thinking? She's the best thing that's ever happened to me. I love her.'

He frowned and gave his head a little shake. 'I can't believe I just said that. I don't think I've told anyone that before, apart from my mother, which is totally different. *I love her.*'

He cautiously reached out to ruffle the dog's ears again. 'What if she doesn't love me?' he asked. 'I'm going to look the biggest fool if I gush out what I feel and she just laughs in my face.'

Scraps let out a long doggy sigh and settled his head back down on his paws.

'I'm not going to tell her over the phone or in a text message,' Andreas said with steely determination. 'I'm going to track her down and talk to her face to face. She thinks she can outsmart me but she's wrong.'

He got to his feet and dusted off his hands. 'If you want to come inside I guess I could make an exception just this once,' he said. 'But no jumping up on the sofas and you are absolutely banned from any of the beds, do you understand?'

The little cottage by the sea on South Harris in Scotland was a perfect hideaway. The long, lonely windswept beaches on the island gave Sienna plenty of time to walk and think about her future—her lonely future without Andreas. She had kept her phone on for the first week, hoping he would call or at least text, but he had cut her loose like the trophy wife he had fashioned her into and, even more galling, she had allowed it to happen.

But now was different.

Now it was time for her to rebuild her life, a life that did not include him, a life without love and passion and fulfilment—a wretchedly lonely, miserable life, the opposite of the one her twin sister was living. How could two people so identical in looks have such disparate lives?

She had phoned Gisele, so as to avoid causing her sister any undue worry but she had refused to say where she was. She knew Gisele would immediately tell Andreas. She wasn't ready to talk to him yet. As far as she was concerned, he'd had his chance and he had blown it.

Sienna had since turned her phone off, only checking it once a day for messages. The second week there were literally hundreds of texts and missed calls from him each day. The messages had progressed from calm and polite pleas to get her to call him, to shouting tirades interspersed with colourful obscenities.

She deleted them all, only wishing she could delete all her memories of him so easily.

She lay awake at night as the wind howled against the shore, whipping up the waves like galloping white horses. She spent hours thinking of Andreas, of his touch, the way his hands felt against her skin, the way his mouth felt against hers, the way his body felt as it claimed hers.

Sienna had been on the island almost a fortnight without once setting eye on a newspaper. She had avoided reading anything on the web browser on her phone as well. She didn't want to know what the press were saying about her and Andreas. But while she was walking on Scarista beach that morning she had briefly turned on her phone and found a message from Gisele alerting her to an article that had come out a day or two before regarding the sex tape scandal. Apparently the man involved had given an exclusive interview to a journalist. He had seen the news of Gisele and Emilio's wedding and had obviously thought he could cash in on the situation by giving a no holds barred tell-all interview.

Sienna read the interview with a churning feeling in her stomach. It brought it all back: the shame and disgust she felt at herself. The way the man told it, she had acted like a drunken slut.

Despair clawed at her chest as she stood on the windswept beach. Was there anywhere she could run, far enough away to hide from this? Was this never going to go away?

But then she pressed on the second link Gisele had sent her.

French-Italian tycoon Andreas Ferrante is pressing charges of slander against Eric Hogan over Mr Hogan's claim that he slept with Mr Ferrante's wife Sienna Baker in London two and a half years ago. The case is likely to be long drawn-out and expensive but Andreas Ferrante says he will not stop until his wife's name is cleared. Police are making further enquiries regarding a possible drink spiking charge on Mr Hogan following the recent revelations of witnesses.

Sienna's heart was beating so fast she could barely breathe. She read the article again, her eyes prickling with tears.

Andreas had stood up for her.

He had publicly defended her. He was fighting her

battle for her, not even counting the cost in money, let alone the cost to his fiercely guarded privacy.

Sienna was heading back to the cottage to pack when a tall, imposing figure came striding towards her. She knew immediately who it was. She felt a shiver run over her flesh as soon as he came into view. The wild wind was whipping at his sooty black hair and his unshaven face looked as thunderous as the brooding sky above.

'You'd better have a damn good reason for not returning any of my calls,' he ground out. 'Do you have any idea of the trouble you've caused? I've spent tens of thousands of euros looking high and low for you. Why couldn't you have just told me? Just one phone call or text. God damn it, was that so hard?'

Sienna just stood there looking up at him. Her gaze drank in his features.

He had stood up for her.

'OK, so give me the silent treatment; see if I care,' he said. He shoved his windswept hair back with one of his hands. 'Just answer me one thing. Why did you run away like that?'

'How did you find me?' she asked.

'Gisele told me she thought she heard bagpipes in the background when you called her,' he said. 'That narrowed it down considerably. The rest I left up to a private investigator. Do you have any idea of what the press have been saying?'

Sienna peeled a strand of hair away from her mouth. 'I haven't seen anything in the press until this morning,' she said. 'I'm sorry about the embarrassment I've caused you.'

'I'm not talking about that,' he said, glaring at her fiercely. 'I've taken care of that sleaze ball. He won't be saying anything about you ever again. How could you think I wouldn't be out of my mind with worry over you? Do you realise what a fool you made me look in front of my staff when I turned up there at the villa and you'd already been gone a week?'

'I'm sorry but I didn't want you to talk me out of it,' Sienna said. 'Anyway, you could have called me. I was giving you a dose of your own medicine.'

'You realise you won't get a penny because of this,' he said still glowering at her. 'You defaulted. I get everything.'

'You've always *had* everything, Andreas,' she said. 'The irony is I've spent most of my life envying rich people like you. I wanted it all: the nice houses and the designer clothes, the jewellery and the fabulous holidays. I thought they would make me happy, that they would make me feel a sense of belonging. But I've come to realise possessions and prestige can never make up for what's most important in life. They're nothing when you don't have love.'

His eyes narrowed in anger. 'You think I don't love you?' he said, shouting above the howling wind. 'I've just spent the last fortnight without proper sleep or food. God knows what's happened to my business because I haven't put a foot inside my office or my workshop. And don't get me started on that contract I just forfeited. I've been too busy trying to track you down to do a thing about it. How dare you stand there accusing me of not loving you?'

Sienna swept her tongue over her wind-chapped lips as her heart went pitter-pat. 'You love me?' she said. 'You're not just saying it to save face and get me to come back?'

'I'm saying it because it's true, damn it!' he said. 'I love your madcap sense of humour. I love your mess. I love the way you tamed a flea-bitten mongrel dog that no one else wanted. I love your smile. I love your laugh. I love your cheekiness. I love the way you nearly always have a spark of mischief in your eyes. I love the way you feel in my arms. I love the way you say one thing and mean the total opposite.' He drew in a breath and released it in a whoosh before he added, 'Have I left anything out?'

Sienna gave him a sheepish smile. 'I think you've just about covered it,' she said.

He let out a laugh and grabbed her, hugging her close to his chest, breathing in the salty sea air that had clung to her hair. 'You little minx,' he said. 'I love you so much it hurts.'

She eased back to look up at him. 'Where does it hurt?'

'Here,' he said, placing one of her hands over his heart.

Sienna blinked back tears. 'I've been so lonely and sad since Gisele and Emilio's wedding. I couldn't live the lie any more. I didn't think it was right. Your father was wrong to set things up the way he did. It was cruel and manipulative.'

'I know, *ma petite*,' he said, gently cupping her face so he could stroke her cheeks with his thumbs. 'I felt like that too. Seeing the love Emilio has for your sister unnerved me. All of my life I have avoided emotional commitment. I've always set the agenda in my relationships. But with you it was different. I couldn't control what I felt. I refused to confront it. I don't think I really understood how much I loved you until I saw the way Scraps behaved after you left.'

'Is he OK?' Sienna asked. 'I cried like a baby when I left him. My eyes were red and swollen for days.'

Andreas smiled at her. 'He's decided that the barn is no longer suitable accommodation,' he said. 'He's taken up residence in the villa. He has a particular penchant for lying on the sofa watching mind-numbing reality TV shows.'

Sienna smiled back as she looped her arms around his neck. 'That's my boy,' she said. 'I always knew he could be tamed. I just had to be patient.'

Andreas held her close against him. 'I want us to have a proper wedding. I want you to wear one of those fairy tale dresses with a big floating veil, and even glass slippers on your feet if you want. Whatever you want, just tell me and you shall have it.'

Sienna let out a sigh of contentment as she gazed into his hazel eyes. 'What more could I want than you?' she said.

'What about babies?' he said, his expression sobering for a moment. 'You said you didn't want children.'

'Now that you mention it, maybe a baby or two would be nice,' she said.

He kissed the end of her nose. 'I quite fancy the idea of you being pregnant,' he said. 'I think we should get working on that right away. What do you say?'

'Sounds like a plan.'

He held her aloft for a moment. 'Do you realise you haven't actually told me you love me?' he said. 'Here I am shouting it from one end of the beach to the other but you haven't said it back.'

'I love you,' Sienna said, smiling up at him radiantly. 'I love you with all my heart. I think I've always loved you, even when I hated you. Does that make sense?'

He gave her an indulgent smile. 'From you, my adorable little scatterbrain, it makes absolutely perfect sense,' he said and covered her mouth with his.

* * * * *

DESERVING OF
HIS DIAMONDS?

To Carol Marinelli: not just a fellow author but
a fun friend.

CHAPTER ONE

EMILIO was sitting in a café in Rome not far from his office when he finally found out the truth. His chest seized as he read the article about twin girls who had been separated at birth due to an illegal adoption. The article was journalism at its best: an intriguing and poignant account of how identical twins had finally been reunited, quite by chance, after a shop attendant mistook one for the other in a Sydney department store.

One mistaken for the other...

Emilio ignored his coffee and sat back in his chair and looked out at the bustling city crowds wandering past. Tourists and workers, young and old, married and single—everyone going about their business, totally unaware of the shock that was consuming him until he could scarcely breathe.

It hadn't been Gisele in the sex tape.

His throat felt as if a spanner were going down sideways. He had been so adamant about it, so stubborn. He had not listened to Gisele's protestations of innocence. He had *refused* to listen. She had begged and pleaded with him to believe in her, but he had not.

He had got it wrong.

She had cried. She had screamed. She had pummelled

at his chest with tears pouring down her face, and yet he had walked away. He had cut all contact with her. He had sworn on his life he would never see or speak to her again.

He had got it wrong.

Emilio's company had almost folded over the scandal. He'd had to work so hard to get back to where he was today. Eighteen-hour, sometimes twenty-four-hour days, sleepless nights, endless travel, jet lag so bad he didn't sleep properly any more, no matter how utterly exhausted he was. He went from project to project like an automaton, putting in the hours, signing up the deals, paying off the debts and then finally banking the millions, his drive to succeed knowing no bounds.

And for all this time he had blamed Gisele.

He had fuelled his hatred of her every day since. It had festered inside him like a gangrenous wound. He had felt it in every pore of his body. Every time he had thought of her the temperature of his wrath had risen. It had burned like a roaring furnace deep inside him. It had blazed like wild flames through his veins. Some days it had almost consumed him. It had been like a fever he could not control.

His gut clenched with a fist of guilt. He had always prided himself on never making an error of judgement. He aimed—some would say ruthlessly—for perfection in every area of his life. Failure was anathema to him.

And yet with Gisele he had got it wrong.

Emilio looked at his phone. He still had her number in his contacts. He had left it there as a reminder to trust no one, to let no one under his guard. He had never thought of himself as the sentimental type, but when he brought her details to the screen his fingers shook slightly as they hovered over her name. Somehow calling out of the blue to say sorry didn't seem the right way to handle things. He owed her a face-to-face apology. It was the least he could do. He wanted to erase that mistake, to draw a line through it and move on with his life.

He clicked on his phone's rapid dial instead and called his secretary. 'Carla, cancel all of my appointments for the next week and get me a flight to Sydney as soon as you can,' he said. 'I have some urgent business to see to there.'

Gisele was showing a first time mother the handmade christening gown she had embroidered when Emilio Andreoni came in. Seeing him standing there, so tall, so out of place in her baby clothes boutique made her heart leap to her throat like a gymnast on an overused trampoline.

She had practised this day over in her head just in case he took it upon himself to apologise once he found out about her long-lost identical twin. She had imagined how vindicated she would feel that he would have to admit he had got it wrong about her. She had imagined she would look at him and feel nothing, nothing but the bitter hatred of him for his cruel and ruthless rejection and his inexcusable lack of trust.

And yet that first glimpse of him sent a shockwave through her that made her feel as if the floor beneath her feet were suddenly shifting. Emotions she had bolted down with bitter determination suddenly popped against their restraints. One by one she could feel them spreading through her, making her chest ache with the weight of them. How could it physically hurt to see someone face to face? How could her heart feel pain like a stab wound at seeing his tall, imposing frame standing there? How could her insides clench and twist when his coal-black eyes met hers?

Gisele had seen him in the press several times since their break-up and although each time it had made her feel a tight sort of ache, it had felt nothing like the raw, claw-scraping pain of this.

He still had the same darkly tanned olive skin. The same Roman nose, the same penetrating dark brown eyes, the same intractable jaw that right now looked as if it hadn't seen a razor in the last thirty-six hours. The slightly wavy black hair was a little longer than the last time she had seen him—it was curling around the collar of his shirt and it looked as if his fingers had been the last thing that had moved through it. There were bruiselike shadows beneath his thickly lashed bloodshot eyes, no doubt put there by yet another sleepless night out with one of his one-night stand bimbo bedmates, she imagined.

'Excuse me…' she said to the young mother. 'I won't be a minute.'

Gisele walked over to where he was standing next to the premature baby clothes. He had one of his hands on a tiny vest that had a pink rosebud with little green leaves embroidered at the neck. The vest looked so tiny against his hand and it occurred to her then that Lily would have been too small for it when she had been born.

'Can I help you with something?' she asked with a brittle look.

Emilio's eyes meshed with hers, holding them captive. 'I think you know why I am here, Gisele,' he said in that deep, rich voice she had missed so much. It moved along her skin like a caress, settling at the base of her spine like a warm pool of slowly spreading honey.

Gisele had to fight hard to keep her emotions in check. This was not the time to show him she was still affected by him, even if it was only physically. She had to be strong, to show him he hadn't destroyed her life with his lack of trust. She had to show him she had moved on, that she was self-sufficient and successful. She had to show him he meant *nothing* to her now. She drew in a breath and lifted her chin, keeping her voice cool and composed. 'Of course.' She gave him an impersonal on-off movement of her lips that was nowhere near a smile. 'How could I forget? The two-for-one sale on all-in-one suits we have on at the moment. You can have blue, pink or yellow. I'm afraid we're all out of the white.'

His gaze never once wavered from hers; it was as dark and mesmerising as ever. 'Is there somewhere we could talk in private?' he asked.

Gisele straightened her shoulders. 'As you can see I have customers to see to,' she said, indicating with a waft of her hand the young woman browsing along the racks.

'Are you free for lunch?' he asked, still watching her steadily.

Gisele wondered if he was studying her for flaws. Could he see the way her once creamy skin had lost its glow? Could he see the shadows below and in her eyes that no amount of make-up could disguise? He had always prized perfection. Not just in his work but in every facet of his life. He would find her sadly lacking now, she thought, in spite of her name and reputation finally being cleared. 'I own and run this business,' she said with more than a hint of pride. 'I don't take a lunch break.'

Gisele saw his dark critical gaze sweep over the baby wear boutique she had bought a few weeks after he had cut her from his life just days before their wedding. Building it up from yet another struggling suburban retail outlet to the successful exclusive affair it was now had been the only thing that had got her through the heartbreak of the past two years.

Some well meaning friends, along with her mother, had suggested it would have been better to have sold the business as soon as she had been told Lily wasn't going to make it, but somehow, in her mind, holding on to the shop was a way to hold on to her fragile little daughter for just that little bit longer. She felt close to Lily here, surrounded by the handmade blankets and bonnets and booties she made for other babies to wear. It was her only connection now with motherhood and she wasn't going to relinquish it in spite of the pain it caused to see those brand-new prams being pushed through the door day after day. No one knew how hard it was for her to look and not touch those precious little bundles inside. No one knew how long at night she clung to the bunny blanket she had made for Lily's tiny body to be wrapped in during those few short hours of her life.

Emilio's eyes came back to connect with hers. 'Dinner then,' he said. 'You don't work past six, do you?'

Gisele watched in irritation as the young mother left

the shop, no doubt put off by Emilio's brooding presence. She sent him a glare. 'Dinner is out of the question,' she said. 'I have another engagement.'

'Are you involved with someone?' he asked, pinning her with his eyes.

She worked hard at keeping her composure. Did he really think she would have dived headfirst into another relationship after what he had done to her? She often wondered if she would ever feel safe in a relationship again. But she daren't admit to her singleton status. She had a feeling he wasn't just here to apologise and to clear the air between them. She could see it in the dark magnetic pull of his gaze. She could sense it in the atmosphere, the way the air she shared with him thickened with each breath she took into her lungs. Damn it, she could even feel it in her traitorous body as it reacted to his dark, disturbing presence the way it had always done in the past. Her senses went on full alert, her legs giving a little tremble as she thought of how he had taught her all she knew about physical intimacy, how it had been his body and his alone that had shown her what hers had been capable of in giving and receiving pleasure. 'I can't see how that is any of your business,' she said with a hoist of her chin.

A muscle flexed beside his mouth. 'I know this is hard for you, Gisele,' he said. 'It's hard for me too.'

'Meaning you never thought you'd ever have to apologise to me for getting it wrong?' she asked with a cutting look. 'Hate to say I told you so.'

His expression immediately became shuttered, closed off, remote. 'I'm not proud of how I ended things,' he said. 'But you would have done the same if things were the other way around.'

'You're wrong, Emilio,' she said. 'I would have looked high and low for an alternative explanation for how that tape came about.'

'For God's sake, Gisele,' he said roughly. 'Do you think I didn't look for an explanation? You told me you were an only child. *You* didn't even know you had a twin. How was I supposed to come up with something as bizarre as that? I looked at that tape and I saw you. I saw the same silver-blonde hair, the same grey-blue eyes, even the same mannerisms. I had no choice but to believe what I was seeing.'

'You *did* have a choice,' Gisele said, shooting him a blistering glare. 'You could have believed me in spite of, not because of, the evidence. But you didn't love me enough to trust me. You didn't love me at all. You just wanted a perfect wife to hang off your arm. That wretched tape tarnished me so I was of no further use to you. It wouldn't have mattered if the truth had come out in two minutes or two hours instead of two years. Your business was always going to be the priority. You put it before everything.'

'I put my business on hold to come out here to see you,' he said, frowning at her broodingly.

'You've seen me, so now you can jump back on your private jet and fly all the way back,' she said, sending him a haughty look as she spun on her heel.

'Damn it, Gisele,' he said, snagging one of her arms to stall her.

Gisele felt the steely grip of his long, strong fingers on her bare arm as he turned her back to face him. His touch was like a flame. It seared her skin like a brand. Every nerve flinched beneath her skin. She felt her stomach go hollow as his eyes locked on hers. She didn't want to lose herself in that glittering dark gaze. Not again. Once was enough. It had been her downfall, falling for a man with the inability to love and trust.

She didn't want him this close.

She could smell the heat of him, the sharp and heady cocktail of musk and male and lemon-based aftershave that made her nostrils flare and tingle. She could see the black pepper of the stubble on his jaw and her fingers suddenly itched to feel that sexy rasp under the soft pads of her fingertips. She could see the grim line of his beautifully sculptured mouth. The mouth that had wreaked such havoc on her senses from the very first time he had kissed her. She only had to close her eyes to remember how it felt to have those hard, insistent lips press down on hers...

She snapped out of her reverie like an elastic band that had been stretched too far. That same mouth had vilified her cruelly. Her ears still rang with his hateful, unforgettable, unforgivable words. There was no way she was going to let him off lightly, if at all. Her life had come undone the day he had cut her adrift. She had been so devastated and alone. Her happy future had suddenly been ripped away from her without warning. She had been shattered by his accusations. She had been left so raw with pain she had barely been able to drag herself through each agonising day.

Finding out she was pregnant a couple of months after she had returned to Sydney had been her only glimmer of hope in that very dark place she had found herself in.

But then that hope had been cruelly dashed a few weeks later at the second ultrasound. She had always wondered if that was her punishment for not telling Emilio about the pregnancy. He had forbidden all contact after their break-up, but she had been too devastated and hurt to even try.

And too angry.

She had wanted to punish him for not believing in her. She still wanted to punish him. It was like a rod of steel inside her. The only thing holding her upright was her fury and resentment and hatred towards him. Nothing was going to melt it.

'Why are you making this harder than it already is?' Emilio asked.

Gisele needed the trench of her anger to hide in and the deeper and dirtier the better. 'You think you can breeze in here and issue some half-hearted apology and I'll forgive you?' she asked. 'I'll *never* forgive you. Do you hear me? *Never.*'

The line of his mouth was grim. 'I don't expect you to forgive me,' he said. 'I do, however, expect you to act like an adult and hear me out.'

'I'll act like an adult when you stop restraining me like an out of control child,' she said, shooting him a livid look. 'Let go of my arm.'

His fingers softened their hold but he didn't release her. Gisele felt her heart give a nervous flutter as the broad pad of his thumb slid down to her pulse. Could he feel the thud of those hit-and-miss beats? She surreptitiously moistened her mouth but his gaze caught the movement. His eyes darkened, the pupils disappearing into the chocolate-brown of his irises. She knew

that look so well. It triggered a visceral reaction in her
body. The pulse of longing was like a lightning strike
to that secret place between her thighs. Every erotically
sensual moment they had ever shared flashed through
her brain like a film on fast-forward. Those sensually
provocative images made a mockery of every paltry attempt she had made to keep herself immune. What hope
of immunity when one look from those dark eyes made
her blood rush through her veins at breakneck speed?

'Have dinner with me tonight,' he said.

'I told you I already have an engagement,' she said,
not quite meeting his eyes.

Emilio tipped up her chin with his other hand, his
eyes dark and penetrating as they held hers. 'And I know
you are lying,' he said.

'What a pity you weren't such a hotshot detective
two years ago,' she threw back resentfully as she finally
managed to break free. She stood and pointedly rubbed
at her wrist, still glaring at him.

'I'll pick you up at seven,' he said. 'Where do you
live?'

Gisele felt a bolt of panic rush through her. She didn't
want him at her flat. That was her private sanctuary,
the one place she felt safe enough to let out her grief.
Besides, how would she explain all the photos of Lily?
It was much better to leave him ignorant of their baby's
short life. She wasn't ready to tell him. She would *never*
be ready to tell him. How could she cope with the pain
of him telling her she should have had a termination as
she had been advised? It had been hard enough hearing it from her mother and some of her friends. Emilio

wouldn't have wanted a child who wasn't perfect. It wouldn't have suited his plan for a perfectly ordered life.

'You don't seem to be getting the message, Emilio,' she said with a defiant look. 'I don't want to see you again. Not tonight. Not tomorrow night. Not ever. You've apologised. End of story. Now, please leave before I have you evicted by Security.'

His expression was faintly mocking. 'What Security?' he asked. 'Anyone could walk in here and empty your cash register while your back was turned and you wouldn't be able to do a single thing to stop them. You don't even have CCTV cameras installed.'

Gisele pressed her lips together, hating him for pointing out what he obviously perceived as a flaw in her personality. Her mother…*her adoptive mother*, she corrected herself, had communicated much the same thing only a few days ago, saying she was far too trusting with her customers. It didn't come naturally to Gisele to mistrust people, but then wasn't that why her life had ended up the way it had? She had been so naive and trusting with Emilio and it had backfired spectacularly.

Emilio continued to study her for a lengthy moment. 'Have you been ill recently?' he asked.

Gisele suddenly froze, caught off guard by that dark penetrating gaze that refused to let hers go. 'Um…why do you ask that?'

'You look pale and much thinner than when we were together,' he said.

'Not quite up to your impeccable standards any more?' she said, giving him a hardened look. 'What a lucky escape you had in calling off our wedding. It wouldn't suit your image to be married to a frump, now, would it?'

Another heavy frown appeared between his brows. 'You misunderstand me,' he said. 'I was simply commenting on your pallor, not your lack of beauty. You are still one of the most beautiful women I have ever seen.'

It was amazing how easily cynicism came to Gisele now. In the past she would have blushed and felt incredibly flattered by such a compliment. Now all she felt was a simmering fury that he was trying to charm her into forgiving him. He was wasting his time and hers. *Forgiveness* was a word she had long ago deleted from her vocabulary.

She walked over to the shop service counter and barricaded herself behind it. 'You can save your shallow compliments for someone who will believe them enough to fall into your bed,' she said. 'It's not going to work with me.'

'Is that why you think I am here?' he asked.

Gisele felt herself being swallowed by that charcoal-black unreadable gaze. The air seemed to be charged with an erotic energy she had no control over. Her hands gripped the edge of the counter for support, her heart beating too hard and too fast as his hooded gaze slipped to her mouth.

She held her breath in that infinitesimal moment as his gaze rested on her lips.

His gaze was like a touch. It burned her with its intent. She felt the tingle of her lips as if he had reached across the counter and pressed his mouth to hers...

But her best friend cynicism came to her rescue just in time. 'I think you are here to clear your conscience,' she said. 'You're not here because of me. You're here because of you.'

His expression gave no clue to what was going on behind the screen of his dark eyes, but a tiny nerve twitched at the edge of his mouth as if it were being tugged by an invisible needle and thread.

It seemed a very long time before he spoke.

'I am here for both of us,' he said. 'I want to wipe the slate clean. Neither of us can truly move on with our lives with this lying like a festering sore between us.'

Gisele put up her chin with cool hauteur. 'I *have* moved on with my life,' she said.

His eyes challenged hers for endless seconds, but when he finally spoke his voice was gruff. 'Have you, *cara*? Have you really?'

Was it his unexpectedly gentle tone or his use of an all too familiar endearment that made her throat suddenly close over as if someone had gripped it and cruelly squeezed? She blinked against the sting of tears, once, twice, three times before she was confident they were not going to break through. 'Of course,' she said coldly. 'Or would you rather I said I'd been pining for you forlornly ever since you cut me from your life?'

'That would indeed be a punishment I would not like to have inflicted on me,' he said with a rueful movement of his lips. 'It would make the guilt I feel all the harder to bear.'

Gisele looked at him standing there, so tall, so assured, the master of all he controlled. Was he really feeling guilty or just annoyed at being wrong for once in his life? He was a fiercely proud man. She had met no one prouder or more stubborn. 'You can sleep easy,

Emilio,' she said. 'After the way you treated me I put you out of my mind as soon as I stepped off the plane. I haven't thought of you in months.'

He held her look for a heartbeat longer than she would have liked. 'I'll be in town for the rest of the week,' he said, handing her a business card. 'If you change your mind about meeting with me, please feel free to call me at any time.'

Gisele took the silver-embossed card with a hand that trembled slightly as it came in contact with his. She curled her fingers around the card until its edges bit into her palm. 'I won't change my mind,' she said with steely determination wrapped around each and every word.

She waited until he had left before she let out her breath in a long ragged stream. She looked at the card she had crushed in her hand. A sharp corner had broken the skin of her palm; a very timely reminder that if she allowed Emilio Andreoni too close again she would be the only one to get hurt.

CHAPTER TWO

A COUPLE of days later Gisele received a visit from her landlord, Keith Patterson. For a heart-stopping moment she wondered if she had somehow overlooked paying her rent, but then she remembered she had seen the electronic transfer of the funds on her accounts profile page only the week before.

'I know this is short notice, Miss Carter,' Keith said after the usual polite exchange of greetings, 'but I've decided to sell the building to a developer. I got an offer too good to refuse. The wife and I lost a fair bit in the global financial crisis and we need to refinance ourselves for our retirement. This offer couldn't have come at a better time.'

Gisele blinked at him in alarm. While her profit turnover was good and her bank overdraft manageable, finding other premises would no doubt involve a rise in rent. She didn't want to overstretch herself, especially as she had only recently employed an assistant. So many small businesses folded due to having too many overheads and not enough income. She didn't want to become another statistic of economic disaster. 'Does that mean I have to move out?' she asked.

'That will depend on the new owner,' Keith said.

'He'll have to get council approval before he does any alterations. That could take weeks or a couple of months. He gave me his card for you to contact him to discuss the lease.' He handed her a silver-embossed card across the counter.

Gisele's heart dropped like a stone inside her chest even before she saw the name on the card. 'Emilio Andreoni bought the building?' she asked in a shocked gasp.

'You've heard of him?' Keith asked.

She felt her face grow warm. 'Yes…I've heard of him,' she said. 'But he's an architect, not a property developer.'

'Maybe he's diversifying his interests,' Keith said. 'I've heard he's won numerous awards for his designs. He seemed mighty keen to buy the place.'

'Did he give you a reason for his enthusiasm?' Gisele asked, boiling with anger inside.

'Yes, he said it held sentimental value,' Keith said. 'Maybe a relative of his owned it in the past. Some Italians used to have a fruit shop here in the fifties. I can't remember their name.'

Gisele ground her teeth. Sentimental value indeed! She knew for a fact Emilio had no living relatives, or at least none he wanted to associate with. He had told her very little about his background, but she sensed it hadn't been much like hers. She had often wondered if that was another reason he had wanted to marry her. Her blue-blooded pedigree had appealed to him. How ironic that it turned out she and her twin were the products of an illicit affair their father had had with a housekeeper while he and his wife were living in London.

Once Keith Patterson had gone Gisele looked at the business card lying on the counter. She drummed her fingers on the glass surface, her teeth almost going to powder as she considered her options. She could tear up the card into tiny little pieces as she had a couple of days ago, or she could call the mobile number on it and arrange a showdown. If she tore up the card he would surely come in to see her and she would be caught off guard just as she had been before.

She decided it would be better to see him on her terms this time around. She picked up the phone and started dialling.

'Emilio Andreoni.'

'You bastard!' Gisele spat before she could stop herself.

She heard the sound of a leather chair squeaking as he shifted position. She imagined him with his feet up on the desk, his ankles crossed casually, his head laid back against the headrest and a self-satisfied smile on his mouth.

'Nice to hear from you, Gisele,' he said smoothly. 'Have you changed your mind yet about meeting with me one last time before I leave?'

Gisele almost broke the phone with the pressure of her fingers as she gripped it in her hand. 'I can't believe how ruthless you're prepared to be in getting your own way,' she hissed at him. 'Do you really think by charging me an exorbitant rent it will make me hate you less?'

'You're assuming I'm going to charge you rent,' he said. 'Maybe I'll lease the premises to you without charging a cent.'

Gisele's heart clanged against her rib cage. 'Wh-what did you say?'

'I'm offering you a business proposition,' he said. 'Meet with me and we'll discuss it.'

She felt a shiver of apprehension trickle down her spine like a single drop of icy water. 'I'd rather turn tricks on the nearest street corner than have anything to do with you,' she threw back.

'Before you reject an offer you really should discuss the terms and conditions more thoroughly,' he said. 'You might be surprised at some of the benefits.'

'I can just imagine some of the benefits,' Gisele said, her voice liberally laced with scorn. 'A rent-free premises in exchange for my body and my self-respect. No thanks.'

'You really should consider my proposal, Gisele,' he said. 'It wouldn't do to put at risk everything you've worked so hard for, now, would it?'

'I've lost everything before and survived,' she said, throwing a verbal punch.

She heard it land with a sharp intake of his breath. 'Don't make me play dirty, Gisele,' he gritted. 'I can and I will if I have to.'

Gisele felt that icy shiver again. She knew just how ruthless he could be. She knew he had ways and means to make things very difficult for her, even more difficult than when he had thrown her out of his life so callously just days before the wedding she had planned with such excitement and anticipation. She still remembered the horror of that moment. She couldn't even look at a wedding gown now without feeling that gut-wrenching sense of despair. But she was not going to roll over for him. 'I don't want or need your help,' she said. 'I don't care if I have to beg on the streets. I will not accept anything from you.'

'I recently designed a holiday retreat for one of Europe's largest retail giants,' Emilio said. 'With a click of a computer mouse I could make your business expand exponentially. Your shop will not just be a local enterprise. It will instantly become a global brand.'

Gisele thought of the expansion she had planned over the next few years. How she had imagined building her business to spread to other suburban outlets and to the larger department stores and, more importantly, increasing her online presence. The only things that had been holding her back were secure finance and the right contacts.

She fought with her resolve. She wanted to say no. She wanted to slam the phone down in his ear. But turning her back on him would mean turning her back on the sort of success most people could only dream about. But then, doing any sort of business deal with Emilio would mean contact with him.

Contact she didn't want, wouldn't *allow* herself to want.

Her stomach slipped like a cat's claws on a highly polished surface.

Maybe even intimate contact...

'Think about it, Gisele,' he said. 'You have a lot to gain by allowing me back in your life, even if it's only temporarily.'

'What do you mean, temporarily?' she asked warily.

'I would like you to spend the next month with me in Italy,' Emilio said. 'It will give us a chance to see if we can still make things work between us. I will, of course, pay you an allowance for the time we spend together.'

'I'm not spending the next minute with you,' Gisele said with a fresh upsurge of resolve. 'I'm hanging up right now so don't bother call—'

'It will also be the perfect opportunity for me to introduce you to the right contacts,' he said. 'How does a million dollars for the month sound?'

Gisele's mouth opened and closed. She couldn't seem to get her voice to work. Her heart was pumping so hard and so fast she felt as if it were going to explode out from between her breasts and land on the floor in front of her.

A million dollars.

Could she do it? Could she survive a month living with Emilio? She had shared his bed with love in the past. How could she do it this time with hatred?

Would he *want* her to share his bed?

A shiver ran over her skin. Of course he would want her to. Hadn't she seen his desire for her burning in his dark eyes when he came into the shop? Couldn't she hear the spine-tingling rumble of it in his voice now? 'I...I need some time to think about this,' she said.

'What's to think about?' he asked. 'You win either way, Gisele. If after a month we both feel there's no point in carrying on any further, you will be free to go. No strings. You can take the money and leave.'

She chewed at her bottom lip for a moment. 'And you're happy to have me back in your life, hating you the way I do?' she asked.

'I understand your feelings,' he said. 'But I feel we both need to be sure we're not making the biggest mistake of our lives by not exploring the possibility of a future together.'

Gisele frowned. 'Why are you doing this?' she asked. 'Why not leave things as they are?'

'Because as soon as I saw you the other day I knew we had unfinished business,' he said. 'I felt it and I know you did too. You can deny it but it won't make it any less real. You might hate me but I felt your body react to mine. You still want me just as much as I still want you.'

Gisele hated that he knew her body so well that he could read its most subtle of signals. What hope did she have of coming out of this with her pride intact? 'I want another day or two to think it over,' she said. 'And if I agree, I won't accept less than two million.'

'I can see why you have done so well for yourself in the time we've been apart,' Emilio said musingly. 'You drive a hard bargain. Two million is a lot of money.'

'I have a lot of hate,' she shot back.

'I will look forward to dismantling it,' he said.

Gisele felt her insides clench with unruly desire. 'You haven't got a hope, Emilio,' she said. 'You can pay all you like for my body but you will never have my heart.'

'Your body will do for now,' he said with smouldering intensity. 'I will send a car for you on Friday evening. Pack your passport and some clothes if it is a yes.' And with that the phone line went dead.

As Emilio's driver pulled up in front of her block of flats Gisele told herself she was saying yes for one reason and one reason only. She wanted to make Emilio's life as miserable as she could for the next month. She would enjoy every minute of making him regret the way he had treated her. He would not find her such an easy conquest this time around. She was not the sweet, shy, rather naive virgin he had met and swept off her feet two years ago. She was older and wiser, harder and more cynical. More battle scarred and dangerously, scarily angry.

Also, being in Europe for a month might give her the opportunity to get to know the sister she had never met until a couple of weeks ago. Sienna was currently living in London, which was a whole lot closer to Rome than Sydney.

Gisele felt her chest tighten as she thought of all the lost years, all the lost confidences and closeness she and Sienna should have had together. Selfish adults who had not stopped to think of the long-term consequences of such a reckless and self-serving deception had stolen it from them.

She was still coming to terms with the heartbreak of finding out the truth. It wasn't just about the sex tape scandal mix-up, although that was heartbreaking enough. She felt her whole life had been a lie. She didn't know who she was any more. It was as if Gisele Carter, the Sydney born and bred only child of Richard and Hilary Carter, had suddenly vanished, vaporised into thin air.

Who was she now?

She was not her mother's daughter. And yet she was not her biological mother's daughter either as she had never felt her mother's arms or ever felt the brush of her lips on her skin, or if she had in those first early days after birth she had no memory of it now.

She had been handed over like a package, a one-way delivery, never to be returned to sender. How had her mother, Nell Baker, chosen which baby to keep and which one to give away? Had she done it willingly or had she done it for the money?

A little dagger of guilt pierced Gisele as she thought of what she had led Emilio to believe *she* would do for money. He thought he could pay any amount to have her back in his life and back in his bed but he was in for a big surprise. She gave a grimly determined smile as she pressed down on the suitcase to snap the locks closed. Once the month was up Emilio would be just as glad to see the back of her as he had been the last time.

She would make sure of it.

Emilio was waiting in the hotel bar when Gisele came. He felt the jolt of awareness hit him like a punch to his abdomen. He had met hundreds of beautiful women but no one had that powerful physical effect on him just by walking into the room. And yet she hardly seemed to be aware of how every male head turned and looked at her.

Her simple but elegant cream dress was nipped in at the waist with a black bow at the front that drew attention to how slim she was. He suspected he could now span her waist with his hands. Her silver-blonde hair was pulled back in a smooth knot at the back of her head, showcasing the swanlike grace of her neck. She was wearing make-up but it was so skilfully applied it looked entirely natural. She had subtly highlighted the grey-blue of her eyes with eyeliner and a brush of smoky eyeshadow, and her lush lips were shiny with pink-tinted lipgloss. It made him want to lean down and press his lips to hers to see if she still tasted the same. He could smell her perfume, her signature summery honeysuckle scent that had clung to his skin for hours after making love with her. He had missed that fragrance. It never smelled quite the same on anyone else.

He stood to greet her, and even though she was wearing shiny patent black killer heels he still towered over her. 'Did you bring your passport?' he asked.

She gave him a churlish look from beneath her lashes. 'I almost didn't, but the thought of two million reasons why I should made me see reason.'

Emilio allowed himself a small smile of satisfaction. She was here under duress but at least she was here. He led her to a quiet corner in the bar with a gentle hand at her elbow. He felt her bare skin shiver in response to his touch and an arrow of need staked him in his groin. Her skin was so soft and creamy, like silk against his fingers. 'What would you like to drink?' he asked. 'Champagne?'

She shook her head. 'I'm not celebrating anything,' she said, shooting him another look. 'White wine will do.'

Emilio ordered their drinks and, once they had been served, he leaned back in his seat to study her ice-maiden features. He knew he deserved her ire. He had thrown her out of his life with a callous and ruthless disregard for her feelings. He had been so convinced she had betrayed him. The red mist of anger he had felt had blinded him to anything but what he believed she had done. The image of her with that man taunted him and had done so until he had found out about the discovery of her identical twin.

Seeing her in the flesh again had brought back all the

reasons he had wanted to marry her in the first place. It wasn't just her natural beauty or grace or poise. It wasn't just her softly spoken voice and the way she nibbled at her bottom lip when she was feeling uncertain, or the way she sometimes twirled a loose strand of hair around one of her fingers when she was concentrating on something. It was something in her eyes, those incredible were-they-grey-were-they-blue eyes that had warmed and softened the first time she'd looked at him. What man didn't want the woman he had chosen to be his wife to look at him like that?

As far as he had been concerned, Gisele had been perfect wife material, sweet and gentle, biddable and loving. The fact that he hadn't been in love with her was irrelevant. For his whole life love had been an emotion he had never been able to rely on. In his experience, people used the words so freely but their actions rarely backed them up. The sex tape scandal had reinforced to him how pointless it was to love someone, for people *always* let you down. But in the end he had been the one to let *her* down. He had destroyed her love with his lack of trust in her. But he was determined to get her back. He would make it up to her in a thousand different ways. He couldn't allow a failure like this to blot his life. It felt like a giant ink stain on his soul. He had made the error and it was up to him to do whatever it took to fix it.

And he would do *whatever* it took.

He knew she still wanted him. He had seen it that first day in her shop, the way her body spoke to him in its own private language. His own intensely visceral response to her had sideswiped him. He had thought he had put his desire for her behind him, but it was back with a vengeance as soon as he had laid eyes on her. It was an aching, pulsing need to feel her in his arms again. He couldn't wait to take her upstairs and prove to her they still had a future, that the past could be permanently put aside, erased as if it hadn't happened. She was playing coy with him but he was sure once he kissed her she would melt, just as she always had in the past. He could not tolerate any other outcome.

Failure was not an option.

'I have arranged a flight for tomorrow,' he said. 'We leave at 10:00 a.m.'

Gisele gave him a brittle look. 'You were that certain I'd come?'

He returned her look with measured calm. 'Let's say I know you well enough to be quietly confident,' he said.

'You don't know me any more, Emilio,' she said with another hardened look. 'I'm not the same person I was two years ago.'

'I don't believe that,' Emilio said. 'I know we all change a bit over time but you can't really change who you are deep inside.'

She lifted a slim shoulder in a devil-may-care manner. 'Maybe in a month you'll change your mind,' she said and took a sip of her drink.

'Is your sister still here in Sydney?' Emilio asked.

'No, she flew back to London ten days ago,' she said, looking into the contents of her glass with a little frown. 'The press were hounding her. They were hounding us both. I found it a little scary…' She bit her lip and drained her glass as if she wanted to stop any more words coming out of her mouth.

'It must have been a very difficult time for you both,' he said.

She lifted her gaze to his; her eyes were like stormy grey-blue ice cubes, hard, cold and resentful. 'I'd rather not talk about it if you don't mind,' she said. 'I'm still trying to sort it out in my head. So is Sienna.'

'Perhaps you can invite her to stay at my villa for a few days,' Emilio said. 'I would like to meet her.'

She gave another shrug of indifference. 'Whatever.'

Emilio signalled for the waiter to refresh their drinks. He sat back in his seat and observed Gisele as she tucked an imaginary strand of hair behind her ear, another one of her I'm-out-of-my-depth-and-trying-not-to-show-it mannerisms. She was not as immune to him as she tried to make out. He had seen the flare of female interest in her gaze. He had felt the shiver of reaction on her skin when he had touched her. One kiss would prove he could have her back where he wanted her.

'Tell me about your shop,' he said. 'How did you come about buying the business?'

She dropped her gaze to the drink the waiter had just set before her. 'When I came back…from Italy I…I wanted a secure base,' she said. 'I liked the idea of working for myself. Having more control, that sort of thing. I'd sold some items to the owner in the past and she gave me the first option of buying.'

'It's a big commitment for a young woman of just twenty-five, or twenty-three as you were then,' Emilio said. 'Did your parents help you?'

Gisele put her glass down. 'At first, but then things got a bit tricky after my father got sick. He had a few debts we didn't know about until after he'd died. Bad business decisions, a bit of gambling with the stock market that didn't pay off as well as he'd hoped. I had to help my mother…I mean Hilary out.'

Emilio put his drink down on the coaster on the table between them. 'I'm sorry I didn't send a card,' he said. 'I'd heard he was terminally ill. I should have made contact to offer my condolences. It must have been a very difficult time for you and your mother.'

She looked back at the contents of her glass; the grip of her fingers was so tight around the stem he wondered if it would snap. 'He took eight and a half miserable months to die,' she said. 'Not once in all that time did he ever say anything about me having a twin sister.' She looked at him at that point, her grey-blue gaze blazing with anger. 'Both my parents knew our relationship had broken up because of that sex tape but still neither he nor my mother said a word. I can never forgive them for that.'

Emilio carefully removed the wineglass from her stiff fingers and put it to one side. 'I can understand your anger towards them but our relationship broke up because I didn't trust you,' he said. 'If anyone is to blame it is me.'

Gisele met his gaze in the long silence that ensued. 'You know what really upsets me?' she asked.

'Tell me,' he said, still holding her gaze.

'How did they choose?' she asked.

'You mean who got which twin?' he asked.

Gisele blew out a hissing breath. 'I can't get it out of my mind,' she said. 'How did they do it? How could my mother, my biological mother, give me up? And how could my father ask it of her? And not only that, what was my adoptive mother thinking by agreeing to bring up her husband's love child? Did she have no self-respect?'

Emilio bent his forearms on his thighs so he could reach Gisele's tightly knotted hands. He took them both in one of his, stroking the tension away as best he could. 'Have you asked her about it?' he said.

She looked at him with flashing eyes. 'Of course I've asked her,' she said. 'She said she did it to keep my father happy. She spent their whole married life trying to make him happy but it never worked.'

'From what you told me, your family always seemed so perfect to me,' Emilio said, still stroking her hands. 'You never said anything about them being unhappy together.'

Gisele looked down at their joined hands and hastily pulled hers away. She sat straighter in her seat, ramrod straight, angry straight, keep-away-from-me straight. 'I never liked admitting it to anyone but I always felt I wasn't good enough for either of my parents,' she said. 'I tried my best but nothing I did or achieved seemed to please them. My mother wasn't the maternal type. She never liked cuddling me or playing with me. She employed a nanny to do that. Now I understand why. I wasn't her child.' She drew in another painful-sounding breath and continued, 'My father was just as bad. Deep down, I think he really wanted a son. My mother certainly couldn't give him one, but then his mistress gave him two daughters so he chose one. But I've often wondered if he thought he'd chosen the wrong one or whether he wished he had just walked away from both of us. He was stuck in a loveless marriage until the day he died, out of guilt presumably. All of those long stone-walling silences between him and my mother over the years suddenly made a whole lot of sense.'

Emilio frowned. He had never heard Gisele talk so honestly about her childhood. He had thought she had come from a reasonably happy and stable home. He had envied her background, given the bleak misery of his. It made him realise how little he had known her, even though he'd been days off marrying her. He had been struck by her beauty but had given little thought to who she was, what she valued and how she wanted her life to run. He had swept her off her feet, dazzled her with his wealth and charm, and yet had not known for a moment how deeply insecure she really was. It was like looking at her for the first time. The same beauty was there but so too was a fragility that he had not seen the first time around. But then she had been devastatingly hurt and he, to his shame, had done that to her, even more so than her parents. He wasn't sure how he could ever fix that terrible mistake but he was determined to try. 'How is your sister dealing with this?' he asked.

Gisele let her stiff shoulders drop. 'She's a lot more chilled about it than me,' she said. 'I guess growing up with a single mother who was known to be a bit of a tearaway has toughened her up rather a lot. It sounded like Sienna was the parent rather than the child most of the time. She told me there were always a lot of men coming and going in her mother's life. It can't have been an easy childhood but she just made the best of it.'

'Is she disappointed she didn't get to meet your father?'

'Yes and no, I suppose,' Gisele said, frowning a little. 'I think she would've given him a serve for what he did. She's a bit of a straight shooter. I think I could do with some lessons from her, actually. It's about time I learned to speak up for myself.'

'I think you're doing rather a good job of it,' Emilio said with a crooked smile. 'Perhaps I am wrong after all. Maybe you have changed.'

Her eyes glittered as they held his. 'You'd better believe it.'

Emilio allowed a little silence to pass before he spoke. 'Did you give the keys and all the relevant paperwork for your shop to the driver?'

'Yes.'

'Good,' he said. 'Your new assistant will hold the fort until you decide what course of action to take. I've already spoken to her about it.'

She frowned at him. 'What do you mean?'

He held her look for a moment. 'You might decide to stay on in Italy,' he said. 'It would be imprudent not to prepare for that possibility.'

She gave him a disdainful look. 'You must get really exhausted carrying that monumental ego around. Do you really think I will step back into your life as if nothing has changed? You're paying for a month and that's all you're going to get.'

Emilio fought back his temper. He was not used to her being so obstructive and defiant. In the past she had been so willing to fit in with his plans. Where was the sweet young woman he had chosen as his bride?

'Would you like another drink?' he asked after a tense pause.

'No… Thank you.' She pushed the glass away with another little frown pulling at her brow.

'I thought we could have dinner in my suite,' he said.

She looked at him with startled eyes. 'Why not in a restaurant?' she asked.

'I thought it might be more private.'

Her eyes narrowed. 'You can quit it with the whole seduction routine, Emilio,' she said. 'It won't work.'

Emilio felt his groin tighten as she threw the challenge down with her flashing gaze. 'You think not?' he asked.

'I know not,' she said with a lift of her chin.

He held her gaze, hot, hungry desire leaping like flames in his body. This new feisty Gisele was turning him on. There was something about her newfound defiance that thrilled him. It stirred his blood, making it surge through his system like rocket fuel. There was one thing he loved more than anything and that was a challenge. He had left his dirt-poor background behind with the same gritty determination to succeed no matter what it cost. He had put himself through school and then university, working day and night to cover the expense. He had made his fortune by rising to the demands of difficult clients and completing next to impossible projects. He had nearly lost it all after the scandal, but he had clawed his way back.

Gisele was another next to impossible project but, just like all the rest, he was determined to succeed.

Nothing and no one was going to stand in his way.

CHAPTER THREE

GISELE stood like a statue of marble as Emilio escorted her up to his suite. She could smell his aftershave; it stirred deep memories she tried desperately to suppress. She felt as if she were stepping back in time. How many times had she stepped into an elevator to accompany him up to his penthouse suite in hotels all over Europe? The erotic images that thought triggered made her skin prickle all over and she had to bite her lip until it hurt to block them from her mind.

Back then she had been so eager to please him. She knew right from the moment she had met him that he was a proud and strong-willed man but she had never questioned him, never stood up to him and never challenged him. She had just loved him, completely and desperately. How had she allowed herself to become so vulnerable? The power balance of their relationship had been wrong. She had loved him too much and he hadn't loved her at all.

It was only his pride that wanted her back now. She knew it wasn't about her as a person. He wanted the world to know he was setting the record straight. His offer of a one-month trial seemed to prove it. A man with his high profile could not afford to be seen as acting unfairly. The press had gone wild with the story of Sienna and her being reunited. She was surprised he hadn't already informed the media of his intention to resume his relationship with her.

The elevator stopped and Emilio held the doors back for her with an outstretched arm. Gisele moved past him, determined not to show how unsettled she was. Her stomach was twitching with nerves. Everything about him unsettled her. He seemed to see much more than she wanted him to see. What if he sensed she was hiding something from him? How long before he guessed the pain in her eyes had been put there, not just by him, but also by the loss of their child? The child whose soft pink bunny blanket that still held a faint trace of her sweet baby smell was folded inside her suitcase? She hadn't been able to leave that final link with Lily behind. Her mother...*Hilary*, she quickly amended, had said it was unhealthy to keep holding on. She had said Gisele should put it all behind her, pack the blanket away so she could finally move on.

Gisele wasn't ready to move on.

She didn't think she would ever be ready to move on. What would Hilary know anyway? She hadn't physically given birth to a child only to have that child's life snatched away. She didn't know, *couldn't* possibly know what it felt like...

'Relax, *cara*,' Emilio said as he opened the door to his suite. 'You look like you're about to be devoured by a wild beast.'

Gisele stalked past him. 'I have a headache,' she said and it wasn't a lie. The pain behind her eyeballs had gone from a dull ache to a pounding that felt as if a team of jackhammers on steroids had taken up residence inside her skull.

His brows moved together. 'Why didn't you say something earlier?' he asked.

'I'll be fine,' she said, licking her lips to give them some much-needed moisture. 'I probably shouldn't have had that second drink. I don't have a good head for alcohol.'

'When was the last time you ate?' he asked.

The fact that she had to think about it didn't go unnoticed by him, Gisele thought as she saw that dark frown deepen across his brow. 'I can't remember,' she said. 'It wasn't a priority. I had to get things sorted at my flat and at the shop.' She threw him a resentful scowl. 'You didn't give me much time.'

'I'm sorry but I have to get back to Rome for a project I'm working on,' he said. 'The client is a big one. I had to work hard to get the contract. It's worth several million.'

Gisele thought of all the money he earned from his designs. She suspected he hadn't come by it easily. He was a prime example of the adage that anyone could do anything if they had enough determination. And the one thing Emilio had in spades was determination. She could see it in the glittering depths of his dark eyes and the strong lines of his jaw, both hinting at the implacability of his nature. In the days and weeks ahead she would be going head to head with that intransigent personality. Who would eventually come out on top? She gave a little involuntary shiver. It was a nerve-jangling thought.

'I'll have dinner sent up immediately,' he said. 'The porter brought up your things earlier,' he said. 'Would you like me to get a housemaid to unpack it for you? I should have thought of it before.'

'No,' Gisele said, perhaps a little too quickly. She saw his eyebrows lift. *Yes, definitely too quickly.* 'We're… um…leaving tomorrow, in any case.'

He held her gaze for an infinitesimal moment. 'Would you prefer the guest suite tonight?' he asked.

Gisele gave him a flinty look. 'Where else did you expect me to sleep?'

He came up close and brushed her hot cheek with the backs of his bent knuckles. 'Do you really think you'll be sleeping in the spare room for the entire month?' he asked.

She brushed his hand away as if it were an annoying fly. 'I haven't signed anything that requires me to sleep with you.'

'That reminds me.' He moved away from her and opened a briefcase that was lying on a table near the window. He took out a document and brought it over. 'You should read it before you sign it,' he said, his expression now inscrutable. 'The full amount we agreed on will be transferred to your account on the completion of your stay.'

Gisele looked at the sheaf of papers, wishing she could walk away. But two million dollars was not the sort of money she could turn her back on right now. She took pride in her success so far; it had helped her cope. How much better would she feel if her baby wear became even more successful? What else did she have in her life other than her shop? It wasn't as if she was ever going to get married and have a family now. That dream was long gone.

She took the papers and sank to the nearest chair, casting her eyes over the words printed there. She read it in detail but it was as straightforward as he had said. After the month was up she would be two million dollars richer and would owe him nothing. She signed it with a hand that wasn't quite steady. 'There,' she said, shoving the papers at his chest.

He put them to one side before he faced her again. 'So, it looks like we have a deal.'

She lifted her chin. 'Yes,' she said. 'You just signed away two million dollars.' *For nothing.*

His lips moved up in a curl that had a hint of mockery about it. 'How long do you think you will hold out, mmm? A week? Two?'

She glared at him fiercely. 'If you want a bedmate then you'll have to look elsewhere. I'm not interested.'

'You're planning your own little payback, aren't you?' he asked, still with that sardonic half smile.

Gisele felt a betraying flush stain her cheeks. 'I don't know what you're talking about,' she said.

'You think I don't know how your mind works?' he asked. 'You plan to make me suffer every minute of the time we spend together. But do you really think that by snipping and snarling at me it will make me want you less? Don't fool yourself, Gisele. You will sleep with me again, not because I paid you, but because you just can't help yourself.'

Gisele thought she couldn't hate him more than at that moment. She wanted to slap his arrogant face for assuming she had no self-control, no discipline and no self-respect. 'I hate you with every cell in my body,' she snarled at him like a cornered cat, all claws and bared teeth. 'Do you realise that? I *hate* you.'

Emilio's calmness riled her even further. 'The fact that you feel something for me is good,' he said. 'I can handle anger. It is far better than cold indifference.'

Gisele was determined she would show him just how cold and indifferent she could be. 'OK then.' She kicked off her heels and began to unzip her dress. 'You want me to sleep with you? Then let's get it out of the way right here and now.'

He stood there watching her silently, hardly a muscle moving, apart from his eyes. She saw the flare of his pupils, the primal signal of male attraction as she stepped out of her dress, leaving it in a puddle of fabric on the floor. She was standing in just her bra and knickers before him. She had stood in a whole lot less before him two years ago. But suddenly she felt naked in a way she had never felt before. A shiver broke out over her skin and her stomach curdled at the thought of going any further with this.

She put her hands behind her back to unhook her bra but her fingers were suddenly fumbling and useless. She felt as if she was going to cry. The emotions were like a fountain inside her that had been blocked. The pressure was building and building. She could feel it behind her eyes; she could feel it inside her chest, a tight ache that burned like fire.

'Get dressed,' Emilio said curtly as he turned away.

Gisele felt as if he had ripped the ankle-deep carpet out from under her feet. She had been prepared to play him at his own game but he had somehow turned the tables on her. He wanted her but on his terms, not hers.

She felt foolish.

She felt uncertain.

She felt *rejected*.

She watched as he walked over to the bar and poured himself a drink. He tipped back his head and drained his glass and then set in down on the bar with a thump. His shoulders looked tense; the muscles were bunched beneath the fine cotton of his shirt. She remembered how those muscles felt under the soft pads of her fingertips, how she used to massage away those tight knots, how she used to press her mouth to that hot, salty male skin…

Gisele ran the tip of her tongue over her bone-dry lips. 'So,' she said, summoning up what was left of her paltry attempt at cold indifference, 'I take it you no longer require my services this evening?'

Emilio turned to look at her but his expression was difficult to read. 'I will have a meal sent up to you presently,' he said. 'Please make yourself at home. I'm going out.'

'Where are you going?' The question was out before she could stop it and, to her shame, it sounded scarily close to one a jealous wife might have asked.

He turned from the door and raked her with his cold indifferent gaze. 'Don't wait up,' he said and then he was gone.

Gisele picked up one of her shoes and threw it at the door, angry tears spilling from her eyes. 'Damn you,' she said. 'Damn you to hell.'

Emilio entered the penthouse at two in the morning. He had walked the streets of Sydney for hours, determined not to return until Gisele was safely out of his range. His body had ached to take what she was offering so defiantly but he was not going to give her any more reasons to hate him. He would bide his time, waiting for her to come to him, as he knew she would. One night would not be enough for either of them. He was counting on that. He knew as soon as she gave in to the sexual chemistry that sizzled between them she would want more. She was bitter and angry but he knew she would get over it. Time was a great healer and a month was surely long enough to see if what they had shared together before could be resurrected.

The meal he had sent up to the suite looked as if it had been barely touched. He frowned as he looked at the selection of dishes and the undrunk wine sitting on the dining table. Her lack of appetite could have been because of her headache, but he suspected it was more to do with her current I'll-show-you attitude.

He admired her for standing up to him. Not many people did. He had learned on the filthy backstreets of Rome how to intimidate people. Those skills had come in handy in his professional life. What he said went. People didn't argue with him. They didn't challenge or defy him. The women in his life—and there had been plenty—never argued with him. They played by his rules. He always made sure of that. And Gisele had been no different during their time together. She had been biddable and gracious, the perfect companion, the perfect hostess, the perfect woman to be his wife.

Emilio frowned as he wandered over to the windows to look at the harbour view below. Some would say he had selected a trophy wife but he had never thought of Gisele like that. He had genuinely liked having her around. She had been easy company, at ease with him and with others. He was proud to have her on his arm. She moved with such poise and grace, with such natural elegance.

He let out a sigh that pulled on something deep inside his chest. If it hadn't been for the scandal they would have celebrated their second wedding anniversary a couple of weeks ago. Perhaps they might have even had a child by now. They had talked about it. That was another of the reasons he had wanted her as his wife. She had been keen to have a large family, having grown up as an only child. And he had been just as keen. All those years in and out of ill-run foster homes or begging on the streets had made him envious of all those warm, well-lit homes he had wandered past, with their close-knit family units inside.

His envy of other people's homes had been his primary motivation to become an architect. He had been barely ten years old when he had made the decision. He had thought by designing hundreds of dream homes that he would be satisfied, but it hadn't had the effect he'd imagined. He suspected that having his own family would be the only thing that would truly satisfy him. That and that alone would be able to soothe the raw sore of loneliness that constantly oozed deep inside his soul.

He felt it now, the never-ending sense of something missing from his life, of being incomplete. Was that why he had been drawn to Gisele, because of her own previously unspoken of loneliness?

Emilio turned from the window when he heard a

sound behind him. 'You didn't eat your dinner,' he said, just as Gisele was searching for the light switch.

She put a hand up to her throat, her eyes wide with shock. 'I didn't see you there,' she gasped. 'You scared me half to death. Why didn't you put the lights on?'

'Maybe I prefer the dark.'

She clutched the edges of her wrap together close to her chest. 'You could have said something,' she said with an accusing glare.

'I did,' he said. 'I said you didn't eat your dinner.'

She gave him a testy look. 'Maybe I wasn't hungry.'

'You need to eat,' he said. 'You're too thin.'

'You need to keep your opinions to yourself,' she shot back.

Emilio came over to where she was standing. 'Weren't you able to sleep?' he asked.

She flicked some hair back off her face and gave him a defiant stare. 'What's it to you?'

'I'm concerned about you,' he said. 'You look like you haven't slept properly in months.'

'Concerned, are you?' She flashed her eyes at him like blue lightning. 'What a pity you weren't so concerned about my welfare when you tossed me out on the street two years ago.'

Emilio ground his teeth together to stop himself saying something he might regret later. He had always prided himself on his self-control but Gisele's stubborn refusal to meet him halfway was testing his limits. How long was she going to persist with this game of payback? He had made amends. Wasn't it time to move on?

'Would you like me to make you a hot milk drink?' he asked.

She gave a choked bubble of laughter that sounded almost hysterical. 'Yeah, why not?' she said. 'Maybe put a shot of whisky in it for good measure. Two shots. That should knock me out.'

Emilio poured milk into a mug and placed it in the microwave set near the bar. He leant back against the counter as he studied her. 'I know from experience that running a business, even a successful one, is stressful,' he said. 'I've had plenty of sleepless nights myself.'

She curled her lip at him. 'I'm sure you've found plenty of women to distract you from your spreadsheets.'

'Not as many as you might think,' he said.

She gave him a cynical look. 'Well, just for the record, I'm not opening my legs like one of your cheap gold-digging whores.'

'You didn't seem to have any problem with it in the past,' he said. 'And at a cool two million, *cara*, you are certainly not cheap.'

Gisele raised a hand to slap him but he intercepted it, holding her slim wrist with the steel handcuffs of his fingers. 'Don't even think about it,' he warned. 'You might not like the consequences.'

She fought against his hold, clawing at him, but it was like a kitten trying to fight off a panther. He was too strong. He was too close. He was too everything.

'What consequences?' she asked. 'What are you going to do? Hit me right back? Is that what rough, tough Italian guys do?'

His expression tightened. 'I would never lay a finger on you and you damn well know it.'

She gave him a challenging glare. 'You've got five fingers on me right now.'

'And they're staying on you until you stop behaving like a wilful child.'

'I hate you,' she spat at him furiously.

'So you've said.'

'I mean it.'

'I believe you.'

'I want you to die and rot in hell.'

'I believe that too,' he said. 'But trading insults isn't going to make this go away.'

Gisele felt his thighs way too close to hers. She felt the warmth of his body, a radiating heat that her colder flesh craved. She felt his warm brandy-scented breath move like a teasing feather over her face. She felt her breasts go to hard aching peaks as the hard wall of his muscular chest loomed closer. Her lashes lowered as she looked at the line of his mouth. That mouth had kissed her so many times she had lost count. It could be hard and yet so soft, so demanding and yet so giving. 'I hate you,' she said again, but she wasn't sure if she was saying it for herself or for him.

She *needed* her anger.

She needed her rage and fury to keep herself in one piece. It was all she had. The only armour left that she could rely on. It had carried her through for so long.

Emilio cupped the side of her face with the broad span of his hand, his thumb moving over the hollow of her cheek, back and forth in a mesmerising rhythm that sent every thought flying out of her head. His eyes moved over her face, taking their time before they finally meshed with hers. 'Stop fighting me, Gisele,' he said. 'Don't give up on us before we've had a chance to set things right.'

'Some things can't be fixed,' she said. 'It's too late. Too much time has passed.'

'Do you really believe that?' he asked.

Gisele didn't know what to believe when he was holding her against him, his hard body fitting against her softer one as if no time had passed at all. She felt the hardened ridge of him, the surge of blood that lengthened him in the primal preparation to mate. It was so earthy and real. No amount of denying it could make it go away. Her body was responding to him in its own secret way. The silky moisture of her inner core was reminding her that she was no less immune to him than she had ever been. It didn't matter how much she hated him. It didn't matter how much she told him she wanted nothing more to do with him. Her body had its own needs and wants and they were overriding every other rational thought she tried to cling to.

'I believe you're only doing this because you're worried what the press and your precious business colleagues will think if you don't try to make amends,' she said, looking at him defiantly. 'It's all for show. The one-month reconciliation. You'll appear to do the right thing by me but it will all be for nothing because I won't come back to you for good. No amount of money will ever induce me to do that.'

He pulled her roughly up against him, his expression hard and bitter and thunderously angry. 'Then I'd better get my money's worth while I can, hadn't I?' And then his mouth crashed down on hers.

It was a blistering kiss, no hint of softness about it. Gisele felt its impact from the top of her prickling scalp to her toes curling into the carpet at her feet for purchase. His lips ground against hers with bruising force, making a dam inside her break its bounds. She kissed him back with all the fury that was inside her. She felt the demand of his tongue at the seam of her mouth and didn't hesitate in allowing him in.

She *wanted* him in.

She wanted to duel with him until they were both breathless with need. She wanted to taste him, to savour that essential maleness that had always sent ripples of delight through her body.

She wanted to hurt him. She wanted to remind him of what he had thrown away. She used her teeth, and not just little nippy bites either. She bit down on his lower lip and held on like a tigress with a prized piece of prey.

He bit her back, the alpha-male-taming-his-mate action sending a rapid blast of heat straight to her core. She tasted blood and wasn't sure if it was his or her own. She felt the rough graze of his stubbly jaw against her face as he changed position. His hands were clutching her head, his fingers buried deep in her hair, holding her captive to his sensual assault.

Gisele's hands moved up from lying flat against his chest to rediscovering the thick silkiness of his hair. He shifted against her urgently, his body so thick and full she felt her body quiver in reaction. Raw need clawed at her, an ache that was so tight and ravenous it burned inside her.

She wanted him.

She wanted him even though she hated him. She wanted the savage thrust of his possession to make her feel alive again. Oh, dear God, please make her feel *alive* again...

Emilio suddenly pulled away from her, his hands dropping from her as if she were a carrier of some deadly disease. He wiped at his mouth with the back of his hand, grimacing as he saw a smear of blood. 'Is that yours or mine?' he asked.

'Does it matter?' Gisele asked with an arch look.

'Actually it does,' he said, frowning darkly. 'I didn't intend to hurt you.'

She challenged him with her gaze as she touched a finger to where her bottom lip had borne the brunt of his kiss. 'Didn't you?'

He took a clean folded handkerchief out of his pocket and stepped back into her body space, lifting her chin as he gently held the cool cotton against her lip. His eyes were unfathomable coal-black pools as they held hers. 'It doesn't have to be this way between us, Gisele,' he said in a husky tone.

She took the handkerchief from him and moved away, turning her back on him. 'It's not going to work, you know,' she said. 'Nothing is going to change my mind. I will never forgive you.'

She heard the rustle of his clothes as he moved. Then she felt his hands come down on the tops of her shoulders and her whole body shivered in reaction. She closed her eyes, summoning her resolve. Where was it? What was happening to her that she wanted to turn around and melt into the warm protection of his broad chest? 'Don't…' she said, squeezing her eyes even tighter.

'Don't what?' he asked.

'You know what,' she said, suppressing a sigh of delight when his fingers began to massage the tightly knotted muscles of her neck and shoulders. If he was running true to form, any minute now he would slip the wrap from one of her shoulders and press his warm lips to her needy flesh. God help her if he did. She would have no power left in her to resist him.

'You want me, Gisele.' His still-aroused body brushed against hers from behind.

'You think.'

'I know.'

She turned and glared at him hotly. 'I want this month to be over so I can finally be free of you.'

His eyes roved her face, looking for what, she wasn't quite sure. She schooled her features into cool indifference, her version of it anyway. 'You should go to bed,' he said, brushing his thumb ever so gently against her bottom lip. 'It's a long flight tomorrow, even when travelling First Class.'

'What?' she said with a mocking look. 'No private jet any more?'

His expression remained inscrutable. 'Owning a private jet is no longer my measure of a successful person,' he said. 'I have other things I would rather spend my money on.'

'Such as?'

His hand dropped from her face as he stepped back from her. 'Good night,' he said. 'I'll see you in the morning.'

'It *is* morning,' she said, just to be pedantic and annoying, but it was a wasted effort on her part as he had already left the room.

CHAPTER FOUR

OF COURSE she didn't sleep. Not even the chemical cocktail the doctor had prescribed to help dull the nightmares about Lily had any effect on her tonight. Gisele tossed and turned and watched as the clock went round, her mind racing with thoughts of Emilio and the month ahead and how on earth she was going to get through it.

In the end she gave up. She padded over to her suitcase and took out Lily's blanket and cradled it against her chest as if her tiny baby were still alive and breathing, wrapped inside it. Tears rolled down her cheeks unchecked. How many nights had she spent doing exactly this? When was this searing pain ever going to ease?

She must have dozed off for she suddenly heard the rap of Emilio's knuckles on her door. 'Time to get up, Gisele,' he said. 'It's 7:00 a.m.'

'I'm awake,' she called out as she struggled upright off the bed. She put Lily's blanket safely back in her suitcase before heading for the shower.

Emilio was pouring himself a cup of coffee when Gisele came in. She had a stoic look about her as if she were being led to the gallows and was determined not to beg for last-minute mercy. 'Sleep OK?' he asked.

'Out like a light.'

He doubted it. She had damson-coloured shadows under her eyes and her face was deathly pale. 'You should have something to eat,' he said, waving a hand towards the food he'd had delivered to the suite.

'I'm not hungry.'

He drew in a breath. 'You think by going on a hunger strike that it's going to help things?'

She shot him a glare. 'I'm not on a hunger strike. I'm just not hungry.'

'You're never hungry,' he snapped at her in annoyance. 'It's not normal. You need food. You'll fade away to nothing if you don't eat.'

'What would you care?' she asked. 'Your last girlfriend was much thinner than me. It *was* a swimwear model you were dating last month, wasn't it? Or have I got her mixed up with that London socialite with the big boobs?' She tapped a finger against the side of her mouth as if trying to prod her memory. 'What was her name again? Arabella? Amanda? Ariel?'

Emilio ground his teeth as he pulled out a chair for her. 'Sit.'

She gave him a castigating look. 'You know you could have saved yourself a heap of money by buying a dog to obey your commands.'

'I thought it would be much more fun training you,' he said through tight lips. 'Now, sit and eat.'

She sat with a toss of her head. 'At least I don't pee on the carpet,' she said.

'I wouldn't put it past you,' he muttered.

She picked up a rasher of bacon and dropped it on

her plate. 'So did you sleep?' she asked. 'You don't look like it. You look like hell.'

'Thank you.'

She stabbed the bacon with her fork. 'You're welcome.'

Emilio watched her as she nibbled at the bacon. Her small white teeth and those luscious lips of hers had kept him awake for what had been left of last night. He tore his gaze away and refilled his coffee cup. 'Do you want coffee or tea?' he asked.

'Tea,' she said and, rolling her eyes, added, 'Sorry for being so *un*-Italian.'

'You're not sorry at all,' he said, putting a steaming cup of tea in front of her. 'Do you want milk or sugar?'

She raised her brows at him. 'You don't remember how I take my tea?' she asked. 'Or have there been so many women since me you're getting us all a little mixed up?'

Emilio pressed his lips together. He wasn't proud of how many women there had been. It was just like her to twist the knife as much as she could. 'You take it black with one sugar,' he said.

She pressed her finger to the table and made a buzzing noise like that on a game show. 'Wrong answer.'

He frowned. 'Are you sure?'

She gave him a look. 'Yeah, I'm sure.'

'So when did you give up the sugar?' he asked.

'I did that when I was…' She stopped and dropped her gaze to her plate.

'When you were?' he prompted.

She pushed back from the table. 'I have to get my things together,' she said. 'I haven't packed.'

'You haven't unpacked,' he pointed out wryly.

'I have to do my…my hair,' she said, ruffling it with one of her hands. 'It's a mess.'

'It looked perfectly fine until you just did that,' he said.

'I have to do my make-up.'

'You're wearing make-up,' he said.

She bit her lip and then winced and put her fingers up to her mouth.

Emilio felt his gut clench. 'Does it hurt?' he asked.

Her eyes fell away from his. 'I've felt worse pain.'

A little silence passed.

'I'm sorry,' he said heavily.

'For what?' she asked, shooting him another cut glass look. 'Buying me back into your life or throwing me out of it in the first place?'

Emilio held her brittle gaze for a lengthy moment. 'I have already told you I'm not proud of how I handled things back then. This is my chance to make it up to you.' He let out a rough-edged sigh. 'It must have been terrible for you the night I asked you to leave.'

'It wasn't a highlight of my time in Italy, that's for sure,' she said, affecting a couldn't-care-less pose. 'But what doesn't kill you makes you stronger, right?'

Emilio swept his gaze over her thin frame. 'You don't look stronger, *cara*,' he said softly. 'You act it but you don't look it.'

She seemed to be actively avoiding his eyes. 'I'd really prefer it if you didn't call me that,' she said.

'I always called you that in the past.'

'This is not the past,' she said tightly. 'This is now. It's different now.'

'Not so different,' he said. 'We are together again.'

She flashed him a defiant glare. 'Only for a month.'

He picked up his coffee and took a sip before he responded. 'Maybe you'll like it so much you'll change your mind and stay.'

'And do what?' she asked. 'Hang off your arm and your every word like some besotted bimbo with no mind of her own? No, thanks. I've grown up. I want more for my life than to be a rich man's plaything.'

Emilio buttoned down his anger with an effort. 'You were going to be my wife, not my plaything,' he said.

Her eyes clashed with his. 'Why did you ask me to marry you, Emilio?' she asked. 'Why not one of the many other women you'd been involved with before me? Why was I so special?'

He put his coffee cup down with a little thwack. 'I think you already know the answer to that, Gisele.'

'It was because I was a virgin, wasn't it?' she asked. 'What a novelty in this day and age to have a woman no one else had ever had. I was a perfect candidate as your future wife. I was perfect until that scandal broke and then suddenly I wasn't worth anything to you. I was soiled. Used goods. Imperfect. And there's nothing you like less than imperfection, is there?'

Emilio pushed himself away from the counter, the set to his mouth grim. 'We need to leave in less than an hour,' he said. 'I hope I don't need to remind you that your behaviour towards me will be under intense scrutiny as soon as we leave the privacy of this hotel. I will not tolerate your insults or your childish attempts to pick a fight in front of any member of my staff, or the press, or indeed the public. If you want to have a showdown with me, then at least have the decency and poise to keep a lid on it until we are alone.'

Gisele looked at him in alarm. 'You don't expect me to act as if I'm still in love with you, do you?'

He gave her a look that would have sliced through steel. 'That's exactly what I expect,' he said. 'We're meant to be trying to resurrect our relationship.'

She felt her stomach shift uneasily. 'I can't do it,' she said. 'I can't pretend to feel something I no longer feel.'

'You will have to,' he said implacably. 'I'm not paying two million dollars for you to look daggers at me while the whole world looks on. If you can't meet the terms, then tell me now and I'll tear up the agreement. It's up to you.'

Gisele hesitated, caught between wanting to walk away and wanting to prove something to him and to herself. Could she do it? Could she act the role she had played for real with such embarrassing enthusiasm in the past? It was just a month. Four weeks of playing for the press. In private she could be herself. She could hate him a thousandfold and no one would be the wiser. 'All right,' she said, mentally crossing her fingers that she was doing the right thing. 'I'll do it.'

Thankfully, the Australian press had not been present when Gisele and Emilio left the hotel for their flight. But it was a completely different story when they landed in the Leonardo da Vinci Airport in Rome. As soon as they stepped through Customs the paparazzi swarmed like bees. Gisele felt under siege as it brought back horrible reminders of the time when the scandal had broken. The camera flashes made her flinch, and her heart was racing so much she felt as if she was going to faint.

She had pretended to sleep on the plane rather than try and make polite conversation with Emilio, but it was all catching up with her now. She felt tired and sick and way too much out of her depth to cope with the barrage of comments firing like machine gun bullets at her. She had always found the intrusion of the press rather daunting from the moment she became involved with Emilio. She had felt as if she was under scrutiny all the time. The speculation on what she wore, how she looked or whether she was smiling or frowning was something she had never got used to. Rumours about their relationship would appear from time to time, which Emilio had laughed off, but Gisele—although she had pretended otherwise—had been distressed by the lack of privacy.

Emilio spoke in Italian, asking the press to keep back to give Gisele some room. His arm came around her protectively, and if it hadn't been for their terse exchange before they left the hotel, Gisele would have been tempted to believe he truly cared about her welfare rather than his reputation.

'Signor Andreoni—' a journalist pushed through the cluster of cameras with a microphone '—does this mean you and Signorina Carter will be getting married as soon as possible?'

'We are enjoying some time together before we make any firm plans,' Emilio answered.

Gisele had learnt a bit of Italian while she had lived with Emilio but it wasn't enough to follow every rapidly spoken word, although she did hear the word *matri-*

monio—marriage. What exactly was he telling the press?

'Signorina Carter?' The same journalist turned the microphone in Gisele's direction but this time spoke in English. 'Is it good to be back with Signor Andreoni?'

Gisele stumbled over her reply. 'Um… I'm very happy…'

'It has been two years since your very public break-up,' the journalist continued. 'You must be feeling very relieved the truth has finally come out about who exactly it was in that sex tape.'

Gisele felt uncomfortable talking about her sister's private life. Sienna had seemed reluctant to go into any details other than to say the press had blown it up to be much more than it actually was. Gisele suspected that ignominious incident had been devastating for her twin, although Sienna pretended otherwise. 'I'm happy that I've found my sister,' she said. 'That's been the most important outcome of such a difficult time.'

'Is your twin sister planning on spending some time with you now that you are going to be living in Italy?' another journalist asked.

'I'm not planning on stay—'

Emilio cut Gisele off. 'We are both looking forward to spending time with Sienna Baker. Now, if you will excuse us, we have to get moving.'

'Signorina Carter, one more question…' Yet another journalist rushed after them.

'Basta,' Emilio said and then repeated it in English. 'That's enough.'

He spirited her away to the waiting car, physically blocking the swarm of press as she got in. 'Remember what I said earlier about what you do and say to me in public,' he said.

Gisele caught the driver's watchful eye in the rear-view mirror. A glass partition separated her and Emilio from the front of the car but it was hardly what one would call being in private. She forced herself to sit with a relaxed pose beside Emilio even though she wished she had the courage to thrust open the door and throw herself out of his life, both literally and figuratively.

She drew in a sharp little breath as she looked out at the scenery passing by. The Colosseum suddenly appeared and a tight ache settled in her chest. She could still remember the excitement of her first trip to Italy after she had met Emilio while she was doing a needle-work course at the London School of Embroidery. They had met at an art exhibition she had been invited to by one of the girls she had met doing her course, whose boyfriend couldn't make it at the last minute. Gisele had been in two minds whether or not to attend but in the end had decided to go so that her new friend wouldn't have to go alone. Within minutes of walking into the small privately owned gallery she had met Emilio's gaze from across the room. She could still recall the way her heart had fluttered in her chest as he moved through the knot of people to get to her. He had been head and shoulders above all the other men, not just in stature, but also in looks and in his proud, almost aristocratic bearing. She had thought he must be Italian royalty at the very least, and why he should single her out was beyond her comprehension. But single her out he had, and within a week she had been swept off her feet and totally, blissfully in love.

'I have a new housekeeper,' Emilio said into the silence that had fallen. 'Her name is Marietta.'

'What happened to Concetta?' Gisele asked with a frown.

His mouth tightened briefly. 'I fired her the day after you left.'

'Why?' she asked. 'I thought you said she was the best housekeeper you'd ever had.'

'She was.'

'So why'd you fire her?'

'She overstepped the mark in telling me I was a fool for throwing you out,' he said. 'I fired her on the spot.'

'Way to go, Concetta,' Gisele said. She pushed her tongue against the inside of her bottom lip as she studied his brooding expression. 'You didn't think to ask her to come back to you along with me?'

His brows moved together over his eyes as he looked at her. 'She wouldn't come back,' he said.

Gisele gave him a saccharine-sweet smile. 'Maybe you should've offered her two million dollars.'

He didn't answer but she saw his jaw flex just before he turned and looked out of the window.

The driver pulled up in front of Emilio's villa in the exclusive area near the Villa Borghese parklands. Gisele felt another pang as Emilio helped her from the car. She had been totally blown away by the magnificent building two years ago and she felt exactly the same way now. Built on four levels with gorgeous formal gardens and a huge fountain set in the middle of the circular driveway, it looked every inch the private residence of a person who had very much made their way in the world.

Emilio gave the driver instructions about their luggage before leading Gisele to the front door, which magically opened, revealing a neatly dressed Italian woman in her fifties with a welcoming but deferential smile on her face. '*Bentornati*, Signorina Carter,' she said. 'Welcome back. Congratulations on renewing your engagement.'

'*Grazie,*' Gisele said, taking the housekeeper's hand and returning her smile with an effort. *Engagement? What engagement?* Anger bubbled up inside her. What on earth did Emilio think he was doing? She could hardly have it out with him in front of the housekeeper. She stood with a frozen smile on her face, furious with him for putting her in such an invidious position.

Emilio spoke to Marietta in Italian before turning to Gisele. 'Marietta will unpack your things while you have a rest,' he said.

Gisele faltered as she thought of Lily's blanket inside her case. 'Um… Do you mind if I do it myself? I haven't brought much with me anyway. I feel…um… embarrassed. I need some new clothes. There hasn't been much money for extras just lately…'

He studied her flushed features for a pulsing moment, his eyes dark and unreadable. 'You have no need to be embarrassed,' he said. 'I will see to it that you have all the clothes you need.'

'I'd still like to unpack my own things,' she said. 'I've got out of the habit of having people waiting on me.'

He held her look for another beat or two. 'As you wish.'

Gisele let out a breath of relief as he turned and issued Marietta another set of instructions. She didn't want anyone handling Lily's blanket. No one had touched it but her. She didn't want to lose that last trace of her baby's scent...

Emilio turned back and took Gisele's hand and toyed with the knuckle of her ring finger as he held her gaze. 'We have a little job to do, *si*?' he said. 'I have your engagement ring in the safe in my study.'

'So you managed to fish it out of the fountain, then?' she asked with an arch look.

'It took three plumbers, but yes,' he said. 'I finally managed to locate it.'

Gisele waited until they were alone in the study where his safe was before she let fly. 'How *could* you lead your housekeeper to believe that we're engaged? I haven't agreed to that! I've only agreed to come here for a month but not as your fiancée.'

Emilio's expression remained calm, as if he were dealing with a small, wilful child. 'Relax, *cara*,' he said. 'There is no need for such hysterics.'

'I am *not* hysterical!' Gisele shrieked with a stamp of her foot for good measure.

His brows snapped together. 'Keep your voice down.'

She clenched her hands into fists and spoke through tight lips. 'You've done this deliberately, haven't you? You're making it impossible for me to deny we have a formal relationship by making me wear your stupid ring.'

'*Cara*, you're tired and overwrought,' he said. 'You're not making sense. Of course you will have to wear my ring while you are here. People will not accept our reconciliation as the real thing if we don't appear to pick up where we left off.'

She glowered at him. 'You think by putting that ring on my finger it gives you automatic licence to sleep with me, don't you?'

'You will sleep with me, ring or no ring,' he said. 'We will be sharing my room. I will not have it any other way. I don't want the servants to suspect anything is amiss.'

Gisele's heart tripped in her chest like a pony's hoof in a pothole. 'I'd rather sleep on the floor than share a bed with you.'

'It seems to me you don't sleep anywhere,' he returned wryly. 'Your little closed-eye routine didn't fool me on the flight, *cara*. That's obviously why you're being so obstreperous now. You're acting like a little child who has been kept up way past her bedtime.'

She swung away from him in fury, flustered because he saw too damn much. She was worried because she didn't trust herself not to turn to him during the night. If her nightmares about Lily hadn't been enough to deal with, so many times over the past two years she had found herself reaching for him during that half-awake, half-asleep phase of fitful rest. Her need for him had not automatically switched off just because he had thrown her out of his life. If anything, it had smouldered under the surface, building in intensity as each lonely month had passed.

Gisele heard the sound of the safe being opened and drew in a breath for composure. This would be another emotional hurdle for her to negotiate. How different would this be from when he had slid that ring onto her finger after he had asked her to marry him? She didn't want to think about how eagerly and excitedly she had accepted his proposal. She had gushed in enthusiasm and he had looked down at her with the sort of indulgent amusement that made her cringe now. How gauche she had been, how foolishly romantic to think he had adored her even a fraction as much as she had adored him. He hadn't loved her at all. She had simply ticked all the boxes for him under the compartment in his life marked: Find Suitable Wife.

'Give me your hand,' Emilio commanded.

Gisele turned around like a statue on a plinth, her body tense from head to foot. 'I don't suppose you're going to do a rerun of your proposal?' she said.

His eyes glinted as he took her hand in his. 'I had thought of it but decided against it.'

'Why?' she asked. 'Because you were worried I'd say no?'

He slid the ring onto her finger, holding it there with the warmth of his finger and thumb, his eyes still meshed with hers. 'Ah, but *would* you say no?' he asked.

'Why don't you give it a shot and see?' she challenged him.

He gave a little chuckle that was spine-tinglingly deep. 'I'm sure if the price was right you would agree to marry me,' he said, bringing her hand up to his mouth and pressing his lips against her bent fingers.

Gisele felt a butterfly wing–like flutter pass over the floor of her belly. She disguised a swallow as she felt his lips move to the sensitive skin of the underside of her wrist. She wanted to close her eyes and lose herself in his magical touch. The sensation of his warm velvet lips made her skin shiver in reaction. 'Stop it,' she said, not really meaning it and pretty sure he knew it.

He slid his tongue over her leaping pulse, a sexy lick that sent a dart of pleasure straight to her core. She suppressed a tiny whimper, determined not to show him how much he affected her by his proximity, by his touch, by his astonishing ability to dismantle her defences. Her legs felt like dampened paper, barely strong enough to hold her upright. Her spine was loosening, vertebra by vertebra, until she felt sure she would melt into a pool at his feet. Where was her resolve? Where was her anger when she needed it? They were like cowardly soldiers retreating from the frontline of battle.

'You taste like summer,' Emilio said against her wrist. 'Like frangipani and honeysuckle.'

Gisele shivered as his teeth gave her a playful but gentle bite. Her breasts peaked with longing, her insides contracting with need. How was she going to resist him if he kept this up? It was torture to be so near him and not respond the way she wanted to. 'I need a shower...' she said.

'Have one with me.'

The images those words conjured up! She had to fight with everything within her to keep them from flooding her mind. But it was impossible to eradicate every single one. She felt the heat build inside her at the memory of his hard body driving into her as the water cascaded over them: the memory of his hot, clever mouth feasting on her intimately and the memory of her doing exactly the same to him. Just thinking about the earthy rawness of it made her cheeks grow warm. 'I don't think so,' she said, trying to pull away.

His eyes came back to hers as he held her firm. 'It

won't be long before you change your mind, *cara*. We both know that, don't we?'

She glared at him, spitting out the words one by one. 'Let. Me. Go.'

He pulled her up against him, pressing a brief hard kiss to her mouth before he released her. 'Go and have your rest,' he said. 'I'll see you at dinner.'

Gisele felt unsettled and disoriented when he stepped away from her. It was a feeling almost like being cast adrift. She felt strangely empty without his hands holding her against him. That too-brief kiss had made her feel hungry for more. She swept the tip of her tongue over the tingling surface of her lips, the tantalising taste of him making her insides clench with longing. She didn't realise she was still standing there in a zombie-like daze until she heard the soft click of the study door, signalling Emilio had left.

Walking back into Emilio's bedroom suite was something Gisele had been silently dreading for all the memories being there would stir up, but when she pushed open the door she was surprised to see everything had changed. The decor was completely different, even the bed ensemble and the light fittings and soft furnishings. She wondered if he had done it deliberately, somehow purging his room of her presence after he had sent her from his life.

The master suite now had a Venetian theme to it with the boldest of gold and black in the fabric of the curtains and bed linen. Crystal lamps encrusted with onyx and gold were stationed either side of the massive bed, and the priceless thick carpet on the floor continued the theme.

The en suite bathroom was fitted out in highly polished black marble with gold tap wear and golden-framed mirrors. There was a large shower with two showerheads and a deep marble-surrounded bath and a heated towel rack with several snowy-white towels with a black-and-gold trim neatly folded there.

It was decadent and rich and luxurious, the perfect setting for seduction, Gisele thought as she came back to the windows that led out onto a balcony that overlooked the gardens.

She opened the French windows and went out to breathe in the warm spring air, the clovelike scent of roses drifting towards her from below. The rear gardens were much the same as before, lots of clipped hedges and herbaceous borders and roses everywhere. A lavender pathway led to another fountain, larger than the one at the front. The sound of the water splashing had always had a soporific effect on her. She had spent many nights lying in Emilio's arms listening to that wonderfully relaxing sound as she drifted off to sleep, dreaming of their future together…

She stepped out of her reverie by leaving the balcony and closing the doors, turning the key as a reminder to herself that the past was no longer accessible.

She found another room farther down the hall. It was decorated in tones of milky coffee and white, with large windows overlooking the gardens.

Once she unpacked her things from her suitcase and stored them in the wardrobe, she found a drawer to put Lily's blanket and photos in and gently closed it.

The aching tiredness she felt was suddenly so over-whelming she was barely aware of kicking off her shoes before she curled up like a comma on the feather-soft bed and closed her eyes...

Emilio searched through several bedrooms before he found Gisele lying sound asleep on the bed in the room furthest from his. Her silver-blonde hair was spread out over the pillow, her slim body barely making an inden-tation on the mattress. She looked like an angel lying there, a sleeping angel with features so perfect and yet so pale she didn't seem quite real. How was he to get through the wall of her anger? He had to dismantle it brick by brick, getting her to slowly warm to him again.

Looking back now, he could see how truly devastated she had been when he had cast her from his life. At the time he had read her body language as a greedy little gold-digger whose plans to wed a rich man had been thwarted at the last minute, but now he could see her shattered expression for what it was: a young woman who had loved and loved deeply, who by a quirk of fate had suddenly found her life in ruins through no fault of her own.

Where had she gone?

Who had she turned to?

How must she have felt to have her life ripped out from under her without warning? He didn't like think-ing about it. She would have been feeling so shocked and frightened, so upset that she hadn't been able to get him to see reason. Even worse, anything could have hap-pened to her that night. In her state of high emotional distress she could have come to some sort of harm and he had done nothing to protect her. He had cast her out of his life as if she had been nothing more than some trash he no longer had any use for.

He had got it so horribly wrong.

Emilio watched the soft flutter of her lips as she gave an inaudible murmur and the way one of her hands seemed to be searching for something on the bed next to her. Her face suddenly contorted as if she was having a terrible nightmare. She started to thrash about, her cries soft but heart-wrenching. 'No…oh, no, please *no*…'

'Gisele, shh, it's all right,' Emilio said softly as he perched beside her and captured her flailing hands.

Her eyes sprang open and she jerked upright. She seemed momentarily disoriented but then her expression turned hostile. 'What are you doing here?' she asked, pulling her hands away from his.

'I hate to point out the obvious, but this is my villa and you are in one of my bedrooms,' Emilio said.

She brushed her hair out of her eyes with an angry movement of her hand as she gave him a resentful scowl. 'You shouldn't sneak up on people like that,' she said.

'I didn't sneak up on you,' he said. 'It looked like you were having a bad dream. You were crying out in your sleep so I came over to comfort you.'

She bit down on her lower lip, a soft flush rising in her cheeks as she averted her gaze from his.

Emilio turned her chin so she had to meet his eyes. 'Do you often have bad dreams, *cara*?' he asked.

A shadow passed over her blue eyes. 'Not often… sometimes…'

He caressed her cheek with the pad of his thumb.

'I wish I could wipe out the last two years,' he said. 'I wish I could just reset the clock. I wish I could take back every horrible word I threw at you.'

She didn't answer. She just kept looking at him with that grey-blue accusing gaze of hers.

'What did you do the night I sent you away?' Emilio asked.

'I found a hotel,' she said. 'The press gave me a hard time but eventually I managed to shake them off. I caught a flight back to Sydney the next day.'

'You never tried to contact me,' he said, still stroking her creamy cheek. 'Not even once.'

She gave him a brittle look. 'You forbade me to, remember?'

He studied her for a long moment before dropping his hand from her chin. 'Dinner is in half an hour,' he said as he rose from the bed. 'I'll see you downstairs.'

CHAPTER FIVE

AFTER Gisele had a shower she dressed in a slim-fitting sheathlike taupe-coloured dress and a pair of heels. She dried her hair and scooped it up into a knot at the back of her head and put on a bare minimum of make-up. She looked down at the engagement ring on her finger. It was too loose for her now. The huge diamond kept slipping round the wrong way out of sight. Was that some sort of omen? she wondered.

Emilio was in the *salone* when she came downstairs. He was sipping at an aperitif, looking out of the window to the gardens outside. He turned and looked at her, his gaze moving over her body like a warm caress. 'You look beautiful,' he said.

'Thank you.' Gisele fought for cool poise but a blush crept over her cheeks in spite of her best efforts.

'What would you like to drink?' he asked.

'Um…white wine if you have it.'

He poured her a glass of wine and brought it over to her. She saw his nostrils flare as if he was taking in the fragrance of her perfume. She saw too the way his eyes darkened as they caught and held hers. 'Do you feel a little more refreshed after your rest?' he asked.

'Yes,' she said, taking a generous sip to settle her nerves.

'Why didn't you put your things in my bedroom as I asked you to?' he said.

She gripped her wineglass a little tighter. 'You can't force me to occupy your bed. I need more time. It's a big step for me.'

'Didn't you like the new decor?' he asked.

'It looks like no expense has been spared to rid your bedroom of every trace of my previous occupation of it,' Gisele said with a touch of asperity.

His expression was unreadable as he raised his glass to his lips. 'I thought it was time for a change.'

'Out with the old, in with the new?' she said with a cynical look. 'Did all your subsequent girlfriends like it?'

A brooding frown appeared between his eyebrows. 'If you don't like it then we can occupy another room,' he said. 'But you *will* share a bed with me, Gisele. I will not have any rumours circulating that this is not a proper relationship.'

'How soon did you replace me?' she asked.

A muscle worked in his jaw. 'Gisele, this is not going to help matters.'

'How many?' she asked, feeling a lump rise in her throat.

'I could ask you the same thing.'

'Go on,' she said. 'Ask me.'

The muscle in his jaw worked even harder. 'All right,' he said on an expelled breath. 'How many lovers have you had since me?'

Gisele wished now she hadn't provoked him. Could

she lie just to hurt him? Could she play payback with a host of imaginary lovers, not one of whom would have come close to being as perfect for her physically as him? What was the point? She suspected he would see through it anyway. Hadn't the way she'd responded to him so far given him enough proof that she hadn't moved on?

'There's been no one,' she said after a tight pause.

'Gisele...'

'Don't get me wrong.' She cut him off quickly. 'I've had plenty of opportunities. I just didn't want to rush into anything. You don't have to automatically assume I was waiting for you to take me back because I wasn't.'

He took his drink and moved over to the windows again, his back turned towards her. It was a moment or two before he spoke and, when he did, his voice was rough around the edges, as if it had been dragged up from a place deep inside him. 'Would you believe me if I told you I was thinking of making contact with you even before the press release came out about Sienna being the one in the tape?'

Gisele felt her heart give a little hit-and-miss beat. 'Why?'

He turned from the window and faced her with an in-scrutable look. 'I'm not sure,' he said. 'I guess I wanted to see if you had fared any better than me.'

'What do you mean?'

'Anger and bitterness are pretty corrosive things to be carrying around,' he said. 'I think I got tired of being angry. For two years I was totally consumed with it. I could think of nothing else. I finally got to the point where I wanted to move on. I thought if I contacted you, perhaps met with you face to face to ask you why you'd betrayed me, it might've helped.'

'But I hadn't betrayed you.'

He let out a heavy sigh. 'No,' he said. 'You hadn't. And that's what I have to live with. I made a mistake. It's new territory for me. I'm not usually wrong about anything.'

Gisele looked at the wine in her glass and thought about what he had said about carrying around anger. Her anger had burned like acid inside her. It was still burning, eating away at her, keeping her awake at night. But she wasn't quite ready to relinquish it.

Marietta appeared at that point with the announcement that dinner was ready.

Gisele followed Emilio to the dining room where the long highly polished table had been beautifully set up for a romantic dinner for two. Flowers from the garden made a fragrant centrepiece along with the flickering candles in the candelabra that added to the tone of intimacy. So many times in the past she had sat here at this table and looked lovingly across the table at him. She had pictured their children one day joining them there, their little faces shining with good health and happiness and vigour. How far from her dreams and romantically infused imaginings had she travelled? There would be no happy family now. Not for her at least.

Emilio seated her before he took his own place. 'I've been thinking about your business,' he said. 'Do you outsource any of the needlework?'

'No,' she said. 'I do it all myself. I like working to commission. I think it gives the customer that sense of a personal touch.'

He reached across to pour her some wine. 'But you surely can't expect to keep up with demand if things were to take a sudden upswing?'

'I've managed to keep ahead so far.'

'Yes, but that will change as soon as things take off over here,' he said. 'How will you keep up then?'

She bit her lip. 'I've brought some work with me...'

'Gisele.' He sounded like a world-weary parent speaking to a naive child. 'You can't expect to run things as you have done in the past. You'll have to consider outsourcing. You have no choice. You can hand-pick your needlewomen. You'll still have total control over the standard of your product.'

She flashed him a defensive glare. 'I know what I'm doing. I'm good at what I do. I love my work.'

'The creative side of it is not the problem, *cara*,' he said. 'I've seen your needlework. It's exquisite. You are extremely talented. I'm not saying you aren't. I'm just saying you can't possibly do it all. You need to think about how to meet demands for more of your work, otherwise people will go elsewhere.'

Gisele pressed her lips together before answering. 'OK, I'll think about it.'

He gave a sigh and reached for her hand across the table. 'Look at me, *cara*,' he commanded gently.

She met his gaze with resentment burning in hers. 'I won't allow you to take over my life. I've been doing perfectly fine without you. My shop is the busiest one on that stretch of the street.'

'I know that,' he said. 'You've done amazingly well. I'm just trying to help you do better, to maximise your profits. At least if things don't work out between us you will have a stronger base to go home to.'

Marietta came in with their meal and Emilio deftly steered the conversation into less contentious areas. Gisele made an effort to do the delicious food justice but being in Emilio's presence made her feel nervous and excited at the same time. He could be such charming company when he put his mind to it. She felt the intoxicating lure of it each time he looked at her with that sexy slant of a smile. His eyes took on a dark mesmerising heat as they held hers, the sensual promise in them making every hair on her body stand up and take notice.

After Marietta had served coffee in the *salone* she announced she was leaving for home.

'She doesn't live here like Concetta did?' Gisele asked once the housekeeper had left.

'No,' Emilio said. 'She has a husband and a couple of daughters who still live at home. She likes to spend the nights with them.'

'So if she's not here at night then there should be no problem with me having my own room,' Gisele said.

His expression tightened. 'She is back first thing in the morning,' he said. 'What are you going to do? Run along the hall and jump in beside me just for show?'

She put her coffee cup down and rose to her feet agitatedly. The thought of jumping into bed with him for real was far too tempting. It was all she could think about. Her body burned with hot flames of need and there was nothing she could do to dampen them down. 'Lots of couples don't sleep together,' she said. 'My parents didn't share a bed for most of their marriage.'

He came over to where she was standing. 'That is not how this relationship is going to be run,' he said. He took her hands in his and held them gently but firmly. 'Why are you fighting what is inevitable? I know you were hurt by our break-up. I understand that you're still angry. We have this chance to reconnect but you seem intent on sabotaging every attempt on my part to put things right.'

'Some things can never be put right,' she said, looking down at their joined hands rather than meeting his gaze. Her belly quivered as his thumbs began stroking her fingers, his darker-toned skin against hers a spine-tingling reminder of how very masculine he was and how she couldn't help but respond to his primal call to all that was feminine in her. She could feel the flicker of desire between her thighs, a tiny rhythmic pulse that was like a faraway drumbeat deep inside her, each throbbing second bringing it closer and closer…

Emilio tipped up her chin, his eyes so dark she couldn't make out his pupils. 'Are you fighting me or yourself, *cara*?' he asked.

She sent the point of her tongue out over her lips, testing his hold but it remained firm. 'I hate you,' she said, but somehow the words didn't sound as feisty and determined as they had even a day ago.

'That doesn't mean that the sex between us won't still be good,' he said as his mouth blazed a hot trail over the sensitive skin near her left ear.

Gisele felt her senses go into a tailspin as his teeth gently tugged on her earlobe. It sent a delicious shiver down her spine as he moved back towards her mouth, slowly, tantalisingly, awakening each and every nerve beneath her skin, making her lips tingle in anticipation for the hot, urgent pressure of his. She gave a soft little whimper and turned her head just a fraction, just enough to make that final devastating contact.

His mouth sealed hers but it was nothing like the bruising kiss of the other day. This was a kiss that was sensually soft, exploratory and yet unmistakably commanding and arrantly sexual in its intent. She felt the stroke of his tongue at the seam of her lips and she opened to him, their breaths mingling, their tongues mating in an erotic ritual that sent lightning bolts of need straight to the heart of her femininity. One of his hands slipped to the nape of her neck, the warm cup of his palm causing the entire length of her spine to shudder in delicious response. His mouth changed position, his lips still moving gently against hers, but she still sensed an undercurrent of urgency, of his control still tightly leashed but straining for freedom.

His other hand pressed her in the small of her back, bringing her closer to the pulsing heat of his erection. She felt its thickness, the potent power of it stirring her body into a maelstrom of feeling. Her skin tightened, her heart fluttered, her legs trembled and still the kiss went on and on.

It was so wonderful to *feel* again. To feel alive and vibrant with sexual energy, to feel the way her body inflamed his by its closeness. His hand at her back pressed harder, a low groan emitting from his throat as she rubbed against him, her feminine mound aching to feel his possession. It was a deep ache inside her, a pulsing, throbbing ache that she could feel vibrating in his body as he ground himself against her, hungry for relief.

'I want you,' he growled like a wolf against her mouth, the primal deepness of his voice and the scrape of his teeth as he tugged at her lower lip making Gisele melt like honey under intense heat.

She didn't need to say she wanted him too. Her body was doing all it could to relay the message of how much she needed him to relieve her of this voracious need that was clawing at her insides. She pushed herself closer, her breasts jammed up against the hard wall of his chest, her mouth feeding greedily off his.

Emilio pulled down the zip of her dress, his hands moving over the naked skin of her back in tantalising strokes that made her legs feel as if they were going to go out from beneath her. He deftly unhooked her bra and it slid to the floor along with her dress, leaving her in nothing but her knickers and her heels. He brought his mouth to her achingly tight breast, sucking on her erect nipple before doing the same to the other. Gisele whimpered as her senses screamed in rapture. It was so good to feel him on her naked flesh, to feel the sexy rasp of his masculine jaw with its pepper of stubble on her soft skin.

She took her hands from around his neck and worked her way down his shirt, button by button, tasting the sexy saltiness of his skin with her tongue, teasing each of his flat male nipples with her teeth. He shrugged himself out of his shirt as she moved her hands down to the waistband of his trousers. She ran her hand over the proud jut of his body, her insides clenching with feverish anticipation as he moved against her hand with a guttural groan.

'I knew you would come back to me,' Emilio said in a gravel-rough tone as his lips hovered above her mouth. 'I knew you wouldn't be able to resist.'

The ice-cold water of common sense doused the flames of Gisele's desire at the hint of arrogant assurance in his tone. Did he really think she was *that* predictable? That he only had to beckon to her and she would come running back as if nothing had happened? 'Wait,' she said, dropping her hands from his body.

He frowned at her. 'Is everything all right?'

Gisele took a deep steadying breath and covered her naked breasts with her crossed arms. 'I can't do this,' she said. 'Not like this…not here…'

'Then we'll take it upstairs,' Emilio said.

She sent him a speaking glance. 'No.'

'No?'

'I'm sorry,' she said, bending down to retrieve her dress and her bra, her cheeks so hot they felt as if they had been scorched. She got dressed with as much dignity as she could, putting some order to her hair as she faced him once more. 'I'm sorry, Emilio. I know I should have called a halt earlier. I don't know what I was thinking. Maybe I wasn't thinking. I don't seem to do a lot of that when I'm around you.' She made a self-deprecating movement of her lips. 'I guess that's one thing that hasn't changed in two years.'

He gave her a wry smile as he brushed her cheek with the tip of his index finger. 'I like it when you're not thinking,' he said. 'I like it best when you're just feeling.'

Gisele chewed at her lip. 'It's been a long time for me,' she said softly.

He cupped her cheek with the warmth of his hand, his eyes dark and surprisingly tender as they meshed with hers. 'I know,' he said. 'That's why I want our first time back together to be special. I don't want to rush things just for the sake of it. I want to savour every moment with you.'

'You sound like you missed me,' she said a little wistfully.

His thumb brushed over her bottom lip like a teasing feather. 'Those first few days after you left I was unbearable to be around,' he said. 'The contract I was working on securing fell through. The man I was negotiating with was a very conservative family man. He gave the contract to the other architect who, unfortunately, was my biggest rival. I was so blind with rage I felt sure you must have had something to do with it. I thought you had been planted as a spy.' His mouth twisted. 'I became totally obsessed after that. I had to work hard to make up for the loss of that commission. The first real block of time I've had off since then was when I flew to Sydney to see you.'

Gisele thought of him working himself to the ground in an attempt to put her out of his mind. He had always been an intensely driven man. She had recognised that when she'd first met him. It had inspired her to think of how hard he had worked for his success. He had told her once it had been his dream since childhood to become an architect and he had determined nothing would get in his way. And it hadn't. He had become one of the world's leading and most innovative designers with a string of accolades to his name.

To suddenly find out he had been wrong about the accusations he had hurled at her must have come as a horrid shock to a man with his level of pride. The fact that he had put everything on hold to fly out to see her to make amends was certainly admirable, but she still suspected it was his pride and reputation that was at stake, not his heart.

His heart was for no one. Whatever had happened in his childhood had left scars that cut deep. That was another thing Gisele had suspected right from the start, but she had been determined to be the one to heal him. How deluded had she been to think that the strength of her love could unlock his fiercely guarded heart? He had trust issues that no amount of love would ever heal. She had been a casualty of that lack of trust, and she very much doubted that she was the first or even going to be the last.

'Have you spoken to Sienna about us?' he asked.

'I didn't go into a lot of detail,' Gisele said. 'I didn't want her to feel responsible for what happened between us. You have to remember that although we're identical twins we're virtual strangers. It will take some time to get to know each other properly.'

'Do you like her?' Emilio asked. 'Is she someone you could warm to?'

Gisele thought of her vibrant, vivacious twin, with her generous and impulsive nature. From what she had picked up so far, Sienna had got herself into plenty of scrapes because of her somewhat reckless take on life, but it was impossible not to like her. 'I think she's lovely,' she said. 'She's smart and sassy and sophisticated. But I think the press misrepresent her. They paint her as a hedonist, a wild child without morals. I don't think she's anything like that. I think she's very sensitive but hides it behind the party girl façade.'

'I have a client to see in London towards the end of the month,' Emilio said. 'I'd like it if you came with me. You can introduce me to Sienna and perhaps spend some time with her while I'm at work.'

'I'd like to see her,' Gisele said. 'But I don't want to lie to her about our relationship. Putting on an act for the press is one thing, lying to my sister is another.'

'Perhaps by then it won't be an act, *cara*,' he said, brushing her lip again with his thumb.

Gisele felt the sensitive surface of her lips tingle from the gentle caress. It was true what he had said: she was fighting herself rather than him. Her unruly desires were annihilating her resolve like a hurricane against a house of cards. She had no hope of withstanding him, not while her feelings for him were still so ambiguous. She stepped back from him, giving him a brief on-off smile. 'I think I'll go to bed,' she said. 'Good night.'

Emilio didn't answer but Gisele felt his scorching gaze follow her as she left the room.

CHAPTER SIX

GISELE was pulling back the covers of her bed when she heard the bedroom door open and Emilio came in dressed in a bathrobe, his hair still damp from a recent shower. 'What do you think you're doing?' she gasped in shock.

'Coming to bed,' he said, slipping off the robe.

Gisele's eyes drank in the sight of him: that hard muscular chest, that gorgeous flat washboard abdomen and the arrantly masculine heart of him that was already partially aroused. Her heart gave a jerky kick inside her chest and her throat almost closed over. 'But I told you I—'

'And I told you how things were going to be,' he said before she could complete her sentence. 'We will share a bed for the month even if we don't make love. I will not force myself on you. You should know me better than that.'

She swallowed deeply, wondering if it was possible to share a villa of this size with Emilio without wanting to make love, let alone a bed. It was a big bed certainly, but not big enough for her to avoid those long, strong hair-roughened legs coming into contact with hers. 'That's not the point,' she said, running the tip of her tongue out over lips so dry they felt like ancient parchment.

'What *is* the point, Gisele?' he asked with a glittering look. 'You don't seem to know what you want. One minute you look at me as if you want to throw yourself back in my arms and never leave, and the next you look like you want to claw my eyes out. At some point you're going to have to make up your mind.'

Gisele had thought she had made up her mind but her body had chosen an entirely different path. It was calling out to him now in a secret sensual language he couldn't fail to misinterpret. But in her haste to disguise how much she wanted him she swung away from the bed and in doing so accidentally knocked the glass of water and her pills off the bedside table. The glass landed with a thump on the carpet and the little bottle of pills rolled across the floor and came to a stop right in front of Emilio's left foot.

She watched, dry mouthed, as he bent to pick them up. 'What are these for?' he asked, frowning as he read the label.

'Give them to me,' she said, trying to make a grab for them but he held the bottle just out of her reach.

He frowned as he read the label. 'Sleeping tablets?' he asked, looking at her again.

'So?' she said, throwing him a defensive look. 'Lots of people take them.'

'How long have you been taking them?' he asked.

Gisele folded her arms mutinously, her mouth in a flat line.

'Gisele?' He tipped up her chin, forcing her eyes to

meet his. 'How long have you been taking sleeping medication?'

She let out a shaky breath. 'A while…a few weeks… a couple of months maybe…'

'Sleeping tablets are meant to be a temporary thing,' Emilio said reprovingly. 'You shouldn't be on them any longer than a few weeks. They're highly addictive.'

Gisele rolled her eyes. 'You sound just like my doctor.'

He caught her just before she made to turn away from him. His eyes were dark and a concerned frown sliced deep into his forehead. '*Cara*, did *I* do this to you?' he asked hollowly.

Gisele thought of the weeks after his rejection when she had done nothing but sleep most days as well as the nights. She had slid into an abyss of depression that had made every little task an impossible feat. Having a shower hurt her skin. Brushing her hair felt like torture. Getting dressed in street clothes made her muscles ache. Walking to the front door had seemed like a marathon. Getting through each day felt like a lifetime. The warm, secure nest of her bed had been a reprieve from a life she didn't think she could live without him in it.

And then she had discovered she was pregnant. The news had pulled her out of her depression. She had started to look forward to life again with hope and a tentative happiness that had all too soon been torn away from her.

Was Emilio to blame that Lily had died?

For a while she had felt as if he was, but over time she had come to realise no one was to blame. It was just one of those things, or so the doctors had said—a genetic abnormality, a mistake of nature.

'No...' Gisele said in a voice so soft it was more of a whisper. 'No, it's not because of you.' It was the sound of Lily crying that haunted her sleepless nights. The only way to escape the torture of hearing that tiny mewling cry was to numb herself to sleep. Not that it always worked.

Emilio looked deeply into her eyes as if he wanted to see into the very heart of her. His eyes were pitch-black, still etched with concern as he cupped her face. 'Is it because of the business? Your father's death? Finding out about Sienna?'

Gisele put her hand on his to peel it off her face and stepped backwards, wrapping her arms about her body. Should she tell him about Lily? She could feel guilt nipping at the heels of her conscience. Didn't he have the right to know he had been a father, even for such a short time? She would have to tell him one day. What if he somehow found out by some other means? The thought was terrifying. Wouldn't it be better to hear it from her rather than someone else? But how could she drop that sort of bombshell into the conversation? Her chance to tell him had been right at the start. She couldn't talk about it now. Not like this, with no preparation. 'I...I've just been under a lot of stress,' she said. 'It's no one thing but everything, I guess.'

'You should wean yourself off them,' he said, still frowning. 'I don't like the thought of you drugging yourself to sleep. You never used to have any problem sleeping.'

She gave him a wry look before she could stop herself. 'As I recall, we didn't always do a lot of sleeping.'

The words seemed to hang in the air for a moment, the erotic images they conjured up gathering around like ghosts from the past.

Gisele saw the flare of heat in Emilio's eyes as he took in her scantily clad body. She had slipped off her wrap just before he had come in and her creamy satin nightgown left very little to the imagination. She felt the tight buds of her nipples pressing against the soft fabric and knew he could see them too. Her belly gave an excited flutter as his eyes skimmed her lower body, the heat in her core liquefying as if he had touched her there. His body responded to her as if she had stroked her fingers along his length. She saw him swell and rise, the sheer power and potency of him taking her breath away.

'No, we didn't, did we?' Emilio asked with a smouldering look as his eyes slowly came back to mesh with hers.

Gisele drew in a quick breath, her chest feeling prickly and tight. The heat from his body radiated out and touched her like a caress. Her skin felt tingly and supersensitive, as if all the nerves had repositioned themselves on the outside of her body. 'Don't do this, Emilio,' she said in a hoarse whisper.

'Don't do what, *cara*?' he asked as he shrank the gap between their bodies by taking half a step. 'This?' He touched his lips to the skin of her neck just below her ear, not a kiss, not a bite, but something sinfully and sexily in between.

She shivered as his tongue grazed her skin as he

moved down to the fragile scaffold of her collarbone.
'Or this?' he asked as his breath moved over her like a
sultry summer breeze.

Gisele's lower body ached to move forwards to find
his. It was like a magnetic field she had inadvertently
stepped inside. It was pulling her inexorably towards
him. She could sense him there, thick and hard, pulsing with the same longing that was making her heart
race and her breathing become shallow and uneven. His
feet touched hers, a sexy bump of toes that sent a shockwave of forbidden pleasure right through her body. She
felt him then against her belly, the blunt head of him as
scorching as a naked flame against her skin.

He worked his way back up towards her mouth,
slowly, each brush of his lips setting her skin alight.
'This is what used to keep us both awake, remember?'
he said just above her quivering mouth.

Gisele moistened her dry lips, her heart hammering
as he slipped a hand beneath the curtain of her hair. The
sensations shimmering down her spine made her dizzy
with need. She remembered it all. It had never left her.
How he made her feel. How he could set her aflame with
just a look.

How much she still wanted him.

Time stood still for a heart-stopping pause.

She prepared herself for the press of his mouth; her
eyelashes came down, her lips were softly parted, her
breath had stilled…

But Emilio suddenly broke the spell by stepping
backwards and moving to where he had dropped his
bathrobe.

Gisele blinked a couple of times in bewilderment as

she watched him shrug himself into it and tie the cord around his waist, seemingly untouched by what had just transpired between them. How could he leave her like this? Was he doing it deliberately to prove how little he needed her? That she was just another woman he could have sex with if he could be bothered?

He was the *only* person she wanted to be intimate with. She couldn't imagine wanting anyone else the way she wanted him. Her body felt as if it *belonged* to him. It had belonged to him for more than two years.

'I'll give you the rest of the week to settle in,' he said. 'I'll make up some excuse for Marietta for why we're not sharing a room.'

'And after that?' she asked.

His eyes pulsated as they locked with hers. 'I think you know what happens after that,' he said in a gravel-rough, oh-so-sexy tone.

Gisele felt her belly do another crazy little tumble turn but she hid behind her increasingly fragile armour of pride and haughtiness. 'You think two million dollars is going to be enough to make me enjoy being back in your bed?' she asked.

His mouth curled up at the corners in a confident smile as he opened the door to leave. 'I'll make sure of it,' he said and, with a soft click of the lock falling in place, he was gone.

Gisele spent the night in a fitful state of tossing and turning. Emilio's promise had made her so edgy and agitated she hadn't had a hope of sleeping a wink in spite of her pills. Her body had been so uptight with longing she had felt like a tightly coiled spring. She hadn't been able to rid her mind of his aroused naked body so close to hers, *touching* hers. How dared he entice her like that with his mouth and hands, only to step back from her as if she was nothing to him? It made her so angry she had been so close to giving herself to him. It made her absolutely furious to think he knew how weak she still was. He was playing with her, toying with her like an angler with a fish on his line. He was biding his time before he reeled her right in.

She would show him.

She deliberately lingered in her room, taking an extra-long shower, dawdling over her hair and light make-up, determined to keep her distance for as long as she could, hoping he would have long ago eaten breakfast and headed off to work.

She walked down the stairs with an assured smile hovering about her mouth. She would show him how little she needed him. She would keep herself busy all day, sending him the clear message she wasn't waiting around for him to crook his finger and summon her back to his bed.

Marietta was on her way out to the terrace with a tray of fresh rolls and fruit. 'Signor Andreoni is waiting for you,' she said. 'You like tea, *sì*?'

'Grazie,' Gisele said, forcing a smile. It looked as if she wasn't going to be able to escape Emilio's disturbing presence after all. It was almost eleven in the morning. He was not one to linger about the villa. He had never taken a day off in the past. He had even worked most weekends, leaving her for long periods on her own.

He was sipping a cup of coffee when Gisele stepped out onto the sun-drenched terrace. He looked fabulously rested, his skin glowing from good health and his eyes clear. He was dressed in black trousers and a white business shirt but it was rolled back over his tanned forearms in a casual manner, making him look even more arrestingly handsome.

He put down his cup and rose to his feet, pulling out a chair for her. '*Cara*, you look like you had a rough night,' he said. 'Your little pills not working, hmm?'

She gave him a gimlet glare as she plonked herself down on the chair. 'Why aren't you at work?' she asked.

'I took the day off to spend it with you,' he said. 'That's what a newly reconciled couple would do, is it not?'

'You shouldn't have bothered,' Gisele said crossly, flicking her napkin across her lap. 'I don't feel like being around you or anyone.'

'Too bad,' he said, picking up his coffee cup again. 'We will be expected to be seen out and about together.' He took a sip of his coffee, looked at the contents frowningly for a moment before looking at her again. 'I have a business function to attend this evening. I thought we could go shopping for you to find something suitable to wear.'

'I can go shopping by myself,' she said, shooting him a look across the table. 'I don't need you to carry my bags.'

Emilio placed his cup back down on its saucer with unnerving precision. 'Gisele,' he addressed her sternly, 'you are walking a very fine line. I am trying to be patient with you but there is only so much leeway I'm prepared to give.'

Gisele saw the steely determination in his dark eyes

and had to look away. 'What did you tell Marietta about me sleeping in the other room?' she asked to fill the heavy silence.

'I told her you have a snoring problem.'

Her eyes flew back to his. *You what?*

He gave a little shrug as he brought his cup towards his mouth. 'It's OK, *cara*,' he said. 'Lots of people snore.'

'I don't!' she said, bristling with outrage. 'Why didn't you tell her it was *you* with the problem?'

'Because I'm not the one with cold feet about sharing a bed, that's why,' he said smoothly.

Gisele scowled as she took a roll and tore it into little pieces. 'You could've thought of something a little less demeaning,' she said. 'Snoring sounds so…so unsexy.'

'Are you going to eat any of that roll or just play with it?' Emilio asked.

She pushed the plate with the decimated roll to one side. 'I'm not hungry.'

He challenged her with his narrowed coal-black gaze. 'Are you doing this deliberately to annoy me?' he asked. 'Because, if so, it's working.'

Gisele felt a little frisson race down her spine. She liked the sense of power it gave her to get under his skin. He was still in control but she could see the leash on it was straining. There was a muscle pulsing at the corner of his flattened mouth and his eyes had hardened to chips of black ice.

The air between them seemed to crackle like electricity along a wire.

'You are not leaving this table until you've had something to eat,' he ground out. 'Do you hear me?'

She glared back at him. 'If you want me to eat, then why don't you stop deliberately upsetting me?'

The sound of Marietta's footsteps sounding on the flagstones broke the tense moment.

Emilio sat back and visibly forced himself to relax and Gisele did the same. She sensed the housekeeper's intrigue and wondered how much she had overheard of their heated exchange. How well did Emilio know this new housekeeper? Concetta had been the soul of discretion. Was that why Emilio was so determined that Gisele should occupy his room? Journalists on the hunt for a story paid well for leaks and for photo opportunities. Marietta could exploit the situation if she sensed a lack of harmony between them, and clearly Emilio was fully aware of it.

'Here is your tea, *signorina*,' Marietta said as she placed a teapot beside Gisele, her gaze watchful.

'*Grazie*, Marietta,' Gisele said, trying to smile but not quite managing to pull it off.

'Is everything all right?' Marietta asked, hovering about the table.

'Everything is fine,' Emilio said firmly.

Once the housekeeper had left he raked a hand through his hair. 'I don't mean to upset you, Gisele,' he said. 'This is a difficult time for both of us. There are adjustments and compromises to be made. I want this to work. I really do.'

'Why?' she asked.

He frowned as if she was suddenly speaking a different language, one he couldn't understand. 'Because what we had was good,' he said. 'You can't deny that.'

'I do deny it,' Gisele said. 'What was good about me

having to sign a prenuptial agreement? Where was the trust that most good relationships are built on?'

'I've worked hard for my money,' he said. 'I have the right to protect my interests. If you were so unhappy about it, why didn't you say something at the time?'

Gisele looked away again, embarrassed that she had been so biddable back then. She had felt terribly hurt when he had told her about it but she had kept her feelings well hidden. She had signed the wretched agreement with a heavy heart, wondering if he would ever trust her, or anyone, enough to believe they weren't going to rip him off or betray him in some way.

'Gisele?'

She blew out a breath and set about pouring a cup of tea for herself. 'Can we just forget it?' she asked. 'It's not like we're getting married now. It's irrelevant.'

'It might not be so irrelevant if we do decide to make our reconciliation permanent,' he said.

Gisele's cup rattled against the saucer as she put it back down. 'Are you crazy?' she asked. 'There's no way I would ever agree to marry someone who didn't love me enough to trust me.'

'Love and trust are two different issues,' he said. 'They don't always come hand in hand.'

'Well, they come hand in hand to me,' she said, picking up her cup again and cradling it in her hands.

He studied her with an inscrutable look on his face for what seemed like an endless moment. 'You think I didn't care about you, *cara*?' he asked.

Gisele felt her heart contract. Like a lot of people, he cared about a lot of things but it didn't mean he couldn't imagine life without them. He had lived quite well without her for two whole years. 'Where was that care when you threw me out of your life without giving me the benefit of the doubt?' she asked.

His expression tightened. 'I can do no more than apologise,' he said. 'I was wrong and I have admitted it. What else do you want me to do?'

Love me, Gisele thought. 'Nothing,' she said, lowering her gaze from his. 'There's nothing you can do.'

He reached across the table and took her hand in his. 'Where's your engagement ring?' he asked.

Gisele met his gaze across their joined hands. 'I left it upstairs. It doesn't fit me properly any more. I'm frightened I'm going to lose it.'

He frowned as he stroked where her ring should have been. 'Then we'll have to get it readjusted so it does fit,' he said.

'Why did you keep it?' she asked after an infinitesimal pause.

He released her hand and leaned back in his chair, his face like stone. 'It's worth a lot of money.'

'I know, but you could have sold it,' she said. 'Why didn't you?'

He pushed back from the table and got to his feet. 'I have a call to make,' he said curtly. 'The driver will be here in ten minutes. Don't be late.'

Gisele let out a long breath as she watched him stride across the flagstones and back inside the villa. There were times when she wondered why she had given her heart to such a complex and unreachable man.

'Signor Andreoni asked me to tell you he will meet you for a late lunch,' the driver said when Gisele went out to the waiting car. 'He has some urgent business to see to. He gave me this to give you.' He handed her a credit card and a piece of paper with the details of a restaurant on it.

'Why couldn't he have told me himself?' she asked, feeling annoyed.

The driver shrugged. 'He is a very busy man. He never stops working.'

'I don't need you to drive me,' she said. 'I'm happy to walk.'

'Signor Andreoni insisted on me escorting you.'

'Have the morning off,' Gisele said, placing the credit card and note in her purse.

'But I will get fired if I don't—'

'No, you won't,' she said with determination. 'I'll deal with Signor Andreoni. Ciao.'

Emilio was already waiting at the restaurant when Gisele came in. She hadn't done much shopping, other than pick up a dress and shoes for that evening, but she hadn't used Emilio's card. She refused to be sent off like an overindulged child by a too-busy parent.

She weaved her way through the busy restaurant towards him, conscious of his dark brooding gaze focused solely on her. 'Hello, darling,' she said, offering her cheek for a perfunctory kiss for the sake of onlookers.

Emilio took her face in his hands and planted a hot, drugging kiss on her mouth. Gisele felt her senses spin like a top, round and round and round until she was barely able to stand up. She had to place her hands on his hard chest to steady herself. She stepped back when he released her, sure her face was as red as the single rose in the centre of the table.

'You don't look like you've had a very successful shopping spree,' he said as he seated her.

'I don't like spending other people's money,' she said, throwing him a look over her shoulder. 'If I want to buy clothes then I'll buy them for myself.'

'You seem very determined to disobey my instructions,' he said as he took his own seat opposite her.

'You seem to have trouble accepting that I will not be told what to do,' she tossed back.

He drew in a little breath. 'Careful, *cara*,' he said. 'We are in public now. Keep your claws sheathed until we are alone.'

Gisele had to fight not to glower at him. She picked up the menu and buried her nose in it. 'How did your urgent business go?' she asked.

'Fine.'

A stiff silence passed.

Gisele wondered if his urgent business had been female. A sick feeling opened up in her stomach like a canyon. She hated thinking of him with someone else. For two years she had tried *not* to think about it. Did he have a current mistress he was keeping as backup? Her chest tightened painfully at the thought. So many rich men led double lives. Was he one of them?

'I have something for you,' Emilio said.

Gisele put the menu down again. 'What is it?'

He handed her a jeweller's box, his expression as blank as a sheet of paper. 'I hope it fits.'

She opened the black velvet box and looked down at the staggeringly gorgeous diamond sitting there. It looked frightfully expensive and yet it was much simpler than the one he had given her previously. 'I don't understand...' She looked up at him again. 'I thought you were going to get the old one adjusted?'

'I thought you might like this one instead,' he said. 'But if you don't then you can choose your own. It doesn't matter either way to me.'

Gisele bit her lip as she took the ring out of the box and slid it on her finger. It was a perfect fit and suited her hand so much better than the old one. She had never really liked the previous one but she hadn't had the courage to say so. It had been too heavy and cumbersome for her hand, too flashy, and the claws had caught at the finer fabrics of some of her clothes. This one, with its delicate setting, looked as if it had been designed for her and for her alone. She brought her gaze back to Emilio's. 'It's beautiful,' she said. 'It's the most gorgeous ring I've ever seen.'

He gave a dismissive grunt and picked up his menu. 'What would you like to eat?' he asked.

Gisele looked at him as he flicked through the menu, as a cricket ball of bitterness and hate slowly loosened in her chest. 'Was *this* your urgent business this morning?' she asked, holding up her hand.

He put down the menu and looked at her with a brooding frown. 'Can we get on with the meal or are you still on a hunger strike?' he asked.

'Was it, Emilio?'

'I had several things to see to,' he said, shifting in his chair as if someone had put marbles beneath him. 'That was one of them.'

'It was very thoughtful of you,' she said softly.

'Think nothing of it,' he said, turning another page of the menu with a look of acute boredom on his face. 'It's just a prop, anyway. I didn't want people to talk about why you're not wearing an engagement ring.'

She chewed at her lip as she looked at the sparkling diamond, watching as the light caught at it from a thousand different angles. 'Looks like a pretty expensive prop,' she said.

He closed the menu with a little snap. 'It's just money.'

She met his gaze across the table. 'Do I get to keep it after I've…you know…got through this?' she asked.

'"Got through this"?' he said, with a rueful quirk of his mouth. 'You make it sound like something dreadful you have to endure, like torture or a prison sentence.'

Gisele pursed her lips as she examined the diamond again. 'I don't know…maybe there are some compensations to be had.'

'Well over two million at the last count,' he muttered.

She flicked her gaze back to his. 'So, do I get to keep it?'

'What will you do with it?' he asked with a curl of his lip. 'Sell it or toss it in the nearest fountain like you did the last time?'

Gisele held his mocking gaze for a beat before she picked up her menu. She still couldn't work out why he had taken the time and effort to choose her such an exquisite ring. Was she fooling herself he cared more than he was letting on? She wasn't used to thinking of him being hurt by their break-up because he had been the one to end their relationship. She had thought he had only orchestrated this temporary reunion for the sake of appearances.

But what if he really *did* want a fresh start? What if the new ring was his way of communicating that? Was it crazy of her to look for love where hate had resided for so long?

What if he had only bought the ring to lure her back into his bed? It was way too soon to be jumping to any conclusions over his motivations. She had to tread carefully or risk everything all over again. 'I think I'll keep it as a souvenir,' she said. 'A girl can never have too many diamonds, now, can she?'

His expression hardened all the way to his dark-as-night eyes. 'I'm surprised you didn't keep the old one,' he said. 'The sale of it could have set you up for a year or two at least.'

'I found it much more satisfying to throw it away,' she said. 'It seemed appropriate, given the circumstances.'

His mouth tightened even further as he held her look. 'You're never going to let it go, are you?'

'Is that why you bought the ring?' Gisele asked. 'You thought a little bauble would soften me up enough to occupy your bed once more? You'll have to try harder, Emilio. I'm not that easy for the taking.'

He elevated one dark brow as he ran his smouldering gaze over her indolently. 'That wasn't the message I was getting last night,' he said. 'You were hot for it as soon as I kissed you.'

Gisele felt the heat rise from her neck to pool in her cheeks. She pushed against the table and got to her feet, all of her movements stiff with outrage. 'Excuse me,' she said. 'I need to use the Ladies' room.'

'Don't even think about it,' Emilio said before she had even stalked two paces from the table.

She turned and looked at him haughtily. 'Excuse me?'

'I know how your mind works, Gisele,' he said. 'But running away is not going to help things.'

'I'm not running away,' she said, shooting him a livid glare. 'I'm simply removing myself from your hateful presence.'

His expression became as unmalleable as marble and his voice just as hard and unyielding when he spoke. 'If you walk out of this restaurant without me I will call every contact I have in Europe and tell them not to touch you with a barge pole. The knock-on effect will follow you all the way back to Australia. Can you imagine what the press will make of that?'

Gisele felt the scorch of his glitteringly determined gaze as it warred with hers. It made the backs of her knees tingle with a sensation like pieces of ice chugging through her veins.

Dared she call his bluff?

What if the press dug a little deeper into her private life? Somehow she had managed to keep Lily's birth and death out of the public arena. She couldn't bear having her grief splashed over the press for the world to see.

It was a king hit to her pride to resume her seat but she didn't see what other choice she had. She threw him a look of undiluted venom. 'Happy now?' she asked.

'You've turned into quite a little spitfire, haven't you, *cara*?' he said. 'Taming you is turning out to be quite diverting.'

'Would you like me to sit up and beg while you're at it?' she threw back.

'No,' he said, giving her another smouldering look.

'I'm much more interested in you rolling over and playing bed.'

Gisele felt the incendiary heat of his play on words at the very base of her spine. How could he reduce her to such a quivering wreck of need with just a look or a teasing comment? 'You might be in for a disappointment,' she said with deliberate coolness. 'What if I don't live up to your lofty expectations?'

He sat back and surveyed her features at his leisure, pausing for a moment on her mouth before his eyes came back to mesh with hers. 'I'm sure you haven't lost your touch,' he said. 'I still remember what you feel like wrapped around me.'

She gave him a cynical look to disguise the way her insides were coiling with red-hot lust. 'All cats are black in the dark.'

'I've met a few cats in my time,' he said. 'But none purr quite the way you do.'

'I might scratch and bite instead,' she said, crossing her legs to try and control the surge of longing that was rippling through her. 'Or I might just go through the motions to get it over with. Lots of women do.'

His lips curved upwards in a glinting half smile. 'Do you really think I wouldn't be able to tell if you were faking it?'

Gisele shifted her gaze from his, her face flooding with colour all over again. He had known her body so well. Every pulse point, every curve and indentation, every sensual hotspot had been his to tease and please. Her body had sung for hours afterwards. The memory of his touch was still on her skin. It was still *in* her body. She could feel it even now, the on-off pressure of aching need building deep inside her. She would have no hope of holding back her response even if she wanted to for the sake of her pride. Hadn't last night proven that? He had been the one to call a halt, not her. She had been incapable of it. Desire had consumed her common sense. It had always been that way with Emilio. She had no defences against the attraction she felt for him. She suspected he knew how fragile her armour was. How could she keep herself safe from further heartbreak? 'Can we please talk about something else?' she asked, darting a glance either side in case other diners were listening in.

'What are you embarrassed about, *cara*?' Emilio asked. 'That I know your body almost as well as I know my own?'

'You don't know it *now*,' Gisele insisted.

He leaned across and picked up her left hand, bringing it up to his lips as his eyes held hers in a mesmerising trance. 'Then perhaps it is time I reacquainted myself with it, hmm? The sooner the better, don't you think?'

Gisele's whole body shivered as his lips brushed the tips of her fingers. The diamond he had placed on her hand glittered as a reminder of the contract he had drawn up between them: two million dollars for a month of her time. 'Why didn't you do so last night?' she asked. 'You had the opportunity. Why didn't you take it while you had the chance?'

He stroked his thumb across the soft dish of her palm, sending powerful lightninglike sensations all the way up her arm. 'You weren't ready last night,' he said. 'It wouldn't have been fair to take advantage of you when you were tired and overwrought.'

'I might never be ready,' she said with a pert lift of her chin. 'What will you do then?'

His coal-black eyes caressed hers until she wondered if she was going to disappear in their bottomless depths and never come out. 'You'll be ready,' he said with bone-melting conviction. 'Your body is already there—it's just your mind that has to catch up. I'm prepared to wait until it does.'

Gisele pulled her tingling hand out of his. She buried her nose in the menu and chose a dish she had no real appetite for, just so she didn't have to meet Emilio's percipient gaze. It unnerved her how well he could read her. But, even more disturbing, it *touched* her that he hadn't exploited her last night. So many men would have taken advantage of her vulnerability but he hadn't. How was she supposed to hate him if he didn't do hateful things?

'You don't seem to be enjoying that,' Emilio said a little while after their meals had been served. 'Would you like me to order something else for you?'

She put down her fork, which she had been using to push the rich, creamy food around on her plate. 'I'm sorry,' she said. 'I guess I'm just not hungry.'

He looked at her for a long moment, his expression dark and serious. 'Does my presence upset you so much?' he asked.

Gisele made a rueful movement with her lips. 'It's not just you…it's the situation between us. It feels… I don't know… I'm not sure what you want.'

'I want you.'

She felt his statement brush along her spine like a caress. 'Apart from that, I mean.'

'You mean in the long term?'

She ran her tongue over her tinder-dry lips. 'I'm not sure we want the same things now.'

'Isn't it a little early to be worrying about that?' he asked. 'At this point we need to take each day as it comes. We have to try—surely you see that?'

Gisele nailed him with her gaze. 'How much of this is about restoring your good reputation with the public?'

His brows moved together over his eyes. 'Is that what you think this is?' he asked. 'Nothing but a publicity stunt?'

She let out a wobbly breath. 'I don't know… How can I know? You bought me a beautiful ring and yet you've never said anything about your feelings. Not before and not now.'

'What do you want me to say?' he asked. 'You hate me. You've said it several times. What would be the point in me saying what I feel? It's not going to change how you feel, is it?'

She took a breath and dived straight in. 'Did you *ever* love me?'

His expression turned to stone, muscle by muscle. 'I was prepared to marry you, wasn't I?'

Gisele looked at him in disdain. 'So I'm supposed to feel grateful that you selected me from a line-up of hundreds, if not thousands, of potential candidates?'

'Why are you bringing this up now?' he asked.

'I want to know what you felt for me back then,' she said. 'I want to know what foundation our relationship was built on.'

He scraped a hand through his hair. 'It was built on a mutual desire to build a life together. We wanted the same things—children, a solid family base and a secure home life. All the things most people want.'

'Most people want to be loved,' she said with a sigh. 'It's what most people want more than anything.'

'I realise that, Gisele,' he said. 'I would be lying if I said I didn't want it too. I've wanted it all my life but I've learned that it doesn't always happen just because you want it to. It also doesn't last, or at least not in my experience.'

Gisele could sense the conversation was over even before the waiter appeared to clear their plates. Emilio's expression had closed over like a page being turned in a book. She knew it would be pointless pushing him to reveal more of his childhood. She wondered how many people had come and gone in his life to leave him so cynical about love. Had people made promises and not kept them? Said words that had no actions to back them up? Children were so trusting and relied heavily on the adults around them for stability and security. Had *he* grown up feeling he had no one he could truly rely on, no one he could trust to have his best interests at heart?

'Luigi will drive you back to the villa,' Emilio said. 'I have some paperwork to do at my office.'

'So you didn't fire him?' Gisele asked with a sheep-ish look.

He put a hand to her elbow as he escorted her out of the restaurant. 'He's on notice,' he said.

'Oh, but you mustn't do that,' she said, a frown puckering her brow as she stopped to look up at him. 'He's probably got a family to feed. It was my fault. I wanted to avoid the press. I wanted to melt into the crowd rather than turn up in a flash car and draw attention to myself.'

He smoothed the tiny frown away from her forehead with his finger. 'I don't like it when my orders are disobeyed,' he said, 'especially by members of my staff.'

'Thank God I'm not on the payroll...' She flushed and sank her teeth into her bottom lip. 'Well, maybe I am, now that I come to think about it.'

Emilio brought her chin up. 'You are not a member of my staff.'

'What am I then?' she asked.

His eyes measured her gaze for a long moment. 'Try and rest this afternoon,' he said and brushed a light kiss on her lips. 'Tonight might be a late night.'

Gisele got in the waiting car, but when she turned from adjusting her seat belt Emilio had already gone.

CHAPTER SEVEN

EMILIO watched later that evening as Gisele came down the stairs towards him. She was wearing a simple but elegant fuchsia-pink cocktail dress with a matching chiffon wrap. She had skilfully styled her hair into a smoothly coiffed up-do that gave her a regal air. He had never seen her look more beautiful as she smiled at him, albeit briefly. Her smile was like sunshine breaking through the clouds on a bleak day. He had forgotten how wonderful it made him feel to see it. It was like a spill of warm fluid inside his chest, slowly spreading until all the places inside him were no longer echoing with emptiness.

It was a big step for him, taking her with him tonight. He had thought about going alone, like he usually did. Few people outside the charity knew how deeply he was involved and why. Over the past year or so he had felt the need to stop ignoring where he had come from and do something to help others escape the hell he had escaped. He had done it through sheer grit and determination but he had come to realise others didn't always have the confidence or willpower to do it.

Giving Gisele a glimpse of his former life would be uncomfortable for him but that was the price he had to pay for wanting to make a difference. It wasn't easy facing the dark shadows of his past. He always came away from these things feeling unsettled. He felt as if those ghostly shadows were reaching out of the darkness to drag him back to the gutter and leave him there, cold and shivering and alone.

Emilio took Gisele's hand as she stepped off the last stair and brought it up to his mouth, pressing his lips against the soft skin of her bent knuckles. 'You look stunning,' he said. 'Pink suits you.'

She gave him another fleeting smile. 'Thank you.'

He reached for the jewellery box he had left on the hall table. 'I have something for you to go with your ring.'

Her eyes looked at the box and then up at him with a little frown. 'You shouldn't be spending so much money,' she said.

'I have the right to spoil my fiancée, don't I?' he asked.

He opened the box and she touched a finger to the diamond-and-sapphire necklace glittering there. 'I'm not really your fiancée,' she said. 'It's just a game of pretend to the press.'

'We could make it real,' Emilio said.

Something flickered in her grey-blue gaze before she turned so he could put the necklace about her neck. 'You want the old Gisele back but she's gone, Emilio,' she said. 'You can't get her back, no matter how much money you spend trying.'

Emilio put his hands on her slim shoulders once he had fastened the necklace, breathing in the summery fragrance of her until he felt intoxicated. He felt her skin lift in a shiver beneath his fingers, just as it always used to do. He liked that he still had that effect on her. He liked the way her body instinctively reacted to him, in spite of what she said to the contrary. 'Is the money issue worrying you?' He turned her back to face him. 'The fact that I paid to have you back in my life?'

She gave him a pensive look. 'It's not about the money...not really...'

'What, then?' he asked.

Her eyes dropped from his to study his bow tie. 'You want everything to be as it was,' she said. 'But I'm not sure life comes with a reset button. You can't just pick up where you left off and expect things will be exactly the same as they were before. Things change. People change... *I've* changed.'

Emilio studied her for a moment with an uneasy feeling in his stomach. She said she had changed and she had. She didn't eat. She didn't sleep. She looked pale and frail. He had done that to her. *He* had been the one to change her. How could he change her back? He wanted it all to go away. A fresh start was what they both needed. It was no good looking back. He, of all people, knew that. It didn't change things, brooding about what could have or should have been. Moving forwards was the only way to heal the past. He was living proof of it. Perhaps tonight would help her to see that.

He tipped up her chin again. 'Let's just take it from here and see how it goes, shall we?' he said. 'No promises. Just time to explore what we have now, instead of what we had then, OK?'

She moved her lips in a semblance of a smile but

her eyes looked as if a cloud had passed through them. 'OK,' she said and slipped her hand in his as he led her out to the car.

When they arrived at the luxury hotel where the dinner was being held, Gisele realised the function wasn't actually anything to do with Emilio's architecture business but was rather a fundraising event for a homeless kids' charity he had set up over the past year. She found out through the course of the evening that he had developed a drop-in centre in the city where young people could get a meal and a shower and a bed. His charity also offered educational and vocational schemes to help kids get off and keep off the streets. Counselling services were provided as well as drug and alcohol rehabilitation for those in need.

Gisele spoke to several young people who had benefited from the charity personally. They told her stories of how they had come to be on the streets—desperately sad and heart-wrenching stories of neglect and abuse. It was an unsettling reminder of how little she knew of Emilio's background.

He had told her almost nothing about his past. Had she known him at all back then? Had *he* grown up like some of these young people? Why else had he set up such a charity? What had happened to him on those dark, dangerous streets? What sort of horrendous horrors had he witnessed or experienced? She wondered how he had survived it. How had he overcome such desperate odds to be the successful man he was today?

What had happened in the past year or so that he had decided to do something as big as this? She'd always suspected he deliberately shied away from his past, that he wanted to leave it well behind him. But putting himself out there in such a public way spoke of a deeply moving concern for others less fortunate than himself. It was such a change from the super-successful businessman persona he presented to the world. He was no longer using his wealth to show how far he'd come up in the world; rather he was reaching back down into his dark past to help others climb out of it.

One of the young volunteers, called Romeo, told her how Emilio did a lot of the hands-on work himself on the streets, speaking to kids to help them realise there were other options for them other than crime or prostitution or gang warfare.

'He's not afraid to get his hands dirty,' Romeo said. 'I was one of the first he helped get off the streets. He helped me see a better future for myself. He taught me that you mustn't let what happens to you define you. It's how you handle it that counts. You must be very proud to be his fiancée, *si*?'

Gisele hoped her smile didn't look too unnatural. She was still feeling so incredibly shocked. The world Emilio came from couldn't be more different from hers. She couldn't imagine how hard it must have been for him to drag himself from such a rough start in life to achieve all that he had. So many obstacles must have stood in his way. How had he overcome them? 'Yes, I am,' she said, 'very proud.'

After a few more words of conversation, Romeo got called away to help with serving food.

Emilio came back over with a drink for her. 'I hope

Romeo wasn't telling tales out of school,' he said. 'He has a tendency to exaggerate.'

'Is this how you grew up?' Gisele asked, looking up at him with a shell-shocked expression. 'Like some of these kids? Why didn't you tell me?'

'Lots of people have it worse than I did,' he said with a dismissive shrug as he took a sip of his drink.

'Why didn't you tell me about your charity?' she asked. 'You've not said a word to me about any of this. In fact, this morning you said this was a business function.'

'Does it matter?' he asked.

'Of course it matters,' she said. 'I thought I'd be forced to speak to stuffy old businessmen and their wives, and instead I'm meeting young people whose lives you've saved from God only knows what.'

'Romeo would have made it without my help,' Emilio said. 'He just needed a leg-up.'

'Who helped you?' Gisele asked. 'Who was your leg-up person?'

His eyes became shuttered. 'Some people need more help than others,' he said.

'So you did it all on your own?' she asked.

He touched her on the elbow to position her to face a man who was approaching them with a camera. 'The official photographer is coming over for a photo for the newsletter,' he said. 'Put on your happy face.'

Gisele schooled her features back into happy fiancée mode as Emilio put his arm around her waist, drawing her into his hard warmth. She felt her skin react to his closeness, to his smell, to the sense of protection he offered. It was hard not to want to get closer, to start to imagine a future where she would always be by his side, helping him help others. He had mentioned they could make their 'engagement' real again, but how could she give him what he wanted most? The one thing he had always been clear on was that he wanted a family, but there was no way she could risk going down that path again.

The evening soon drew to a close. Emilio escorted her out to the waiting car, but he barely spoke on the way back to the villa. He spent most of the short journey staring straight ahead, his eyes blank, the different-coloured lights of the city passing over his features like a special-effects film, making his handsome face take on grimly distorted shadows and angles.

Although he had cleverly evaded answering her question about his background, Gisele wondered if he was thinking of the life he had left behind, the life of poverty and neglect and unspeakable cruelty that lurked on the underbelly of the eternal city. She thought of him as a young teenager out there, huddled under a bush or park bench, cold, hungry, thirsty, terrified, lost and alone. It made her heart ache to think no one had protected him, no one had taught him how to love.

'I think it's amazing what you've done,' she said into the silence.

He frowned and looked at her as if he hadn't realised anyone was sitting beside him. 'Sorry, did you say something?' he asked.

She gave him a soft smile and took one of his hands in hers. 'It must feel good to have made a difference,' she said. 'To think that you're responsible for so many young people getting a chance to live a decent life—

a life they would never have been able to have without your help. It must make you feel very satisfied.'

He rolled his thumb over the diamond on her finger before meshing his gaze with hers. 'In my experience money fixes just about everything,' he said. 'You just need enough of it.'

Gisele felt a little frisson scuttle down her spine at the glittering darkness of his eyes. 'I guess you have to decide which projects are going to be worth pursuing,' she said. 'You wouldn't want to be throwing good money after bad.'

His half smile had a hint of ruthlessness to it. 'I don't take on projects unless I'm sure I'll succeed with them,' he said.

'Success isn't always up to you, though, is it?' she said. 'Other people or circumstances can influence outcomes in spite of what you've planned.'

His bottomless brown eyes moved from hers to slowly gaze at her mouth. She felt her lips tingle and fizz, her heart stepping up its pace as he touched her bottom lip with the pad of his thumb. 'Overcoming obstacles is part of the challenge,' he said, returning his eyes to hers. 'The harder they are, the more satisfying they are when accomplished.'

Gisele felt another shimmery sensation move down her back as the car drew to a halt outside his villa. There was a premonitory weight to the air as he helped her from the car. His fingers as they curled around hers sent livewires of electricity along her arm. She followed him into the villa, all her senses on overdrive as he led her to the *salone*.

'Would you like a nightcap?' he asked.

Gisele sent her tongue out in a quick darting movement to moisten her paper-dry lips. 'Um…I think I might give it a miss,' she said. 'I think I'll go on up to bed.'

'As you wish,' he said, moving to the bar to pour himself a finger of whisky.

She hovered for a moment, not sure why, but unable to tear herself away. She watched as he lifted the glass to his lips, how they rested against the rim and then how his strong throat moved up and down as he swallowed the liquid.

He put the glass down and looked at her. 'Is something wrong?' he asked.

'No… I… It's just I wanted to say thank you for this evening,' she said. 'I had a good time. It was very… revealing.'

He picked up his glass again. 'Don't go out making me out to be a hero, *cara*,' he said grimly. 'I'm anything but. You, of all people, should know that.'

'I think you care much more than you let on,' she said.

He gave a grunt of something that might have passed for mocking laughter. 'Got me all figured out, have you, Gisele?' He took another swallow of his whisky, a generous one this time.

'I think you hide who you really are and what you really feel behind that I-couldn't-give-a-damn façade,' she said. 'I think that deep down you're afraid you're going to get let down so you do everything possible to protect yourself.'

He put the glass down with a crack that sounded like a gunshot. His eyes were blazing with a heat that threatened to consume her. She felt the lick of the flames as he raked her with his gaze, an incendiary heat that ran along her flesh like a river of fire. 'You should've gone to bed while you still had the chance,' he said, moving towards her.

Gisele stood her ground, determined not to be threatened by his devilish and roguish manner. 'You don't scare me, Emilio,' she said. 'You might scare the warlords and the pimps and the drug dealers of the backstreets of Rome, but you don't scare me.'

'Such brave words,' he said, taking a handful of her hair and pulling it free from its restraining clip, unleashing with it a flow of sensations that showered over her like the sparks from exploding fireworks.

Gisele sucked in a much-needed breath. He was so close. He was *too* close. She could feel *him* there: the heat, the hardness, the need that was as hungry as hers. It was pressing against her, calling her body into play. A call she could not resist, even if she wanted to. It was too primal, too overwhelming and way too rampant to be held back any longer.

He tugged her towards him with a roughness that thrilled her as much as it terrified her, pelvis against pelvis, need against need. She could not hide behind her smart comebacks now. Witty words were no defence for the onslaught of feeling that was rushing through her like a tumultuous tide. There was nothing between their bodies now but the desire that had always pulsed and throbbed between them. 'Such brave, foolish words,' he said and then his mouth came down on hers.

Gisele revelled in the fiery heat of his kiss. He took control from the start and refused to relinquish it. He thrust through the seam of her mouth with a bold stroke of his tongue and she whimpered in submission as she gave him total access. He explored her thoroughly, staking his claim, leaving her in no doubt of who was in charge. Teeth and tongues collided, hands groped and grabbed, clothes were unzipped, unbuttoned and at one stage even torn.

'If you don't want this then you'd better tell me now,' Emilio said as he all but slammed her up against the nearest wall.

'I want this,' she said against his mouth, her lips nibbling at his, her hands searching for him, aching to feel him. 'I want this. *I want you.*'

He groaned deeply as she finally found him, her fingers closing around his hot, hard heat, rediscovering the length of him, the strength and power of him. She felt him shudder as he fought for control. He was just as she remembered him: sleek and hard, an intriguing combination of satin and steel.

Somehow she was naked from the waist down; she couldn't remember how it had happened but it didn't matter. There was barely time for him to put on protection before he positioned her and drove into her with a force that sent her head back against the wall, a gasp exploding from her lips as she welcomed him all the way. He grunted with deep male satisfaction and her skin rose in a fine layer of goose bumps as she held him to her. He rocked against her savagely, deep pumping actions that made her body sing with delight, a rapturous melody that struck on chords that had been played in the distant past.

She didn't take long to reach the summit. She only

teetered there for a moment before she lifted off, her body convulsing around his, squeezing, contracting, milking him of his essence in those few blissful seconds where common sense and rational thought had no place, no foothold.

He followed close behind, a shudder going through him that ricocheted through her as she held on to him.

Long seconds passed.

'Sorry,' Emilio said against her neck, still breathing heavily. 'I probably rushed that a bit.'

'No,' she said, sliding her hands over his back and shoulders. 'You don't need to apologise.'

After a moment or two he eased back to look at her. 'You OK?'

Gisele wondered what he was really asking as she looked into the black unreadable pits of his eyes. 'I'm fine,' she said. 'It was...amazing...'

He pushed himself away from the wall, his expression rueful as he dealt with disposing of the condom. 'It wasn't supposed to happen this way,' he said, raking a hand through his hair in a distracted manner. 'I wanted it to be better than a rough grope against a wall. I wanted it to be memorable.'

Gisele stepped forwards and placed a gentle hand on the side of his face, loving the feel of his raspy skin under the softness of her palm. 'It *was* memorable,' she said. Being back in his arms was unforgettable. She knew she would have to live off the memories all over again, but at least she had this time with him.

He studied her for a moment before placing his hand over hers, holding it to his jaw. 'I want you in my bed,' he said. 'I want to wake up in the morning with you beside me.'

How could she say no to him when he made her feel things she'd thought she would never feel again? He might not love her but he wanted her.

He might *never* love her. Some people were just incapable of it and, from what she had picked up about his past, it certainly hinted that he might be one of them, too damaged to open himself to anyone else. It was a heart-wrenching thought but it was something she would have to accept. She could not stay with him permanently without the love she needed, but for now this felt right. She looped her arms around his neck and looked up into his dark eyes. 'Make love to me,' she said softly.

Emilio lifted her and carried her to his bedroom, laying her down as if she was the most precious cargo he had ever had in his possession.

'Emilio...' The soft sound of her voice was like a caress over his skin.

'I'm here, *cara*,' he said, threading his fingers through her hair. 'I'm here.'

'Did you miss me?' she said, looking into his eyes with her grey-blue ones. 'Did you miss doing this with me?'

He pressed a soft-as-air kiss to her mouth. 'I've missed everything about you.'

And he had, desperately. His life had seemed so pointless and empty without her in it. He had worked like a man obsessed over the past two years but none of it had given him any real sense of purpose. He had made money—lots of money; more than he had dreamed possible—but it hadn't filled the gaping hole she had left in his life. The charity helped a bit but it wasn't enough. He wanted more. He wanted her.

He kissed her again, a long drugging kiss that stirred up deeply buried longings that he could no longer ignore. He wanted to feel her convulse around him again in ecstasy, he wanted to feel her grasp hold of him as if he was her only lifeline—the only person on this earth who could make her feel complete.

He peeled back the spaghetti-thin straps of her dress to press a kiss to her bare shoulder. Her skin tasted of summer, an exotic tropical fragrance he had always and only associated with her. He worked his way around to her neck, lingering on the sensitive flesh there, delighting in the way she wriggled beneath him, her soft gasps of pleasure fuelling the raging fire of his need. It was a blistering furnace of want, hot flames leaping beneath his skin, making him aware of her in every cell of his body. She was his nemesis, the completion of him, the missing other half that he had been seeking for most of his life.

'I want you,' he said, pressing a hot kiss to the skin just shy of her earlobe. 'I want you so badly I can't think straight. It's all I can think about. How much I want you back in my arms.' He moved his mouth to the soft temptation of hers.

'I want you too,' she whispered back, her soft lips moving around to play with his in a cat and mouse game that set his senses on overload.

At least he had her desire for him to build on, Emilio thought. It was the one thing he could count on. She might say how much she hated him but her touch and the press of her lips against his told another story entirely.

He felt the sexy tug of her teeth, the way they pulled on his lower lip in a tantalising bite that made his spine tingle. He nipped her back gently, sucking on her lip and then stroking his tongue over the plump softness until she whimpered and did the same back. Their tongues met and mated in a moist duel of wanton need, each one seeking the other in sensual combat.

Emilio slipped the other strap of her dress off her shoulder and planted a kiss to the creamy softness of her skin. She tilted her head, her long hair falling back over his hand where it rested in the middle of her slender back. She made a soft noise of acquiescence, a murmur of want, of need, of red-hot desire, and his blood surged in response. No one made him feel more of a man than she did.

He uncovered her breasts and gently cupped one of them with his hand while his mouth continued to explore hers. She arched up into his palm, her erect nipple driving into the centre of his palm, her slender hips inciting his to press down to meet her feminine softness. He ached to fill her with his presence but this time he wanted to take things slowly, to savour each moment. He stroked his fingers against her folds, delighting in the scented moistness of her body that told him she was more than ready for him. But still he took his time, gently stretching her with a finger, feeling the tight clasp of her body around him.

'Please…' she begged breathlessly.

'Not yet,' he said against her mouth. 'You know how much better it is when we both wait.'

She writhed restlessly beneath him, pushing her body up to meet his, her mouth ravenous as it fed off his. He kissed her back with the same intensity while his fingers continued their gentle exploration. He felt her swell beneath his touch, the tight pearl of her need so delicate and yet full of such feminine power.

Her hands began to search for him and when they found him he groaned out loud in pleasure. Her soft fingers stroked along his length at first before she made a sheath with her hand and rubbed him up and down, slowly at first and then with increasing vigour. He felt all his senses roar for release and had to fight not to explode right there and then.

She wriggled some more, grasping the cradle of his hips with her hands, positioning herself beneath him. 'Now,' she said. 'I want you *now*.'

He quickly found another condom and applied it before he positioned himself above her with the bulk of his weight supported by his arms as he surged into her with a deep thrust that drew a gasping breath from her body and a guttural groan of pleasure from his. He felt her body wrap around him, the tight ripples of her flesh massaging him, torturing him, luring him into the deep swirling pool of blessed oblivion. He held himself back from it with an effort; no one challenged his ironclad control more than her. The physical act of sex always became something more with her. It was not just a joining of bodies; it reached him on a level he had not experienced with anyone else. It felt as if each time they made love she reached inside his battered soul with her soft fingers and soothed the torn and ragged edges until they didn't ache any more.

He felt it now, the way she stroked the muscles of his back with her gentle hands, long, smooth, gentle movements that made his flesh turn to gravel with goose bumps. He felt it in the soft but urgent press of her mouth against his, the way her lips were both gentle and insistent, her tongue searching and yet submissive to the driving command of his.

He moved within her, the slide of his flesh in hers slick and sexy, slow and then fast, her body rising to meet each downward movement of his, her legs wrapping around his hips as she urged him towards the edge of rapture.

He caressed her with his fingers to heighten her pleasure. He knew exactly what she needed to take that final plunge into paradise. She was hot and wet and swollen beneath his touch. He kept caressing her, softly and slowly, varying the pressure until he felt her finally give in to the pleasure her body craved. She threw her head back against the pillows and let out a high-pitched cry as her body convulsed around his. He felt every milking movement until he had no choice but to pour himself into her, his body finally collapsing with spent pleasure against hers when he was done.

She continued to stroke his back in the aftermath. He felt those softly padded fingertips move up and down his spine as he eventually got his breathing back under control.

'I'm assuming you're still on the Pill,' he said as he eased himself up on his elbows to look at her. 'Condoms are not always reliable, especially putting them on as haphazardly as I did earlier.'

Her eyes flickered before moving away from his to

concentrate on a point just below his chin. 'I'm sure it's not going to be a problem…'

'Are you currently using contraception?' he asked.

Her gaze met his briefly before skittering away again. 'I'm on a low-dose pill to regulate my cycle,' she said. 'It's been out of whack since…' Her teeth sank into her lip before she continued. 'Since we broke up…'

Emilio felt another dagger-sharp probe of guilt assail him. Gisele had done it tough since he had thrown her out of his life. So much had happened to her: the death of her father and the revelation of her twin sister, all the while juggling the demands of building up her business. No wonder she didn't sleep properly at night. She had said it wasn't his fault but how could it *not* be? Her life would have been completely different if he had stood by her.

He wanted to fix it all, to wipe out all the wrongs, but he sensed it wasn't going to be as simple as that. There was a streak of stubbornness in her that hadn't been there before. He understood how she would want to protect herself from being hurt again, but he wanted to break down her defences so she would come back to him, not because of her need for money, but because she valued him and the future they had planned together more than her pride.

He wanted her as the mother of his children. He couldn't imagine anyone else. He had never considered anyone else. He looked forward to becoming a father. He longed for a family to love and protect. He had dreamed of her swollen with his child. The images had mocked him over the past two years, but now it was something that was just within his grasp if only he could get her to put aside her pride and admit to her own yearnings. She was born to be a mother. She loved anything to do with babies. She just had to trust him enough to let go of the past so they could move forward.

Emilio played with the ends of her silky hair, running it through his fingers, watching as her features relaxed in enjoyment. 'You know how we talked about having a family one day?' he said.

She flinched as if he had slapped her. Then she pulled her hair out of his fingers and, using the flat of her hand against his chest, pushed him away from her. He watched in bemusement as she got off the bed and reached for a wrap, tying it roughly around her middle. 'Was it something I said?' he asked.

'I've changed my mind,' she said, spearing him with a glance. 'I don't want to have children.'

Emilio swung his legs over the bed and reached for his bathrobe, coming over to where she was standing with her arms folded tightly across her body. 'What are you talking about?' he asked. 'You adore children. You own and operate a baby wear shop, for God's sake. You spend hours doing exquisite embroidery and smocking on baby clothes. What do you mean, you've changed your mind?'

She gave him a defensive look. 'I mean exactly what I said. I've changed my mind,' she said. 'People do. I did.'

Emilio looked at her as if she had suddenly turned into someone else. Where was the young woman who spoke so excitedly of having a family? Two years ago she had talked to him about baby names, what sex their children might be, what they would be like, *who* they would look like. They had even talked about her coming off the Pill as soon as the honeymoon was over.

He was thirty-three years old now. He didn't want to leave it much longer before he became a father. He had hoped Gisele would settle back into his life and within a month or two everything would be back to normal. He had planned that once things had settled down between them they would marry and start a family. It was unthinkable to him that she wouldn't fall in with his plans. He hadn't factored in her refusal to give him the family he wanted so desperately. That would be admitting defeat.

Failure.

That word was like a ghost that stalked him. That word haunted him like no other. It was an invisible but all too real enemy from his childhood, the same one that had followed him out of back alley dumpsters in search of food and shelter. It had taunted him; it had tortured him with thoughts of not being good enough, not strong enough, not determined enough to get out of that hellhole. He had fought it off; he had wrestled it to the ground, determining he would never allow it back in his life.

He would not fail.

He would find a way to change Gisele's mind. Whatever it took, however long it took, surely she would change her mind. 'Has this been a recent decision or one you've thought about for a while?' he asked.

'What does it matter when I made the decision?' she said. 'I've made it and I'm not unmaking it.'

'Gisele, you know how much I want a family,' he said. 'You've known that from the start. It's one of the reasons I asked you to marry me. I saw a future with us as parents, building a family unit together.'

'Just because you've made bucket loads of money doesn't mean you can automatically have anything you want,' Gisele said. 'Life isn't like that.'

Emilio tunnelled a hand through his hair. 'Look, I know you got terribly hurt by our break-up. It came out of the blue and shook you badly. Having a child is a big commitment in any relationship, let alone one that caused you so much pain in the past. But we can make it work. We'd make great parents. You'll be a fabulous mother. I just know it. I've always known it.'

She gave him a glittering glare. 'I'm not going to be a breeding machine for you or for any man,' she said.

'For God's sake, Gisele,' he said, frowning heavily. 'When have I ever referred to you as such? I want you to be the mother of my children. That's an honour that I have never asked of any other woman.'

'You'll have to ask someone else to do it because I'm not going to,' she said, shooting him a look that would have felled a lesser man.

Emilio felt his jaw tighten with frustration. How could he make her see reason? Was a month going to be long enough to make her change her mind? Was she doing this just to get under his skin? If so, she couldn't have picked a better weapon. He hadn't told her anything about his past. He had told no one. The loneliness he had felt, not having a proper home and family, not belonging, being constantly hungry, cold and dirty. The shame of not even knowing who his father was. The shame of being an outcast because of the poverty that had been all he had ever known. 'Is this about money?' he asked, barely managing to control his anger. 'You want more money? You want a business deal instead of a proper relationship? Is that what you want?'

Her expression turned bitter. 'That's what we already have, isn't it?'

'That's not what we have and you damn well know it,' he said, frowning at her furiously. 'You made love with me, not because of the money we agreed on, but because you wanted me. It wouldn't have mattered what amount of money I gave you. I don't believe you would have sold yourself. You're not that sort of woman.'

She turned away, her arms still wrapped tightly around her body. 'I don't want to talk about this any more,' she said. 'I'm only here for a month. That's what we agreed on. I haven't signed up for anything else.'

Emilio let out a harsh breath. 'I want a future with you, Gisele, and I want a family. Don't make me choose between one and the other.'

He saw her back and shoulders stiffen. 'I can't give you what you want,' she said.

'Can't or won't?' he asked cynically. 'You want to punish me for how I hurt you. I get that, I really do. I understand that was part of the reason you agreed to come to Italy with me. You saw it as a chance to be as difficult and demanding as you could so I would let you go at the end of the month with no regrets.'

She swung back round to face him, her expression taut with anger. 'And why shouldn't I punish you?' she asked. 'You broke my heart, damn you. I *hate* you for that.'

Emilio put his hands on her shoulders. '*Cara*, if you

truly hated me you would never have shared that bed with me just now,' he said.

'It was just sex,' she said with a worldly toss of her head. 'It's been a while for me. I wanted relief and you provided it.'

'I don't believe it was just sex.'

'Women can do it too, you know,' she said. 'We can separate emotion from sex when we need to.'

'Is that so?' Emilio asked with a curl of his lip.

'Yes,' she said, chin up, eyes defiant.

His hands tightened on her shoulders as he pulled her closer. 'Then if that's the case, you won't mind having sex again just for the heck of it, will you?' And then he brought his mouth down heavily on hers.

Gisele had fully intended to block his kiss by keeping her lips firmly closed, but just one stroke of his tongue had her opening to him with flagrant need. She felt the sexy thrust of his tongue against hers, calling hers into a tango that sent shivers racing up and down her spine. Her body was pressed tightly against his aroused one, the hardened probe of his erection searing her belly with the erotic promise of his potent possession. She returned the heat and fire of his kiss with wanton disregard for her pride or principles. She wanted him with a hunger that was beyond her control. It raced through her veins with breakneck speed, lifting her skin in earthy delight as he tore open her wrap as if it were made of tissue paper. His hands cupped her breasts, his thumbs rubbing over her nipples until they were tight and aching all over again.

He eased the ache with the hot, moist cavern of his mouth, sucking on her until her back was arched in pleasure, her hands clutching his head for support as the fiery sensations tore through her.

Her hands got to work on his bathrobe, pulling it off him while her mouth went back in search of his. She grabbed at him greedily, delighting in the hard sheath of his flesh and the way it throbbed under the caress of her fingers.

He picked her up and carried her to the bed, dropping her in a sexy tangle of limbs, his weight coming down over her, his body spearing hers with a hard thrust that knocked the air right out of her lungs. She heard him give a primitive male grunt of pleasure as her body wrapped around him, a sound that made her shudder all over in delight. He set a furious pace but she was with him all the way. She clawed at the skin on his back, she grabbed his taut buttocks and drove him on with a feral urgency she had no idea she possessed.

It was wicked.

It was racy.

It was thrilling to have him so close to losing control.

She felt the tension in her body rise with every rough surge of his body within hers. She felt her orgasm approach like a speeding train. She couldn't have done anything to stop it if she had tried. It smashed into her, tossing her high in the air, rolling and rolling her in a whirlpool of heady, blissful sensation that surpassed anything she had felt before in his arms.

He came with a stabbing thrust and a shout of pleasure that made her skin shiver. She felt the pulsing of his body as he discharged his essence, anointing her, branding her as his.

He rolled off her and lay with his chest heaving, his

body totally spent and the scent of their coupling fragrant in the air.

Gisele wasn't sure what to say, so said nothing. She was still struggling to get her breathing under control. Her body was still tingling from the sensual assault of unrivalled ecstasy. She wanted to hate him, but how could she when he made her feel this way? He had dismantled every one of her defences with his hot, drugging kisses and his fiery possession. She squeezed her legs together and felt the stickiness of him. It was such a stomach-hollowing reminder of the passion that still flared between them. Would it ever go away? Would *she* be able to walk away once the month was up?

Emilio turned back to her, propping himself on one elbow as he toyed with the wayward strands of her hair. 'I want you to move into my room,' he said.

Gisele quickly hid a nervous swallow. She had wanted some space but he clearly wasn't going to be satisfied unless she was in his arms every night. The intimacy of it terrified her, not because she didn't want to sleep with him. She did. It was just that she knew she would fall in love with him all over again if he got too close.

'What, now?' she asked.

'Not right this minute,' he said, rolling her so she was lying on top of him. 'I have other plans for you just now.'

'Oh?' she said with a coolness she was nowhere near feeling. Her body had already betrayed her. It had welcomed him with slick moistness, gripping him so tightly she could feel the hot, hard length of him filling her completely. She couldn't just lie there without moving. She just *had* to feel the delicious sensation of being in control. She rode him all the way to heaven and back, finally collapsing over him when she had shattered into a million pieces. She felt him plunge himself deeper and deeper before he let go with a raw groan of ecstasy.

And then, without the need for anything other than the sheltering circle of his arms, she fell soundly asleep...

CHAPTER EIGHT

EMILIO lay awake for long hours, watching Gisele sleep. She was purring softly like a kitten beside him. She had curled up against him, one of her arms thrown across his chest in the way she had used to do. He stroked the silky flesh of her arm, thinking how much he had missed moments like this. She was the first woman he had wanted to spend the entire night with. He had never felt comfortable doing that with any other lover. The physical closeness of sex became something deeper with her. Her natural sensuality was something that had attracted him from the first moment he had met her.

He had loved that she had been a virgin. It was perhaps a little old-fashioned of him to have been so ridiculously pleased, but he admired her for not putting herself out there for just anyone. All the women he had slept with had been experienced. It had stopped him in his tracks to think Gisele had waited until she felt she had met the right man to give herself to.

He had been that right man.

She had waited until she was absolutely sure she was ready for that level of intimacy. He had enjoyed tutoring her. He had always thought there was something highly sacred about her giving herself to him. It wasn't just her body she had given him, but her trust.

It had been such a precious gift, one he had savoured and treasured...until the sex tape scandal had erupted and he had mistakenly believed her virginal status had all been a hoax, a deliberate ploy to gain his confidence in her—an act to put a ring on her finger and a steady income in her bank account. His extensive experience of gold-diggers and social climbers had made his judgement skewed. He had not for a moment considered Gisele had been innocent. That was the thing that still plagued him the most. He had not looked long and hard enough for another explanation. He had gone with the pack on calling her out as little more than a high-priced whore.

It pained him to think of the way he had let her down. Would she ever forgive him? Did the fact that she had let her guard down enough to be intimate with him again mean she was softening towards him? Or had she only done it to ease her conscience about taking the money he had promised her? Was the only thing tying her to him two million dollars? It was a disquieting thought and one he couldn't readily dismiss from his mind.

She moved against him, stretching one leg and then the other before her eyes slowly opened. 'Have I been sleeping?' she asked, struggling to an upright position, her blonde hair all tousled like a bird's nest around her shoulders.

Emilio smiled and brushed a strand of hair out of her eyes. 'Like a baby,' he said.

Something flickered in her eyes before she lowered them, her fingers plucking at the edge of the sheet covering her chest. Her face had taken on a stricken look. He even saw the colour leach out of her face.

Emilio propped himself up on one elbow. 'Are you OK?' he asked.

'Why wouldn't I be OK?' she said, affecting an indifferent tone.

He trailed a gentle finger down the slope of her linen-creased cheek. 'Did I hurt you?' he asked. 'Things got pretty intense there last night.'

She still didn't look at him but her cheeks filled with colour again. 'No, of course not.'

He tipped up her face with a finger beneath her chin. 'Still just sex?' he asked.

'Of course,' she said with a haughty look. 'What else could it be?'

His eyes continued to study her as he outlined the contours of her mouth with the tip of his index finger. 'Liar,' he said. 'It's never been just sex, has it, *cara*?'

She pushed against his chest and rolled away from him, reaching for a bathrobe and tying the ends around her waist, her lips pressed tightly together as if she didn't trust herself to answer. She gave him a final chilly look and stalked across the room.

'Where are you going?' he asked.

'I'm going to take a shower,' she said with a little flash of her gaze. 'Is that OK or should I have asked permission first?'

Emilio frowned at her. He was getting a little tired of her game-playing. One minute she was sobbing with pleasure in his arms and the next she acted as if she couldn't wait for the month to be over. He wanted their relationship to settle down, not be a constant battlefield.

He wanted the past put behind him. It wasn't his way to dwell on things. He had to move forwards. There was no other choice. 'Do what you like,' he said, throwing off the bedcovers as he rose from the bed. 'I'll see you downstairs.'

When Gisele came downstairs Marietta had set out the breakfast things and the morning papers out on the terrace. She sat down and poured herself a cup of tea, but just as she was lifting it to her mouth she saw there an English paper sticking out from beneath the Italian one. She pulled it out and looked at the headline below the main news item. The cup in her hand fell with a loud smashing clatter to the flagstones of the terrace. Her heart jerked, stopped and then started to stutter. Her breathing stalled for so long her head swam.

She heard the firm tread of Emilio's footsteps come out on the terrace. 'Gisele?' he said. 'Are you all right? Have you burnt yourself?'

She pressed the paper to her thumping chest, unable to get a single word out past the sudden constriction of her throat. Her heart was thudding sickeningly, a kick-blow beat that was as painful as it was erratic.

There were two photos. One was of Emilio and her at lunch yesterday. The shot showed her looking crossly at him. It wasn't very flattering to her at all, but that wasn't the worst of it.

The other photo...*oh, dear God...* How had it happened? How had the press sourced a photo of her at her baby's grave? Had someone followed her there the last time she had placed flowers on Lily's grave?

She tried to think through the haze of pain inside her

head. The cemetery had been a little busier than usual that day. Had someone recognised her and cashed in on the opportunity to sell the shot to the press? She knew there were websites where members of the public could sell phone pictures of celebrities: candid shots, catching people off guard with no make-up on or having an intimate argument with a partner—private moments made public for cash. Not that Gisele thought of herself as a celebrity in any shape or form, but re-establishing her connection to Emilio made her an instant target. Was this how life was going to be for the next month? Her still raw, agonising grief splashed over every paper for others to gawk at?

To have her private pain made so public was devastating. She couldn't bear it if her tragic loss was going to be cheap fodder for the press. Lily's short, precious life would be wrapped around someone's fish and chips or vegetable scraps—discounted as yesterday's news.

How on earth would she bear it?

Emilio's dark gaze went to hers. 'What on earth's the matter?' he asked.

She opened and closed her mouth, her lips too dry to make them move. She felt sick. She was *sure* she was going to be sick. Her insides were churning with such anguish and despair she felt as if she was going to drop in a faint. She vainly tried to keep the paper against her chest but her hands were shaking so much she could do nothing but watch in sinking heart-stopping dread as Emilio took it from her.

Time seemed to come to a standstill as he unfolded the newspaper. Even the sound of the paper crackling as he opened it was magnified a thousand million times.

And then she saw as his eyes went to what was printed there. Every word was carved on Gisele's brain like a cruel tattoo: *Andreoni Reconciliation Haunted by Tragic Death of Love Child.*

Gisele saw the flinch of Emilio's dark gaze, the camera shutter flick of shock, surprise and disbelief. Every muscle on his face seemed to freeze for an infinitesimal moment.

There was no movement.

No sound.

She couldn't even hear him breathing.

But then the column of his throat moved up and down, once, twice.

'What?' His one word was a rasping gasp, a choked, strangled sound that contained so much agony it resonated in her trembling body like a loud echo.

She could feel his tension. She could feel every tight band of muscle in his body. His face was ashen. He looked as if he had aged a decade right before her eyes.

She hadn't wanted him to find out like this. She'd wanted to work up to it, to make sure she had a more secure footing with him before she told him what she had gone through.

She slowly released the breath she hadn't even realised she had been holding. 'I was pregnant when I left you two years ago,' she said. 'I didn't find out until a couple of months after I got back to Sydney.'

His throat moved, rose and fell again as if he was trying to swallow something that didn't quite fit inside his oesophagus. 'Pregnant?' he said hollowly.

'Yes...'

The silence was so intense she heard him draw in a

breath. She even heard the sound of his hand against his skin as he dragged it downwards over his face, catching on his stubbly regrowth.

His eyes took on a haunted look. 'You had a baby?'

Her throat tightened over the word. 'Yes…'

He swallowed again. '*My* baby?'

For a moment all she could do was just stare at him as the hurt of his question smashed against her heart like a knockout punch. Then she took a breath and sent him a look that would have stripped wallpaper off a wall. '*How* can you ask that?' she said. '*How can you?*'

His expression contorted with remorse as his hand came back up to rub over his face. 'Sorry, I wasn't thinking,' he said. 'Of course it was mine. Forgive me.' He dropped his hand back by his side. He looked completely floored, dumbstruck, shattered. 'Was it a girl or a boy?'

'A girl,' Gisele said, squeezing back tears.

'What happened to her?' he asked in that same raspy croak.

She let out another painful breath. 'I found out at sixteen weeks there was a problem,' she said. 'I was offered a termination. But I wanted to give her a chance. There was a slim chance she might've made it. I wanted her to make it. I *wanted* it more than anything but she didn't live past a few hours. Six hours, twenty-five minutes and forty-three seconds, to be precise. Not much of a lifespan, is it?'

Emilio felt as if he had been hit with an anvil that had come out of nowhere. He had not seen it coming. Nothing could have prepared him. He stood there in a shell-shocked silence as his thoughts ran riot, each one pointing a finger of blame at him.

Gisele had been pregnant when he had cast her from his life. He had thrown her out on the streets while she had been carrying his child.

A child he would never meet.

A child he would never touch or hold in his arms.

A child he would never know.

What had stolen his child's life from him? What had gone so terribly wrong that she had been advised to terminate the pregnancy?

He thought of his tiny daughter suffering. Had she felt pain? Distress? His gut twisted with anguish. Why hadn't he been told?

'What was the problem?' he asked. 'What happened to her?'

'She had a genetic abnormality,' she said. 'Some of her organs hadn't developed properly. There was nothing they could do to fix it.'

His little daughter had never stood a chance. Would it have been different if he had been there? Could he have saved her? He would have shifted heaven and earth to do so.

Frustration and grief besieged him. He felt the weight of it like a straitjacket made of lead. His emotions—emotions he had never allowed space enough to breathe—were now gasping for air until his throat felt as if it had been scraped raw with rusty razor blades.

'What caused it?' he asked hoarsely.

She looked down at her hands. 'Who knows? The doctors said it was just one of those things but I've always wondered if it was something I did or didn't do...'

Emilio felt another smashing blow of guilt assail him. If it was anyone's fault, wasn't it his? The stress she had been under would have been enough to jeopardise the baby's development.

His baby.

'Why didn't you tell me you were pregnant?' he asked. 'I could have helped you. It might have made all the difference. Did you ever consider that? Why did you keep my own child's existence a secret from me? Surely I had the right to know?'

She gave him a hardened look. 'Have you forgotten your parting words to me?' she asked. 'You said you never wanted to see or hear from me again. I had no reason to suspect you didn't mean it.'

'Did you even try and contact me?' he asked. 'Did you even give me a chance to do the right thing by you and the baby?'

She glared at him, her grey-blue eyes flashing with accusation. 'And have you pressure me to get rid of her because there was something wrong with her?' she said.

Emilio opened and closed his mouth, trying to locate his voice. His chest felt as if someone had landed a heavy blow to it, knocking the air right out of his lungs. How could she think so lowly of him? Didn't she know anything about him? 'Did you really think I would've asked you to do that?' he finally said.

'I wasn't prepared to risk it,' she said. 'You strive for perfection in everything you do. I wasn't sure how you would handle the news of a baby that wasn't perfect in every way, especially since our relationship had ended so bitterly. I thought you'd be better off not knowing. I thought you wouldn't want to know.'

Emilio kept looking at her in bewildered dismay. Did she know him so little that she thought he would not want to give his child every possible chance at life? He would have done anything—*anything* and *everything* within his power. 'What sort of man do you think I am?' he asked. 'Do you really think I would've rejected my own flesh and blood?' *Like my mother did to me.* The words were like a flashback of horror. He blinked to make it go away. 'I would never have done that, Gisele. Never in a million years.'

She bit down on her lip and swung away, her arms going around her body protectively. 'I had enough trouble dealing with everyone else's opinions on what I should do,' she said. 'I didn't think I could cope with your input as well.'

Emilio swallowed against a king tide of regret. 'You should have told me,' he said. 'Damn it, Gisele, do you realise what this is like for me, finding out like this now, and via the press, for God's sake?'

She swung back to face him, her expression full of bitterness. 'So this is all about you, is it, Emilio? What about me? What about what I suffered? You have no right to tell me *how* you feel. As far as I'm concerned, you brought it on yourself.'

Emilio felt his spine tighten with anger. He had never felt so blindingly angry. He was angrier than when he had thought she had betrayed him two years ago. How could she be so cold and callous to deny him the knowledge of his own daughter? 'You did it deliberately, didn't you?' he said. 'You could have told me but you chose not to because you knew that would hurt me far more than anything else. It was your chance to punish me for not believing you. It was a perfect payback. And it worked, goddamn you. You couldn't have thought of a better revenge.'

She gave him a defiant look. 'You always think the worst of me. It's your automatic response, isn't it? Blame first, ask questions later.'

'Were you *ever* going to tell me?'

A flicker of guilt came and went in her gaze. 'I wasn't sure how to bring it up. It's not easy talking about it… about her…'

'You should've told me the day I came to see you at the shop,' he said. 'I came all that way to apologise. I did my best to make it up to you. You should've at least met me halfway.'

She threw him a withering look. 'Some apology that turned out to be,' she said. 'We both know I wouldn't be here now if it hadn't been for the money you offered.'

Emilio ground his teeth until his jaw ached. He felt blindsided by pain and a sense of loss that was unlike anything he had felt before. He was unaccustomed to being bombarded with such deep emotions. Emotions were something *other* people felt. He had cauterised his heart a long, long time ago. He wasn't supposed to feel like this. He'd always made sure he never did.

He had *never* felt so out of control.

How could he ever right the wrongs of the past? Gisele had lost their baby. She had suffered that loss all by herself. He hadn't been there for her. He hadn't protected her or provided for her. He could see now how a simple *sorry and let's try again* wasn't going to cut it. Nothing could make up for that loss. There was nothing he could do to bring their child back. A chasm of pain and bitterness divided him from Gisele now. Was there any bridge that could span that canyon of bitterness? Was there any amount of money or machinations on his part that could fix things? The powerlessness he felt was like being thrown back on the streets all over again. 'I'm sorry,' he said, but his voice sounded nothing like his own. It was hollow and empty, lifeless, soulless.

Dead.

A long pain-ridden silence passed.

'I have some photos,' Gisele said quietly.

Emilio blinked himself back to the moment. 'Of the baby?'

'I brought them with me...' She lowered her gaze from his. 'I have her blanket too. She spent her short life wrapped in it. I would have buried her in it but I didn't want to part with it.'

A spasm of pain gripped Emilio's chest again. 'You have it *with* you?' he asked.

She gave him a defiant look. 'I suppose you'll think it's weird or sick or pathetic of me, but I've never felt ready to let that final link with her go.' Her eyes suddenly filled with tears. 'Do you know what it feels like when people ask you if you have kids? What am I supposed to say? I had one but I lost her?' She choked back a sob. 'I don't even know if I'm supposed to call myself a mother or not...'

Emilio reached for her and enfolded her in his arms, pulling her stiff little body close, resting his chin on the top of her head as he rocked her gently in his arms as she quietly sobbed. He couldn't speak for the roadblock of emotion in his chest. He thought of her holding on to her baby as long as she could. How had she endured such heartbreak? Who had supported her? How could she have juggled the demands of running a small business with the tragedy of carrying a child that had never been given a guarantee of making it? And how cruelly ironic to have been surrounded by constant reminders of what she had lost?

Baby wear.

His stomach plummeted as he thought of all those tiny outfits, all those little vests and booties and bonnets and christening gowns. Could she have chosen a harder way to navigate her way through her loss? Seeing other mothers day after day with their babies. Helping those mothers choose outfits for their little ones. How on earth had she done it? No wonder she hated him. No wonder she had asked for more money. 'No, I don't think it's weird or sick or pathetic,' he said.

She leaned back to look up at him with reddened eyes. 'You…you don't?'

He shook his head, feeling humbled by all she had suffered. His anger seemed so pointless and inappropriate now. Hadn't she suffered enough without making her feel guilty for not contacting him? Besides, there was every chance he might have blocked her attempts to speak to him. His stubbornness had helped him in his business life but he had paid a high price for it in his personal one. 'I think you're still grieving,' he said, blotting a tear as it rolled down her cheek. 'You'll know when it's time to finally say goodbye.'

Her bottom lip started to quiver again. 'My mother… Hilary thinks I'm a basket case,' she said. 'She thinks I'm morbid. But what would she know? She's never lost a baby. She's never even *had* a baby.'

'That's not true,' Emilio said. 'She had you. Not in

a physical sense, but she was the one who stood by you and reared you. She might not have been the best mother in the world, but at least she didn't leave you on some cold, rat-infested doorstep in the middle of winter to fend for yourself when you were less than four years old.'

The silence reverberated with the horror of his words.

Emilio wished he hadn't blurted that out. This wasn't about what he had suffered. This was about her. About her loss. About her devastation. He had put his behind him a long time ago.

'Your mother left you on a *doorstep*?' she asked with wide incredulous eyes.

He stepped away from her. 'You think you're hard done by? I know it's been tough on you, finding out about a long-lost twin. I know it must have been devastating to find out your mother is not really your mother. But she's your mother in every sense that's important. You can't cut her from your life just because you don't share the same genetic make-up. It wasn't her fault. It sounds to me like she did the best she could, given the circumstances.'

She looked at him narrowly. 'Have you been talking to her?'

'No, but I can imagine what she feels like. She's been shut out of her child's life due to circumstances beyond her control. At least her child is still alive and breathing. I don't even know my child's name.'

'I called her Lily,' she said softly.

His throat rose and fell again.

Lily.

'Can I see the photos?' he asked.

She gave a nod. 'I'll go and get them.'

Emilio turned and bent to pick up the shattered remains of Gisele's cup. There was no way the fine china could ever be put together again, which was just like his heart felt right now…

Gisele took the photo album out of her drawer and cradled it against her chest for a moment. Emilio's statement about his childhood had shocked her to the core. She couldn't bear thinking about him as a little boy, cast aside, frightened, alone, vulnerable. How could his mother have done that to him? Who had taken care of him? Had anyone? Was that why he was so closed off and so determined to put the past behind him? He couldn't stomach thinking about his wretched childhood. It was something he wanted to forget. And yet he had set up the charity, throwing himself into the hands-on work with the strength of character she was only now coming to understand.

She put the album back down and took out the soft pink blanket she had so lovingly made for Lily, holding it up to her face for a moment, breathing in that sweet baby smell. She wondered what Emilio had been wrapped in, whether he had ever been loved and cherished even a fraction of the way she had loved and cherished Lily. It was too painful to think he might have never been welcomed, never loved or wanted. How could he have been if he had been left to fend for himself at less than four years old?

When Gisele came back Emilio was standing looking out over the gardens. He turned when she came in, even though she was sure she hadn't made a sound. His eyes went straight to the album she carried. She handed it to him silently, her throat closing over with emotion.

His large hands held the album as if it was the most precious item in the world. She watched as he stroked his fingers over it reverently where she had placed a photo of Lily on the cover inside a pink-and-white embroidered heart. It was a moment she knew she would never forget. He might not have been there for her pregnancy and Lily's birth and all too short life, but he was a father in every sense of the word, meeting his daughter for the very first time. His dark brown eyes melted, a sheen coming over them like the glisten of wet paint. His expression was one of wonder and deep, heart-squeezing emotion. She had never seen him with his guard down. She had never seen such softening of his features, with such raw humanity on show.

He turned the first page and there was the one taken straight after birth, with Lily's tiny body still vernix- and blood-streaked, her minuscule mouth open like a baby bird, but she hadn't had the strength to make much more than one mewling cry.

There was another one after the nurse had washed her. She was wrapped in the pink blanket, looking almost normal. When that photo had been taken Lily had had less than four hours of life left. So little time to say all she needed to say to her. She'd had to pack a lifetime of mothering into a few short hours…

'She looks like you,' Emilio said in a gravel-rough tone.

'I thought she looked like you,' Gisele said.

He met her gaze and her heart contracted when she

saw the glimmer of moisture shining in his eyes. She hadn't expected him to care about a baby he had never known about until now. She hadn't expected him to feel the way she felt when she looked at photos of Lily. She had assumed it was different for men. They didn't have the physical connection with their offspring that mothers did. But it looked as if he was grieving every bit as much as she was. She saw the agony etched on his face.

'She looks like both of us,' he said in a low, deep, pain-filled burr.

She bit the inside of her mouth to keep control of her emotions. 'Yes...'

'Can I...?' He cleared his throat and began again. 'Can I have these copied?'

She nodded. 'Of course.'

'How much did she weigh?' he asked after a long aching silence.

'Just under four pounds. She was like a doll. I could hold her in one hand. See in that picture?' Gisele pointed to the one where Lily's tiny frail body lay in her hand.

He touched the photo, his long finger making their baby look even tinier in comparison. 'She's beautiful,' he said. 'I wish...I wish I'd been able to hold her. To touch her. To smell her. Photos are so one-dimensional.'

Gisele handed him the blanket she had been clutching against her chest. She had never let anyone else touch it before now. 'I can still smell her on this,' she said. 'It's faint but when I close my eyes I can imagine I'm still holding her. I made it for her. She was wrapped in it as soon as she was born. It was the last thing she was wrapped in before she...' She swallowed before she could continue. 'Before I dressed her for the burial.'

He took the blanket and held it up to his face, closing his eyes as he breathed in the lingering trace of their baby's sweet, innocent smell. A mixture of talcum powder and newborn baby, a fragrance so precious Gisele wished she could stop it from ever fading.

She watched as a single tear rolled down Emilio's cheek. She felt for him then in a way she had not felt before. For so long her anger had shut down her feelings for him. How must he feel to have missed out on their baby's short but precious life? She felt dreadful for not telling him now. She had misjudged him, just as he had misjudged her. Would he ever forgive her?

After a long silence he handed the blanket back to her. 'Thank you.'

'Emilio...' Gisele met his tortured gaze. 'I'm sorry I didn't make the effort to tell you. I realise now how wrong that was of me. I should've at least tried.'

His mouth twisted ruefully. 'I probably would've cut you off before you could tell me. I was too proud, too stubborn. I made a bad situation a whole lot worse.' He pulled a hand down over his face again; it made a sound like sandpaper. 'I've handled all of this appallingly. From day one I've been so wrong, so unforgivably blind.'

'We've both made mistakes,' she said softly.

'I don't know how to fix this, any of this,' he said with a haggard look in his eyes. 'For the first time since I was a small child, I find myself totally defeated, powerless. I can't turn any of this around.' He sighed again, a deep serrated sigh that sounded painful as he exhaled. 'You were right, *cara*. Life doesn't come with a reset button.'

Gisele swallowed the lump of emotion clogging her throat. 'I'm so sorry…'

'For what?' he asked, frowning at her. 'What did you do? You're the innocent one in all of this. I was the one in the wrong. None of this would have happened if I'd trusted you.' He walked to the windows and looked out over the gardens, his back a stiff plank of self-recrimination.

'I've been thinking about what you said…' Gisele cradled Lily's blanket close to her chest. 'About if things had been the other way around?'

He turned to look at her, his expression so full of pain it was agonising to witness it. 'Don't try and make excuses for me, Gisele,' he said. 'You would've handled it differently. We both know that. This is my wrongdoing, not yours. I have to live with it. I got it wrong and apologising is not enough. But then, it was never going to be enough, was it? You always knew that.'

Gisele wasn't sure what to say, although she didn't think she could have spoken even if she had known. Her throat had closed over completely, her eyes were burning with more tears and her heart was compressed by the weight of sadness that she had carried for so long. Sharing it with Emilio hadn't halved it; rather it had *doubled* it. She felt his pain as well as her own. She had learned to manage her grief. She had no idea how to manage his. The misery of his childhood had been bad enough; now he had the loss of his child to deal with. It didn't seem fair, but then what in life was fair?

Emilio came over to stand in front of her again. 'I know it's a lot to ask you to stay on in Italy after this,' he said. 'But I will do my utmost to protect you from the media. I can handle the business meetings for you. I can meet with the executives on your behalf. You can stay here, within the privacy and protection of the villa. You don't have to go out in public at all.'

'I'm not sure hiding away is going to solve anything,' Gisele said. 'I'm not sure how the press got hold of that photo, but if they've got that one, they probably have more. I don't want to become a victim and I certainly don't want to be seen as one either.'

'So you're still happy to stay the full month?' he asked.

Giscle studied his expression for a microsecond. She thought about leaving. She thought about packing her bag and walking away, drawing a line under her relationship with him, never to look back. He was giving her permission to do so. Could she do it? But, more to the point, did she *want* to do it? He had, for the first time ever, revealed something about the horror of his childhood. How much more might he tell her if she stayed on the full time? Wouldn't it help her to understand him better? She *wanted* to understand. 'I'll stay on,' she said.

He put his hands on her shoulders, his fingers cupping her gently in an embrace that touched on something deep in her soul. He had touched her in a thousand different ways in the past, but somehow this was different. His charcoal-dark eyes held hers for a long mesmerising moment before he bent his head and briefly but tenderly brushed her mouth with his. 'Thank you,' he said. 'I will do everything in my power to make sure you don't regret it.'

CHAPTER NINE

OVER the next week the meetings Emilio had set up went off brilliantly. Gisele came out of each one with a renewed sense of purpose and vision for her work. It was all happening so fast but she was happy to be swept along with it, as it was just the distraction she needed.

In private, Emilio was tender but distant. She knew he was still coming to terms with the knowledge of being a father to a child he would never meet. She found it hard to reach out to him. Part of the reason was because she was frightened of talking about it in case he brought up the topic of having another child. It was the proverbial elephant in the room. It made her conversations with him stilted. She knew she sounded distant and removed but she couldn't do anything to stop it.

But, in spite of her assiduousness at avoiding the subject, there was a heart-stopping moment when she was confronted with how much Emilio had missed out on by not knowing about her pregnancy and how dearly he still wanted a family of his own. They had been visiting one of the main baby wear outlets in an exclusive department store. Gisele was showing the manager some of her samples and had not realised Emilio had moved to a selection of infant toys farther along. The store manager excused himself to speak to a staff member about something urgent and that was when Gisele's gaze went to where Emilio was standing. He had picked up a soft teddy bear dressed in a pink tutu, his expression so wistful she felt an ache that took her breath away. She bit her lip and turned away, relieved when the manager came back from dealing with his little crisis so she didn't have to deal with her own.

After the first day or two the press's interest in her relationship with Emilio had died down a little, but not enough to make her feel totally at ease. The sense of living under a microscope was petrifying at times. She wondered how big-name celebrities coped with it. And yet Emilio seemed to handle it all in his stride. But then he seemed to know what places the paparazzi frequented, cleverly managing to avoid them. He took Gisele to quiet, off the radar restaurants where the food was magnificent and the wines like nectar. As the days passed, she felt she was gradually getting to know the real Emilio, not the super-successful architect, but the *real* man. The man behind the mask he wore in public. He was making an effort to lower his guard with her, perhaps because he had sensed her closing off from him.

It came home to her in a powerful way when they were walking back from having dinner in one of the less trendy suburbs of Rome. They suddenly came across a young girl who was obviously stoned on some drug. She staggered up to Emilio, teetering on her shabby and scuffed high heels, her skin-tight skirt showing more than was decent of her scarily skinny thighs. She said something lewd in Italian and put a hand out to Emilio's chest. He covered the girl's scabby hand with his and pulled it off his chest, but he still held it within his. He spoke to her like a concerned father would do to a wayward daughter.

Gisele watched in amazement. Although she couldn't understand much of what he had said, she could tell that he hadn't berated the girl. He took her to one side, out of the way of passers-by, chatting to her for a minute or two before he made a call to his homeless kids' hotline. Within a few minutes a van arrived and one of the youth workers came over and escorted the girl into the vehicle, presumably to take her somewhere safe.

Gisele came over to where Emilio was standing watching as the van drove down the street. She looped her arm through his and moved her body close to his. 'You seemed to know her,' she said.

He drew in a ragged breath and released it. 'Yes, her name is Daniela and she's been in and out of our detox programme three times,' he said. 'She wants to beat the cycle but she's got so much going against her—the wrong family, the wrong friends and the wrong beliefs about herself.' He turned and looked at her, his expression haunted. 'I'm terrified I'm going to find her dead in some back alley one day. The police will write her off as just another overdose.' He scraped a hand through his hair and continued. 'Do you know the thing that gets me the most? She could have been *anything* she wanted. She's bright and beautiful but look where she's ended up. How can I stop her from self-destructing? How many young women are out there just like her? Some of them have children. Do you realise that? Who is looking after them while their mothers are out working the streets?'

Gisele swallowed tightly. *He* had been one of those

little children. She knew it, even though he hadn't said anything further about his childhood. She had tried to get him to open up over the past week but he had seemed reluctant to reveal anything else. 'You're doing all you can, Emilio,' she said. 'You're doing more than anyone I know to try and help.'

'It's not enough.' He stalked a few paces away, his hand going back to his hair, making it stick up in disarray. 'Goddamn it, it's not enough.'

She went over to him and hugged him from behind. He was so rigid with frustration, but eventually he softened and turned to face her. His expression looked as if he had come to some sort of definitive decision—a decision he had taken a long time to make. 'I want to show you something,' he said.

'What?' she asked.

He took her hand and led her down a side street and then another and then another. It was a labyrinth of dark alleys and shadows, of scuttling rats and strewn and rotting rubbish. Gisele's skin crawled but she clung onto Emilio's strong hand, somehow feeling safe in a world that she had never visited before. A world she had not even known existed. She felt ashamed that she hadn't made herself more aware. How had she lived for twenty-five years and not have known that life for some people was a daily struggle for basic survival? It made her grievances over the lies she had been told about her origins pale in comparison.

Eventually they came to a back alley that had only one working streetlight. The insipid light it cast was just enough to show the disrepair of the buildings, the neglect that spoke of desperate people in desperate times.

Emilio led her to the front of a run-down building that was abandoned. No lights shone from inside. Graffiti-sprayed slats boarded the windows up. It looked like a soulless body, a shell of something it had once been but would never be again, no matter how much money was thrown at it.

'This is where my mother left me,' he said in a tone-less voice. 'I was a month or two off turning four. I remember it as if it were yesterday.'

Gisele gripped his hand, her throat so tight with emotion she couldn't speak. She let the tears run down her face as she looked at the worn step. She imagined Emilio as a little child, not even of school age. What had he felt to be left here? To watch in bewilderment as his mother walked away, never to return?

'She was a teenager, barely out of childhood herself,' Emilio said into the silence. 'She probably didn't know who my father was. I've heard since there were four or five possible candidates.'

'Oh, Emilio…'

'She told me she would be back.' His hand suddenly gripped Gisele's so tightly she felt her bones protest but she wouldn't have indicated that for all the money in the world. She stood there silently, watching as the memories flashed through his haunted gaze.

'She *promised* me she would be back,' he said. 'I believed her. I waited for her. I waited for her for hours. Maybe it was days. I can't remember now. I just remember the cold. It was so cold.' He gave an involuntary shudder. 'It crept into my bones. Do you know, there are some times when I can still feel it?'

Gisele put her arms around him and held him close,

trying to reach inside him to the little abandoned, be-wildered child he had once been. 'Oh, Emilio,' she said, her voice breaking over a sob. 'I can't bear that you went through that. I can't bear to think of you so alone and so helpless.'

His arms were like steel bands as they wrapped around her. He crushed her to him, his head buried against her neck. She breathed in the essence of him, the pain and the wretchedness, drawing into her being the lost, lonely soul he had hidden from everyone for so long.

After a long moment he set her from him. 'I don't want other kids to go through what I did,' he said. 'I don't want them to spend their lives wondering where their mother went to that night and why she didn't come back—to not know if she's alive or dead. I don't want them to wonder if every man of a certain age they pass on the street is the father they never met.'

'You're such an amazing person, Emilio,' Gisele said, putting a gentle hand to his face. 'I don't think I've ever met a more amazing person.'

'I've never shown anyone this place,' he said gruffly. 'Not even the shelter workers know this is where I came from.'

'Thank you for showing me,' she said. 'It makes me admire you all the more.'

He gave her a twisted look and linked his hand with hers. 'Let's get out of here,' he said. 'This place gives me the creeps.'

Emilio closed the door of the villa when they got home and turned off the exterior lights. 'You go on up to bed, *cara*,' he said. 'I'm going to call the shelter to make sure Daniela is settling in OK.'

'I'll wait for you,' Gisele said.

He brushed the underside of her chin with his finger. 'Wait for me upstairs,' he said. 'I promise I won't be long.'

He watched as she made her way up the stairs; every now and again she turned back to look at him over her shoulder. Her grey-blue eyes were full of the longing he could feel pumping through his own veins.

Telling her about his childhood had felt good. It had felt cathartic. It made him feel as if that part of his life was truly behind him. Gisele had not been repulsed by his wretched background but rather had embraced him with the sort of acceptance he had been hungering for all of his life.

After he made his call he went upstairs and opened the door of the master suite. Gisele had showered and was now wearing his bathrobe. It was way too big for her, almost covering her from neck to ankles, but even so he could tell she was naked beneath it. 'You're wearing my bathrobe,' he said.

'Yes,' she said with a coy smile. 'What are you going to do about it?'

He pushed the door behind him closed. 'I'm going to take it off you.'

Her eyes teased his. 'What if I put up a fight?'

A glint of amusement lit his gaze as he came towards her. 'Then it will be twice the fun.'

She gave a little squeal when he scooped her up in his arms, carrying her caveman style to the bed, where he gently dropped her. He stood back and dispensed with his clothes, watching as her pupils flared as each layer hit the floor. He came back to her and tugged the ties of the bathrobe free, watching as it fell away from her body. He feasted his eyes on her beautiful breasts, the cherry-red nipples already tightly budded. He bent his mouth to each one in turn, tasting her, suckling on her, delighting in her unrestrained response. 'Some fight you're putting up,' he said teasingly.

'Maybe I can't resist you,' she said, toying with the hair on his chest with her soft fingertips. Her hands moved lower, tantalising him with her touch. He sucked in a breath as she closed her fingers around him. How could one woman's touch work such intense magic on him? He wanted her so badly it was like a raging fever in the surging river of his blood. He pressed her back down and came over her with his weight supported by his elbows. 'Am I too heavy for you?' he asked.

'No,' she said, pulling his head down so she could press her mouth to his.

Her tongue danced with his, darting away and then coming back for more. Her lips were impossibly soft, like velvet against his.

He stroked his hands down her body, delighting in the silk of her skin before going to the heart of her womanhood. She was so warm and wet and he was so hard and aching he couldn't resist sinking into her. She gave a little gasp and he immediately stilled. 'Sorry, did I hurt you?' he asked.

'No, it's just you're so big and I'm still a little out of practice…' Her cheeks took on a rosy hue that he found so incredibly endearing.

He went to pull out but she stalled him with her hands on his buttocks. 'No, stay,' she said softly. 'I want you.'

He took it slowly, conscious of her tender muscles accommodating him. She felt so wonderful, so silky and yet so tight. She lifted her hips for each downwards thrust, urging him on, her hands caressing his back and shoulders, her mouth like fire on his. He caressed her breasts, taking his time over each one, his tongue rolling over her nipples, stroking along the highly sensitive undersides where he knew her nerves danced triple time. She writhed with pleasure as he continued his sensual feast on her body, his teeth and tongue working in tandem to bring about maximum excitement for her. She became more and more restless as her need grew, her body rising to meet his as he sank deeper into her. He felt the tension grow in her, the way her thighs gripped him around the waist, her body open to him in wanton abandon as she sought the ultimate in human release.

'Now...' she gasped brokenly against the hot damp skin of his neck. 'Oh, please *now*...'

He played her with his fingers, his touch light but sure. He knew exactly what she needed to go over the edge. He had taught her himself how to relax into the whirlpool, to let it carry her into oblivion. She had been hesitant in the past; she had been almost frightened of the overpowering sensations clamouring in her body, but he had gently coaxed her into embracing what her body craved. Now as he felt every contraction of her body as she orgasmed, the pulses of her flesh triggered his own cataclysmic release. He fell forwards, pumping through those precious few seconds of bliss as her body welcomed him home.

He lay in the quiet aftermath, still with her in the circle of his arms, her silver-blonde hair splayed out on his chest. He heard the rhythmic sound of her breathing, the way on each soft breath out it blew across his chest like a feather dancing ahead of a teasing breeze.

He closed his eyes, sighing deeply as he breathed in the fragrance of her hair and skin, the taste of her, vanilla-sweet on his tongue.

It was the closest he had ever felt that he had finally found somewhere to call home.

CHAPTER TEN

WHEN Gisele woke the next morning she was disappointed to find Emilio wasn't beside her. But as she lay there covered in fine Egyptian cotton, in that richly furnished suite, she thought about why he worked so hard and so tirelessly, why he drove himself day after day after day. Visiting the bleak desolation of that back alley and finding out the true horror of his childhood had finally made her understand why Emilio was so driven and determined. In the past she hadn't fully comprehended his ruthless ambition, but now she saw it for what it was. All the long hours he worked, his single-minded focus on projects that kept him awake at night were not to make him become yet another mega-rich self-indulgent man, but rather a passionate quest to make the world a better place for others less fortunate than him. He wanted to be successful so he could help others escape the life he had once led.

After her shower Gisele went downstairs in search of Emilio but Marietta informed her he was taking a call in the study. 'I have served breakfast in the breakfast room this morning,' the housekeeper added. 'It looks like it is going to rain.'

'*Grazie*, Marietta,' Gisele said and went through to the delightfully appointed east-facing room to wait for him.

With an unnerving sense of déjà vu, she moved to where the newspapers had been laid out on a sideboard close to the table. The Italian paper had a large photograph of Emilio and her coming out of the baby wear department. She remembered the moment so clearly. She had been carrying some of her samples and Emilio had put his arm around her protectively as they came out on the busy street. Someone had been taking a photo with their phone but Gisele had thought they were taking it of a friend standing at the front of the store.

Her heart started to gallop as she picked up the English paper, where the caption was emblazoned there above the very same photo: *A New Baby for Award-winning Architect and his Australian Bride-to-be?*

Gisele went hot and then icily cold. Panic streaked through her. Her heart tripped. Her breath caught. Her hands and fingers tingled as if she was losing her blood pressure.

The elephant wasn't just in the room.

It had escaped. It was everywhere, stalking her. Crowding her, pressuring her to do something she could not do.

'I'm sorry about that,' Emilio said as he came in. 'I was just making sure Daniela had booked into rehab... *Cara?* What's happened?'

Gisele thrust the paper at him. 'I can't do this,' she said. 'I can't live like this. *I can't do this.*'

Emilio glanced at the paper briefly before putting it to one side. 'It's just a bit of speculation,' he said. 'You know the games the journalists play.'

'*Speculation?*' She glared at him. 'Is that what you call it? I call it pressure.'

'*Cara*, no one's pressuring you to do anything.'

'Aren't they?' she asked, starting to pace the floor in agitation. 'What about you and all your talk about having a family? It's what you want. You told me.'

'I do want a family but we'll take things slowly until you get used to the idea of—'

'Stop it!' Gisele put her hands over her ears. 'Don't say it. Don't tell me I'll get used to the idea of having another baby. I don't want to hear it.'

'Gisele, you're overreacting,' he said.

'Don't tell me I'm overreacting!' She felt close to hysteria. She had been in that scary place before and didn't want to go back. She struggled to get her emotions under control. 'I saw you looking at that teddy bear.'

He frowned at her. 'What teddy bear?'

'The pink one with the tutu,' she said, her heart racing so wildly she could feel it knocking against her rib cage. 'In the shop we visited the other day. You picked it up and looked at it. I could *see* it, Emilio. I could see how much you want another baby.'

'*Cara,*' he said soothingly. 'Can we talk about this some other time? You're upset just now. I can understand that. It was a horrible shock to you to see that article. You'll feel different in a few days' time.'

'I *won't* feel different,' she said. 'I'll never feel different. You have to accept that.'

A muscle worked in his jaw. 'Gisele, I'd rather not discuss this with you in this state of mind.'

'I'm not in a state of mind!' she all but screamed at him. 'I can't do it, Emilio. I'm *not* doing it. I'm not going to be speculated on and pressured and cajoled into a relationship I'm not sure I can handle any more.' She stopped pacing, snatched in a scalding breath and added impetuously, 'I want to go home.'

He stood very still, barely a muscle moving, except for that tiny one in his jaw. His eyes gave nothing away; they were onyx-black, fathomless. 'You are free to leave any time you want, Gisele,' he said. 'I am not holding you here by force.'

Gisele swept her tongue over her lips. Her heart gave an extra beat—a sickening thud that reverberated throughout her body like a church bell struck too hard. 'What did you say?'

'If you want to leave, then leave,' he said. 'I'll get Marietta to pack your things while I book you a flight.'

'But…but what about the rest of the month?' she asked. 'What about the money?'

'You've earned every cent,' he said with a slight curl of his lip. 'You owe me nothing.'

Gisele wondered if she'd heard him correctly. Was he really sending her away without a single word of protest? Had all they had shared in the past couple of weeks been reduced to a business deal that had now ended?

What about what they had shared last night?

What about what *he* had shared?

He had let her into the private hell of his childhood. Didn't that mean he cared about her? But how could he truly care about her if he was happy to let her leave? 'But I don't understand…'

'I'll have my legal people contact you with the details of the handover,' he said in his cold and detached businesslike manner that was so at odds with her seesawing emotions. 'You'll own the building and the business outright. You will be able to employ more assistants as things expand. I have engaged a web-designer to help you set up a better online presence. People will be able to order and buy from you online once it's set up.'

Gisele couldn't think beyond the fact he wanted her to go. If he wanted her to stay then why wasn't he saying it? Was it because deep down he wasn't able to forgive her for not telling him about their baby? Had last night brought that home to him afresh? The fact that he had never got the chance to meet his child in the flesh, just like he hadn't met his father? Or was it that he didn't want her in his life any more because he didn't want to be reminded of the pain they had both suffered? Was that it?

No, there was more to it than that, she realised with a sickening jolt.

He didn't love her.

He had never loved her. He was *never* going to love her.

'What about the press?' she asked, clutching at whatever straws she could. 'Won't they make a fuss about… about everything ending like this?'

He gave a careless shrug. 'I'll release a statement saying things didn't work out between us,' he said. 'Don't worry about it. I'll make sure they leave you alone. I'll get Luigi to take you to the airport.'

'So…' She moistened her lips again, trying her best to appear as casual as he was being about it all. 'So, I guess this is goodbye.' Oh, how it hurt to say the word! *Please let this not be goodbye,* she thought. *Don't send me away. Not again. Not like this.*

The shutter was still down over his face, every muscle locked down now. 'Yes,' he said. 'This is goodbye.'

She gave a little nod of assent. What else could she do? She had told him she wanted to go. He had virtually *commanded* her to leave. He had his driver waiting on call. Her bags would be packed within minutes. What was she waiting for? She hadn't wanted to come in the first place. She was only here under sufferance.

Why, then, when she left him standing there, did it feel as if her world had shattered into a thousand pieces all over again?

Three weeks later...

Gisele was hanging some new stock in her shop when Hilary, her mother, came in. Hilary had only been to her shop a couple of times, barely staying long enough to look around. It was the first time Gisele had seen her mother since she had come back from Italy. She had spoken once or twice on the phone to her but the conversation had felt stilted and awkward.

'The shop looks lovely,' Hilary said.

'Thank you.'

There was a little silence.

'You look very thin, Gisele,' Hilary said. 'Are you sure this new expansion's not too much to handle? It's a lot to take on.'

'I can handle it,' Gisele said, hanging another baby jacket on the rack.

Hilary let out a little sigh as she picked up a jacket with a row of baby rabbits stitched around the bottom.

'I know you're still upset and angry,' she said. 'I don't blame you. What your father did was wrong.'

Gisele turned and looked at her. 'What you both did was wrong. You told just as many lies as he did. You *lived* a lie.'

Hilary's eyes suddenly filled with tears as she held the baby jacket against her chest. 'I know, and every day of it I was terrified the truth would come out,' she said. 'I wanted you to know the truth right from when you were little but your father wouldn't hear of it. I didn't trust Nell Baker. I lived in dread that she would turn up and insist on having you back. I guess that's why I was always so distant and stiff with you. I was never sure if I was going to have you snatched out of my arms.'

Gisele had never seen her mother shed tears before. Not a single one. Hilary had always been so stiff upper lip about everything, so stoic, so in control, so emotionally detached. 'I never felt like you really loved me,' Gisele said. 'I never felt like I was good enough for you.'

'Oh, my darling,' Hilary said. 'I loved you so much. I loved all of my babies.'

Gisele frowned. 'Babies? What babies?'

Hilary fondled the tiny jacket in her hands. 'I had four miscarriages in the first couple of years of our marriage. I felt such a failure. Each time my hopes would soar and then it would all be over. I tried so hard not to get attached but I loved each one so very much.'

'Why didn't you tell me?' Gisele gasped. 'Why didn't you tell me when I lost Lily?'

Hilary's lower lip trembled. 'I lost my babies when they were just a few weeks along. You lost a full-term baby. How could I tell you I understood a fraction of what you were going through? I felt ashamed of not being able to be a proper mother. At least you were a mother, even if it was only for a few hours.'

'You *are* a proper mother,' Gisele said, with tears rolling down her face. 'You're the only mother I've got and I love you.'

Hilary's arms gathered her close. 'I love you too, my precious daughter. I love you too.'

Emilio pushed the computer mouse away in frustration and got stiffly to his feet. He stared sightlessly out of his office window. Almost a month had passed since Gisele had left and he still couldn't focus on work or indeed anything. He couldn't remember the last time he had slept more than a couple of hours. He had forgotten the last time he had eaten a full meal. He moved through each day like an automaton.

His life felt empty.

He felt empty.

Even the weather had joined him in his misery. The promising start to spring had been replaced with a capricious sun that had stayed behind brooding clouds for days and days. The drizzle of intermittent rain was a poignant reminder of the aching sadness he felt deep in his soul.

He hadn't cried since he was six years old, when a particularly unfeeling foster carer had told him his mother was never going to come back. He had thought his tear ducts would have dried up from lack of use. But no, they were working all right. He only had to look at the photos of his little daughter for the tears to fall.

He had wanted to do the right thing by Gisele. Seeing

how distressed she was about the thought of having another child with him had made freeing her his only option. It had been the right and most honourable thing to
do. But it hurt so damn much! Was this wrenching pain
never going to go away?

He had received an email from her with a polite thank
you for the help with the expansion of her business. He
had stared at the typed words, looking for a clue between the lines, but there had been nothing. But then
what else had he expected? If she had loved him, she
wouldn't have wanted to leave him. But she had gone
as soon as she had been given the chance.

His secretary, Carla, came in with his afternoon coffee. He didn't even bother turning from the window.
She brought it in every afternoon, even though he never
touched it. It would sit on the desk, forming a skin over
the top as it went cold. 'Leave it on the desk,' he said
tonelessly.

'There's a parcel for you,' Carla said. 'It came by registered mail. It's marked private.'

Emilio turned and looked at the package she had
placed on his desk next to the cup of coffee. 'Who's it
from?' he asked.

'It's from Signorina Carter,' she said. 'Do you want
me to open it?'

Emilio felt a fist tighten over his heart. 'No,' he said,
raking an unsteady hand through the thickness of his
hair. 'That will be all, Carla. You can have the rest of
the day off.'

'But what about the Venturi Project?' she asked,
frowning at him. 'Don't you have a deadline on that?'

Emilio gave a negligent shrug. 'It'll get done when

it gets done. If they're not happy with that, tell them to get someone else.'

Carla's finely groomed brows rose. *'Sì, signor,'* she said and left with a soft click of the door.

Emilio traced a finger over Gisele's neat handwriting where she had printed his name on the package. It was probably the jewellery he had given her. He'd been expecting her to send it back. He was surprised she hadn't left it behind the day she had left. He could imagine she wouldn't want any physical reminders of their relationship.

The package was securely wrapped with packing tape. He worked at it methodically. He could have used the silver blade of his letter opener but this time he preferred to do it by hand. He wanted to touch where her hands had touched. It was ridiculously sentimental of him, but that just about summed him up these days. He peeled back the tape and opened the cardboard box where a tissue-wrapped parcel lay nestled safely in a bed of Styrofoam cushioning.

His hands shook uncontrollably as he peeled away the tissue wrap to find the pink hand-embroidered blanket his tiny daughter had spent her short life wrapped in. Emotion burned like fire at the back of his throat as he cradled it gently in his hands. He felt as if he were holding his own heart.

There was a single sheet of paper in the box, neatly folded over. He took it out and opened it to read:

You said I would know when I'm finally ready to say goodbye. You were right. Gisele.

Emilio felt a juggernaut of emotion assail him. He hadn't been there at the beginning of their daughter's short life or at the end, but he was to be with her for ever more. Gisele had given him that privilege. How much had it cost her to do so? She had sent him her heart.

A lightning bolt of realisation hit him.

She had sent him her heart.

Mio Dio, what had he done? He had sent her away when all he had ever wanted was to have her close. Why hadn't he told her how he felt? Would it have hurt to have at least said the words? Even if she had still left, it would have been better for him to tell her he loved her. She deserved to know she was the only woman he had ever loved, *could* ever love.

He had been a coward. A pathetic coward, not man enough to own his need for her. Too frightened to feel like that little abandoned boy he had once been, he had kept his feelings locked away. He hadn't even admitted them to himself, let alone to her.

How could he have been so stupid?

So stubborn?

So blind?

He pressed the intercom on his desk. 'Carla? Are you still there?' he asked.

'*Sì, signor,*' his secretary said. 'I was just tidying my desk.'

'Get me a flight to Sydney,' he said. 'I don't care how much it costs. You can even hire a private jet. Buy one if you have to.'

'Urgent business again, Signor Andreoni?' Carla asked.

'No,' he said. 'This is personal.' *This is my life. This is my love. This is my everything.*

Emilio saw the 'Closed' sign on Gisele's shop as the taxi drew up outside. His heart slipped like a Bentley on black ice. But then he realised it was only seven-thirty in the morning. In his haste to get here he'd forgotten the time difference. He kicked himself for not having phoned first. But he had wanted to see her face to face. He *ached* to see her face to face.

He directed the driver to Gisele's home address and waited with a thudding pulse for the journey to be over. He mentally rehearsed his speech. He had been awake for the entire flight, thinking about what he would say, but in the end he knew he really only had three words to say to her: *I love you.*

The taxi turned the corner into her street and Emilio's stomach nosedived when he saw the 'Sold' sign on her flat.

He stumbled out of the taxi, issuing a brusque order over his shoulder for the driver to wait.

There was no answer when he pressed the doorbell. He peered through gaps in the drawn blinds but there was no sign of her being inside.

'Can I help you?' an older female voice asked.

Emilio swung around to see an elderly lady with a walking frame standing by the letterboxes. 'I'm looking for Gisele Carter,' he said. 'Do you know where she is?'

'She left a little while ago,' the old lady said.

Panic gripped Emilio by the throat. 'Left?'

'Yes, she's taking a holiday before she moves to her new home,' she said. 'She's meeting her mother and her sister in Queensland. A tropical island, I think she said. I can't remember the name of it now.'

Emilio mentally groaned. How many tropical islands were there in Queensland? *Hundreds*. How on earth was he going to track her down? 'When did she leave?' he asked.

'You just missed her,' the old lady said. 'She only left half an hour or so ago.'

'Do you know what airline she was booked on?' Emilio asked as he walked quickly backwards to the waiting taxi. 'It's really important. I need to see her. I'm going to tell her I love her. I'm going to ask her to marry me.'

The old lady smiled as she told him the carrier's name. 'I think I remember now the island,' she said. 'Hamilton Island—yes, that's the one.'

Emilio rushed to the gate lounge after he had cleared Security but it was empty. The illuminated board said the flight was closed.

He was too late.

He scraped a hand through his hair and stumbled to the window overlooking the tarmac. The plane was backing out, preparing its journey down the runway, its lights along the wings flashing in preparation.

A choked-up feeling seized his chest. He couldn't breathe. He planted his hands on the glass in front of him for support.

He was too late.

He rested his head on the window. He *knew* this feeling. It was the same feeling he had on that step. He remembered all too well the feeling of being abandoned, of having no one to turn to, of not knowing what was going to happen next. The uncertainty, the bleakness, the loneliness, the aching emptiness...

'Emilio?'

The skin on the back of his neck prickled. He was imagining it, just like he had imagined his mother's voice, reaching out to him in the dark while he had been sitting on that cold stone step for all of those long, lonely, terrifying hours.

He slowly turned and saw Gisele standing in front of him. She looked pale, wraithlike, just like a ghost. Was his mind playing tricks on him? It must be. He blinked a couple of times but she didn't disappear. 'You sold your flat.' *What an inane thing to say*, he chided himself.

'Yes,' she said. 'I felt it was time to move on.'

He shifted his weight from foot to foot. 'I thought you were on that flight.' *Even more banal*. Why couldn't he just say what he wanted to say?

'My flight isn't for another forty minutes,' she said. 'I'm going to Heron Island. Mum and I are meeting Sienna there. Mum thought it might be a good chance for us all to get to know each other. It leaves from the other gate down there.' She pointed farther down the concourse.

'Oh... I thought you were going to Hamilton Island,' he said. 'Your neighbour said... The board said the flight was closed... I saw it leaving.' He stopped because he was rambling like a tongue-tied lovesick fool.

Gisele rolled her lips together, looking just like a shy, uncertain schoolgirl. 'I was coming back from the restroom and saw you standing here,' she said. 'I thought I must be imagining things. Why are you here?'

'I wanted to see you,' Emilio said. 'I wanted to thank you for…for giving me our daughter's blanket.'

A shadow passed over her face before she lowered her gaze. 'She was made in Italy,' she said in a tiny whisper-soft voice. 'I thought it was appropriate that a part of her rested there too.'

Emilio felt his emotions rise like a flash flood within him. He had no control over it. His chest ached with the pressure. It was building to a crescendo. He felt every tidemark. They were etched indelibly on his soul. He brushed away the tears that were falling with the back of his hand. 'What if you still need to hold her sometimes?' he asked.

Her bottom lip quivered uncontrollably. 'It's your turn to hold her.'

'She needs both of us to hold her,' he said, gulping back a ragged sob. 'No one can take your place. No one can *ever* take your place. She loves you. *I* love you. I've always loved you. Please come home, *cara*. Come back to me. Come back to us.'

She paused for an infinitesimal moment before she stumbled towards him, a flurry of arms and emotions that he welcomed with every cell of his being. He had never felt so close to another human being. Her arms wrapped around his waist, but he felt them around his heart. *'Il mio prezioso,'* he said. 'My precious one. I thought I had lost you for ever.'

Gisele clutched at him, terrified he would suddenly vaporise, that she would open her eyes and find this was all a dream. Had he really said those wonderful, amazing words? She looked up at him with tears streaming from her eyes. 'Do you really love me?' she asked. 'You're not just saying it?'

He grabbed her hand and pressed it against his thudding heart. 'I love you, *tesore mio*,' he said. 'My life is meaningless without you. I can't imagine how I will cope if you don't say you will marry me. You will, won't you? Marry me, I mean?'

She smiled at him with immeasurable joy. 'Of course I will marry you,' she said. 'I can't think of anything I want more. I love you.'

He crushed her to him again, holding her tightly, as if he never wanted to let her go. 'You are everything to me, *cara*,' he said. 'I am ashamed of how long it has taken me to realise how much you mean to me. How can you ever forgive me for taking so long to come to my senses? How can you ever forgive me for how I misjudged you, which started this crazy affair in the first place?'

'Don't torture yourself any more,' she said. 'We were both victims of circumstances beyond our control.'

Emilio held her from him so he could look into her eyes. 'I was such a fool. I can't believe I got it so wrong. If only I had stopped and thought about who you were as a person, your values, the strength of character you had demonstrated so many times. I ignored all of that. And then, to add insult to injury, I practically forced you back in my life. I wanted to wipe the slate clean but you taught me that it's not always possible. The hurts and blows and mistakes of life are things you sometimes have to carry with you. You can't erase all of them. Those are the very things that make us who we are.'

Gisele stroked his lean cheek with her hand. 'I love who you are,' she said. 'I love everything about you.'

He rested his forehead on hers. '*Cara*, I want you to know that if you can't bear the thought of having another baby, then that is fine. God knows I've got enough on my hands with all the street kids I'm taking in. Daniela has brought in some of her friends. Having you will be enough. More than enough.'

Gisele blinked back fresh tears. 'For all this time I could never imagine going through a pregnancy again,' she said. 'I couldn't bear the thought of going through that terrible loss again. But this time you'll be by my side. I think I could handle just about anything with you standing beside me.'

He cupped her face in his hands, his gaze soft and tender as it held hers. 'And that's exactly where I plan to be for the rest of our lives,' he said. 'By your side, loving you, protecting you and worshipping you with my body and my soul.'

Gisele closed her eyes as his lips sealed hers in a kiss of promise and hope and healing. She wrapped her arms around his waist, leaning into his strength, delighting in the feeling of being loved and cherished.

It was like finally coming home.

Sienna Baker was sitting by the pool on Heron Island, sipping a Manhattan when she got the text message from Gisele. She picked up her phone and, propping her sunglasses on her forehead, squinted against the bright sunlight as she read the words: *Sienna, sorry, slight change of plan. Mum's on her way but I'm off to Italy to prepare for my wedding. PS Will you be my bridesmaid? Gisele X*

* * * * *

MILLS & BOON
True Love

Romance from the Heart

Celebrate true love with tender stories of heartfelt romance, from the rush of falling in love to the joy a new baby can bring, and a focus on the emotional heart of a relationship.

MILLS & BOON

THE HEART OF ROMANCE

A ROMANCE FOR EVERY KIND OF READER

MODERN

Prepare to be swept off your feet by sophisticated, sexy and seductive heroes, in some of the world's most glamourous and romantic locations, where power and passion collide.
8 stories per month.

HISTORICAL

Escape with historical heroes from time gone by. Whether your passion is for wicked Regency Rakes, muscled Vikings or rugged Highlanders, awaken the romance of the past.
6 stories per month.

MEDICAL

Set your pulse racing with dedicated, delectable doctors in the high-pressure world of medicine, where emotions run high and passion, comfort and love are the best medicine.
6 stories per month.

True Love

Celebrate true love with tender stories of heartfelt romance, the rush of falling in love to the joy a new baby can bring, and focus on the emotional heart of a relationship.
8 stories per month.

Desire

Indulge in secrets and scandal, intense drama and plenty of hot action with powerful and passionate heroes who have it all: wealth, status, good looks…everything but the right woman.
6 stories per month.

HEROES

Experience all the excitement of a gripping thriller, with an intense romance at its heart. Resourceful, true-to-life women and strong, fearless men face danger and desire - a killer combination!
8 stories per month.

DARE

Sensual love stories featuring smart, sassy heroines you'd want as a best friend, and compelling intense heroes who are worthy of them.
4 stories per month.

To see which titles are coming soon, please visit

millsandboon.co.uk/nextmonth

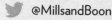